Studies in Global Science Fiction

Series Editors

Anindita Banerjee
Department of Comparative Literature
Cornell University
Ithaca, NY, USA

Rachel Haywood Ferreira
Department of World Languages and Cultures
Iowa State University
Ames, IA, USA

Mark Bould
Department of Film and Literature
University of the West of England
Bristol, UK

Studies in Global Science Fiction (edited by Anindita Banerjee, Rachel Haywood Ferreira, and Mark Bould) is a brand-new and first-of-its-kind series that opens up a space for Science Fiction scholars across the globe, inviting fresh and cutting-edge studies of both non-Anglo-American and Anglo-American SF literature. Books in this series will put SF in conversation with postcolonial studies, critical race studies, comparative literature, transnational literary and cultural studies, among others, contributing to ongoing debates about the expanding global compass of the genre and the emergence of a more diverse, multinational, and multi-ethnic sense of SF's past, present, and future. Topics may include comparative studies of selected (trans)national traditions, SF of the African or Hispanic Diasporas, Indigenous SF, issues of translation and distribution of non-Anglophone SF, SF of the global south, SF and geographic/cultural borderlands, and how neglected traditions have developed in dialogue and disputation with the traditional SF canon.

Editors
Anindita Banerjee, Cornell University;
Rachel Haywood Ferreira, Iowa State University;
Mark Bould, University of the West of England

Advisory Board Members
Aimee Bahng, Dartmouth College;
Ian Campbell, Georgia State University;
Grace Dillon (Anishinaabe), Portland State University;
Rob Latham, Independent Scholar;
Andrew Milner, Monash University;
Pablo Mukherjee, University of Warwick;
Stephen Hong Sohn, University of California, Riverside;
Mingwei Song, Wellesley College.

Emmanuel Buzay

Contemporary French and Francophone Futuristic Novels

The Longing to be Written and its Refusal

Emmanuel Buzay
University of Massachusetts Amherst
Amherst, MA, USA

ISSN 2569-8826   ISSN 2569-8834   (electronic)
Studies in Global Science Fiction
ISBN 978-3-031-16627-3   ISBN 978-3-031-16628-0   (eBook)
https://doi.org/10.1007/978-3-031-16628-0

Credit line: alengo/Getty Images

This Palgrave Macmillan imprint is published by the registered company Springer Nature
Switzerland AG.
The registered company address is: Gewerbestrasse 11, 6330 Cham, Switzerland

The Sirian picked up the little microbes once more. He still spoke to them with great kindness, despite being privately a little vexed to find that the infinitely small should have a pride almost infinitely large. He promised to write a fine work of philosophy for them, in suitably tiny script, in which they would discover the nature of things. True to his word, he gave them the volume before leaving. It was taken to Paris, to the Academy of Sciences. But when the Secretary opened it, he found nothing but blank pages. "Aha," said he, "I suspected as much."

—Voltaire, Micromégas

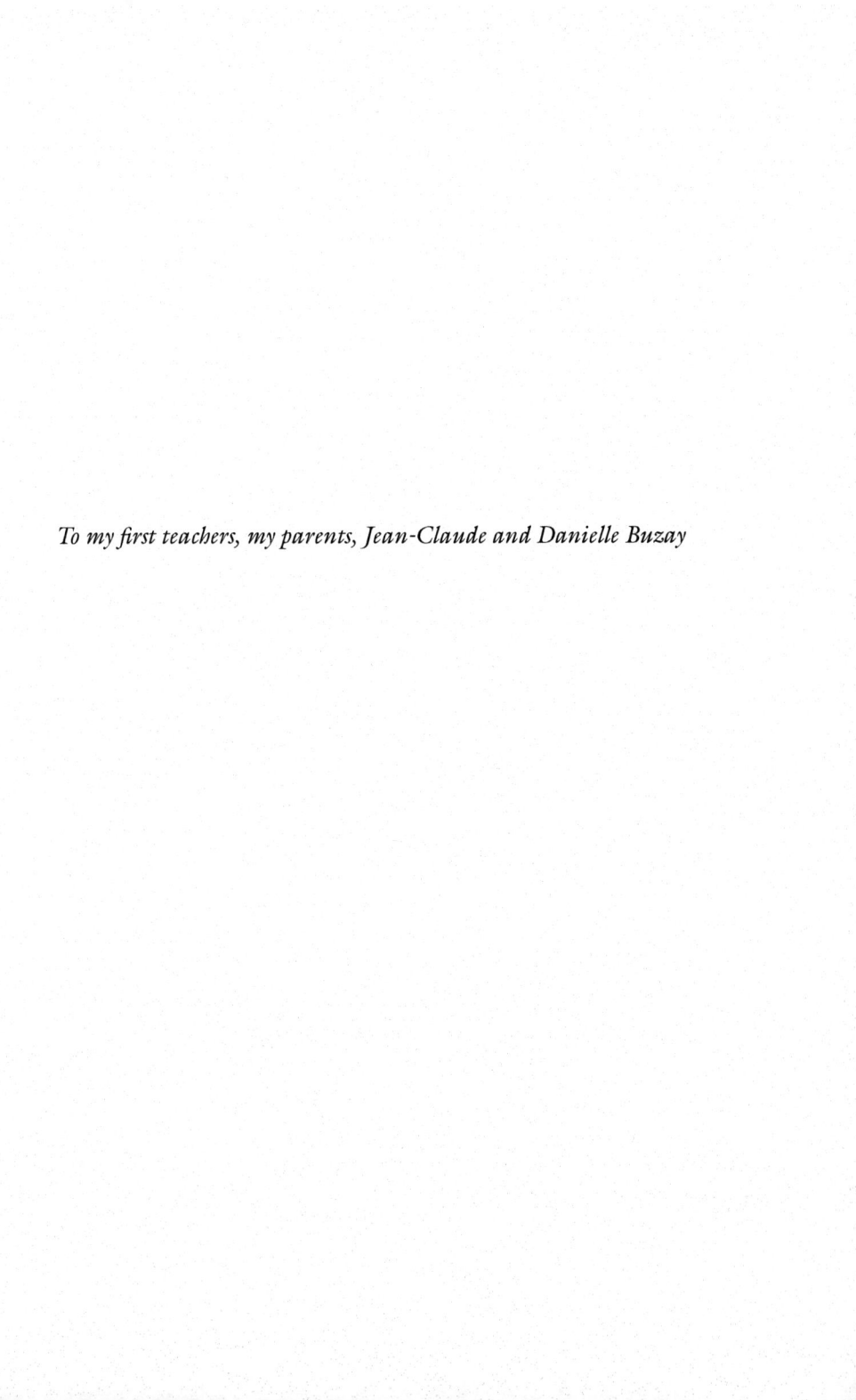

To my first teachers, my parents, Jean-Claude and Danielle Buzay

Acknowledgements

Writing a book is a long process, and this one was no exception. The roots of this book dig deep into my past—as far back as my adolescence when my aunt, Jocelyne Král (*in memoriam*), gave me a copy of Kate Wilhelm's *Juniper Time*, which launched me on a winding path through the worlds of science fiction from which I have yet to emerge. The essential ideas I develop here grew from my doctoral studies, first those in France, directed by Jacques Perriault (*in memoriam*), and more specifically in my dissertation, which was nourished by the insights of my teachers and colleagues at the University of Connecticut, most especially through the guidance of my advisor, Anne Berthelot, whose impressive breadth and depth of knowledge repeatedly improved my work, in addition to the advice of my other dissertation committee members, Éliane DalMolin and Roger Célestin. As a beginning academic at the University of Massachusetts—Amherst, my colleagues in the French and Francophone Studies section of the Department of Languages, Literatures, and Cultures have continued to support my work, giving me the time and space to develop and mature the ideas I began with my dissertation, even during this unprecedented period of the Covid-19 pandemic. I must also add that as a native French speaker, the idea of writing this book in English was incredibly daunting, but thanks to the editorial work, both of Rose Ernst, and of my wife, Elisabeth Buzay, I have confidence that my sometimes-rough prose has been smoothed out—and that any remaining errors are my own. I am also very thankful for Allie Troyanos' flexibility and understanding as Executive

Director and Head of Literature at Palgrave Macmillan. Finally, I owe my thanks to my extended family—my parents, Jean-Claude and Danielle Buzay, and my in-laws, Eric and Judy Herbst, in particular—for helping me to have the space and time to work, as well as supporting me over the past years as I have grown my ideas from their initial stages into the completed book they have become. Many thanks, at last, to my wife, Elisabeth, for our many discussions and her help editing, and to my children, Julia, Gabriel, and Margo, for inspiring me.

Peyrilles (France), July 15, 2022

CONTENTS

CHAPTER 1

Introduction

The past is latent, is submerged, but still there, capable of rising to the surface once the later imprinting unfortunately—and against ordinary experience—vanished. The man contains—not the boy—but earlier men, he
thought. History began a long time ago.
Philip K. Dick, *Ubik*

The Longing to be Written and its Refusal is a book of ideas based on the
interwoven fabric of my non-academic professional and academic experiences, which have occurred in the wide-ranging fields of Information
Science and Communications, diplomacy, multimedia center manage-
ment, and, of course, French and Francophone literature. This book provides a new understanding of French and Francophone contemporary
science fiction, and more specifically reveals how, in the wake of Cyrano de
Bergerac's and Voltaire's philosophical tales, this genre's metafictional features and the metaphors of the book related to nature, the world, and the
universe address, question, and reframe the mythologies of the creation of
writing. Furthermore, this text questions why these mythologies matter,
allowing us to understand the idea of humanity, as well as recent claims of
the advent of a posthumanity.

These reflections all started for me at the end of the first stage of my
academic life at the University of Paris 3—Sorbonne Nouvelle, after first
earning a Master's degree in contemporary French literature and then a

© The Author(s), under exclusive license to Springer Nature
Switzerland AG 2022
E. Buzay, *Contemporary French and Francophone Futuristic Novels*,
Studies in Global Science Fiction,
https://doi.org/10.1007/978-3-031-16628-0_1

professional Master's degree in publishing focused on editorial techniques and professional writing, and thanks to which the emphasis on linguistics, computer science, and publishing uses and practices provided me the opportunity to be accepted for a long-term internship at the Éditions Larousse publishing house. Shortly after this experience, I completed my French national service by working in Canada as a linguistic attaché at the French Embassy in Ottawa in the early 1990s, where the cultural adviser had the choice between keeping me in Ottawa to write memos, draft telegrams, and organize cultural missions and sending me to Alberta to support an association of French teachers. Thanks to my internship at Éditions Larousse, I was asked to remain in Ottawa in a position that not only included more responsibility, but also allowed me to have a first-hand view of the French cultural missions in Canada. The language industry, a field in which Canada played a predominant role at the time, was one of the areas that I was asked to closely observe, and it was in the course of this mission that I selected two key French scholars—Jean-Pierre Balpe and Pierre Lévy, specialists in hypermedia and literary studies in relation to computer networks—who were invited to travel to Canada for a lecture tour of several Canadian universities that I organized and scheduled.

Clearly something of importance was in the air, and when the French diplomatic presence in North America became aware of the surge in significance of the Internet, as a wider audience started to use it through the World Wide Web in 1993–1994, I witnessed the diplomats' geopolitical concerns. Returning to France in the second half of the 1990s was somewhat turbulent, due to the economic crisis, and when I was looking for a job, I faced a dilemma: I could either work part-time for publishing companies or find a full-time position if I were willing to test the waters in one of the new professional activities that were emerging with the expanding use of the Internet. It was by choosing the latter that I found myself working as a multimedia manager in charge of a cybercafé that was part of the Videothèque of Paris (known as the Forum des images starting in 2000), a cultural institution that began as an archive dedicated to the cinematographic memory of the city, although it has since expanded its mission to encompass a wider range of medias and cultural events. Although very pleasant, this work was not necessarily challenging, even if it had the advantage of placing me at the forefront as an observer of how people used the new media of the Internet, as well as what their expectations of it were. Furthermore, the Internet appeared to be a positive development that served the public good in innovative ways, as well as supporting idealistic claims such as providing free, worldwide access to libraries, museums, and other institutions.

The confrontation in perspectives that I saw between the earlier political point-of-view and the on-the-ground experiences of Internet use had a lasting impact on my understanding of this technology and my desire to study its implications. Indeed, the shift was huge between what, in the realm of French diplomacy, I had glimpsed of the potentialities of the Internet from a geopolitical perspective and, at the Forum des images, the ever-evolving media environment that fostered new projects and new economic developments. These differences led me to wonder more and more about their coexistence, and in 1999 to start a Diplôme d'études approfondies (the academic coursework and diploma completed in the French university system prior to the research work of a doctorate) in Information Science and Communications Studies while still working at the Forum des images. Of all the classes I took, my favorite seminar was very quickly the one given by Professor Jacques Perriault. Interestingly, Perriault used to be a computer scientist before earning a doctorate in Information Science and Communications Studies for which his dissertation was entitled *Machines à communiquer: logique des fonctions, logique des usages* (*Communication machines: logic of functions, logic of uses*). Perriault's work was particularly appealing to me due to his unique interdisciplinary approach to usage logic that put into dialogue Seymour Papert's constructionist learning theories and anthropologist André Leroi-Gourhan's understanding of human evolution based on technology. I still have vivid memories of the key points Perriault emphasized as he tried to understand the magnitude that the Internet was then taking on in contemporary society. In his seminars, Perriault repeated frequently that any technology in its deployment required a *symbolic engine* that necessitated a methodological approach[1] that included taking into account a long-term

---

[1] In 2015 in an interview (Perriault) (Jacques Perriault, « Retour sur la logique de l'usage », *Revue française des sciences de l'information et de la communication* [https://journals.openedition.org/rfsic/1221], 6 | 2015) with Professor Alexandre Coutant in communication studies at UQAM, Jacques Perriault revisited his concept of the "logic of use" of communication technology (Perriault and Schaeffer) and qualified the tenets of his approach by calling it "socio-cognitive" and "anthropological," before quoting Pascal Boyer's definition of cognitive anthropology in his preface to *The Naturalness of Religious Ideas: a cognitive theory of religion* in its French edition (Boyer, *La religion comme phénomène naturel*), of which the English-language original is: "... the study of cognitive processes [...] [allowing] us to reformulate many classic problems of anthropology and to put forward more precise hypotheses about the acquisition and transmission of cultural representations" (Boyer, *The Naturalness of Religious Ideas*, xi).

view of history. Furthermore, at that time, he thought that the *symbolic engine* of the Internet had something to do with the desire to participate in the emergence of a planetary consciousness.

The link between a form of writing and technologies was one of the aspects of Perriault's methodology that most struck me. It was the historic process of Internet based on a *symbolic engine*, among the many ideas developed in Perriault's seminars, that revealed his hypothesis that Internet was the result of a "reticular writing" made of hybrid forms of languages and technologies, a notion that referred to the work of the French archaeologist, historian, and linguist, Clarisse Herrenschmidt. I was attracted by this notion and by Herrenschmidt's views which ended up being a determining factor for me in the context of my present work—and indeed in this book—although I did not know at first how they could fit in my own research agenda. When I finally decided to start a PhD with Perriault in 2002, having started a new position as multimedia manager in the Parisian suburb of Nanterre, Perriault's intention was to have me study either the uses of the Internet in the municipal Internet public accesses I was managing at the time or the politics in norms and standards in communication technologies, given my previous experience in diplomacy. However, I did not find these subjects appealing, and so I met with him several times to envision the possibilities of other subjects, before finally deciding, due to my position's professional workload that I had underestimated, in addition to our differing perspectives, that completing the doctorate in those conditions would not be possible for me. Ironically enough, despite the disappointment I felt at the time, in addition to his teachings and writing, one of our meetings about potential doctorate research topics that was fruitless in that regard, nonetheless eventually served as the basis for my current study and the hypotheses I develop in this book, and so, despite our differences of opinion, I remain truly indebted to and appreciative of Perriault's influence.

The essential discussion concerning research topics that I had with Perriault was a moment that crystallized for me a tie between literature and technology that I continue to explore to this day. I had been reading a collection of short stories for teenagers entitled *Les Visages de l'humain*[2] (*Faces of the Human*) that questions posthumanism, and while discussing with Perriault the main goals of my new job, for which I had to help the Nanterre public libraries organize events for the young public, our discus-

---

[2] *Les Visages De L'humain: Anthologie.* Paris: Mango-Jeunesse, 2008.

sion eventually touched on the uncanny figure of the automaton, which I have always found fascinating. Upon hearing this, Perriault suggested that I read the scientific review *Culture technique* archived in the Arts et Métiers Library, which might help me to broaden my research to include the work of other researchers in Information Science and Communications Studies, before reflecting on the past to explore this topic... When I responded, "So I will look in the archives as far back as the 17th century," satisfied with myself for having understood his suggestion, he shocked me by raising his eyebrows and answering, "No, probably as far as antiquity!" A few years after this meeting, when I knew that I would probably be starting a new cycle of studies due to an upcoming move to the USA, I followed Perriault's advice, went to the Arts et Métiers Library, and found a 1982 article written by Juliette Grange, "L'ange automate" ("The Automaton Angel")[3] in the *Culture technique* archives, that made a strong impression on me concerning the *symbolic engine* to which Perriault referred, and allowed me to tie these notions into the French and Francophone literature studies I later undertook at the University of Connecticut.

When I began my PhD at the University of Connecticut, my very open-minded advisor, Professor Anne Berthelot, assured me that I could incorporate the specific theoretical lenses I had been developing in the fields of Information Science and Communication Studies to treat a French contemporary literary subject related to posthuman ideology that would focus on works in the science fiction genre. It is odd to explain how Information Science and Communication Studies research done by computer scientists and engineers began to provide a solid framework in my literary research, but it did it based on a specific interest I had for literary science fiction that began as a teenaged reader and developed over the years, as my curiosity to comprehend the soft power of new medias such as the Internet grew and changed.

Now, on a sidenote, I have to say that I am not a typical science fiction reader. In high school, in the 1980s, I read a number of science fiction works that remain linked together in my mind, not only due to the fact that I read them at a similar moment, but also because of some basic similarities in their messages and meaning. These books, which I read in French, are: Jules Verne's *20,000 Leagues under the Sea*, Vercors's *We Shall Know Them*, René Barjavel's *Ravage*, and Pierre Boulle's *Planet of the*

[3] Grange, Juliette, « L'ange automate—Histoire des robots au XIXe siècle. » Culture Technique N°7—1982. http://hdl.handle.net/2042/30780.

Apes. I was particularly attracted by the way these works address what makes a civilization worthy and by the philosophical tone of their contents—in fact, Boulle, for one, claimed multiple times that *Planet of the Apes* was not a science fiction novel, but a philosophical tale. While such readings were not really encouraged in the classical French educational system, the reading in translation of dystopian novels was acceptable, and so my science fiction readings resonated with those I read in school, such as *Brave New World* by Aldous Huxley, *1984* by George Orwell, and *Fahrenheit 451* by Ray Bradbury. All of these works eventually played a key role in the constitution of the group of works that I study in this book. But if there is one book that truly was the seed from which this selection grew, it is one I read at an even younger age, in middle school, which left a deep impression on me and that I have reread several times in its French translation: *Le Temps des genévriers*[4] or *Juniper Time*[5] by Kate Wilhelm. At that time, besides the exotic (to me) setting of this novel in California and in Oregon, and the fascinating characters, including both Native Americans and the two protagonists (a young female linguist and young astronaut) who have in common astronaut fathers who help build a space station as the world faces a catastrophic drought, what struck me was the importance of language, since a message engraved on a gold plate from some supposed extraterrestrial form of life had to be decoded, although readers understand at the end of this science fiction novel that it is a fake message. I especially remember the scene when, sitting under a juniper tree in the Oregon desert, Jean, the female linguist, fully envisions the power of a message in an unknown language to the point that "one person could say a few magic words and change everything" (Wilhelm 244), and I think that I kept in mind this idea of a strange, new media that used ancient technologies, thus bridging the gap between civilizations and holding up a mirror that we desperately need in times of crisis. In sum, then, this is the path I followed to arrive at my interest in a very specific form of SF: those works that use languages or forms of medias as a plot device.

To return to my doctoral studies and the notions I developed through my research that are continued here in this book, in addition to explaining my interest in science fiction as a genre, I also should detail further how my insights about and fascination with automatons that first started in the Arts et Métiers Library built up the framework of my research. These

[4] Wilhelm, Kate, and Sylvie Audoly. *Le Temps Des Genevriers: Roman.* Paris: Denoël, 1980.
[5] Wilhelm, Kate. *Juniper Time: A Novel.* New York: Harper & Row, Publishers, 1979.

insights eventually led to another understanding of the significance of messages and our own humanity in science fiction works, just as it did in Wilhelm's *Juniper Time*: in other words, in the science fiction texts upon which I focus, messages exist that mirror who we need to think and/or believe we are. This understanding formed over time and included work in a variety of areas that slowly came together to form my current interpretations. One key moment in this evolving understanding occurred in a research paper I wrote during my doctorate that concerned how Gaby Wood's chapter, "Magical Mysteries, Mechanical Dreams," in her book *Edison's Eve. A Magical History of the Quest for Mechanical Life*, partially inspired the graphic novel written by Brian Selznick, *The Invention of Hugo Cabret*, which was about the fictional life of the French moviemaker Georges Méliès, who turned the pieces of an automaton into one of the very first movie cameras. In my readings for this research paper, I discovered the first pages of the French engineer and scientist Jean-Claude Heudin's *Les Créatures Artificielles: Des Automates Aux Mondes Virtuels (Artificial Creatures: From Automata to Virtual Worlds)* (26–28), which were about the myth of Pandora, and revealed a thought process that was strikingly similar to Perriault's approach, as well as referring to Philippe Breton's *À L'image De L'homme: Du Golem Aux Créatures Virtuelles (In the Image of Man: From Golem to Virtual Creatures)*, which represents a theoretical cornerstone in the (hypo)thesis that I am going to unfold over the course of this book. At the core of Breton's study is the idea that artificial creatures, along with communication and information technologies more widely speaking, help humanity in the process of self-reflection by making avatars of itself. This leads Breton to the following reflection: "The look that is given to the most contemporary techniques of computer science is less devoted to the tool than to the project that gave birth to it and to its meaning in a global narrative that sees the human in the artificial,"[6] and he later explains how theological and mythological texts matter in the understanding of modern technological advances, given the fact that "[t]hese texts continue an ancient narrative and, as in every epoch, this one comes to be lodged in the means of expression that seems

---

[6] Translations of texts originally written in French are mine, unless otherwise noted. « Le regard qui est porté sur les techniques les plus contemporaines de l'informatique est moins consacré à l'outil qu'au projet qui lui a donné naissance et à sa signification dans un récit global qui voit de l'humain dans de l'artifice » (Breton 8).

the most legitimate."[7] Either qualified as "global" or "ancient," this narrative is not clearly defined in *In the Image of Man: From Golem to Virtual Creatures*, but having finally read Clarisse Herrenschmidt's *Les trois écritures: langue, nombre, code* (*The Three Scriptures: Language, Number, Code*)—this scholar whose work as a linguist and archeologist was highly praised in Perriault's seminars—my hypothesis extended to include the notion that the mythical narratives, to which Herrenschmidt refers in her chapter, "Writing as a double of mankind" (189–219), show "some analogy between the modalities of the emergence of the human race and the writing system that notes the language in which it was written,"[8] echoing Breton's thoughts on "a global narrative" and "an ancient narrative," which are at the origin of the development of contemporary information technologies that can modify our humanity and help us better understand dystopian uses of sciences.

My book, thus, bases itself on the theoretical background detailed above, which allows for new and useful interpretations of the contemporary French and Francophone science fiction novels I have selected to study. My selection focuses on works that transport their readers "into a fantasy world where the protagonists, unbending in their resolve, overcome ever more surprising obstacles" (Pavel 292) and wonder how to inhabit that world despite such obstacles. My book's central idea is that futuristic novels are unique in their dual identity, which deems science fiction to be a genre that allows readers to *think* about how we are a "narrative species" (Levinson 107), as Paul Levinson, another scholar in communication and media studies, reminds us in *The Soft Edge: A Natural History and Future of the Information Revolution*. Furthermore, I will argue that science fiction novels are based on scientific extrapolations or technological issues—but also reactivate the mythologies that represent writing as the "double of mankind" (for example in mythological writings such as *Genesis*, works about Pandora, *Gilgamesh*, and Mesopotamian poetry), an approach inspired by Herrenschmidt's investigations—by questioning, reframing, or subverting the metaphors of the books (the book of nature, the book of the world, and the book of the universe) to

---

[7] « Ces textes continuent un récit ancien et, comme à chaque époque, celui-ci vient se loger dans le moyen d'expression qui paraît le plus légitime » (Breton 105).

[8] « … quelque analogie entre les modalités de l'émergence de l'humain et le système d'écriture qui note la langue dans laquelle il fut rédigé » (Herrenschmidt 193).

allow humanity to reflect upon itself and the meaning of its mutations through technology. By doing so, *Contemporary French and Francophone Futuristic Novels. The Longing to be Written and its Refusal* sheds a new light on the metafictional aspects of futuristic novels. It examines the fictional minds of characters and their conceptions of resistance to the anticipated worlds they inhabit. More specifically, from the fictional readers' points of view, it provides a critical approach to the mythologies of writing I previously mentioned, in the wake of the French philosophical tales by authors including Cyrano de Bergerac and Voltaire, to question the traditionally expressed formulations of the mythologies of writing, that is, of the metaphors of the book, in order to rethink the idea of humanity within its limits.

More than in countries like Canada and Belgium, in France where science fiction has until recently been slow to find academic legitimacy, as exemplified by Serge Lehman in his article "La Légende du processeur d'histoire"[9] ("The Legend of the History Processor"), science fiction is certainly not univocal, and at the end of the twentieth century as well as at the beginning of the twenty-first century, it appears to be fragmented into sub-genres which gain all the more relevance as they relate, renew, or subvert the standards of general literature, with the exception of some well-known French and Francophone science fiction writers. The selection of books that I have chosen to illustrate the ideas that I have just presented illustrates this case in point, and in addition, these books all have in common the fact that they feature fictional readers whose readings make them resistant and discordant in relation to their society and cause them to act in the worlds in which they evolve before widening the scope of their understanding, as they find out that they have woven themselves into narratives that they can accept, revisit, or even reject. All these novels overlay a *sense of wonder* that defines science fiction for many readers and includes reading experiences that ask, according to Thomas Pavel, "whether, in order to uphold ideas in a world that does not guarantee their supremacy, individuals must simply resist the world, act to change it, or concentrate on overcoming their own failings" (Pavel 18). In these circumstances, books are metaphysical compasses not only for fictional readers to teach

---

[9] Lehman Serge, « La Légende du processeur d'histoire », Cycnos, vol.22.1(La science-fiction dans l'histoire, l'histoire dans la science-fiction), 2005, mis en ligne en novembre 2006. http://epi-revel.univ-cotedazur.fr/publication/item/609.

them how to inhabit their respective worlds, but also for science fiction readers who enjoy the *estrangement* such readings invite, and which is often driven by the "familiarity-strangeness paradox" as Anne Besson defines it:

> In all logic concerning a paradox, it made us describe a circle: from a fiction grafting its imaginary continuation on a real science, we pass to a fiction which wants to be more broadly of the same status as the scientific, to the point of authorizing its verification, but while remaining an inescapably and ostensibly fictional fiction, and which is finally going to be able to assume this fictionality to hold the contradiction in the definition of the fiction itself. […] The opposition science/vs/fiction is not reduced, but transposed in the terms knowledge-imagination, stability of knowledge-evasion through dreams, familiarity-authenticity, a contradiction this time not only accepted but even taken on as the framework of the definition of the genre.[10]

The "familiarity-strangeness paradox" that Besson identified is present in mainstream science fiction, dystopian speculative fiction, and transgressive fiction, in different ways. The gap is maximal—or at times "indeterminate"—between "familiarity" and "strangeness" in mainstream science fiction, whereas this gap is much smaller in the case of the dystopian speculative fiction; in the case of transgressive fiction, the "familiarity-strangeness" paradox is subverted and tends more toward a form of avant-garde writing that reflects on the act of writing.

My selected works include a variety of texts illustrating these three types of science fiction texts. Two mainstream science fiction novels setting up post-apocalyptic dystopias—*The Silent City* (2002) by Elisabeth Vonarburg and *Les Derniers Hommes* (*The Last Men*) (2005) by Pierre Bordage—revisit the mythological bedrocks of the narratives of *Genesis* and the *Apocalypse* in the Bible and give particular consistence to the biblical

---

[10] « En toute logique concernant un paradoxe, il nous a fait décrire un cercle: d'une fiction greffant sa continuation imaginaire sur une science réelle, on passe à une fiction qui se veut plus largement de même statut que le scientifique, au point d'autoriser sa vérification, mais tout en restant une fiction inéluctablement et ostensiblement fictive, et qui va enfin pouvoir assumer cette fictionnalité pour porter la contradiction dans la définition même de la fiction. (…) L'opposition science/vs/fiction n'est pas réduite, mais transposée dans les termes savoir-imagination, stabilité de la connaissance-évasion par le rêve, familiarité-altérité, contradiction cette fois non seulement acceptée mais même assumée comme cadre de définition du genre. » Anne Besson. "Les paradoxes science-fictionnels: état des lieux critique(s)". Jean Bessière (éd.).Littérature, représentation, fiction, Honoré Champion, 2007. 233.

metaphors of the book that are approached from a similar point of view in both books in their comprehension of the laws of Nature. Additional works can be classified as dystopian speculative fiction in the vein of the dystopias mentioned before by Huxley, Orwell, and Bradbury: *The First Century After Beatrice* (1995) by Amin Maalouf, *Globalia* (2005) by Jean-Christophe Rufin, and *Our Life in the Forest* (2018) by Marie Darrieussecq, all of these novels having been written by writers who were already well-known in the French literary landscape. Finally, the examples of transgressive fictions or "transfictions,"[11] as Francis Berthelot termed them, are unique in the way that they both transgress the order of the world and the order of the story, since they constitute "an interface, a kind of nebula surrounding the boundary between general literature and literatures of the imagination, a nebula whose contours are necessarily indistinct" (Berthelot 19). The works that are of this sub-genre are: *The Possibility of an Island* (2007) by Michel Houellebecq and *Songes de Mevlido* (2007) (*Mevlido's Dreams*) by Antoine Volodine. These two French authors have completely opposite points of view and convictions, but these works transgress the order of the world and the order of the story in order to reflect on what it means to be a *last man of writing*, with aspects that are strongly reminiscent of Philip K. Dick's *Do Androids Dream of Electric Sheep* (1968) and *Ubik* (1969). In Houellebecq's and Volodine's works, the two characters are a nihilist posthuman who, under Houellebecq's pen, rounds out his understanding of the *Bible* and an ex-revolutionary, in Volodine's work, who struggles with the *Bardo Thödol*. Even if Antoine Volodine claims not to be a science-fiction writer, many of his novels retain the imprint of science fiction, as Emmanuel Jouanne argued[12] starting in the 1980s with a piece exploring how new French fiction authors, including Volodine, kept on being inspired by Philip K. Dick, an author who particularly at the end of his life worked at the crossroads of science fiction and general literature. Thus, in Dick, as with Volodine in *Songes de Mevlido*, "one 'hallucinates' one's existence, one travels in time, one meets avatars or simulacra of the human being, one manipulates one's levels of consciousness in various ways, and one experiences frequent crises

---

[11] Berthelot, Francis. *Bibliothèque De L'entre-Mondes: Guide De Lecture, Les Transfictions.* Paris: Gallimard, 2005.

[12] Jouanne, Emmanuel et al. How "Dickian" Is the New French Science Fiction? (La nouvelle science-fiction française: est-elle dickienne?). Science Fiction Studies, *[s. l.],* v. 15, n. 2, pp. 226–231, 1988.

as to the certainty of what surrounds us."[13] As for Houellebecq, his ambition, according to Stephen Metcalf, "has been to mingle the libertinage of Laclos with the science fiction of Philip K. Dick,"[14] in the way he describes the sentimental life of his main character, Daniel, before he is cloned. We can see an example of this in the fact that in this novel, poetry revives a desire which withers in the posthuman clones.

The following paragraphs offer an overview of the contents of this book. The opening chapter "Reading the Enigmatic Worlds of Futuristic Novels" focuses on the dual identity of the contemporary French and Francophone futuristic novels studied here and in which metafictionality prevails: on the one hand, science fiction, as well as its subgenres of dystopian speculative fiction and "transfiction" are based on scientific extrapolations and technological issues, but on the other hand, stories of these (sub)genres reactivate mythologies of writing that have existed since time immemorial. Therefore, this chapter explores a distinction between an external approach, in which readers investigate a different world than their own to compare those two worlds (with reference to the notion of "novum" and its variations elaborated by Darko Suvin), and an internal approach leading the same readers to investigate ostensibly dated and historically marked concepts, such as the books of the world and nature. The chapter concludes with an illustration of this second approach through the study of the figure of the last man.

Through an external approach, Chap. 3 "Modalities and Fictional Storyworlds in Futuristic Novels," surveys the different storyworlds of my selected texts, categorized by whether in these worlds the characters act, make others act, or are acted upon, according to possible worlds theories applied to cognitive narratology in *Fictional Minds* by Alan Palmer and his interpretations of Lubomir Doležel's *Heterocosmica*. In relation to the dual structures of these storyworlds suggested by Doležel, in which each (sub)genre's storyworlds pair ability and another modality—those of knowledge (science fiction), duty (dystopian speculative fiction), and a deceptive ability (transfiction), respectively—this chapter depicts

---

[13] « … on "hallucine" son existence, on voyage dans le temps, on croise des avatars ou des simulacres de l'humain, on manipule diversement ses niveaux de conscience, et l'on éprouve de fréquentes crises quant à la certitude de ce qui nous entoure. » Laforest, D. (2008). Les révolutionnaires rêvent-ils de moutons électriques?/*Songes de Mevlido* d'Antoine Volodine, Seuil, 462 p. *Spirale*, (219), 54.

[14] Metcalf, Stephen. "Clones Behaving Badly." *The New York Times Book Review*, 11 June 2006, p. 14.

dissonant fictional minds in action that both gradually become resistant to the world they live in and whose readings make them aware of their different embodiments: mutants (science fiction), witnesses (dystopian speculative fiction), and body-corpora (transfiction).

Shifting from the external approach of the previous chapter to an initial exploration of the reader's internal approach to understanding the metafictional features of the works of these genres, Chap. 4 "The Idea of the Book and Its Symbolism in Times of Change" provides a critical approach to the mythologies of writing in the wake of the French philosophical tales by authors including Cyrano de Bergerac and Voltaire, to question the traditionally expressed formulations of the mythologies of writing. This includes questioning the metaphors of the book (the book of life, the book of nature, and the book of the world) in order to rethink the idea within humanity's limits. It addresses a recurrent concern regarding these very limits at the core of the posthuman ideology that could be summarized as a trend, which I call a "longing to be written," and demonstrates that the symbolism of the metaphors of the book can be either closed or open. Chapter 4 also explains the relationship of insect animalism to metamorphoses and human mutations.

By continuing the internal approach of the reader begun in the previous chapter, Chap. 5 "Regaining Humanity by Learning from Escapes and Detours" explores how this internal approach can be expanded and deepened to include an exploration of the novel's space. The act of making a detour is a source of human singularity and learning. In that sense, this chapter tackles the importance of the body for the characters who seek to cross uncharted territories to regain a sense of memory and escape their worlds. Chapter 5 continues to develop and evaluate how the metaphors of the "book of nature" and the "book of the world" (previously explored in Chap. 4) are essential to an understanding of the digital age and the advent of a posthumanity, as well as the dystopias that preceded them, and explains how in futuristic novels physical manhunts turn into metaphysical manhunts where the act of hunting or the trial of walking—when being hunted—parallel the act of reading.

In Chap. 6, "Encounters with Bodies and Narratives: A Matrix of Contemporary Philosophical Quests," I will discuss three works, *Sulphuric Acid* (2008) by Amélie Nothomb, *The Horde of Counterwind* (*La Horde du Contrevent* (2004)) by Alain Damasio, and *Latium* (2016) by Romain Lucazeau, explore how our corporal postures serve as a matrix for contemporary philosophical quests. Each of these works takes a different approach to an examination of the value and power of speaking and writing. More specifically, in *Sulphuric Acid*, the use of speech and the value of literature are questioned by situations of violence and suffering, which lead readers to question their status as fragile gatekeepers of humanity, topics which I delve into more deeply by using a philosophical framework based on Hannah Arendt's work. In a different approach, in *The Horde of Counterwind* and *Latium*, writing and being able to narrate stories based on a corporeal standpoint are used to show the limits of an embodied consciousness's capacities, whether that embodied consciousness be human or mutant. In a parallel move to that in with the first of the three novels, I examine the influences of Spinoza's and Nietzsche's philosophies in Damasio's work, while for Lucazeau's novel, I do the same with the influences of Plato's and Leibniz's philosophies.

Finally, the conclusion outlines the issues at stake that I have studied thus far and focuses on the spirit of resistance through the body that, despite posthuman desires, resists elimination if such changes do not take into account the collective, a notion that is deeply seated in French and Francophone culture. I then widen my reflection to include the work of the scientist-author David Elbaz, whose incorporation of similar literary motifs in his scientific and popular science works further demonstrates the pertinence of my argument. I close with an argument underlining the importance of a desire-driven body in mediating the world and in renewing the hypothesis that the sense of memory, molded by writing, shapes the imaginary of humanity's potential changes and mutations.

BIBLIOGRAPHY

Berthelot, Francis. *Bibliothèque de l'entre-mondes: Guide de lecture, les transfictions.* Gallimard, 2005.

Boyer, Pascal. *La religion comme phénomène naturel.* Bayard Éditions, 1997.

———. *The Naturalness of Religious Ideas: A Cognitive Theory of Religion.* University of California Press, 1994.

Breton, Philippe. *À l'image de l'homme: du Golem aux créatures virtuelles.* Seuil, 1995.

Herrenschmidt, Clarisse. *Les trois écritures: language, nombre, code.* Gallimard, 2007.

Levinson, Paul. *The Soft Edge: A Natural History and Future of the Information Revolution.* Routledge, 1997.

Pavel, Thomas G. *Lives of the Novel: A History.* Princeton University Press, 2013.

Perriault, Jacques. "Retour sur la logique de l'usage." *Revue française des sciences de l'information et de la communication,* no. 6, 6, Société Française de Sciences de l'Information et de la Communication, Jan. 2015. journals.openedition. org, https://doi.org/10.4000/rfsic.1221.

Perriault, Jacques, and Pierre Schaeffer. *La logique de l'usage: essai sur les machines à communiquer.* L'Harmattan, 2008.

Wilhelm, Kate. *Juniper Time.* Harper and Row, 1979.

CHAPTER 2

Reading the Enigmatic Worlds of Futuristic Novels

In the early 1990s, the development of the Internet was popularized by the first uses of the World Wide Web information system, and with this, utopian worldviews grew in number. Subsequently, some French scholars in Media and Communications Studies, such as Pierre Musso and Yves Jeanneret, among others, started to research the imaginary sources that could explain the development of such (new) technologies. In *Télécommunications et philosophie des réseaux: La postérité paradoxale de Saint-Simon,* Pierre Musso (1998) conceptualized the success of the idea of the "network" and its expansion as the secular form of "communion" from a positivist point of view. Yves Jeanneret examined the imaginary bedrock at the origins of science fiction through the lens of the meaning of "scientific marvel" as a proto-science fiction that emphasizes that anticipation as a genre seems to be characterized by a "dual identity" binding the empowerment of technological knowledge to the reactivation of ancient mythologies:

> Scientific Marvel [translates] better the dual identity of the work of anticipation: supported by real knowledge, a condition of plausibility, it reactivates the myths of an immemorial imagination. The growing powers of technology

© The Author(s), under exclusive license to Springer Nature Switzerland AG 2022
E. Buzay, *Contemporary French and Francophone Futuristic Novels,* Studies in Global Science Fiction, https://doi.org/10.1007/978-3-031-16628-0_2

give tangible character to deep fears and senseless aspirations, while capacity for imagination is projected, symmetrically on real innovation (Jeanneret 25).[1]

Such a trend is certainly exhibited less nowadays than in the nineteenth century, but still prevails. Here, I will focus this notion of "dual identity" and apply it to my study of the metafictional features that trigger a sense of "self-understanding,"[2] as Margaret Atwood coined it. In the book selection I examine, I will focus on their twofold aspects by reconceiving the use of metaphors, such as the *window* and the *mirror*, as they were introduced by Albert Wendland in reference to science fiction:

> ... my focus might be summarized by speaking of science fiction as either a window or a mirror, showing, respectively, 'worlds without' or 'worlds within'. The worlds created in science fiction are clearly inside us, but they are also attempts to depict something outside, to be—as much as possible— genuinely alien and new. In other words, science fiction can act as a *mirror* or as a *window* depending on how it is maneuvered by the author. It is like a pane of glass that can behave in two ways. If held so that the light shines directly through it onto the author's creations, the reader is sometimes fooled into thinking that glass is not there, that he is seeing genuine aliens, genuine futures, genuine other worlds that have nothing to do with him, the wonders of other places and times, of pure escape, of playing in the presumed sensation of difference. But if held in a slightly different way, a pane of glass also reflects, and the onlooker might catch a glimpse of himself, might see his own image even stronger than that of the new scene (Wendland 6–7).

While Wendland associates conventional science fiction with the window and experimental science fiction with the mirror, I argue that those two metaphors can designate two seminal phases in the reading process of a same work of science fiction and that I will term these phases a *window stage* and a *mirror stage*, each of which I will examine in more detail in the following sections. I suggest that there is an external approach, in which readers investigate a different world other than theirs to compare

---

[1] « Merveilleux scientifique [traduit] mieux la double identité de l'œuvre d'anticipation: étayée sur un savoir réel, condition du plausible, elle réactive les mythes d'un imaginaire immémorial. Les pouvoirs croissants de la technique donnent un caractère tangible à des peurs profondes et à des aspirations insensées, tandis que se projette, symétriquement sur l'innovation réelle une charge d'imaginaire » (Jeanneret 25).

[2] "By 'myth' I mean a story central to our self-understanding" (Atwood 54).

the two worlds, and an internal approach that explores how ostensibly dated and historically marked concepts such as the book of the world and the book of nature broaden their reading, in the retelling of "myths of an immemorial imagination", as per Yves Jeanneret.

LOOKING FOR CLUES: THE INVESTIGATIONS ENTRUSTED TO THE READER

In the window stage, the reader's mind has to fill in the gaps in the author's creations. By inferring the rules of new worlds in which a full spectrum of enigmatic alterities are staged, this reader builds up fictional worlds based on a futuristic framework illustrating the science fiction notion of *cognitive estrangement*, in "the sense that something in the fictive world is dissonant with the reader's experienced world" (James et al. 5); which makes, according to Umberto Eco, most science fiction narratives "narrative[s] of hypothesis and abduction" (Eco, Umberto). This reading process applied to futuristic novels with their conventions, paradoxes, and multiple expectations, arises from a "Model Reader" (1979)—to keep using Eco's terminology—who hypothetically adopts the author's worldview by assuming a "cooperative principle in narrativity" (Eco 256). This reading process also presupposes "a specific encyclopedic competence" (Eco 7) that has recently been studied with great detail in French and Francophone science fiction studies by two scholars whose books, namely *L'Empire du pseudo: Modernités de la science-fiction* (*The Empire of Pseudo: Modernities of Science Fiction*) (1999) by Richard Saint Gelais and *La science-fiction: Lecture et poétique d'un genre littéraire* (*Science Fiction: Reading and Poetics of a Literary Genre*) (2006) by Irène Langlet, complement each other in terms of their use of abductive reasoning in science fiction poetics.

While the Model Reader encompasses a whole spectrum of knowledge, characters, places, objects, or uses, given the actual historical context of mainstream literature that Umberto Eco calls an "encyclopedia," what is implied with science fiction literature is not the same, since knowledge, characters, objects, or places result in cognitive estrangement, under the guise of instability, which critic Richard Saint-Gelais describes as follows: "in science fiction [...] the reader has no other choice but to make encyclopedic readjustments: additions, deletions, or alterations then make it impossible to strictly identify the reader's previous encyclopedia and the one posed or presupposed by the text, that is to say [...] the *xenoencyclopedia*"[3] (Saint-Gelais, *L'empire du pseudo* 140)—stemming from "xénos," which means "alien" in ancient Greek. (I will return to the role of the reader in more detail to illustrate the possible fictional storyworlds that I will examine in Chap. 3.) For this reason, readers must adjust their understanding to take into account this instability.

Any reader of science fiction must therefore make "encyclopedic readjustments" in order to understand the text, and these readjustments require different cognitive activities. All of the cognitive activities analyzed by the semiotician Charles Sanders Peirce in *Elements of Logic*—deduction, induction, and abduction—encourage the use of this xenoencyclopedia in the reader's mind, but abduction best defines the work of the reader in recent science fiction, which can be defined as an "enigma genre, where the elucidation concerns not the culprit of a crime but the coherency of a world or an imaginary world"[4] (Langlet 51).

While in the process of deduction, the statement of a rule tends to explain the unfolding of phenomena, in the induction process the phenomena observed or retained during an analysis are valuable examples and come to confirm the statement of a rule. Abduction, for its part, by soliciting more willingly a logical analysis, completes the two cognitive operations mentioned previously in the sense that the observed phenomena participate in the formulation of hypotheses, rather than rules, that will be confirmed or overturned by later observations.

For Langlet, abduction is a pleasurable activity that consists of "elaborating diegetic and/or encyclopedical hypotheses, in the double network of the imagination of the reader and the fabric of the novel"[5] (Langlet 57), and this "abductive pleasure", as she coins it, has an influence on the way she reframes and adapts the notion of "novum" elaborated by Darko Suvin. Although Suvin argues that the science fiction literary genre has primarily been conceived as "the narrative dominance or hegemony of a fictional '*novum*' (novelty, innovation) validated by cognitive logic" (Suvin, *Metamorphoses of Science Fiction* 63) to conduct a criticism of

---

[3] « … en science-fiction où le lecteur n'a d'autre choix que de procéder à des réajustements encyclopédiques: ajouts, retraits ou altérations rendent alors impossible une identification stricte de l'encyclopédie préalable du lecteur et de celle posée ou présupposée par le texte, c'est-à-dire (…) la *xénoencyclopédie* » (Saint-Gelais, *L'empire du pseudo* 140).

[4] « … genre[s] à énigme, où l'élucidation concerne non pas le coupable d'un crime mais la cohérence d'un monde ou d'un imaginaire » (Langlet 2006, 51)].

[5] « … élaborer des hypothèses diégétiques et / ou encyclopédiques, dans le double réseau de l'imaginaire du lecteur et du tissu romanesque » (Langlet 57).

society in the 1970s, this notion has gradually evolved to broaden the horizon of the cognitive estrangement experienced by the reader, as summarized by Istvan Csicsery-Ronay in his review of Langlet's book for *Science Fiction Studies*:

> ..., Langlet's use of the term novum is not identical to Suvin's. Where Suvin looks in each science fiction text for an overarching new event or object that dominates the global relations of the narrative, Langlet considers each strange device encountered by the reader—a word, a phrase, a pseudo-document—a novum. The difference this makes for analysis is significant. For Suvin, the goal of critical reading is to arrive at the dominant new idea of an science fiction work, the better to use it as a tool for social criticism. Reading for him is a form of dis-enchantment. For Langlet, the goal is to trace the ways the reader builds up coherent imaginary worlds in response to enigmas distributed throughout the science fiction text, at every level of textuality. Reading is guided construction (Csicsery-Ronay).

In the first part of her book entitled "Outils de mécanique science-fictionnelle" ("Tools of science fictional mechanics"), Langlet distinguishes three categories of novums—a term she uses interchangeably with those of alterities or strangeness—in a continued analysis of the hegemonic feature of the novum expressed by its various dimensions[6] (Langlet 17–123). These three types of novums create their own forms of cognitive estrangement as the plots unfold in contemporary French and Francophone futuristic novels, that is, in the genre of science fiction and two of its subgenres, dystopian speculative fiction and "transfiction".

These three categories can be designated, on a scale, as: lexical (on the level of individual words), discursive (on the level of sentences), and empirical or global (on the level of the entire narrative) novums. Though this novum scale exists in all of the genres or subgenres of futuristic novels studied here, each of these genres or subgenres tends to have a preponderance of one type of novum: Lexical novums are often found in anticipation novels that refer to traditional science fiction in order to tie

---

[6] "...it is possible to distinguish various dimensions of the *novum*. Quantitatively, the postulated innovation can be of quite different degrees of magnitude, running from the minimum of one discrete new 'invention' (gadget, technique, phenomenon, relationship) to the maximum of a setting (spatiotemporal locus), agent (main character or characters), and/or relations basically new and unknown in the author's environment" (Suvin, *Metamorphoses of Science Fiction* 64).

scientific questions and issues into the framework of the narrative. Discursive novums usually stage discussions about behavior in the anticipated world in the dystopian speculative fiction genre. Finally, global or empirical novums (a designation describing the global rules, technological stages, and values of an entire society) underline the total discrepancy of the enigmatic features of the anticipated world in transfiction novels.

Furthermore, these distinctions also follow a certain number of divides in terms of their fictional worlds. In the case of utopian and dystopian worlds, the division can be seen between science fiction novels with their utopian worlds, and speculative fiction and transfiction novels with their dystopian worlds. On the one hand, science fiction novels address the legacy of a utopia often expressed and summarized by the use of lexical alterities; whereas on the other hand, the two subgenres of speculative fiction and transfiction novels, which are closer to mainstream literature and are usually more accepted by French and Francophone readers than science fiction, tend to entail dystopian worlds through their use of discursive and global novums, respectively. The introduction of post-apocalyptic settings divides these genres and subgenres differently. In this case, science fiction and transfiction novels are similar in their post-apocalyptic settings, about which readers must resolve lexical and global novums. Dystopian speculative fiction works, however, tend to occur before an apocalypse (if the topic is even mentioned) where discursive novums prevail to reveal the darkest perspectives of a near-future society.

Post-apocalyptic utopias are particularly suited to science fiction novels. In this context, the understanding of the lexical novums, as well as the ways they are reconsidered and reinterpreted, go hand in hand with the progression of the novel's plot, and solicit the reader's cognition and memory. The "becoming artifact" of the principal characters of the novels by Pierre Bordage and Élisabeth Vonarburg thus imposes the tempo of the narration. While at times this "becoming artifact" enlightens the reader concerning that which is enigmatic in the story, at others it contradicts or illustrates the projects of societies whose choices have been riddled with dramas or risks in a post-apocalyptic context. Will the actions of one character or another be the cause of a new apocalypse? To what extent can a utopia be critical? Regardless of the answers to these questions, one thing is certain: the lexical novums that echo these interrogations between "becoming artifact" and societal projects support a mimetic vision of history in which mankind keeps control of the events that occur.

As Carl Malmgren pointed out "some novums are inherently more telling or potentially more fruitful than others, [but] (...) almost any novum, successfully deployed and elaborated, can be turned to cognitive advantage" (Malmgren 29). At the bottom of this ranking appear lexical novums such as the "^{GM}order", the "Eskato", or the "Verb", in *Les Derniers Hommes* by Pierre Bordage, whose explanation is progressive and belongs to the most mimetic examples of science fiction. In this case, these terms designate a succession of threats against a humanity that survived a third world war. Readers' awareness of what the "^{GM}order" represents starts at the first pages of the novel when they realize that the nomadism of the last human tribes is the result of the poisoning of a genetically modified world where a people named the "Aquariots" trade water with the other tribes. The genetically modified world is the initial founding threat of a seemingly dystopian world of survivors in which abduction gradually invites readers to comprehend this change in the world as a consequence of a literal reading of the Apocalypse of John from the Bible:

> The scientists of World War 3 genetically modified insects and other species, like eels, to turn them into weapons," says Ismahil. "But unlike traditional weapons, it was impossible for them to control their proliferation. They therefore created a new order, the ^{GM}order[7] (Bordage 614).

The literal reading of the biblical text constitutes a setting and provides direction in the fictional investigation whose retrospective and prospective inquiries are embodied by the two characters of Ismahil and Solman through their resistance to this order. This refusal is reflected in Ismahil by the decision he made, when he was a young scientist before WW3, not to join an underground society with a "positivist" outlook—the "Eskato", "a secret para-religious type of organization that [sees] in contemporary science the possibility for the accomplishment of Christ's miracles"[8] (Bordage 529)—which he intuits is destined to unleash cataclysms.

For his part, Solman's refusal strikes back at this elitist organization differently since he acts at the end of the novel as a virus, making the choice

---

[7] « Les scientifiques de la Troisième Guerre mondiale ont modifié génétiquement les insectes et d'autres espèces, comme les anguilles, pour en faire des armes, dit Ismahil. Mais contrairement aux armes traditionnelles, il leur était impossible d'en contrôler la prolifération. Ils ont donc créé un nouvel ordre, l'ordre^{GM} » (Bordage 614).

[8] « ... une organisation secrète, de type parareligieux qui [voit] dans la science contemporaine la possibilité d'accomplissement des miracles du Christ » (Bordage 529).

of dying at the very moment when the "Eskato" tries to incorporate him into a device regulated by "a genetic computer program"[9] (Bordage 662) called the "Verb" if he agrees to forget his companions and his vocation as a prophet in their midst. Through this sacrifice, the dystopian order of the world's last men is overthrown and the rejection of the mediation by the book in the conduct of human affairs is replaced by a natural vitalism that (again) becomes a utopia that resonates with discussions that date back to Enlightenment about the noble savage and the state of nature:

> At dawn, they decided to burn the body. "And the book," added Wolf. "One cycle ends. Men must renounce their old beliefs and fall back into Mother Nature's hands"[10] (Bordage 670).

Even if *The Silent City* first takes on the dimensions of a dystopia before taking the final form of a utopia, the "abductive pleasure" mentioned previously by Irène Langlet does not follow a linear path in Élisabeth Vonarburg's work simply because her characters' points of view are more complex since she makes explicit the meaning of the lexical novums she uses and then blurs their meaning as she unfolds the plot of the novel. For the reader who already knows her work, especially the cycle of *Tyranaël* which precedes *The Silent City*, "it is as though the systematization of the process of explaining the novums, which appeared within the framework of one point of view, by the indications gleaned from another point of view, was deconstructing the process in question"[11] (Langlet 85). As they are reinterpreted throughout the novel, the most important lexical novums referred to in words such as "ommachs," "Project," and "Cities" often bring the inferences of these narrative points of view to the formulation of a "critical utopia," a kind of narrative that mostly has been inherited from the trends of the 1970s, in reaction to the dystopian culture at that time:

> The imaginative exploration of better, rather than worse, places found a new form in the "critical utopia." "Critical," in this sense, incorporates an

---

[9] « … programme génétique et informatique » (Bordage 662).

[10] « À l'aube, ils décidèrent de brûler le corps. "Et le livre, ajouta Wolf. Un cycle s'achève. Les hommes doivent renoncer aux vieilles croyances et s'en remettre entre les mains de mère Nature" » (Bordage 670).

[11] « … tout se passe comme si la systématisation du procédé consistant à expliquer les novums, apparus dans le cadre d'un point de vue, par les indications glanées dans un autre point de vue, déconstruisait le procédé en question » (Langlet 85).

Enlightenment sense of critique, a postmodern attitude of self-reflexivity, (...). Shaped by ecological, feminist, and New Left thought, the critical utopia of the 1970s—represented by writers such as Ursula K. Le Guin, Joanna Russ, Marge Piercy, Samuel R. Delany, Ernst Callenbach, Sally Miller Gearhart, and Suzy McKee Charnas—combines vision and practice... (Baccolini and Moylan 2).

As a lexical novum, "ommach" refers once to a remote automaton controlled by either men or women at the last stage of their life and another time to an independent automaton. In Vonarburg's novel, this linguistic innovation thus starts to point out "a corporal artifact" that former scientists, who are protected and hidden in a secret City, after a nuclear war, use in order to inspire fear in other men who are outside and to conduct genetic experiments to repopulate the earth with enhanced individuals. In addition, "ommach" can be the abbreviation of "homme-machine" which means "machine-man" and in French sounds like the adjective "hommasse", the translation of which could be "mannish," an attribute that is usually applied to female characters. All these interpretations open the way to abduction.

Pulled between the process of individuation and the constraints of the social contract in this novel, focal characters in Vonarburg's novels often seek a personal liberation that is part of broader questions relating to their identity. According to this writer, since their origins, men and women are "ontological artifacts" (Vonarburg, "Les femmes en tant qu'artefactes dans la science-fiction moderne" 155), who tend to renew or modify the idea of humankind through a similar impulse, which leads them to transgress their mechanical and organic limitations. "For all, female and male artifacts, the desired evolution goes from dependence-subjection to liberation: to become, so to speak, auto-artifacts by integrating and transcending these different fabrication planes"[12] (Vonarburg, "Les femmes en tant qu'artefactes dans la science-fiction moderne" 155).

The framework of *The Silent City*'s setting is one of a critical utopia in which, as mentioned earlier, two human communities enter into debatable relationships: on one side, there is a form of humankind that has regressed to the stage of a tribal society and, on the other side, there is a group of

---

[12] « Pour tous, artefacts féminins ou masculins, l'évolution désirée va de la dépendance-sujétion à la libération: devenir pour ainsi dire des auto-artefacts en intégrant et en transcendant ces différents plans de fabrication » (Vonarburg, "Les femmes en tant qu'artefactes dans la science-fiction moderne" 155).

scientists sheltered in a hidden city who are eager to prolong their existence by all means possible. At the core of this "critical utopia," a new form of becoming, given the lexical novum of "Project," is created not by the androids' manipulations, but by those of one of the geneticists. Throughout this novel, the question being asked is what kind of ties this project can develop between the City and the other "Cities," this term of "City" being another lexical novum indicated by the use of a capital letter, which designates a societal project that is also potentially controversial:

> But he will tell her later, he'll talk about his research, his Project. She'll understand. A new race capable of surviving in a transformed world. Human beings who won't be afraid of wounds, illness or radiation. Cellular regeneration, and in the final analysis, total mastery of the life process. Probably not immortality: the malevolent dream of the Cities will die with their last inhabitants. But a long and healthy life, a death without decrepitude[13] (Vonarburg, *The Silent City* 16).

This project in fact entails a new form of becoming—embodied by the focal character of Elisa. Her creator, a geneticist named Paul, and Richard Desprats, another scientist, then go on to debate about the topic of Elisa and her descendants and what is to be done with them. The dynamics of Élisabeth Vonarburg's novel play on this opposition between these two scientists' points of view in more than one way. On one level the opposition is between the "Project" and the "City(/ies)," while on another level it is between the genetic engineering attempts initiated by Paul and the computer programming plans conceived by Richard Desprats.

This opposition develops as the narrative continues. In the beginning, from Paul's point of view Elisa and her descendants are called upon to repopulate aging cities before being spread outside among those primitive human tribes who must be kept under control; however, this elitist worldview is reprehensible to Richard Desprats, who pleads for a "deactivation" of other "Cities" of the same kind, as well as for a decolonization or a non-intervention among those outsiders. After

---

[13] « Mais il lui dira, plus tard; il lui parlera de ses recherches, de son Projet. Elle comprendra. Une nouvelle race, capable de survivre dans un monde transformé. Des êtres humains qui ne craindront ni blessures, ni maladies, ni radiations. La régénération cellulaire, et tout au bout, la maîtrise totale des processus vitaux. Pas l'immortalité, sans doute: le rêve maléfique des Cités mourra avec leurs derniers habitants. Mais une vie longue et saine, une mort sans décrépitude » (Vonarburg, *Le silence de la cité* 21–22).

Desprats' apparent death (in actuality he continues to "live" in the form of an "ommach"), a shocking development occurs when Paul realizes that Elisa can be androgynous. This discovery leads Paul to question what should be done with her, instead of supporting her completely as he had previously done. Indeed, the opposition that Paul and Desprats initially cultivated affects the development of the character of Elisa, and she eventually decides to kill her creator, Paul. Her reflections in the narrative suggest that she moves beyond the logic of these two opposing points of view that had influenced her for a long time. She eventually comes to her own decisions, of which the most important one is to silence the "City" where she was born and raised, without destroying it.

Dystopian speculative fiction that takes place in a pre-apocalyptic period invites readers to participate in an exercise of extrapolation where cognition and memory support most of the comparisons between their period of time and a near future. In these circumstances, the goal of dystopian speculative fiction is less to imagine a "becoming artifact" developed by technologies than to denounce a societal project (which predates it) and criticize its share of media devices.

In the futuristic societies of the anticipation novels written by Jean-Christophe Rufin, Amin Maalouf, and Marie Darrieussecq, discursive novums supersede lexical novums. Whether it is the misuse of syllogisms in *Globalia*, the substitution of letters for numbers in *The First Century After Beatrice*, or the equivalencies between words to teach the robots mental human associations in *Our Life in the Forest*, readers' abductive pleasure causes them to keep on interrogating the articulation of the problematics of language with the description of dystopian societies by imagining how to fill the gaps left for interpretation in the narrative.

These generally totalitarian societies, in which the use of speech and of the body is similarly constrained and forced, are either anti-utopias, in the cases of Rufin and Maalouf, or a "simple dystopia" for that of Darrieussecq, according to a distinction made by Darko Suvin:

> Dystopia in its turn divides into anti-utopia and what I shall call "simple" dystopia. Anti-Utopia finally turns out to be a dystopia, but one explicitly designed to refute a currently proposed eutopia. It is a pretended eutopia—a community whose hegemonic principles pretend to its being more perfectly organized than any thinkable alternative, while our representative "camera eye" and value-monger finds out it is significantly less perfect than an alternative, a polemic nightmare. "Simple" Dystopia (so called to avoid

inventing yet another prefix to topia) is a straightforward dystopia, that is, one which is not also an anti-utopia (Suvin, "Theses on Dystopia 2001" 189).

In the works studied here, what would be considered an anti-utopia? An anti-utopia is an apparently utopian society whose reality is the opposite and which occurs in speculative fiction works whose characters discuss this world in order to explain what is wrong with it, as opposed to merely providing an overview of a dark situation. This is illustrated in the novel by Jean-Christophe Rufin, *Globalia* (2004), whose formulation of lexical novums is mostly inspired by the anti-utopian argument of his two essays: *L'empire et les nouveaux barbares. Rupture Nord-Sud* (1991) and *La Dictature libérale* (1994).

The reflection developed around the idea of establishing "*limes*,"[14] a Latin word meaning the geographical frontiers that separate conflicting identities, is key in the formulation of the lexical novums "Globalia" and "no-zones," of which main characters in this novel seek to make sense throughout their quest. This is the reason why Baïkal, his girlfriend Kate, and their companion Puig repeatedly return to the place that is the secret origin of a territorial division, until they discover, in hidden books and plans, that the label "Globalia" refers to the obverse and reverse sides of the very same propaganda exercise. Indeed, under the guise of a sham, "Globalia" does not designate a wide territory, but rather a group of "secured atolls" ("*atolls sécurisés*") (Rufin, *Globalia* 339), excluding the world outside of it and calling those places "no-zones."

Similarly, Rufin's portrayal of the character of Baïkal in the role of a necessary enemy for democracy is a fictional prototype of one of his political science theses, which stipulates that the conservation of our modern democracies requires the active presence of a heroic and marginal

---

[14] "The limes is a strange and paradoxical line: it is not an ordinary border. It splits two worlds and at the same time unifies each of them. The couple installed by Polybe draws its power from there: it is through their opposition that the two face-to-face universes, the Empire and the barbarians, are defined and solidified. Even if they were completely shattered, the exterior peril that they represent for each other binds them together and makes them persevere in their being." [« Le limes est une ligne étrange et paradoxale: ce n'est pas une frontière ordinaire. Elle sépare deux mondes et en même temps unifie chacun d'eux. Le couple installé par Polybe tire sa puissance de là: c'est par leur opposition que se définissent et se solidifient les deux univers face à face que sont l'Empire et les barbares. Quand même ils seraient totalement éclatés, le péril extérieur qu'ils représentent l'un pour l'autre, les rassemble et les fait persévérer dans leur être »] (Rufin, *L'empire et les nouveaux barbares* 164–65).

enemy.[15] As conceived by the character of Ron Altman, who is the key architect of the Globalian society, the depiction of this "New Enemy" ("Nouvel Ennemi") (194) must be the subject of a marketing promotion campaign based on the necessity to nurture, according to this same character, a "good enemy":

> Without threat, without enemy, without fear, why obey, why work, why accept the order of things? Believe me, a good enemy is the key to a balanced society. That kind of enemy, we do not have one anymore[16] (93).

That being said, if the progression in the plot of *Globalia* was only limited to the progressive clarification of the lexical novums "Globalia," "no-zones," and then "good and new enemy," this novel would risk falling into the category of "thesis novels," which is avoided in this case by the "discursive novums," since the fictional investigation essentially resides in the articulation of a problematics of language with an attempt to resist a totalitarian society.

Through a serious attempt to explore the "no-zones" and the discovery of what characterizes "Globalia" in its antagonism with the forbidden territories, the character of Baïkal, as a "good and new enemy" almost despite himself, gradually substitutes the constrained use of speech and the body with an individualized appropriation of language and gestures. And the readers who keep up with these circumstances are invited to identify the different forms of flawed reasoning that endorse the Globalian propaganda, like the following message which appears repeatedly on the walls of a prison:

> "Globalia, where we are lucky enough to live," proclaimed the psychologist, "Is an ideal democracy. But the natural tendency of human beings is to

---

[15] "The real democratic hero, the one who goes up on the central stages and who the people listen to, is the one who had tried to escape society, to destroy it, and to destroy himself by all means possible: the junkie, the homeless person, the terrorist, the delinquent. In this game, the most central is the furthest away…" [« Le véritable héros démocratique, celui qui monte sur les scènes centrales et que le peuple écoute, c'est celui qui a tenté par tous les moyens de fuir la société, de la détruire et de se détruire lui-même: le toxicomane, le sans domicile fixe, le terroriste, le délinquant. À ce jeu, le plus central est le plus éloigné… »] (Rufin, *La Dictature libérale* 265).

[16] « Sans menace, sans ennemi, sans peur, pourquoi obéir, pourquoi travailler, pourquoi accepter l'ordre des choses? Croyez-moi, un bon ennemi est la clé d'une société équilibrée. Cet ennemi-là, nous ne l'avons plus » (93).

misuse their freedom, that is to say, to infringe on that of others. THE GREATEST THREAT TO FREEDOM IS FREEDOM ITSELF. How can we protect freedom against itself? By ensuring security for everyone. Security is freedom. Security is protection. Protection is surveillance. SURVEILLANCE IS FREEDOM[17] (67).

In a media environment spearheaded by computer programs and video monitoring devices, such flawed reasoning is supported by expressions like "the right to" ("le droit à …") (33)—to designate precisely what the characters in the novel are deprived of—and the "Social Protection" ("Protection sociale") (33)—referring to the Ministry of the Interior. These phrases are two of the most important discursive novums that best represent the anti-utopian project of the Globalian society. Not content to intrigue readera and encourage their abductive reasoning, these discursive novums are then solicited each time that a new expression of the same kind appears and enriches a "linguistic straitjacket" from which the main characters manage to escape.

Midway between fiction and essay, Amin Maalouf's anti-utopian argument differs somewhat from Jean-Christophe Rufin's in the field of anticipation literature. Indeed, Maalouf's novel *The First Century after Beatrice* (1993) precedes two of his essays addressing this topic of anti-utopias, *In the Name of Identity: Violence and the Need to Belong* (2001) and *Disordered World: Setting a New Course for the Twenty-first Century* (2011).

In *The First Century after Beatrice*, the principal lexical novum which triggers strangeness is simply labeled "substance" and first is understood to be a chemical product that favors the selection of male children over female children, and then is expanded to reveal that this product has an enlarged toxicity due to its prescription and use, which results in tensions and antagonisms between the North and the South. Even if the utopian background is not authoritarian like in *Globalia*, the narrator describes an idyllic period before the dissemination of the "substance," which again seems to be the culmination of a positivist utopia:

---

[17] « Globalia, où nous avons la chance de vivre, proclamait le psychologue, est une démocratie idéale. Or la tendance naturelle des êtres humains est d'abuser de leur liberté, c'est-à-dire d'empiéter sur celles des autres. LA PLUS GRANDE MENACE SUR LA LIBERTÉ, C'EST LA LIBERTÉ ELLE-MÊME. Comment défendre la liberté contre elle-même? En garantissant à tous la sécurité. La sécurité, c'est la liberté. La sécurité, c'est la protection. La protection, c'est la surveillance. LA SURVEILLANCE, C'EST LA LIBERTÉ » (67).

We all thought that, by degrees, the whole Earth was about to be touched by Grace, that all nations would soon be able to live in peace, freedom, abundance. From now on, History would no longer be written by generals, ideologues, despots, but by astro-physicists and biologists (Maalouf, *The First Century After Beatrice* 3).

Successively described as "flat capsules, shaped like beans, which in fact are called 'Scarab beans'" (10), and then an "anti-girl vaccine" (57), a "toxic substance" (123), and finally even as a "pernicious substance" (57) that is supposed to embody the North's contempt for the South, the meaning of this lexical novum evolves. As this meaning is reinterpreted, it is moving forward what Amin Maalouf's narrator calls "the North-South Divide—the 'horizontal fault-line'" (147) or "the line dividing moral values" (162) that the two essays mentioned earlier further analyze as "the emergence of a world in which differences of identity have taken over ideological differences" (Maalouf, *Disordered World* 65). If the use of the lexical novum of "substance" with reference to this "horizontal fault-line" first drafts an anti-utopian argument that extends beyond the frame of the fiction, the success of the staging of the plot comes primarily from "discursive novums" set up by the author when the character of the narrator unfolds his worldview as an entomologist. Because the title *The First Century after Beatrice* establishes a chronological order and serves as the first discursive novum, to what extent is this worldview original? By using letters (instead of numbers) to name the chapters of his novel, Amin Maalouf sets up a twofold writing project in which the diary of his narrator-entomologist describes how the use of a substance created to avoid the birth of female children pushes humankind to its limits. In addition to this diary, the novel also includes excerpts from the narrator's girlfriend's journalistic investigations and their daughter Beatrice's comments when she comes of age. I argue that readers wonder on the one hand about the discursive novum concerning the book's division into chapters identified by letters that include the full alphabet in 26 sections from A to Z instead of numbers, and on the other hand why the three sources of writing are interwoven throughout the novel. As a result, a larger question arises about what this discursive novum concerning letters can reveal better than the more typical use of numbers to identify chapters:

My job allows me to read the image of the butterfly or the scarab or the trap-door spider in the larva. I look at the present, and I perceive the image of the future, isn't that wonderful? And the journalist? Where does his passion lie? Is it solely in the observation of human butterflies, human spiders, their hunting and their love affairs? No. Your job becomes sublime, incomparable, when it allows you to read the image of the future in the present, but masked, coded, in a dispersed order[18] (Maalouf, *The First Century After Beatrice* 35–36).

Perhaps one might think that the abductive pleasure of reading this novel is based on the ability to "perceive the image of the future" more than the development of the anti-utopian argument, which solidifies the separation between scientific progress and civilizational development. And from the narrator's point of view, the impossibility to communicate this type of insight to other observers on a larger scale gives a dramatic orientation to the story, after the media failed to alert people of an emergency situation:

> You sometimes imagine that with so many newspapers, radios, TV channels, you're going to hear an infinite number of different opinions. Then you discover it's just the opposite: the power of these means of communication only amplifies the dominant opinion of the time, to the point when it becomes impossible to hear any other bell ringing (…) The media reflects what people say, people reflect what the media says. Aren't people ever going to tire of all these destroying effects of distorting mirrors?[19] (Maalouf, *The First Century After Beatrice* 104–05).

From the writing project of the journalist, who, for a long time, is unable to warn the world about a coming disaster, to the entomologist's project that seeks to read the contours of this disaster while waiting for a cataclysm, the questioning of a society with an excess of media is shown,

---

[18] « Mon métier me permet de lire dans la larve l'image du papillon, ou du scarabée, ou de la mygale. Je regarde le présent, et je discerne l'image du futur, n'est-ce pas merveilleux? Et le journaliste, où donc réside sa passion? Est-ce dans la seule observation des papillons humains, des mygales humaines, de leurs chasses et de leurs amours? Non. Ton métier devient sublime, inégal, quand il te permet de lire dans le présent l'image du futur, car le futur se trouve tout entier dans le présent, mais masqué, mais codé, mais en ordre dispersé » (Maalouf, *Le premier siècle après Béatrice* 63).

[19] « —On s'imagine parfois qu'avec tant de journaux, de radios, de télés, on va entendre une infinité d'opinions différentes. Puis on découvre que c'est l'inverse: la puissance de ces porte-voix ne fait qu'amplifier l'opinion dominante du moment, au point de rendre inaudible tout autre son de cloche. (…)—C'est bien cela! Les médias reflètent ce que disent les gens, les gens reflètent ce que disent les médias. Ne va-t-on jamais se lasser de cet abrutissant jeu de miroirs? » (Maalouf, *Le premier siècle après Béatrice* 170).

in order to reveal its blindness. The anti-utopian argument elaborated from a scientific hypothesis becomes even more visionary when the deficiencies of communication prove to be the inabilities of the fictional beings to read between the lines in order to decode their future. Does this mean that interpersonal communication is merely a sham? Marie Darrieussecq places a counter-wager with her novel *Our Life in the Forest* in which the opportunities for change are fostered by dialogues between a variety of characters, as opposed to an elite of isolated cultured people as is the case for Amin Maalouf's entomologist narrator.

With this "simple dystopia" that follows in the steps of great dystopian tales such as *Brave New World*, *1984*, and *Fahrenheit 451*, Marie Darrieussecq uses a stream of consciousness style to describe the situation of a woman who finds refuge in a forest with her clone who she calls "269017510200880-Thingamajig" (Darrieussecq, *Our Life In The Forest* 48), using a lexical novum to ironically criticize the dehumanization her clone is subjected to, as her other companions of misfortune have been as well. Having taken the name of Viviane as she becomes a fugitive—which echoes the name of the figure of the Brocéliande forest fairy—this female character, actually named Marie, works as a psychologist in an authoritarian, anonymous, and connected society. Confronted with the clinical case of a patient who can no longer fall asleep and whose job is to help robots to understand mental associations whose forms, which I argue are discursive novums, are indicated by the use of the equal sign ("=") between several words, Marie discovers the nature of digital labor and reflects on the types of links and learning that differentiate humans from machines or robots, which makes her formulate witty associations previously summarized by her patient undergoing analysis:

> Patient zero, the cliker. Are you aware of what a cliker does? Their job is to teach the robots all our mental associations, so that one day they'll be able to make them instead of us. Which would allow them to work empathetically, et cetera. (…) the job consists of staying seated in front of your device, an cliking every match between words and images, or words and sounds, or sounds and images, or colours and emotions, that sort of thing. (…) It seems like a mechanical process, but it demands concentration and speed. You're endlessly performing a task the mind can do but which discombobulates a robot. And which is nevertheless difficult to conceptualise. The only solution is to multiply the links, *click, click, clik*, until the robot has been supplied with everything we could possibly have thought up until now, everything we could have felt, everything humanity could have experienced.

Blue = sky = melancholy = music = bruising = blue blood = nobility = beheading. *Click, click, click, click, click* » (Darrieussecq, *Our Life in the Forest* 7–8).

After trying to mislead the robots in her conversations with the cliker by using other discursive novums such as metaphors—because "metaphors produce bugs in robots" (41), she escapes with the help of her former patient. As she flees, Marie also organizes the escape of her clone, who was plunged into a coma at the beginning of the novel to serve as a potential organ reserve. Under the cover of the forest, a place of refuge, Marie then finds a space for personal expression and rethinks her relationships with others. In the past, as a child, Marie had started drawing pictures to get close to her clone, remembering "I drew myself and Marie. I drew *us*"[20] (49), with an unusual use of the first plural pronoun, a discursive novum that speaks volumes about the symbiotic relations that exist between Viviane/Marie 1 and Marie 2. As an adult, then, the forest becomes the place that makes her rethink the limits of her condition based on a rediscovery of reading and writing to explore how to free oneself from a transhumanist ideology. Readers' abductive reasoning in this work is mostly applied to the discursive novums that point out mental associations with the equal signs or the unconventional use of pronouns; these novums are complementary as they require readers to become aware of the (lack of) limits that guarantee humanity's uniqueness, but which must be preserved by all possible means.

This disregard for limits that guarantee humanity's uniqueness occurs frequently in post-apocalyptical transfictions and can even represent their anti-utopian arguments. In the same way, so does the "becoming artifact" of the main characters of the novels written by Michel Houellebecq and Antoine Volodine, determined by an "evolving knowledge" that pushes the boundaries of transfictions and manifests itself in the absence of or in the presence of merely partial intersubjective relations.

Unlike the novels discussed earlier, in transfictions, the trait of "becoming artifact" characterizes the "ultimate man," described by empirical novums that define a global strangeness: a computer programming is explicitly or implicitly applied to these main characters, from which lexical and discursive novums result that attempt to reveal the boundaries of the programming process. From an anti-utopian point of view, the

---

[20] "Je *nous* suis dessinée" (Darrieussecq, *Notre vie dans les forêts roman* 66).

post-apocalyptic qualification attributed to these novels focuses here on the dissolution of the idea of individual choice, when the protagonists wonder about the meaning of their actions and realize that reminiscences about their condition take precedence over individual memories, for reminiscence, more than memory, is "a kind of research that the mind does in the image that the body transmitted to it"[21] (Tadié 26). Revealing of the journey undertaken by Daniel24 and Daniel25 in *The Possibility of an Island* and the main character Mevlido in *Songes de Mevlido*, this reminiscent research is constitutive of the abductive pleasure experienced by readers as they discover that these characters are coded or written artifacts who try to be aware of their current state and limitations.

The Daniel series in *The Possibility of an Island* is a similarly coded character. More specifically, the Daniel series corresponds to the *Type 1 increment* in computer science, when a variable increases by 1 unit regularly in the implementation of a computer program; this series is an example of reproductive cloning, which assumes that conscious activity can be stocked and uploaded. Of all the descendants of the first narrator, Daniel25 is the one who is the most lucid about this process since he describes the post-humanity he belongs to in these terms: "We were ourselves incomplete beings, beings in transition, whose destiny was to prepare for the coming of a digital future" (Houellebecq 156). He even goes further in his contemplation of the meaning of being such a digital reduction, by saying that he and the other clones represent "software fictions" (Houellebecq 238) in anticipation of the "Future Ones," a lexical novum repeated multiple times throughout the novel, leaving readers to develop many possible hypotheses about what this term means.

The computer science increment makes particular sense in the discursive novums that refer to the "life stories" of Daniel24 and Daniel25, which arc intertwined with the 28 subchapters of Daniel1's memoirs, due to the form of this narrative composition. Between the increments and these successive subdivisions, these discursive novums serve as a frame of an anti-utopian reduction that accomplishes the complete opposite of the post-human utopia telling the story of Bruno and Michel, the two "palimpsest brothers" (Clément 94) of Michel Houellebecq's preceding novel, *The Elementary Particles*. Does this mean that this criticism pleads for a reinstatement of a traditional understanding of humankind? Nothing

---

[21] ["La réminiscence est une sorte de recherche que fait l'esprit dans l'image que le corps lui a transmise] (Tadié 1999, 26).

could be less certain, since Anabelle, Michel's bride in *The Elementary Particles*, dies of cancer, and Marie22 and Marie23, the female counterparts of Daniel24 and Daniel 25, are post-human characters who, through poetry, denounce the encroachment of this digital reduction due to the impossibility to communicate outside the frame of the "life stories."

On the margin of the cyberpunk aesthetics inspired by shamanistic rituals, Antoine Volodine also reports on a similar reduction to the extent that the different stories concern the life of Mevlido, a character "programmed to be incarnated into a male baby" (Volodine 420–21) in *Songes de Mevlido*, this eponymous novel. Mevlido's adventures arise almost from what the computer programing calls a *feedback loop*, when he comes to die, "survives," and follows the ways of the Tibetan Bardo Thodol, to whose book I will return to shortly. Here Volodine has been able to somehow revive a legacy of science fiction magic that started earlier with the first novel of William Gibson, *Neuromancer*, as Norman Spinrad, the American science fiction author, pointed out:

> *Neuromancer* is a magician of today (or rather, here, of tomorrow), whose witchcraft is about directly interfacing his protoplasmic neural system with the electronic neural system of the infosphere, using images to manipulate it (and being manipulated by it), the same way that the traditional shamans use images to act, through drugs or dancing, in the traditional mythical spaces (Colson and Ruaud 143).

The *feedback loop* topic seems to be a key media aspect in the cyberpunk genre that can be found, for example, in other narratives such as *All You Need is Kill* by Hiroshi Sakurazaka (also well known for its cinematographic adaptation *Edge of Tomorrow* directed by Doug Liman) that portrays a soldier "caught in a loop" (Sakurazaka et al. 37) of death and resurrection as he is fighting aliens who control time, or more recently in *The Information Theory* (2012) by Aurélien Bellanger, which recounts the evolution of French Internet tycoon Pascal Ertanger who favors the advent of an insectoid humanity after being inspired by the algorithm of the "game of life" created by the mathematician John Conway. The originality of Volodine's approach is the poetic depiction of the exhaustion of his main character in the wake of his Bardo journey, summarized by a feedback loop experiment that also ends up in an insectoid transformation.

In Volodine's work, the exhaustion of the character of Mevlido as an artifact is based on a different empirical novum that defies the laws of the "cognitive estrangement" dear to Suvin by associating the reduction of Mevlido's character to his dreams and shamanic rebirths. Discursive novums such as "What is, he thought?" ("Qu'est-ce que, pensa-t-il?") (Volodine 100) or else "Listen, Mevlido, here is what, says Deeplane" ("-Écoutez, Mevlido, voilà ce que, dit Deeplane") (Volodine 197) appear to be contradictory in the novel. Indeed, the writing sometimes seems computational in a subversive manner and in the text, the writing terms itself "post-exoticism" and includes mentions of imaginary subgenres with the use of lexical novums like "Mudang," "uga," "romance," etc.

In contrast to that of Michel Houellebecq's neo-humans, the reduction of Mevlido does not therefore explicitly question its technological creation, but links this reduction to the development of poetry as do the series of Daniel and Marie in *The Possibility of an Island*. In fact, more rewritten than coded, this reduction especially echoes *The Metamorphosis* by Franz Kafka from an intertextual point of view, except that, unlike Gregory Samsa, Mevlido overcomes the ups and downs of his transformations in order to find the picture of the woman he loved:

> I would like to understand in what form I exist here, in this place where, if we analyze Deeplane's elliptical remark correctly, there is no difference between humans, the beings with six legs, and those who have eight. I am trying to count my limbs, I would like to reach a reliable result. I am getting confused and give up. I still have in mind the bare minimum: my name, Mevlido, the name of the one I love, Verena Becker, and one small certainty—from now on, I am moving inside the dream of the one I love[22] (Volodine 455–56).

But even if Melvido's final physical form coincides with the expected metamorphosis ("A cockroach runs at the base of the wall, seeking refuge under the bed. She doesn't recognize me. She sits on the bed"[23] (460–461)), what matters the most, as in Kafka's novella, may not be so

---

[22] « Je voudrais comprendre sous quelle forme j'existe ici, dans ce lieu où, si on analyse bien la remarque elliptique de Deeplane, il n'y a aucune différence entre les humains, les êtres à six pattes et ceux et celles qui en possèdent huit. J'essaie de compter mes membres, j'aimerais parvenir à un résultat fiable. Je m'embrouille et je renonce. J'ai tout de même en tête le minimum vital: mon nom, Mevlido, le nom de celle que j'aime, Verena Becker, et une petite certitude—désormais, je me déplace à l'intérieur du rêve de celle que j'aime » (Volodine 455–56).
[23] "Un cafard court au pied du mur, se réfugie sous le lit. Elle ne me reconnaît pas. Elle s'assied sur le lit" (460–461).

much the mutation of the focal character as the changing of his surroundings and his environment.

Once Mevlido became a cockroach, it must be noted that the space of
his room coincides for the first time with the space of the street ringing
with protest slogans. In addition to inverting the scene in chapter one
where Mevlido listened from his room to far-away rumblings coming from
the street, this scene uses the first person plural pronoun, resulting in a
unified perspective, just as is the case in the final scene of the book where
Mevlide reaches his lover Verena Becker, another scene incorporating the
first person plural pronoun: "We are listening to what keeps on going on,
in the street, outside. I could not really say where we are, if it is outside or
inside of the world or of somebody" [24] (Volodine 461).

The Broader Scope of the Books of Nature and the World

In the mirror stage, readers are invited to investigate in a different way by
exploring the questioning and reformulation of ancient myths focusing on
the power of speech, which explains why the metaphors of the book of the
world and the book of nature are crucial for French and Francophone
science fiction. In this way, science fiction follows in the traces of
philosophical tales, the best known of which are *The Other World: The
Comical History of the States and Empires of the World of the Moon* (1657)
by Cyrano de Bergerac and *Zadig* (1747) and *Micromégas* (1752) by
Voltaire, as well as two later novels, *The Year 2440: A Dream If Ever There
Was One* (1771) by Louis Sébastien Mercier and *The Last Man* (1805) by
Jean-Baptiste François Xavier Cousin de Grainville.

When it comes to the relations between the dawn of mankind and
technology, the beginning of Stanley Kubrick's movie *2001: A Space
Odyssey* (1968) may come to mind, when the first men-apes discover the
powerful use of bones as weapons, before throwing one of these bones
into the sky where it is transformed through an eloquent match cut into a
twentieth-century spaceship. In a chapter entitled "Freeing of Memory"
from his book *Gesture and Speech*, the French archeologist and
anthropologist André Leroi-Gourhan re-evaluates the importance of

---

[24] "Nous écoutons ce qui continue à se produire, dans la rue, dehors. Je ne saurais trop dire
où nous sommes, si c'est à l'extérieur ou à l'intérieur du monde ou de quelqu'un"
(Volodine 461).

speech in relation to the tool in the understanding of the process of humanization and its dynamic power in community development:

> The whole of our evolution has been oriented toward placing outside ourselves what the rest of the animal world is achieved inside by species adaptation. The most freeing striking material fact is certainly the "freeing" of tools, but the fundamental fact is really the freeing of the word and our unique ability to transfer our memory to a social organism outside ourselves (Leroi-Gourhan 235).

According to the historian Jean Bottéro, with the invention of writing in Mesopotamia, language was empowered to envision the future, for at that time the gods were believed to follow rational rules as they used their writing skills to frame the entire world and all it contained. These religious beliefs defined logocentrism, a new way of thinking that spread from Near Eastern and Mesopotamian cultures to the West:

> The ancient Mesopotamians, between the end of the third millennium and the beginning of the second, developed a completely original method for discovering what would happen to the future. This method was logically embedded in their writing system in its most ancient, never erased or forgotten, form, as I have explained; it was also linked to an old conviction, one that existed unaltered in the land, which identified the name of a thing with the thing itself. For us, a name is a sound from someone's voice that arbitrarily designates something but that in itself is by no means necessarily connected to the thing in question. For the Mesopotamians the name was the object being designated, the vocalized thing when the name was uttered and the written thing when it was written. The person who wrote (and this is the evidence that must have leapt to the eyes of the inventors and then the users of cuneiform writing), while he formed the characters that represented and reproduced objects, thus made and produced those objects themselves. Therefore the gods, creators of everything and who, not only in the beginning but each and every day, produced beings and events, thus also wrote, in their own way, those beings and those events. The entire world, the work of the gods, was similar to a written tablet and like the tablet was full of messages (Bottéro et al. 44).

It is within the framework of these mythological representations that the epic of *Gilgamesh* plays a role. In this epic, there are two pertinent events: the birth of Enkidu, conceived by the goddess-mother Aruru through the god Anu's "dictation," "to which she [Aruru] must conform her modeling operation" in clay (Anonymes and Bottéro 69) and the way the god Enkil used some dirt to create "non-human beings (…) giving us—we might say—the ancestors of Golems, and statues that come to life, and, ultimately, robots" (Atwood 27), as summarized by Margaret Atwood in *In Other Worlds: science fiction and the Human Imagination*. These events reveal the written tablets as a form of media and the first stage of the science fiction imagination. But the second reflexive stage of the metaphors of the book illustrates the concept of "teleology," defined as the "study of the ends or purposes of things" (Blackburn 472) throughout space and time, according to Alberto Manguel:

> Literate societies, societies based on the written word, have developed a central metaphor to name the perceived relationship between human beings and their universe: the world as a book that we are meant to read. The ways in which this reading is conducted are many—through fiction, mathematics, cartography, biology, geology, poetry, theology, and myriad other forms— but their basic assumption is the same: that the universe is a coherent system of signs governed by specific laws, and that those signs have a meaning, even if that meaning lies beyond our grasp. And that in order to glimpse that meaning, we try to read the book of the world (Manguel 2).

Later, the formulation of the metaphors of the book (book of nature, book of the world, book of the universe, and book of life) appears to be central to the poetics of Medieval and Renaissance literatures, as Ernst Robert Curtius explains it in his chapter dedicated to "The Book as Symbol" (Curtius et al. 302–47) in *European Literature and the Latin Middle Ages*, to the extent that the "idea of the Book corresponds to the medieval conception of the Bible, the book that revealed or made present God's transcendent and absolute will, law, and wisdom, a container of the divine plan and itself a sign of the totality of that plan in the world" (Gellrich 31–32). Also, in the wake of the ancient Mesopotamians, who believed in the divine power of writing skills, prophecies like the ones in the Book of Ezekiel and the Book of Revelation by Saint John of Patmos reformulated somewhat similar religious worldviews, since both "Ezekiel and John's images gave rise to an extensive library of biblical commentaries that, throughout the Middle Ages and the Renaissance, see in this double book an image of God's double creation, the Book of Scripture and the Book of Nature, both of which we are meant to read and in which we are written" (Manguel 15).

It is therefore in tension with the understanding of this authority that the French philosophical tales engaged in a new and necessary enterprise. These tales that anticipate science fiction literature introduce and play with a metafictionality that needs to be interrogated; my hypothesis is that contemporary futuristic novels are often a rewriting, a recomposition, or a reinterpretation—more than a deconstruction as understood by Derrida in *Grammatology*—of the teleological structure of writing, expressed traditionally in the formulation of the metaphors of the book.

As such the metaphors of the book are appropriated and reworked in the poetics of futuristic novels where they come to constitute a (sometimes *literal*) reference: bodies are influenced, subject to adventurous changes, or become encoded, *written*, like so much text to be processed. The metaphor of the world-as-book to be deciphered or learned through years of scholarship, dear to major philosophers, gives way in the French and Francophone futuristic novels of my selection to the body as a unit literally encoded through technology. It is this reworking and/or this *literalization* of metaphors that is at the core of a broader scope that lies at the intersection of science, technology, and literature as it addresses once again, but from a different angle, that perennial question concerning the conception or the representation of science and technology by the humanities. And from this perspective, it is the subversion of this teleological structure of writing, first undertaken in the work of Cyrano de Bergerac, *The Other World: The Comical History of the States and Empires of the World of the Moon*, and then continued by other philosophical tales mainly those written by Voltaire in the eighteenth century, that explains the hermeneutic character of futuristic novels and remains the foundation of their composition as a "detection literature" through the present day.

Let us consider therefore the beginnings of French anticipation literature and then its evolution as a proto-science fiction by examining in more detail a selection of works that illustrate these beginnings. In the formation of anticipation literature, at least three texts provide us with the opportunity to examine how satire in the seventeenth century and then the narrative utopias of the eighteenth century can help to explain the scope of the dystopias of the twentieth and twenty-first centuries. In chronological order, they include *The Other World: The Comical History of the States and Empires of the World of the Moon* (1650), a story of an imaginary journey written by Cyrano de Bergerac, the philosophical tale *Micromégas* (1752) by Voltaire, and the first French anticipation novel,

The Year 2440: A Dream If Ever There Was One (1770) by Louis Sébastien Mercier.

While the word "utopia" first refers to a proper noun—the one Thomas Moore chose as the title of his eponymous work in Latin, *Utopia*, in 1516—this word evolved to have, according to its Greek etymology, two different meanings: the non-place or "ou-topos" and the best of places or "eu-topos." Philosophers and writers of the Age of Enlightenment played on these two polarities and the utopia, which was originally two-headed, thus offered a singular dialectic to those who made use of it. Sometimes a modality of thought and sometimes literary genre, the alternation of this conceptual Janus in these conditions weighed heavily in the didactic literature of the seventeenth and eighteenth centuries to formulate what Henri Mattelard considers to be the "creation of a utopia by science and by technology"[25] (Mattelart 54), while simultaneously searching for a universal and quasi-perpetual peace. In response to the idealism of this project, Cyrano de Bergerac's imaginary travel is conceived as a "criticism through derision of the geometric reason of the utopian narrators and of their strictly formed model of life"[26] (Mattelart 55) to depict a lunar world where everything is turned upside down, whether it is a question of language, sexuality, the family, religion, or death.

The explanation of all the societal codes is summarized in the form of a "Wonderful" book that Socrates's spirit hands to the character of Cyrano at the end of his lunar journey:

Having said so, he left me; and no sooner was his back turned, but I fell to consider attentively my Books and their Boxes, that's to say, their Covers, which seemed to me to be wonderfully Rich; the one was cut of a single Diamond, incomparably more resplendent than ours; the second looked like a prodigious great Pearl, cloven in two. My Spirit had translated those Books into the Language of that World; but because I have none of their Print, I'll now explain to you the Fashion of these two Volumes. (…)

As I opened the Box, I found within somewhat of Metal, almost like to our Clocks, full of I know not what little Springs and imperceptible Engines: It was a Book, indeed; but a Strange and Wonderful Book, that had neither Leaves nor Letters: In fine, it was a Book made wholly for the Ears, and not the Eyes. So that when any Body has a mind to read in it, he winds up that

---

[25] La "mise en utopie de la science et de la technique" (Mattelart 54).

[26] Une "critique par dérision de la raison géométrique des narrateurs utopiques et de leur modèle de vie tracé au cordeau" (Mattelart 2009, 55).

Machine with a great many Strings; then he turns the Hand to the Chapter which he desires to hear, and straight, as from the Mouth of a Man, or a Musical Instrument, proceed all the distinct and different Sounds, which the Lunar Grandees make use of for expressing their Thoughts, instead of Language (Bergerac 2016 115–116).

This book looks like a timepiece with its winding mechanism, springs, and hands and has the ability to restitute, as a witness of this strange world, sounds or voices, but contains no written letters. Now the interest of this book consists in its subversion of the teleological features often attributed to the symbolism of the books of nature and the world at this time, as great philosophical works or theological masterpieces, a notion which Hélène Domon summarizes as follows in a book entitled *Le Livre imaginaire* (*The Imaginary Book*):

Cyrano precipitates the debacle of the Book and of all theological organisms and, in the ebb and flow of this debacle, endlessly rocks the constitutive limits of meaning (epistemological limit between right and wrong, ontological limit between being and non-being, high and low hierarchical limit)[27] (Domon 161–62).

There is a parallel between the future of an imaginary world and the limits of the "Book" established by this subversion of the teleological features. These features are often attributed to the symbolism of the books of nature and the world, and their subversion is then taken up again in the eighteenth century by Voltaire's philosophical tales *Zadig* (1747) and *Micromégas* (1752), which display doubts inspired by logocentrism and its mutations.

In *Zadig*, the titular character, a young philosopher in ancient Babylonia, runs into trouble the more he uses his rational mind to find his place in the aristocratic Babylonian society made up of envious people and fools (orientalism and irony apply here to entertain the educated elite who read Voltaire at that time). The scene that best exemplifies the subversion of the teleological features is the one which illuminates the subtitle of this tale in English, "Zadig or the Book of Fate," when, in chapter 18 entitled "The

---

[27] « Cyrano précipite la débâcle entière du Livre et de tout l'organisme théologique et fait tanguer interminablement, dans le flux et reflux de cette débâcle, les limites constitutives du sens (limite épistémologique entre vrai et faux, limite ontologique entre être et non-être, limite hiérarchique haut et bas) » (Domon 161–62).

Hermit," Zadig meets a man, who will later be revealed to be the angel "Jesrad," who first asks Zadig if he is able to read the book he holds in his hand:

> As he walked along, he met a hermit whose white and venerable beard reached down to his girdle. In his hand he held a book, which he was reading attentively. Zadig stopped and made him a low bow, at which the hermit greeted him so mildly and graciously that Zadig was impelled to talk to him and ask him what book he was reading. 'It is the Book of Destinies,' said the hermit. 'Would you like to look at it?' He placed the book in Zadig's hands; but although he knew several languages, Zadig was unable to decipher a single letter of it, which increased his curiosity still more (Voltaire Voltaire, et al. 92).

The fact that Zadig cannot read this book matters because in order to understand its meaning, he decides to follow the hermit in his peregrinations—on the condition that Zadig will not leave the hermit regardless of what the latter does. The hermit goes on to perform terrible actions, whose positive consequences are only subsequently revealed. For example, he sets a castle on fire after being received with hospitality by its owner, but this allows the owner to discover a treasure afterward; the hermit also pushes a child into a river, leading to the child's drowning, but explains his actions later saying that he knows that the child will become a murderer in the future. Eventually, the hermit reveals his angelic nature in the face of Zadig's rage: "'Who told you so, you wretch?' cried Zadig. 'And even if you read the event in that Book of Destinies of yours, who has given you permission, I should like to know, to drown a child that has done you no harm?'" (Voltaire, Voltaire, et al. 96). A dialogue then follows between Zadig and the angel on the effects of providence, punctuated by a series of questions posed by Zadig, all beginning with "But...," which represents the quintessence of Voltairian doubt.

Voltaire's imagery related to the book evolves over the course of his writing, from the "unreadable" book, the Book of Fate (Destinies), in *Zadig*, to become a "blank book" at the end of *Micromégas*. In the philosophical tale *Micromégas*, the main protagonist born on the star Sirius is confronted with his own relativity (he is both micro-small and megas-big, depending on where he finds himself) during his sidereal journey that ends in Paris. There he leaves a book as a present, in a scene that mirrors that at the end of Cyrano de Bergerac's imaginary travel:

He promised to write a fine work of philosophy for them, in suitably tiny script, in which they would discover the nature of things. True to his word, he gave them the volume before leaving. It was taken to Paris, to the Academy of Sciences. But when the Secretary opened it, he found nothing but blank pages. 'Aha,' said he, 'I suspected as much' (Theo Cuffe Voltaire, et al. 35).

It is this perspective of doubt coupled with an invitation to interpretation that characterizes anticipation literature, without the latter perhaps ever having truly abandoned the paradigm of the "liber mundi" as a frame of reference for the plotting of its detective narratives.

Following Cyrano de Bergerac's *The Other World: The Comical History of the States and Empires of the World of the Moon* and Voltaire's *Micromégas*, the criticism of French society under the Ancien Régime that Louis Sébastien Mercier begins in *The Year 2440* also illustrates the idea of a future world that can be seen in the transformation of the written word, with the exception of the fact that the attack on the teleological structure that was readily attributed to the symbolism of the "Book" became much more secularized or no longer was the subject of real quarrels at the end of the eighteenth century. Instead, such attacks were seen as occurring through malicious acts such as auto-da-fés or mutations of the written word, including the appearance of gazettes that delimited the scope of a future world that was more extrapolated than truly imagined.

The Year 2440 by Louis Sébastien Mercier, which features the first truly futuristic French-language utopia, outlines a universal Paris, with a background of reversals and metamorphoses, that oscillates between the eighteenth and twenty-fifth centuries. The architecture of this Paris in the 2440s is "in the image of the reason now governing men"[28] (Mercier 8). The avenues have been widened, many buildings are now human-sized, and, in general, everything is being done to facilitate maximum circulation for people in the Capital's arteries. The revolution of this reorganization, which was, so to speak, a natural outcome, is more a result of the intersection between reason and human nature, of which a "philosopher king" became aware as being needed for the happiness of the greatest number, rather than of an uncontrolled overflow.

This conception of a revolution supports a form of government that presupposes a "public transparency" whose requirements of organic

---

[28] "à l'image de la raison gouvernant désormais les hommes" (Mercier 8).

correspondences cut across the different levels of social hierarchy. Many commentators on Louis Sébastien Mercier's work discuss this ideology of "public transparency" as indeed being the sign heralding a totalitarianism that illustrates, among other examples, a gigantic *auto-da-fé* organized to burn some books and their authors:

> In unanimous agreement, we gathered all the books that we had judged to be frivolous or useless or dangerous together in a vast plain; (...). We set this appalling mass on fire, as an expiatory sacrifice offered to truth, to good sense, to true taste. The flames devoured in torrents the follies of man, the old and the modern. The burning was long. Several authors were seen to be burned alive, but their cries did not stop us at all[29] (Mercier 165).

In addition to its disappearance in the auto-da-fé evoked by Louis Sébastien Mercier, the "object-book," which loses much of its symbolism and whose destruction lays the groundwork for a dystopian horizon, is marked above all by its inability to channel the meaning of the "general circulation" of a utopian society. In these circumstances, gazettes appear to be its replacement, since thanks to this invention "communication was established little by little [and] science flew from one country to another, like bills of exchange" (Mattelart 66).

It can be concluded at this point that the mediation of the "Book," the "book-object," and then recomposed or modified writing determines an important part of the "critical" character of utopias; "critical utopia" here designates, from the twentieth century to the present day, the narrative space through which characters debate the basis of their readings and/or reformulate "stories" in order to eliminate a media device (television, network, or related technologies) or a "becoming artifact" from which they try to escape.

As reason gives way to increasingly misguided institutions in the exercise of power, the notion of a utopia will indeed become more opaque and with it the trust placed in the "educated view" of the ideology of the Enlightenment, which was undoubtedly the perspective that was supposed

---

[29] « D'un consentement unanime, nous avons rassemblé dans une vaste plaine tous les livres que nous avons jugés ou frivoles ou inutiles ou dangereux; (...). Nous avons mis le feu à cette masse épouvantable, comme un sacrifice expiatoire offert à la vérité, au bon sens, au vrai goût. Les flammes ont dévoré par torrents les sottises des hommes, tant anciennes que modernes. L'embrasement fut long. Quelques auteurs se sont vus brûler tout vivants, mais leurs cris ne nous ont point arrêtés » (Mercier 165).

to interpret the blank book at the end of *Micromégas*. This obscuring corresponds to a belief in causes that become more and more abstract by taking a totalitarian form, as Jean-Noël Vuarnet explains in the case of the twentieth century: "More Kantian than Sadian, the totalitarian world of inverse utopias is governed by general imperatives: Law, Order, Reason, a Party, Administration..." (Vuarnet 111). These imperatives are injunctions to be believed, after the disintegration of the "educated view"; the imperatives are resisted by the objectification of the written word as its critical mediation defines it in the poetics of the novel of anticipation.

Finally, my framework to analyze anticipation literature, the ancestor of science fiction, would be incomplete if I did not return to the text of the New Testament's Apocalypse. Synonymous with "revelation," the Book of Revelation traditionally assumes a hermeneutics, or even, in its many adaptations, an interpretation or decoding. In many ways, this "revelation" is about humanity and its limits, with the difference that metamorphoses and that which could be non-human are part of the plan of such a revelation. But beyond the principal biblical intertexts represented by the Book of Daniel and the last book of the New Testament, the Book of Revelation also offers to the authors who draw their inspiration from it a singular generic illumination on time.

Paul Alkon reminds us that anticipation, and with it science fiction, are close to the Apocalypse in their literary treatment of the "'humanization of time'"[30] (Alkon 158) in the chapter of his book, *Origins of Futuristic Fiction*, devoted to the "secularization of the Apocalypse," which essentially comments on Jean-Baptiste Cousin de Grainville's story, *The Last Man* (1805), a work in which the last man, Omegarus, witnesses the disappearance of humanity after having consulted "the Book of Destiny" (Cousin de Grainville et al. 16). For Alkon, the more secularized the Apocalypse is in its thematization, the more its reading and the questions it encourages are anchored in the present: "apocalyptic themes in recent fiction are usually not intended to provide a true vision of the future but to raise disturbing questions about the present..." (Alkon 159).

From this it follows that a certain number of discrepancies produced in reference to the cognitive estrangement presented earlier redouble the search for indices of humanity in order to judge the level of risk and catastrophe of post-apocalyptic narratives where the end of the world is

---

[30] "'Insofar as science fiction is committed to the humanization of time,' according to Mark Rose, 'it naturally tends toward fictions of the apocalypse'" (Alkon 158).

supposed to have already taken place. Since all imaginary (re)beginnings are allowed after the disappearance of civilizations, the more often post-apocalyptic than apocalyptic dystopian novel of anticipation (in science fiction as in mainstream literature) is therefore often addressed to readers whose minds are a priori looking for clues.

In the mirror stage, the mediation of the "Book," of the "book object" or more generally of the written word occupies an essential function in the poetics of the novel of anticipation from this genre's origins to the present day. Indeed, whether they are "books," literary creations integrated into fiction, or "stories" staged or even hybridized by images and incorporated into the regime of the rest of the narrative, this constant within all the works I have selected to study here is represented by the figure "of the book within the book" and is a determining factor in understanding how a novel rethinks humanity and its limits.

THE FIGURE OF THE LAST MAN

The Last Man is a key indicator in detective stories that depends on the previously introduced metaphors of the book; its decoding requires taking into account the pre-apocalyptic, apocalyptic, or post-apocalyptic situation that reveals this figure. As soon as the Apocalypse is a part of a society project or an overview, the figure of the "last man" constitutes the paradigm of a humankind in distress rather than a specific character or his or her story that is being updated. So it is in dystopian speculative fiction, whose narratives take place in pre-apocalyptic situations, like *Our Life in the Forest*, *Globalia*, and *The First Century After Beatrice*, in which the novelistic figure of the last man appears as a dehumanized form living in a totalitarian space.

As for the other novels that are a matter of science fiction and transgressive fiction, the manner in which anticipation novels rethink the limits of the idea of humanity from this determining figure refers back to the characterization of a type of character before extending beyond its system of writing and determining a novelistic expression that prolongs and/or exhausts the motifs that are associated with it. Four novels illustrate the measure and excess of the figure of the last man: *The Silent City*, *Les Derniers Hommes*, *The Possibility of an Island*, and *Songes de Mevlido*.

Understanding the measure and excess at work in these four fictional works supposes the examination of the intertextual characteristics of this figure. In her chapter entitled "Cyborg Conceptions: Bodies, Texts, and the Future of Human Spirit" in *The Enlightenment Cyborg: A History of*

Communications and Control in the Human Machine, 1660–1830, Allison Muri suggests a parallel to this measure and excess and links it to humankind's relation to media when she argues that "Whether a lamentation for the loss of the texture and substance of the book, or an exaltation for a supposed new traversing of boundaries and freedom from hierarchical structures, a predominant conclusion has been that we are altered by our media" (229). This link to media is a key notion that I will later incorporate into my analyses in Chap. 4.

Because it is alternately observer and witness of a world that had disappeared or that was disappearing, the figure of the "last man" who is more than a simple character distinguishes himself more particularly by the mise en scène of his knowledge. This essential character trait explains, for example, that the figure of the "last man" in Pierre Bordage's *The Last Men* is embodied by a character named "Ismahil" whose wanderings throughout the novel are reminiscent of the biblical episode of the casting out of Hagar and her son Ishmael by Abraham (Genesis 21: 9–21). It is by wandering that the character meets the character of Solman, who helps him with the readings of the Apocalypse. The duration of Ismahil's life as a fallen scientist, artificially prolonged and sheltered from numerous conflagrations, also is a form of wandering, until he begins to age and to reveal the ties existing between a totalitarian organization known by the title of the *Eskato* and the book of the Apocalypse of Saint John:

> Solman picked up the Book, stood up, and still supported by Kadija, moved forward toward the old man in a tottering manner. He felt a profound emotion faced with this body finally defeated by the years. The tie between the humanity of the ancient times and the last men was just about to break. With Ismahil, it was an entire segment of history that was sinking into oblivion[31] (Bordage 629).

The same is true of the characters of Desprats and Paul in Élisabeth Vonarburg's science fiction novel, *The Silent City*, which depicts a humankind split into two main groups and confronted with identity mutations after a series of wars and natural disasters: while numerous

---

[31] « Solman ramassa le Livre, se leva et, toujours soutenu par Kadija, s'avança vers le vieil homme d'une manière chancelante. Il ressentait une profonde émotion face à ce corps enfin vaincu par les ans. Le lien entre l'humanité de l'ancien temps et les derniers hommes était sur le point de se rompre. Avec Ismahil, c'était tout un pan de l'histoire, qui sombrait dans l'oubli » (Bordage 629).

"primitive" humans return to a tribal sociability, a grouping of scientists shelter in the shadow of a City to, at the same time, prolong their existence through some robots and exploit the fear that these robots inspire in those that the scientists consider to be "primitive," with the ultimate goal of carrying out genetic experiments.

Desprats and Paul are two scientists who have different goals marked with tensions tied to the relations that their city must maintain with the exterior world, since Desprats, a programmer of robots or other artifacts, and Paul, a geneticist, are literally figures of "last men" who quarrel through-out the novel over the judgment of Elisa, a key character at the origin of an androgynous humanity. Their respective forms of knowledge draw on their rivalry, and the tensions that animate them are, at their origins, stagings, under the cover of a strong of intertextual irony, opposing "Desprats-Sir Arthur" with "Paul-Lancelot," shortly after the "birth" of Elisa:

> Sounding of trumpets. Arthur and Bluebeard approached the table with the fake Serena, and Paul imitated them. Four servants entered, carrying an enormous golden cup that they placed on the table. The sleeping baby was inside, placed on the crimson padding. Paul began to laugh, out of surprise and anger.
>
> "The Holy Grail makes you laugh, Sir Lancelot?" asked Desprats.
>
> "It is not Lancelot who found the Grail, Richard," replied Paul. "Pardon, Sir Arthur, I should say."
>
> "No, indeed, it was his son," smiled Alghiéri. "We are doing what we can. We did not say that you had found the Holy Grail either"[32] (Vonarburg, *The Silent City* 30).

Intertextuality and staging also characterize the reflections of Daniel1, who is a humorist and a professional in the entertainment industry in Michel Houellebecq's *The Possibility of an Island*, a work in which the futurist argument tightens the plot around a semiotic reflection on the

---

[32] « Sonnerie de trompettes. Arthur et Barbe-Bleue s'approchent de la table avec la fausse Séréna, et Paul les imite. Quatre serviteurs entrent, portant sur un pavois une énorme coupe dorée, qu'ils posent sur la table. Le bébé endormi est à l'intérieur, posé sur le capitonnage cramoisi. Paul se met à rire, de surprise et de colère.

"Le Saint-Graal vous fait rire, Messire Lancelot? dit Desprats.

– Ce n'est pas Lancelot qui a trouvé le Graal, Richard, réplique Paul. Pardon, Sire Arthur, devrais-je dire.

– Non, en effet, c'est son fils, sourit Alghiéri. On fait ce qu'on peut. Nous n'avons pas dit non plus que tu avais trouvé le Saint-Graal » (Vonarburg, *Le Silence de la cité* 30).

relationship of the human genre to reading and writing. In this "science fiction" novel that recounts the story of this character alternately with that of his clones who are mandated to read his "life stories" to try to give a meaning to their own existence, Nietzsche, Schopenhauer, Baudelaire, Balzac, and Proust are summoned to flesh out the judgment of an ending world with irony, cynicism, and cruelty. But beyond the reference made to these authors by Daniel1, the neo-human clones write "not only their respective life stories, but also their commentaries on those of their predecessors, which by mirror and mise en abyme effects, create an evident (auto)intertextuality"[33] (Clément, "Michel Houellebecq. Ascendances" 95).

Of all of the readings of Daniel1, who rapidly appears to be the "last man of writing," the poems of Baudelaire occupy an essential function in the sense that they push him to write poetry, too, and therefore have an effect on the societal project of his successors. Opposed to the logic of the "life stories" that aim to progressively anesthetize the neo-humans, poetry persists, indeed, in outlining an "elsewhere" by means of feelings, just like in this poem by Daniel1 whose reading prompts the exile of Marie23 and Daniel25 at the end of the book:

Entered into total dependency,
I know the trembling of being.
The hesitation to disappear,
Sunlight upon the forest's edge.
And love, where all is easy,
Where all is given in the instant;
There exists in the midst of time.
The possibility of an island[34] (Houellebecq 300).

On the edges of the genres of science fiction, fantasy, and magical realism, this semiotic reflection about the relationship of humankind to reading and writing has another take in Antoine Volodine's *Mevlido's Dreams*.

---

[33] "non seulement leur récit de vie respectif, mais aussi leurs commentaires sur ceux de leurs prédécesseurs, ce qui par un jeu de miroir et de mises en abyme crée une (auto) intertextualité évidente" (Clément, "Michel Houellebecq. Ascendances" 95).

[34] « Entré en dépendance entière,
Je sais le tremblement de l'être
L'hésitation à disparaître,
Le soleil qui frappe en lisière
Et l'amour, où tout est facile,
Où tout est donné dans l'instant;
Il existe au milieu du temps
La possibilité d'une île » (Houellebecq 424).

In this anticipation novel where the genre of science fiction is similar to "a simulacrum that permits the transmission of a meaning, perhaps unacceptable, doubtless a rewriting of history"[35] (Ruffel 31), the staged knowledge is that of a writer named Mingrelian whose writing constantly has the main character, Mevlido, confront the traumatizing memory of the slaughter of a woman whom he had loved and who he hopes to rejoin, in some capacity, following his own death.

The difficulty in understanding this novel by Volodine lies in the fact that "Mingrelian is a brother of Mevlido, and, in the course of the writing, there is not the slightest mental or physical difference between them"[36] (Volodine, *Songes de Mevlido* 418). Indeed, this difficulty grows when the reader becomes conscious of the intertexts that inspire this double character who is willing to create a strong visual impression in order to ward off the trauma of a murder scene repeated many times in Volodine's work. Volodine also mentions imaginary literary genres, in an intertextual reference, in *Songes de Mevlido* in that these same imaginary literary genres are defined for the most part in his *Post-Exoticism in Ten Lessons, Lesson Eleven*, a theoretical work that focuses on his genre inventions and indeed claims a new literary aesthetic. Here we can read one such reference in *Songes de Mevlido*:

> The art of Mingrelian, influenced by post-exoticism, plays with the uncertainty, the lack of successful completion, the scrambling of contraries, the void. [...] We like Mingrelian's books. We have liked them since the first one and we had never been disappointed by their manner of telling the world. We like these collections of theatrical sequences, these *entrevoûtes*, these romances...[37] (419).

By these imaginary generic creations that constitute an intertextuality that alternately fragment and recompose the scenes of war or of violence, the figure of "a last man... writer" thus marks a step toward that of the

---

[35] "un simulacre, qui permet de transmettre un sens peut-être inacceptable, sans doute une réécriture de l'histoire" (Ruffel 31).

[36] "Mingrelian est un frère de Mevlido, et, au cours de l'écriture, il n'y a pas entre eux la moindre différence mentale ou physique" (Volodine, *Songes de Mevlido* 418).

[37] « L'art de Mingrelian, influencé par le post-exotisme, joue avec l'incertitude, l'inaboutissement, le brouillage des contraires, le néant. (...) Nous aimons les livres de Mingrelian. Nous les avons aimés depuis le premier et nous n'avons jamais été déçus par leur manière de dire le monde. Nous aimons ces recueils de séquences théâtrales, ces entrevoûtes, ces romances... » (419).

"last man of writing" of Houellebecq and, in the denunciation of the present world, is associated with a position that Marie-Stéphane Devaud presents as the "propositions for a terminal literature" that she summarizes thus:

> Motivated by the past of a militancy of a "soldier without rank" in favor of a more just society, the writer who he became thenceforth opposes an extremely elaborated literary system, in the perfect continuity of his struggle against all forms of subjugation of individuals, to the insidious darkening of the world. A far cry from literary modes, Volodine indeed chose to put into place his own poetics, whose formalist dimension can only be understood if one understands the significance of the interior voice that inspires his fictions, this voice of the last man, of the ultimate resistance to the negation of humanity..."[38] (Devaud).

Besides the intertextual staging of its knowledge, the figure of the "last man" distinguishes itself by the gaps that it multiplies between the characters that incarnate it and the other entities or fictional devices in its continuity, which often are translated by a dramatization of the construction of meaning that the story incorporates. In the novels by Bordage, Vonarburg, Houellebecq, and Volodine, these gaps progressively express a critical knowledge, a power, a prophetism, and a counter-power, respectively, that use all forms of fictional identity mutation as benchmarks.

This excess of the novelistic figure that spreads to the rest of the story is explained for the most part by its exhibition, and then its naturalization in the fiction. On a thematic and formal level, the message of the last man becomes a "revelation," thanks to this metafictional process, to the extent that it clarifies the meaning of the novums that are scattered throughout the fiction, when this message is not simply resolving enigmatic principles. In this fashion, this arrangement causes Ismahil to provide the keys to a critical reading of the text of the Apocalypse to Solman who, like the other members of the tribe of the "last men," is deprived of book

---

[38] « Animé par le passé d'un militantisme de "soldat sans grade" en faveur d'une société plus juste, l'écrivain qu'il est devenu oppose désormais à l'assombrissement sournois du monde un système littéraire extrêmement élaboré, dans la parfaite continuité de sa lutte contre toutes les formes d'asservissement des individus. A mille lieues des modes littéraires, Volodine a en effet choisi de mettre en place sa propre poétique, dont la dimension formaliste ne peut être comprise que si l'on saisit la portée de la voix intérieure qui inspire ses fictions, cette voix de dernier homme, d'ultime résistance à la négation de l'humanité... » (Devaud).

knowledge that dates back to the history of humanity before the explosion of a third world war marked by the dissemination of genetically modified creatures. As the only one able to resituate the expectations demanded by this text in the long-term, the excess of Ismahil as a last man was tied to the disclosure of a knowledge that, formulated in chapters 51–61 of Pierre Bordage's novel, denounced a literal reading of the Bible and explained its consequences:

> Let's say that my hypothesis is the following: the catastrophes that fell upon humanity in an apocalyptic mode during these last two centuries, as if a... being had decided to follow the Book to the letter, to apply it step by step[39] (581).

In *The Silent City* it is also in the excess of the figure of the last man that the character of Elisa tries to free herself from the "programs" and to appropriate the "Project" of cellular auto-generation for herself in order to simultaneously determine the limits and the possibilities of her androgyny, knowing that a marked difference between these two powers exists. While the point of view perpetuated by Paul was, to an extent, her "heritage," whose updating she debated with her androgynous "descendants," the point of view which Desprats perpetuated, even if it did not harm her and perhaps even protected her, corresponded much more to a manipulation about which she ended up becoming conscious:

> And what had Desprats meant to do in each case? She hasn't the slightest idea.
> But that would mean that all the while she thought she was following the ommach, Desprats was following her. She thought she was being led. Was she in fact *free*? Watched but free? The program was following her evolution. Maybe it gave her a little nudge now and then, so she'd be ready when she met Paul once more[40] (Vonarburg, *The Silent City* 95).

Unlike Elisa, the neo-human descendants of Daniel1 moved toward a dim horizon and the biblical and Nietzschean prophecies make *The*

---

[39] « Disons que mon hypothèse est la suivante: les catastrophes se sont abattues sur l'humanité au cours de ces deux derniers siècles sur un mode apocalyptique, comme si une... entité avait décidé de suivre le Livre à la lettre, de l'appliquer étape par étape » (581).

[40] « Et qu'avait prévu de faire Desprats, pour chacun de ces scénarios? Elle n'en a pas la moindre idée. Mais alors, pendant tout ce temps où elle croyait suivre l'ommach, c'était Desprats qui la suivait? Elle se croyait menée, et elle était... libre? En liberté surveillée? Le programme suivait son évolution. Il y a peut-être donné des coups de pouce, même, pour qu'elle soit prête au moment de retrouver Paul » (Vonarburg, *Le silence de la cité* 147).

Possibility of an Island more a "moralizing fable" than a bildungsroman. Indeed, between the biblical prophet whose name signifies "judgment of God" and who announces an Apocalypse, and the identification of Daniel1 with the pronouncement of Nietzsche's Zarathoustra in an ironic mode ("At once I felt a certain sadness as I realized that I had still not given up being what I had been for my entire career: a sort of Zarathustra of the middle classes" (Houellebecq 286)), there is, doubtless, a clarification of the failure of Daniel25, his last clone, who, conscious of his limits at the end of the novel, knows himself to be doubly "coded," both genetically programmed and trapped in the space of the life story of his first "ancestor," which makes him say:

> I then understood why the Supreme Sister insisted upon the study of the life story of our human predecessors. I understood the goal she was trying to reach: I understood, also, why this goal would never be reached.
> I had not found deliverance.[41]

It is worth noting that in this last quotation, Daniel25 uses the French term *"indélivré,"* which includes the word *"livre"* (book), thus further linking the notions of writing and being written—as well as the book—to this figure. In the range of figures that Daniel1 through Daniel25 represent, the focus is less on the figure of the last man, as such, and more on the post-human fictionality of this figure.

This supplementary excess responding to an intensified metafictional activity is even more amplified in Volodine's work. If a desire to multiply the metafictional gaps and to move forward, masked, in the space of the book *Songes de Mevlido* exists, this is likely due more to a form of protection than to a definitive enclosing, in order to outline a poetics of counter-powers that the Quebecker critic Richard Saint-Gelais qualifies as a polytext:

> Volodine's work, to be sure, is a polytext: a structure of generalized and non- hierarchical interconnection, a whole rendered instable by the heterogeneity and the complexity of its constitutive pieces (each text is already a labyrinth), but also, reciprocally, the proper (and in a certain measure, autonomous) operation of each book is always susceptible to be

---

[41] « Je compris, alors, pourquoi la Sœur suprême insistait sur l'étude du récit de vie de nos prédécesseurs humains; je compris le but qu'elle cherchait à atteindre. Je compris, aussi, pourquoi ce but ne serait jamais atteint. *J'étais indélivré*" (my italics) (Houellebecq, *La possibilité* 473).

parasitized by some other, previous or subsequent[42] (Saint-Gelais, "Le Polytexte Volodine" 144).

The measure and excess of the novelistic figure of the "last man," from the intertext to the polytext, thus connects characters' memories through reading before addressing our own memories as the final readers. The "becoming android" of the last men of Élisabeth Vonarburg's work, just like the "becoming artifact" of the character of Solman and that of Ismahil, which expand this notion fall at one end of this spectrum, while in Pierre Bordage's work the steps of a project of society are clearly marked out in which the figures of the last men are inevitable expressions; finally, in a last iteration, the characters of Daniel (1–25) and Mingrelian/Mevlido in Houellebecq and Volodine's works, respectively, invest this figure of the "last man" otherwise, without it being possible for them to embody the limits.

Indeed, as artifacts of projects of dystopian societies of which the understanding totally escapes them and who surpass this figure of the "last man," Daniel (1–25) and Mingrelian/Mevlido correspond instead to this other figure which is that of the "ultimate man," in the sense that the critic Jean Bessière understands it, that is, this "theme designates the situation of the contemporary man who knows, on the one hand, that he is left to his own reflexivity and, on the other hand, that he belongs to a society of which it must be said not that it comes out of history[, …] but that it no longer identifies its start in history"[43] (63).

But the myth of the last man or of the ultimate man, which exists within the limits of measure and excess, in the society projects proposed in these works must be further interrogated in relation to a typology of possible dissonant storyworlds.

---

[42] « L'œuvre de Volodine, à n'en pas douter, est un polytexte: une structure d'interconnexion généralisée et non hiérarchisable, un ensemble rendu instable par l'hétérogénéité et la complexité des pièces constitutives (chaque texte est déjà un labyrinthe), mais aussi, réciproquement, le fonctionnement propre (et dans une certaine mesure autonome) de chaque livre est toujours susceptible d'être parasité par quelque autre, antérieur ou ultérieur » (Saint-Gelais, "Le Polytexte Volodine" 144).

[43] "thème désigne la situation de l'homme contemporain qui sait, d'une part, qu'il est livré à sa propre réflexivité et, d'autre part, qu'il appartient à une société dont il faut dire non pas qu'elle est sortie de l'histoire (…) mais qu'elle n'identifie plus son départ dans l'histoire" (63).

BIBLIOGRAPHY

Alkon, Paul K. *Origins of Futuristic Fiction*. University of Georgia Press, 2010.

Anonymes, and Jean Bottéro. *L'Épopée de Gilgameš: Le grand homme qui ne voulait pas mourir*. Gallimard, 1992.

Atwood, Margaret. *In Other Worlds: Sf and the Human Imagination*. Anchor Books, 2012.

Bergerac, Cyrano de. *The Other World: The Comical History of the States and Empires of the World of the Moon*. Translated by Archibald Lovell, CreateSpace Independent Publishing Platform, 2016.

Blackburn, Simon. *The Oxford Dictionary of Philosophy*. 3 edition, Oxford University Press, 2016.

Bordage, Pierre. *Les derniers hommes*. J'ai Lu edition, 2005.

Bottéro, Jean, et al. *Ancestor of the West: writing reasoning, and religion in Mesopotamia, Elam and Greece*. University of Chicago Press, 2003.

Clément, Murielle-Lucie. *Michel Houellebecq revisité: l'écriture houellebecquienne*. L'Harmattan, 2007.

Colson, Raphaël, and André-François Ruaud. *Science-fiction: une littérature du réel*. Klincksieck, 2006.

Cousin de Grainville, Jean-Baptiste-François-Xavier, et al. *The Last Man*. Wesleyan University Press, 2002.

Csicsery-Ronay, Istvan. *Of Enigmas and Xenoencyclopedias*. Nov. 2012, https://www.depauw.edu/sfs/review_essays/icr118.html.

Curtius, Ernst Robert, et al. *European literature and the Latin Middle Ages*. Princeton University Press, 2013.

Darrieussecq, Marie. *Notre vie dans les forêts roman*. P.O.L., 2017.

———. *Our Life in the Forest*. Translated by Penny Hueston, The Text Publishing Company, 2018.

Devaud, Marie-Stéphane. "Propositions Pour Une Littérature Terminale." *Kritiks*, 26 Aug. 2005, http://kritiks.blogspirit.com/archive/2005/08/26/volodine-le-tenebreux.html

Domon, Hélène. *Le Livre Imaginaire*. Summa Publications, 2000.

Eco, Umberto. "Science Fiction and the Art of Conjecture." *Times Literary Supplement 4257*, 1984, pp. 1257–58.

Eco, Umberto. *The Role of the Reader: Explorations in the Semiotics of Texts*. Hutchinson, 1981.

Gellrich, Jesse M. *The Idea of the Book in the Middle Ages: Language Theory, Mythology, and Fiction*. Cornell University Press, 1988.

Houellebecq, Michel. *The Possibility of an Island*. Translated by Gavin Bowd, Knopf, 2006.

James, Edward, et al. *The Cambridge Companion to Science Fiction*. Cambridge University Press, 2013.

Jeanneret, Yves. "La part de l'imaginaire." *Nouvelles technologies: mythes et réalités. Sciences Humaines,* vol. 59, 1996.

Langlet, Irène. *La science-fiction: lecture et poétique d'un genre littéraire.* A. Colin, 2006.

Leroi-Gourhan, André. *Gesture and Speech.* Translated by Randall White, MIT Press, 1993.

Maalouf, Amin. *Disordered World: Setting a New Course for the Twenty-First Century.* Bloomsbury, 2011.

———. *Le premier siècle après Béatrice: roman.* Grasset, 1999.

———. *The First Century After Beatrice.* Translated by Dorothy S. Blair, Abacus, 1994.

Malmgren, Carl Darryl. *Worlds Apart: Narratology of Science Fiction.* Indiana University Press, 1991.

Manguel, Alberto. *The Traveler, the Tower, and the Worm: The Reader as Metaphor.* University of Pennsylvania Press, 2013.

Mattelart, Armand. *Histoire de l'utopie Planétaire: De La Cité Prophétique à La Société Globale.* La Découverte, 2009.

Rufin, Jean-Christophe. *Globalia.* Gallimard, 2005.

———. *La Dictature libérale: le secret de la toute-puissance des démocraties au 20e siècle.* Hachette, 1995.

———. *L'empire et les nouveaux barbares.* J.-C. Lattès, 1991.

Saint-Gelais, Richard. "Le Polytexte Volodine." *Territoires et Terres d'histoires : Perspectives, Horizons, Jardins Secrets Dans La Littérature Française d'aujourd'hui,* edited by Sjef Houppermans et al., Rodopi, 2005, pp. 142–57.

———. *L'empire du pseudo: modernités de la science-fiction.* Nota bene, 1999.

Sakurazaka, Hiroshi, et al. *All you need is kill.* Haikasoru, 2009.

Suvin, Darko. *Metamorphoses of Science Fiction: Studies in the Poetics and History of a Literary Genre.* Yale University Press, 1978.

———. "Theses on Dystopia 2001." *Dark Horizons,* Routledge, 2013, pp. 199–214. https://doi.org/10.4324/9781315810775-17.

Tadié, Jean-Yves. *Le sens de la mémoire.* Gallimard, 1999.

Volodine, Antoine. *Songes de Mevlido.* Seuil, 2007.

Voltaire, Theo Cuffe, et al. *Micromégas and Other Short Fictions.* Penguin, 2002.

Voltaire, et al. *Zadig; L'ingénu.* Penguin, 1983.

Vonarburg, Elisabeth. *Le silence de la cité.* Editions Alire, 1998.

———. "Les femmes en tant qu'artefactes dans la science-fiction moderne." *Science-fiction et imaginaires contemporains,* edited by Francis Berthelot and Philippe Clermont, Bragelonne, 2007, pp. 153–67.

———. *The Silent City.* Translated by Jane Brierley, Tesseracts Books, 2002.

Vuarnet, Jean-Noël. "L'utopie inverse. Notes sur la prolifération des utopies 1388 du pire." *Saint-Denis: Presses et Publications de l'Université de Paris VIII Vincennes à Saint-Denis*, vol. Théorie-Littérature Enseignement n°3., 1984.

Wendland, Albert. *Science, Myth, and the Fictional Creation of Alien Worlds*. UMI Research Press, 1985.

CHAPTER 3

Modalities and Fictional Storyworlds in Futuristic Novels

Dissonant Minds of Fictional Storyworlds

Worlds envisioned by futuristic novels are hardly ever summarized as static settings framing the actions and outbursts of a few fictional characters. These worlds often intrigue readers through their enigmatic aspects and apparent incoherency, and when their strangeness matters more than the characterization of the characters, this strangeness makes these characters' humanity more striking by contrast. In the books I examine in this chapter, the main features of such enigmatic worlds over time are that they are partly or completely dystopian and reformulate a fundamental question: What makes a future world remain humanized or become dehumanized?

At the outset, readers are invited to distinguish the strangeness of these worlds from the harshness of the laws of these worlds, as well as differentiating between these laws and the main characters' intentions. Most of the time strangeness takes precedence over direct threat in science fiction novels, while dystopian speculative fictions are quicker to point out the danger they want to address, as in the beginning of *Our Life in the Forest*, for example: "I OPENED MY eye and bang, everything came into focus. It was clear. Almost all of us had our halves with us. And it was scary just how clingy my half was. [...] Time to get a grip. I have to tell this story. I have to try to understand it by laying things out in some sort of order. By rounding up the bits and pieces. Because it's not going well. It's

© The Author(s), under exclusive license to Springer Nature   61
Switzerland AG 2022
E. Buzay, *Contemporary French and Francophone Futuristic Novels*,
Studies in Global Science Fiction,
https://doi.org/10.1007/978-3-031-16628-0_3

not okay right now, all that. Not okay at all" (Darrieussecq, *Our Life in the Forest* 1). Finally, transfictions confuse strangeness with harshness and adversity. In the case of transfictions, readers need to pay greater attention to understand the laws of a dystopian world that do not seem to be contradicted by the psychological characterization of the characters, such as in the case of Daniel24's view of the outside world in Michel Houellebecq's *The Possibility of an Island*:

LOOK AT THE LITTLE CREATURES moving in the distance; look. They are humans. In the fading light, I witness without regret the disappearance of the species. A last ray of sunlight skims over the plain, passes over the mountain range barring the horizon to the east, and colors the desert landscape with a red halo. The metal trellises of the protective fence around the residence sparkle. Fox growls softly; no doubt he can sense the presence of the savages. For them I feel no pity, nor any sense of common belonging; I simply consider them to be slightly more intelligent monkeys, and, for this reason, more dangerous. There are times when I unlock the fence to rescue a rabbit, or a stray dog; but never to bring help to a human (Houellebecq, *The Possibility of an Island* 18).

To assess these relations, I use the "possible worlds" semantics that allows us to estimate the level of dissonance between, on one hand, the laws of a world that are supposed to apply to everyone and, on the other hand, the ones that apply to one or several characters who express, to quote an expression of Jean-Noël Vuarnet, a "false note" (Vuarnet 117) by striving to stand out from the crowd. Given that futuristic novels explore in-depth dissonant minds in action that gradually become resistant to the world they live in, I will follow Alan Parker's lead, when he states in *Fictional Minds* that the "possible-worlds approach forms a promising way to unify [...] divergent approaches to fictional minds" (Palmer 36), an approach that follows in the wake of his incorporation of aspects from the possible worlds narrative theorists Thomas Pavel (*Fictional Worlds* (1986)), Lubomir Doležel (*Heterocosmica* (1998)), and Marie-Laure Ryan (*Possible Words, Artificial Intelligence, and Narrative Theory* (1992)).

In order to discover a world whose literary composition strives to disclose itself, I find a definite theoretical advantage in the notion of possible worlds because this notion helps explain the depth of the dissonant fictional minds of the main characters in French and Francophone futuristic novels. These dissonant fictional minds result from the confrontation between the organization of the utopian or dystopian worlds and the actions of those main characters whose dissonance and then resistance are subject to the collaborative participation of readers. Now the questions become: Why is this notion connected to readers? What are its main semantic properties?

First formulated in *Essays of Theodicy* (1710) by the German philosopher Gottfried Wilhelm Leibnitz, the notion of possible worlds was reintroduced in the 1970s by the logician Saul Kripke, who rethought it as a set of proposals made possible through modal relations called "accessibility" between a world of departure and other worlds that would be compared to this first world of departure. In this perspective, every "actual world is [...] surrounded by an infinity of possible worlds, each of them each being in turn the world of reference of a new constellation of possible worlds" (Lavocat 16). The possible worlds semantics that "formalize relations between these worlds" (Lavocat 16) since then has continued to enrich the notion of fiction in the works of Thomas Pavel, Lubomir Doležel, and Marie-Laure Ryan, to name just a few of the main theorists who underpin my argument in this chapter. Indeed, Pavel, Doležel, and Ryan "refer to the possible worlds that are created in worlds of literature and that are also known interchangeably as fictional worlds, narrative worlds, text worlds, and storyworlds" (Palmer 32–33). Unlike those who use the term storyworld interchangeably with that of possible worlds, I will be distinguishing these two terms, as does Alan Palmer, by focusing on the fact that the notion of a storyworld extends the reading experience as it solicits an interpretive commitment on the part of readers that can enrich these experiences and communicate them to other interpreters:

> Within possible-worlds theory, reading—and therefore access to the storyworld—has three elements: the source domain, the real world in which the text is being processed by the reader; the target domain, the storyworld world that constitutes the output of the reader's processing; and the system of textual features that triggers various kinds of reader-held real-world knowledge in a way that projects the reader from source domain to target domain (Palmer 34).

Furthermore, readers' cognitive capacities to interpret provide storyworlds with a certain autonomy beyond the texts in which they find themselves, that is to say, a (fictional) existence. The emphasis on these capacities that are required in order to understand such storyworlds makes this term the most appropriate for my study, due to my focus on the cognitive capacities of both readers and fictional characters as a means of interpretation of these texts. The basis of this term, that is, the notion of fictional "storyworlds," was one I initially borrowed from David Herman,[1] but it has been enriched by Alan Palmer's readings of Doležel's essay *Heterocosmica. Fiction and Possible Worlds* (1998) to fully unpack the processes that connect the reader to fictional minds:

> The reference to the utilization of real-world knowledge in the reading process will bring us [...] to the contribution that cognitive science can make to an understanding of the reading process. Doležel maintains that "fictional worlds are accessed through semiotic channels and by means of information processing" and that readers can do this "by crossing somehow the world boundary between the realms of the actual and the possible" (1998, 20). The reconstruction of the storyworld by the reader "integrates fictional worlds into the reader's reality" (Doležel 1998, 21). [Alan Palmer's thesis being] that the main semiotic channels by which the reader accesses fictional worlds, and the most important sets of instructions that allow the reader to reconstruct the fictional world, are those that govern the reader's understanding of the workings of characters' minds (Palmer 34).

Given the fact that several semantic properties of the futuristic fictional storyworlds constantly solicit the interpretative investment of the reader, it is important to study them. At their "limits," as Palmer terms it, there are three semantic properties that prevail in the building of the storyworlds in the corpus studied here (Palmer 201–03). These properties are: (1) the need for readers to extrapolate based on the "principle of minimal or indeterminate departure," (2) the incompleteness of fictional worlds and beings, and finally (3) the doubly "fictional recentering" function (imparted to the book as an object), which reveals the modal structures of fictional worlds. These three semantic properties appear to be the defining characteristics of the dissonant and resistant fictional consciousnesses

---

[1] "More generally, when compared with cognate narratological terms such as fabula or story, storyworld better captures what might be called the ecology of narrative interpretation. (...) More than reconstructed timelines and inventories of existents, then, storyworlds are mentally and emotionally projected environments in which interpreters are called upon to live out complex blends of cognitive and imaginative response" (Herman et al. 570).

portrayed in the French and Francophone futuristic novels selected here, and perhaps even, in a larger sense, all such works. The progression in the plot of futuristic novels often proceeds through the perspective of a focal character and its fictional mind, which results from the interaction between the text and the readers' reading strategies that are based on either a minimal or an indeterminate extrapolation. This implies that readers evolve at the crossroads of a progressive understanding of the laws of an enigmatic world and the actions of its main protagonists, to the point of exhausting their interrelated insights throughout an investigation. In these circumstances, the interpretation of these fictional storyworlds confronts the orientations of an anticipated world with those of a "real" world or, in other words, these orientations represent a xeno-encyclopedia confronted by the encyclopedia of the reader's world of reference, the "real" world. This form of interpretation requires an original point of comparison, from which the fiction storyworld varies, following a rule that Marie-Laure Ryan calls the "the principle of minimal departure,"[2] which means that "while reading a text and reconstructing a storyworld from it, the reader assumes the minimal possible departure from the actual world unless such a departure is specified or strongly indicated by the text" (Palmer 35).

Since the reconstructed storyworlds differ little from the actual world, this principle of minimal departure applies especially to the dystopian speculative fictions in my selection. The storyworlds of *Globalia*, *The First Century After Beatrice*, and *Our Life in the Forest* result from an extrapolation from our contemporary world and the examination of its societal issues (more specifically, the influence of communication technologies for surveillance and the disparities between the North and the South). The notions introduced here, and in particular these required extrapolations, echo in large part the interpretative work started in the previous chapter with the notion of discursive novums, as well as the considerations of language related to the media devices of our time. However, extrapolations that try to preserve a chronological continuity and a logical order between the storyworlds and the actual world can also

---

[2] This law—to which I shall refer as the principle of minimal departure—states that we reconstrue the central world of a textual universe in the same way we reconstrue the alternate possible worlds of nonfactual statements: as conforming as far as possible to our representation of AW [Actual World]. We will project upon these worlds everything we know about reality, and we will make only the adjustments dictated by the text (Ryan 51).

be distorted, multiply the frames out of focus, and no longer be reduced in these conditions to a simple magnifying glass effect. This blurring becomes even more reinforced in works that occur after the Apocalypse. Indeed, this blurring is, moreover, almost the rule in the storyworlds of science fiction novels and transfictions, such as in the examples of the novels *Les Derniers Hommes* and *The Silent City*, which follow the principle of an "indeterminate departure,"[3] as Richard Saint-Gelais coins it, an aspect that they have in common with *The Possibility of an Island* and *Songes de Mevlido*.

Produced by the discrepancy between the storyworlds and the actual world, this principle of an indeterminate departure reinforces the abductive pleasure readers feel when reconstructing fictional storyworlds whose primary coherence escapes them, from the enunciation of lexical and even more so from that of empirical novums. From the principle of minimal departure to the principle of indeterminate departure, abduction thus increases as it gets more complex, but more importantly, it defines the processing of the fictional minds in their dissonance and resistance, as consciousness is embodied and reveals changes in worlds through actions:

> The processing of fictional minds (…) are bidirectional and interactive in that the information flows are both top-up and bottom-down. A character frame is established on meeting them or hearing of them for the first time (this is top-down). It is then fed by specific information about the character from the text (this is bottom-up). The reader then sets up some initial hypotheses (top-down) that are modified by further information (bottom-up) and so further refined and so on. Minds are mapped from the source domain (the real mind of the reader and in particular their knowledge of other minds) to the target domain of the storyworld within which the reader perceives the fictional minds to function (Palmer 176).

It is in this context that the reflection on natural language developed by the protagonists of dystopian speculative fiction is followed by the questioning of another language: that of computer programming or genetic coding in which the characters of science fiction and transfiction

---

[3] "Similar to the reader of detective novels, but on another plane, the science fiction reader is *on guard*. If the science fictional reading relies on one principle, it is indeed that of the *indeterminate departure*" ["Semblable au lecteur de romans policiers, mais sur un autre plan, le lecteur de science-fiction est *sur ses gardes*. Si la lecture science-fictionnelle repose sur un principe, c'est bien celui de *l'écart indéterminé*"] (Saint-Gelais, *L'empire du pseudo* 218).

are involved. Successively put into perspective by principles of minimal departure and indeterminate departure, the conscious embodiment of the characters in my selection thus acquires an increasingly ambiguous status and is reduced to an impression that attracts readers' attention all the more so because the storyworld in which they interfere tends to be foreign to them. This is the reason why the way in which a character's incarnation determines the discovery of a world's materiality appears to be the main characteristic of futuristic novels. That being said, in order to understand it well, we need to question this dualism further. To do so, the *postures as witnesses* of Baikal, Viviane, and the entomologist narrator, father of Beatrice, who all refuse the reified use of a dystopian world; the *mutant bodies* of Elisa and Solman; and then the *body-corpora* personified by Daniel and Mevlido need to be evaluated from an enlarged semantic perspective to include the incompleteness of fictional worlds and beings.

A significant aspect of Doležel's semantic approach in *Heterocosmica. Fiction and Possible Worlds* is the examination of the incompleteness of fictional worlds and beings distinguishing the categories of fictional worlds or "building blocks" from the modal categories that organize them. Indeed Doležel "takes as a starting point the (theoretical) possibility of worlds made of simple states, then worlds where the only transformations are the work of natural forces, before moving, according to a principle of increasing complexity, to worlds with a single agent and finally to worlds with several agents, where the dynamics of interaction finally become possible."[4] I will reverse this progression in order to follow the organization of subgenres (science fiction, dystopian speculative fiction, and transfiction) through which I have presented the novels studied here. Indeed, this progression does not define real boundaries, but instead identifies trends seen in the worlds extrapolated from science fiction, dystopian speculative fiction, and transfiction, and which are made up of the following constituent units:

> The first, *selection*, determines which constituent categories will be admitted into the world under construction. The world's categorial type is thus fixed: one-person or multiperson world, a world of physical or mental events, a

---

[4] En effet Doležel "prend comme point de départ la possibilité (théorique) de mondes constitués de simples états, puis de mondes où les seules transformations sont le fait de forces naturelles, avant de passer, selon un principe de complexité croissante, à des mondes à un seul agent et enfin à des mondes à plusieurs agents, où la dynamique de l'interaction devient enfin possible" (Saint-Gelais, "Ambitions et limites de la sémantique de la fiction").

world of intentional acting or intentionless processes, a world with nature or without nature, and so on. These types are ideal structures; they combine in many and different ways to create the categorial order of particular fictional narrative worlds (Doležel, *Heterocosmica* 113).

The choice of such units that could correspond either to a "one-person world" or a "multiperson world" does not allow, however, the reconstitution of the extrapolated worlds that I am referring to in this study. Also, rather than considering the two science fiction novels *Les Derniers Hommes* and *The Silent City* as simple restitutions of multiperson worlds, it would be better to qualify this statement and call the worlds in these novels one-person worlds that strive to become complex multiperson worlds. As such, the "becoming mutant" that characterizes Solman and Elisa, who start by isolating themselves from their respective societies, is then subordinated to the achievement of a precise collective project (respectively, the survival of the community of the last men, for Solman, and the regeneration of the human species, for Elisa), which supposes that these characters experience the previously cited binary oppositions, before moving beyond them. Perceived as a response to a hostile physical nature marked by the stigmata of war and by multiple forms of pollution, Solman's and Elisa's "becoming a mutant" culminates, in these circumstances, in a form of a sociality influenced by the exercise of power and the resolution of conflicts. For these reasons, these storyworlds are marked by the expansion of the constituent units of this sociality, which causes them to tend toward a minimum of incompleteness.

In contrast, the storyworlds that emerge from *The Possibility of an Island* and *Songes de Mevlido* more closely resemble multiperson worlds that gradually restrict the possibility of choice to their protagonists and tend to become one-person worlds. This reduction accompanies the dismantling of the subject/object relation from the main characters' perspective, and it explains, among other examples in the novels mentioned above, that Nature collects what remains of Mevlido's and the last of the Daniels' indecisiveness in that the reduction is not truly evolutionary since each of these characters is at the end of their journey. Besides, in these two novels, all forms of society also seem to disappear, and the collapse within these storyworlds illustrates a maximum of incompleteness, as the intentionality of the acts supporting life in society loses its whole purpose.

Finally, the magnifying effect of dystopian speculative fiction almost results from a balance between the binary oppositions identified by

Doležel; this effect assigns the most humanist treatment to the relationships of otherness that assign this or that type of character to a particular society project. In these texts, it is from the perspective of men and women who are nearly our contemporaries that the changes that negatively affect anticipated societies are examined. In this subgenre of science fiction novels, one-person worlds tend to overlap with multiperson worlds, which explains how Viviane in *Our Life in the Forest* and Baïkal in *Globalia*, as well as the entomologist narrator in *The First Century After Beatrice*, give readers the impression of viewing monstrous organizations, which legitimizes their involvement as much as their withdrawal. Whatever the upheavals they experience, they still understand their limitations: Viviane is well aware that she owes her safety to the "cliker," the name she gives to one of her patients, while Baïkal quickly acknowledges that he is no match for Ron Altman, the head of Globalia; lastly, Beatrice's father constantly says that he is only a privileged witness of a human drama. In other words, the incompleteness that qualifies these storyworlds is essentially indicated by the posture of these characters who strangely doubt their function as "heroes," even as they struggle against the dystopian order they intend to challenge.

In order to explain such behaviors, I will relate the worlds' incompleteness to that of the fictional beings, according to Doležel's distinction between intention and motivation, in a reflection about the logic of action:

> Intention is the defining and universal condition of acting, but it is rarely declared by agents and is, therefore, unnoticed by observers of acting (…). We are faced with a curious discrepancy: while in the philosophy of action the problem of intentionality is at the center of interest, empirical studies of acting, including narratology, have hardly noticed its existence. (…) While intention is undifferentiated and ungraded, motivational factors are diverse in both quality and quantity. Because they are habitual features of a person's character, they produce regularities in acting, modes of acting characteristic of individuals and personality types. Whereas intention delimits the domain of acting from nonactional events, motivation is the key to understanding the diversity of acting, the why and how of actions (Doležel, *Heterocosmica* 63).

If intention is the main cause of all the actions that are then normally put into play by motivation, and if these actions are tested in the materiality of the storyworlds over time, then the study of the incompleteness of the beings of fiction can give rise to the following observations. First, it seems that the strange postures of the characters in dystopian speculative fiction are incongruous, because their intentions outweigh their motivations which affect the concrete occurrence of their actions. As they are characterized, Viviane, Baïkal, and Beatrice's father are above all rebellious characters who oppose their societies almost despite themselves. They make others act; they inspire action (or more exactly, they testify in order to make others act) more than act themselves, and it is the primacy of this intention of rebellion over their motivation that perhaps explains why they deny the singularity of their commitments. Since their motivation is confronted with the harsh reality of their societies, it almost never exceeds the empathy they feel for those in whom they keep recognizing themselves. On this point, the endings of the three dystopian speculative fiction works are significant. Feeling the time of her death arriving in the forest, Viviane imagines that her corpse will be inseparable from her notebook, which testifies to the disasters of her time for future generations. Baïkal takes the place of the deceased tribal man "Fraiseur" (a term meaning "miller") and, with his lover Kate, joins this man's tribe in the forest, leaving modern civilization for good. This is also what Beatrice's father does when he imagines finishing his days, staring at a mountain that he sees as "[his] Mount Ararat—the mountain in Armenia where Noah's ark came to rest" (Maalouf, *The First Century After Beatrice* 1991).

Despite the fact that Elisa and Solman are equally empathetic toward their contemporaries, their intentions and motivations are in perfect alignment throughout the narrative and focus on the attainment of specific goals: the deactivation of the City and the destruction of the Eskato organization, both of which are collective artifacts. For these two characters who *act*, not without hesitation sometimes, their "becoming mutant" confirms them in their respective singularity, which makes them fictional beings that are portrayed with a minimum of incompleteness in *The Silent City* and *The Last Men*.

Finally, a maximum of incompleteness applies to the series of Daniels (from 1 to 25) and Mevlido, as fictional beings in the storyworlds of *The Possibility of an Island* and *Mevlido's Dreams*. I explain this characteristic trait of maximum incompleteness by an intention that is shifted, regressive, or simply depersonalized or removed in relation to the characters' erratic motivations that result from this intention, and which these same characters display. The Daniels and Mevlido *are acted upon* by their motivation, and their acts are equivalent to "scripts" (Doležel, *Heterocosmica* 65), as Doležel understands the term, meaning that scripts are similar to artificial intelligence sequences from which manifestations of individuality are gradually diminishing.

In conclusion, if the incompleteness of worlds and fictional beings varies from one text to another, there is, however, a semantic property in which all the futuristic fictional storyworlds of science fiction, dystopian speculative fiction, and transfiction come together. This semantic property is the authentication of the insufficiency of the characters' fictional minds that reveals the full spectrum of the modal system that supports their worlds. This property that corresponds with the doubly "fictional recentering" is imparted to the book as an object, and it stages, beyond the intertextual references and interplays, the importance of fictional readers in futuristic novels.

To support the argument in *Fictional Minds* that a "narrative fiction is, in essence, the presentation of fictional mental functioning" (Palmer 5), Alan Palmer uses Marie-Laure Ryan's concept of "embedded narratives"[5] and extends it as a "key mediational tool" (Palmer 183) to "doubly" envision its effects to the point of characterizing them as "doubly embedded narratives, [that is,] the representations of characters' minds that are contained within the minds of other characters" (Palmer 205). Along with this reflection, I have also borrowed the concept of "fictional centering" from Marie-Laure Ryan and extended the meaning of this term by adding the term "doubly" to it, in a parallel to Palmer's "doubly embedded narratives," thus arriving at the new term of a "doubly fictional recentering" to note how fictional readers access fictional worlds' rules, once reading makes these readers increasingly aware of them. With "fictional recentering," Marie-Laure Ryan describes the interpretative work that all readers do when their understanding of a possible world also takes into account their modes of cultural expression. Doing so, readers "recenter" the relevance of the issues that shape these worlds and that somehow become more "real" for them, in the interlacing of their dreams, desires, and wishes:

---

[5] Marie-Laure Ryan defines her concept of embedded narratives as "any story-like like representation produced in the mind of a character and reproduced in the mind of the reader" (1986, 320). I have considerably extended the meaning of the term by placing it in the context of the parallel discourses described in this study and, therefore, by using it to refer to all aspects of the fictional mind. Ryan explains that for a discourse to evoke a story-world, it must bring a universe to life and convey to the reader the sense that at the center of this universe there resides an actual or real world, a realm of factual states or events (Palmer 188).

For the duration of our immersion in a work of fiction, the realm of possibilities is thus recentered around the sphere which the narrator presents as the actual world. This recentering pushes the reader into a new system of actuality and possibility. As a traveler to this system, the reader of fiction discovers not only a new actual world, but a variety of APWs [Alternative Possible Worlds] revolving around it. Just as we manipulate possible worlds through mental operations, so do the inhabitants of fictional universes: their actual world is reflected in their knowledge and beliefs, corrected in their wishes, replaced by a new reality in their dreams and hallucinations. Through counterfactual thinking they reflect on how things might have been, through plans and projections they contemplate things that still have a chance to be, and through the act of making up fictional stories they recenter their universe into what is for them a second-order, and for us a third-order, system of reality (Ryan 22).

Now for readers who have access to the storyworlds of fictional minds, this "doubly fictional recentering" creates an effect of authenticity.[6] In science fiction, dystopian speculative fiction, and transfiction, the doubly fictional recentering, referred to as a "novel within the novel," expresses itself in three ways: first, it clarifies the actions of the characters based on the rules of their world, next it acts as an intermediary, and finally, it represents a certain form of stability in the narrative regime that guides the progression of the plot.

A pertinent example of this process that stages the book as an object, along with its readers, can be found strangely enough in a videogame whose semantics summarizes the different effects of "fictional recenterings" also at work in anticipation literature. This adventure videogame is named *Myst* and is partially inspired by *The Mysterious Island* by Jules Verne. Created in 1993 by the brothers Robyn and Rand Miller, this game immerses the player in a universe that turns out to be a succession of

---

[6] "When the narrator tells a story, for example, he excludes himself at the same time from a fictional universe of which he is the source: he becomes 'real'. All the novels where the characters are themselves readers of novels play on this process: this reference, at the diegetic level, to the work of fiction, allows the narration to give itself as a metalanguage that is distinct from the literary language, and therefore is *authentic*." ["Lorsqu'un narrateur raconte une histoire, par exemple, il s'exclut du même coup d'un univers fictif dont il est la source: il devient 'réel'. Sur ce procédé, jouent tous les romans où les personnages sont eux-mêmes des lecteurs de romans: cette référence, au niveau diégétique, à l'œuvre de la fiction, permet à la narration de se donner comme un métalangage distinct du langage littéraire, donc *authentique*"] (Jouve 118).

books. As a game, one could say that *Myst*, in these circumstances, represents a reading adventure. After opening the first book, players wander alone on an island where most puzzles to be solved find their solutions in a library that provides them with clues both to understand the actions of the characters and to pass tests and help them to collect the pages of a blue book and a red book. Only these pages will then be likely to release two characters, when these books are completed: these characters are Sirrus and Achemar, sons of Atrus, a third character, their father who is the owner of the island. To reach this point, players must continue exploring the island and following the gameplay in order to realize that Myst as an island is in fact connected to other timeframes of the same place called "Ages," where the player can collect a blue and a red page so as to use them at the end of the game when all these pages can be reunited in order to set free one of the two sons mentioned earlier. Jan Van Looy, who has observed the concurrence of these recenterings in *Myst* prefers, for his part, to speak of "virtual recentering" to analyze how players who engage themselves in the plot *redouble* their attention to repair the world of *Myst*:

> The reason for my adding *Myst* as a case-study and illustration is that it can be interpreted as a comment on its own format and on the virtual structure of a game in general. By constantly referring to the book as a material object and to its fictional worlds, *Myst* demonstrates a preoccupation with the concepts of 'medium' and 'virtuality'. Atrus is put forward as the author of the worlds which the player is to repair ("Virtual Recentering").

In a similar way, the manifestations of "authenticity" linked to the doubly fictional recenterings of the characters in my selected works question or stimulate, through our constant involvement as readers, the idea of repairing a world. It is these recenterings that highlight the interplay of modal structures such as "knowledge," "duty," and "alternative possibilities" in the reconstitution of fictional storyworlds, and which at the very least restore the idea of humanity whose intentions are to inhabit the world.

Dualities and Modal Structures of Fictional
Storyworlds: Knowledge, Duty, and Ability

What connection exists between the perseverance of Solman and Elisa in the accomplishment of their tasks; the fragility of the testimonies of Baïkal, Viviane, and the entomologist narrator father of Beatrice; the poetry of Daniel25; and the dreams of Mevlido? In this plurality of storyworlds, it seems that the *intentional lives* of all these characters are at the heart of the literature of contemporary anticipation in that these conscious lives weaken or diminish in their grasp of the world.

Near or far, the futures portrayed by the science fiction novels are not enigmatic in and of themselves, but because they are interpreted and experienced by characters who *act, testify to make others act,* or *are acted upon,* according to the grasp of their intentional life. In fact, it is the fragility or the reduction of this intentional life in the fictional minds of the characters that actually signals the dystopian features of the worlds they inhabit. In the conception of these storyworlds, a fictional intentional life emerges that invests modalities such as *knowledge, duty,* and (*deceptive*) *ability* that support, in the range of possibilities associated with them, the duality or the indifferentiation between individuals and a plurality of worlds. The structuring dualities of the extrapolated worlds of my book selections presuppose, from the point of view of a logic of action, that the set of modalities initially form an "indissociable whole" in the constitution of the limits of the intentional life that authors delegate to the fictional minds of their characters:

> As constraints of actual human actions, modalities apparently operate jointly; every human action is determined by natural possibilities (agents' abilities to perform certain actions), deontic norms (legal, moral, etc.), by social or individual values (desires) and by the agents' knowledge and beliefs (Doležel, "Narrative Modalities" 7).

The semantics of Doležel's theory of possible worlds, as developed in *Heterocosmica: Fiction and Possible Worlds,* sets out from the outset structuring dualities of "ability" and "knowledge" (science fiction), of "ability" and "duty" (dystopian speculative fiction), and of two conceptions of the modality of "ability" in a dual world (transgressive fiction). All these dualities constitute dissonances of consciousness for the fictional minds in the novels studied in this book. In relation to the dual structures of these storyworlds suggested by Doležel, in which each (sub)genre's storyworlds pair ability and another modality—those of knowledge (science fiction), duty (dystopian speculative fiction), and a deceptive ability (transfiction), respectively—my goal is therefore to study this pattern of dualities in the intentional lives of characters in science fiction, dystopian speculative fiction, and transgressive fiction novels. This intentional life is in fact successively emancipated, disproportionate, and finally quasi-resorbed, as the utopian societies of these storyworlds darken and the intentionality of acts that promote life in these societies loses its *raison d'être*. Indeed, readers, who are collaborating with the text to create an understanding, necessarily consider these dualities or cleavages between the organization of utopian or dystopian worlds and the actions of focal characters.

Furthermore, these terms of knowledge, duty, and ability, as narrative modalities, match the modal semantic system of Doležel. According to this typology, while the modality of knowledge aligns with the macro-constraints of epistemic worlds, the modality of duty complies with the macro-constraints of deontic (and axiologic) world(s), and the modality of ability corresponds to the macro-constraints of alethic worlds.

Since ability, which corresponds to the alethic, is the common feature of all three of the dualities, it is present in all of the works examined in this chapter. These alethic fictions have the distinctive feature of revealing the laws of the possible worlds of science fiction, dystopian speculative fiction, and transgressive fiction novels, in the light of the resistance of the characters who evolve in them. The intentional lives which characterize these characters, that is to say their comprehension of a world whose mystery sums up all the interest of these characters' psychology, implies that readers are the privileged witnesses of a transformation since their comprehension is based on the main protagonists' growing understanding of such worlds and their actions.

From the perspective of a humanization, such a transformation confronts a modal perspective embodied by one or more characters with the order of an alethic world that is alien to them, which supposes an inclusive relationship between modalities that Mattison Schuknetch summarizes in *The Best/Worst of All Possible Worlds?* as follows:

> A combination of the alethic (possible, impossible, and necessary) and epistemic systems generates science fiction and speculative fiction texts; such works frequently ask what may be possible in the future given the current understanding of the actual world's scientific principles (scientific

extrapolation) or what could be possible if such principles were fundamentally altered. [...] Specifically, dystopian texts contain extensive conflict between the modalities of the deontic system, while utopian texts contain a substantial degree of harmony between the same modalities. To put it simply, utopian worlds minimize deontic conflict, while dystopian worlds maximize it (Schuknecht, Mattison 238–39).

This relation of inclusion[7] between modalities is crucial in that it reminds us that the characterization of characters presupposes that they can be endowed with a fictional intentionality, as the vehicles of a world with its own laws. But the semantics of a modal dissonance, in the perspective of a complete dehumanization, can also dissolve the intentional lives of characters to the point of making them undifferentiated from the world they inhabit and make their resistance the story of a transformation backed up by these characters' ultimate testimony.

Ideally, the laws of the futuristic fictional storyworlds are measured by the laws of focal characters who evolve because they are different. It is thus, for science fiction, that the characters of Elisa and Solman, who, while becoming mutant, transform the static or doctrinal knowledge of their respective alethic worlds that determines the possible, the impossible, and the necessary into a more humanized knowledge, as well as gaining access to a better knowledge of themselves. How does this transformation manifest itself? We must remember that these two characters subvert many of the laws of their respective futuristic worlds, as they are at first "foreigners" [8] in them: The androgyny of Elisa is the result of genetic experiments conceived to regenerate a weakened humankind after an apocalyptic war, and Solman is a mutant afflicted by a physical handicap but gifted with a faculty of foresight necessary for the survival of his community.

---

[7] This relation of inclusion between modalities is also illustrated by Peter Stockwell who gives an example of this inclusive pattern in his reading of Malcolm Jameson's short story "Doubled and Redoubled": "The status of each possible world, then, is a matter of character-consciousness, and the other characters, being unaware of the repetition, can be said to occupy different possible worlds of their own belief. In Doležel's (...) terms, 'Doubled and Redoubled' constitutes a set of epistemic worlds held by the different characters, within an *alethic* world (with alternative laws of possibility)" (Stockwell 144).

[8] "The alethic alien is a fictional person whose alethic endowment in some fundamental way deviates from the standard of the world" (Doležel, *Heterocosmica* 119).

Let us consider Elisa's pathway first. In *The Silent City*, the origin of her journey corresponds to a laboratory experiment from which she originates and to which her designer, Paul, would like to reduce her entirely in the scope of his "Project" related to some form of colonialism:

> We have to wait until they're ready Outside. We in the Cities are trustees of a treasure, Elisa. Knowledge. The sciences, the arts, the wisdom of the ages. We are the guardians. You and your descendants will be the guardians. You'll keep the people of the Exterior under surveillance and you'll continue my research. It's very important, Elisa. You've got to learn a lot, work a lot, dearest[9] (Vonarburg, *The Silent City* 25).

All of Elisa's intentional life will consist in departing from this "Project" without following Paul's opponent, Charles Desprats, who would like to destroy these Cities so that they do not interfere anymore with the life of the human communities of the "Outside." But breaking away from the influence of male technological knowledge is overwhelming because it includes the destruction of mythical references of such knowledge, as can be seen in the example of how the "screen culture" of a mainframe computer assimilated to the City gives way to the "literary culture" of the reading of an imaginary book often reminiscent of the *Bible*, even if this later reference is one with which Elisa and her "descendants" can more easily identify.

Readers discover how Elisa "reads" her adventures, her personal evolution, and her responsibilities on a collective level when she uses the term a "baptism of blood"[10] for the second time (Vonarburg, *The Silent City* 199)—the first time this expression referred to the murder she committed against Paul to set herself free—to describe a war between men and women, after having cut herself off from the operations of this City also perceived as a "gigantic, multicellular organism stretching its pseudopods in all directions"[11] (Vonarburg, *The Silent City* 194). She

---

[9] « Nous, dans les Cités, nous sommes les dépositaires d'un trésor, Élisa. La connaissance. Les sciences, les arts, la sagesse de l'humanité. Nous sommes les gardiens. Toi et tes descendants, vous serez les gardiens. Vous surveillerez les gens de l'Extérieur et vous continuerez mes recherches. C'est très important, Élisa. Tu dois beaucoup apprendre, beaucoup travailler, ma chérie » (Vonarburg 36–37).

[10] « … baptême du sang » (Vonarburg, *Le silence de la cité* 309).

[11] « … un gigantesque organisme multicellulaire qui étend ses pseudopodes dans toutes ses directions » (Vonarburg, *Le silence de la cité* 300).

observes an interweaving between her personal evolution and her collective responsibilities—after the departure of the first of her "descendants," Abram, to the "Outside"—that both Abram and her other "children" will eventually reject Paul's "Project," this project that Elisa had tried as best as she could to democratize:

> The Children. Without her. She isn't returning to the community, she's going to a community transformed by Abram's departure, (…). But she is not an avenging angel. Elisa smiles wryly: they have found the tree of knowledge, but it's God who will be judged (*God, Elisa?*) She realizes that she is only half joking, and her smiles fades. Will the children judge *her?* No doubt they already have, years ago. They've never really been taken in her highflown rationalizing. They know what she is, what she wants, what she fears, and they've accepted her for what she is. Do they love her for what she is? But she will judge herself, is already judging herself. Nothing will ever be the same again. The community, the snug dream, the blind Eden, that's over. And who was the serpent, if not herself?[12] (Vonarburg 202–03).

The rejection of this "Project," which was the very reason for Elisa's existence at the beginning of the novel, thus closes her epistemic quest. At the same time, this rejection portrays a more humane and liberated world, as readers discover, under the guise of a scientific and political power, and it is furthermore this very rejection that is a denunciation of the religious intentions that ideologically underpinned it.

Elisa continues to tear off the last masks of a masculine, patriarchal determinism when she evolves, sometimes even taking on the role of God mentioned in the previous quote; just like she began to withdraw from Paul's dreams, when as a teenager she used to sleep with him, in a parallel to Eve being taken from Adam's side or rib. As she evolves, she comes to realize that she is "neither God nor Devil, she is a human being, neither as

---

[12] « Elle ne va pas retourner à la communauté: elle va entrer dans une communauté transformée, par le départ d'Abram, (…), mais ce n'est pas en ange vengeur qu'elle revient ! Elle sourit avec ironie: ils ont touché à l'arbre de la Connaissance, mais c'est Dieu qui va être jugé. *(Dieu, Élisa ?)* Elle se rend compte qu'elle ne plaisante qu'à demi et son sourire s'efface. Les enfants la jugeront-ils ? C'est déjà fait, sans doute, depuis longtemps: ils n'ont jamais été vraiment dupes de ses belles rationalisations, eux. Ils savent qui elle est, ses désirs, ses craintes: ils l'ont acceptée ainsi. Ils l'aiment ainsi ? Mais elle se jugera, elle. Se juge déjà. Non, rien ne sera plus pareil. La communauté, le rêve bien clos, l'Éden aveugle, c'est fini. *Et qui était donc le Serpent, sinon moi-même ?* » (Vonarburg, *Le silence de la cité* 315).

fallible nor as infallible as she would like to think"[13] (Vonarburg, *The Silent City* 203), in this previous observation that is inspired by her acceptance of a demystified knowledge of her nature as an androgynous mutant. "Perhaps *that* is the revelation: to learn that you have to keep tearing yourself away from your illusions, to learn you never stop discovering the lies you tell yourself; to learn how you manipulate yourself. Never stop giving birth to yourself? "[14] (Vonarburg, *The Silent City* 203), she concludes.

In contrast to Elisa, the evolution of Solman's "becoming a mutant" also transforms the static or doctrinal knowledge of his alethic world into more humanized knowledge, but his epistemic quest aims at blending into the biblical narrative, simultaneously appearing to be the fulfillment of a prophecy, not at distancing himself from it by adopting the point of view of science, as Elisa did. As portrayed by Pierre Bordage in *The Last Men* in his visionary capacities, "Solman the cripple"[15] is a character whose empathy and gift of prophecy are joined together to fight two forms of dystopian rationalization: the authoritarian power exercised by the leaders of his own community, the Aquariots, and the enterprise of exterminating the "last men," the community to which he and the Aquariots belong, an undertaking led by a group of posthuman scientists known as the "angels" of the Eskato.

According to the Aquariot dowser Raïma, these rationalizations each contribute to the triggering of the "Last Judgment" of the *Apocalypse*, and when Solman notices the text written by Saint John and then the whole of the Gospels to understand the apocalyptic episode he is experiencing with the other members of his community, his knowledge leads him to increasingly question the meaning of a return to an Edenic dream, that is supposed to be inspired by the biblical prophetism of the apocalypse. Unlike Elisa, the intentional life that animates Solman is, in these circumstances, informed by a religious mythology that is meant to be embodied, given that the scientists of the Eskato were definitely mistaken in their reading of the Bible: "Deeply influenced by the dogmas of the religions of the Book, everyone accepted genetics and computer science,

---

[13] Elle n'est « … ni Dieu ni Diable, […] elle est un être humain, ni aussi faillible ni aussi infaillible qu'elle voudrait bien le croire (…) » (Vonarburg, *Le silence de la cité* 315–16).

[14] « Là est peut-être la révélation, en définitive: apprendre qu'on n'en a jamais fini de s'arracher à ses illusions, jamais fini de se surprendre à se mentir à soi-même, à se manipuler. Jamais fini de se mettre au monde ? » (Vonarburg, *Le silence de la cité* 316).

[15] « Solman le boiteux » (Bordage 9).

the two sciences of the infinitely small, the infinitely powerful, as a necessary means to accomplish prophecies."[16] For Solman who refuses the temptation of a posthuman immortality that the Eskato proposes to him at the end of the novel in order to "close himself to the sweet supplication of the Verb and display his vision,"[17] the fulfillment of biblical prophecies, as he understands it, can only go in the same direction as the renewal of a Christic sacrifice. Just as the Eskato seeks to incorporate him in its computer network, so by sacrificing himself, by accepting to be killed by one of his Aquariot companions, he becomes an entity comparable to a virus, a deadly virus for all the mutants connected to this network and a savior of the "last men," who it allows to return to a Nature no longer marked by the mediation of the Book, but by the spontaneity of the "conservative" nomadism of Solman's tribe.

Without a sacrifice of such an extent, it seems that empathy appears as a relevant mode of confrontation against laws and norms that control the relations of necessity in dystopian alethic worlds. Indeed, many speculative fictions of this kind focus mainly on the deontic dimension of the resistance of characters invested with their sole humanity to subvert the order and agenda of totalitarian societies. When the modalities of permission, prohibition, and obligation take over in the characters' journeys, duty then takes precedence over knowledge and defines their actions by the regime of dualities that bind them:

> The deontic marking of actions is the richest source of narrativity; it generates the famous triad of the fall (violation of a norm-punishment), the test (obligation fulfilled-reward), and the predicament (conflict of obligations), stories retold again and again, from myths and fairy tales to contemporary fiction (Doležel, *Heterocosmica* 121).

From the perspective of the logic of action, the laws of the fictional storyworlds of *Globalia, Our Life in the Forest,* and *The First Century After Beatrice* are mainly defined by the dilemmas and conflicts of obligation that their focal characters experience. As I explained earlier, their intention of revolt, which prevails over their motivation, perhaps explains why they

---

[16] « Profondément marqués par les dogmes des religions du Livre, tous acceptèrent la génétique et l'informatique, les deux sciences de l'infiniment petit, de l'infiniment puissant, comme le moyen nécessaire de concrétiser les prophéties » (Bordage 662).

[17] « ... se [fermer] à la supplique doucereuse du Verbe et [déployer] sa vision » (Bordage 662).

deny their commitments too much singularity. Given the fact that their motivation is not extensive, it almost never exceeds the empathy these characters feel for those in whom they constantly recognize themselves. In other words, for those focal characters who make others act more than they act themselves, the awareness of deontic inspiration is what best encapsulates both their journey and the sense of adversity that they detect and then fight through their presence in the world.

Invited by the most important leader in Globalia to go into exile and join the opposition in order to lead an armed struggle against this regime, Baïkal then becomes aware that he is in fact just a "creature born of the perverse mind"[18] of a man named Altman who makes Baïkal play a "charade of the terrorist chief."[19] Baikal resigned himself to playing this game at the risk of crushing all opposition both inside and outside the borders of their totalitarian society, after having naively imagined a more epic turn during their confrontation:

> Now that he knew the ultimate goal of this conversation, Baïkal understood that they were going to be enemies, that without doubt they already were, that a long and difficult match would oppose him to this man. On this fight would depend his fate, that of Kate, his happiness, and maybe beyond that, the future of a large number of strangers. And despite all the trials that this fight undoubtedly reserved for him, Baïkal felt that he would commit himself to this fight without regret and maybe even with joy. For behind the blows that would strike him, there would be this ageless man, surviving himself in a frightening eternity and with whom he shared, even if it was to fight against it, a similar idea of freedom. [20]

The deontic hero's progress in the world—a world that he opposes with a totalitarian alethic order—is thus modest and often laborious. The

---

[18] "créature née de l'esprit pervers" (Rufin 377).

[19] "comédie du chef terroriste" (Rufin 324).

[20] "Maintenant qu'il connaissait le but ultime de cette conversation, Baïkal comprenait qu'ils allaient être ennemis, que sans doute ils l'étaient déjà, qu'une longue et difficile partie l'opposerait à cet homme. De ce combat dépendrait son destin, celui de Kate, son bonheur et, peut-être au-delà, l'avenir d'un grand nombre d'inconnus. Et malgré toutes les épreuves que ce combat lui réservait sans doute, Baïkal sentit qu'il s'y engagerait sans regret et peut-être même avec joie. Car derrière les coups qui lui seraient assenés il y aurait cet homme sans âge, survivant à lui-même dans une effrayante éternité et avec lequel il partageait, même si c'était pour la combattre, une semblable idée de la liberté" (Rufin 97).

modality of "duty" that defines him is therefore mainly the result of an ethical aim that takes shape more in adversity than in the application of transcendent moral principles in the name of which, a priori, he would like to fight.

This cautious attitude, inspired by the commitments made to others, somehow completes Baïkal's path, while it initiates the path of Viviane, the main character in Marie Darrieussecq's novel *Our Life in the Forest*. In this novel that retraces Viviane's life as a psychologist who is alerted by one of her patients to the dangers of a society under the surveillance of robots and intrusive media, Viviane decides to escape and finds refuge in a forest where she meets her former patient who then becomes her lover. The important factor here undoubtedly lies in the fact that she escapes with her half, her clone, who she refuses to consider as an organ reserve for medical purposes like many other members of this dystopian society do, a decision that corresponds to her moral stance and deontic endeavors. "Sometimes I say to myself that our ultimate aim in life, the most noble thing we can do is to protect our halves" (Darrieussecq, *Our Life in the Forest* 7), she says, before realizing at the end of the novel after a surgical operation where she gets an eye removed that she herself is a clone and a "supply of spare parts" (Darrieussecq, *Our Life in the Forest* 37) for a rich billionaire who lives by the seaside. For Viviane, the need to testify about the loss of a certain idea of humanity following the necessity of writing as a witness is all that remains.

Reduced to the extreme, this breakthrough of the deontic hero also appears in the testimony of the entomologist narrator in the novel written by Amin Maalouf. This breakthrough occurs when the narrator—who presents himself as "a sheltered observer"[21] (Maalouf, *The First Century After Beatrice* 143) throughout the journal he keeps, in order to describe the devastating effects of a "substance" that ensures the pre-eminence of male births over female births in the Third World and then irreversibly everywhere else—observes:

> I was only one among many other witnesses of the events which I am consigning to these pages; I was closer to them than the horde of onlookers, but just as powerless. My name, I know, has been mentioned in books; this was formerly a source of some pride to me. No longer. The fly in La

---

[21] "un spectateur abrité" (Maalouf, *Le premier siècle après Béatrice* 226).

Fontaine's fable, *The Coach and the Fly*, could rejoice because the coach did arrive safely; what would it have boasted of if the journey had ended in a precipice? Such was in fact the part I played: that of a wretched insect flitting ineffectively around. At least I was never either dupe nor accomplice (Maalouf, *The First Century After Beatrice* 1).[22]

If it does not change the course of events, these testimonies, however fatalistic they may be, nonetheless deepen in the fictional minds of Viviane and the entomologist narrator a gap between their awareness and the unfolding of the dramas they deplore by maintaining the idea of a singularity with a human dimension, which is no longer the case in the next two novels that I will examine. In terms of structuring dualities, I note indeed that nothing of this kind remains in the storyworlds of *The Possibility of an Island* and *Songes de Mevlido*, which instead testify to the disintegration of the subject-object relationship of these novels' focal characters due to the "naturalization" of their intentional lives.

This "naturalization" or "becoming mutant" explains that nature collects the uncertainties of Mevlido and of the last of the Daniels, as characters, in that which is more mineral and therefore less evolutionary. This form of naturalization applies to what Lubomír Doležel calls "dyadic worlds." In these types of potential storyworlds, characters illustrate worlds and their systems of dualities, but no longer embody them from a modal point of view:

> These atomic structures, limited in number, combine, alternate, intersect, and overlap in diverse ways to form an unlimited number of composite, molecular fictional worlds (...). The simplest, but very prominent, case is a unification in one fictional world of two domains in which contrary modal conditions reign. (...) All modal systems have the potential for constructing dyadic worlds. The prime dyadic structure of the alethic modality is the

---

[22] "Des évènements que je consigne en ces pages je ne fus qu'un témoin parmi d'autres, plus rapproché que la foule des spectateurs, mais tout aussi impuissant. Mon nom, je le sais, a été mentionné dans les livres, j'en conçus autrefois quelque fierté. Plus maintenant. La mouche de la fable pouvait exulter puisque le coche était arrivé à bon port; de quoi se serait-elle vantée si le voyage s'était achevé dans un précipice ? Tel fut bien mon rôle, en vérité, celui d'un voltigeur superflu et malchanceux. Du moins n'ai-je été ni dupe ni complice" (Maalouf, *Le premier siècle après Béatrice* 11).

mythological world, constituted by a combination of the natural and the supernatural domains (Doležel, *Heterocosmica* 128–129).

In the alethic domain, these confronting situations, which no longer involve the focal characters of a singular presence in the world, are essentially of two types and strangely echo, according to Doležel, Franz Kafka's work. Either they convey a "hybrid world"[23] in which the fictional and mythological worlds are no longer separated by any borders or they correspond to a "visible/invisible world"[24] where control is exercised, and whose ins and outs could not be grasped a priori.

Besides the fact that Antoine Volodine's novel multiplies the absence of predicates in the formulations of his character Mevlido, such as "We never know what…"[25] or even "You will show me the way, the pace that…"[26] and that this character is lost in a "visible/invisible world" ruled by some mysterious "Organs," the hybrid dyadic that Mevlido crosses is especially imbued with the mythology of Tibetan Buddhism that overwhelms the disturbances of his memory and his intention:

> I have the impression that this drum addressed me previously, but that it is far too late for its effect to be profitable or even comprehensible to me. I am closing my eyes, in my memory the image of Linda Siew who was dancing and singing in the rain a few minutes earlier appears. Now, the memory of Linda Siew and the audio document are combined in a harmonious way. Linda Siew is singing the uga, the drum is beating the time of the uga. The rain is crackling. I open my eyes to see what the night is offering us. From

---

[23] "The hybrid world, created by Franz Kafka, has had a tremendous impact on modernist and postmodernist fiction. Because the boundary that divides the fictional world of the classical myth is dissolved, the hybrid world is a coexistence, in one unified fictional space, of the physically possible and physically impossible fictional entities (persons, events)" (Doležel, *Heterocosmica* 187).

[24] "One and the same hierarchy of power is typical of both Kafka's and Belyj's fictional worlds: the visible domain is under the dominion and control of the invisible domain. In Kafka's world, where no intermediate zone is interposed, the pattern of control is relatively simple: the visible-domain inhabitants are under permanent threat of an order, a decree, a decision that originates in the invisible domain and deeply affects their existence" (Doležel, *Heterocosmica* 193).

[25] "On ne sait jamais ce que…" (Volodine, *Songes de Mevlido* 46).

[26] "Vous m'indiquerez le chemin, l'allure que…" (Volodine 249).

the other side of the street, I know that a man has the habit of running a gramophone at night. He always keeps his window wide open... The lamp in his house is lit... The rain is putting vertical streaks on things... But I already said that, I believe.[27]

In Houellebecq's work, the control applied in a transversal way in the only dyadic "visible/invisible world" of *The Possibility of an Island* also presents a disembodied modal viewpoint. In fact, it is based on a belief that erects a system of values in a posthuman society in which readers can only guess at the world in which it operates without really being able to understand its purpose:

IT IS NOT GENERAL PRACTICE to shorten human life stories, whatever the repugnance or boredom they may inspire in us. It is precisely this repugnance and boredom that we must cultivate, in order to distinguish ourselves from the species. It is on this condition, the Supreme Sister warns us, that the coming of the Future Ones will be made possible (Houellebecq, *The Possibility of an Island* 70).[28]

As I explain in detail later in this section, the posthuman clones of this storyworld live "secluded" in the "life stories" of their predecessors expecting that "The Return of the Humid will be the sign of the coming of the Future Ones"[29] (Houellebecq, *The Possibility of an Island* 79), until the practice of poetry definitively disrupts the control exercised by this

[27] "J'ai l'impression que ce tambour s'adressait à moi autrefois, mais qu'il est beaucoup trop tard pour que son effet me soit profitable ou même compréhensible. Je ferme les yeux, à ma mémoire se présente l'image de Linda Siew qui dansait et chantait sous la pluie quelques minutes plus tôt. Maintenant, le souvenir de Linda Siew et le document sonore se comblent de façon harmonieuse. Linda Siew chante l'uga, le tambour rythme l'uga. La pluie crépite. J'ouvre les yeux pour voir ce que la nuit nous offre. De l'autre côté de la rue, je sais qu'un homme la nuit a pour habitude de faire fonctionner un gramophone. Il laisse toujours sa fenêtre grande ouverte... La lampe chez lui est allumée... La pluie pose des stries verticales sur les choses... Mais j'ai déjà dit cela, je crois" (Volodine 175).

[28] "Il n'est généralement pas d'usage d'abréger les récits de vie humains, quels que soient la répugnance ou l'ennui que leur contenu nous inspire. Ce sont justement cette répugnance, cet ennui qu'il convient de développer en nous, afin de nous démarquer de l'espèce. C'est à cette condition, nous avertit la Sœur suprême, que sera rendu possible l'avènement des Futurs" (Houellebecq, *La possibilité d'une île* 100).

[29] "...le Retour de l'Humide sera le signe de l'avènement des Futurs" (Houellebecq, *La possibilité d'une île* 113).

hermeneutic enterprise. In this futuristic storyworld that tells the story in turn of Daniel and his clones, who are instructed to comment on his first "life stories" in an attempt to remove the imperfection of their common ancestor's humanity, poetry indeed opens up an alternative space for questioning.

This poetry inspired by human desire contradicts the advent of these "Futures Ones" about whom Daniel25 makes the hypothesis that "the Future Ones would be beings made of silicon, whose civilization would be built through the progressive interconnection of cognitive and memory processors"[30] (Houellebecq, *The Possibility of an Island* 335) to essentially question the meaning of a possible world at the height of its incompleteness, as the intentions of its characters lose their *raison d'être*.

What should we think of this dystopian reduction inscribed in the order of a dehumanized alethic world? Unlike mainstream science fiction, which often reinvests existing religious mythologies, I agree with Doležel that the "hybrid worlds" and the "visible/invisible worlds" of transgressive fictions have the great merit of creating a modern mythology:

> The modern myth in both of its variants is the product of the secular culture of the twentieth century. Human actions, and, especially, the activities of social institutions, are incomprehensible, but a transcendent, supernatural explanation is either no longer available or lacks authenticity. The senselessness of human actions and historical conflicts, the daily encounters with the bizarre, cannot be explained and redeemed by recourse to divine or demonic forces. The modern myth restates the precariousness of the human condition that the classical myth stated. But now that the gods are dead, humans themselves are responsible for the chaotic world they have created and operate (Doležel, *Heterocosmica* 198).

It seems that many characters' clear-sightedness is as much a hermeneutic enterprise as it is a matter of scientific or societal debates in these

---

[30] "…les Futurs seraient des "êtres de silicium, dont la civilisation se construirait par inter-connexion progressive de processeurs cognitifs et mémoriels" (Houellebecq, *La possibilité d'une île* 472).

futuristic fictional storyworlds. Since this first trend deserves to be clarified, I will explore it further.

DIFFERENCES IN ACTIONS OF FICTIONAL MINDS AS READERS

When confronted with the reification and the becoming an artifact of the human race, the memory of the fictional beings of our corpus emerges all the more from the order of dystopian societies as this memory "refocuses" itself around the figure of the book invested by stories listened to or read.

Along with a theory of possible worlds, the intentional memory[31] experienced by the characters in their unstable futuristic storyworlds is the main motif that depicts a humanity in its resistance and that determines readers' reception of the characters of anticipation novels and understanding of their fictional minds.

The way these characters are understood by readers varies in futuristic storyworlds between a form of hermeneutic reception and a form of modal reception. In other words, readers understand these characters by applying these notions to their fictional minds, to use the terminology of Alan Palmer, as "intermental thinking" and "intramental thinking," respectively. Referring to Vygotsky's understanding of the development of thought[32] in *Mind in Society* (1978), Palmer states that "social norms are always liable to be transgressed by individuals, and the fatal words are a potentially norm-breaking intramental action. Such dissent is characteristic of many aspects of the relationship between intermental and intramental thinking" (Palmer 228–29). These two ways of thinking, "intermental" (between characters through reading) and, as a result of the former, "intramental" (within characters defined by the way a modality is felt and experienced)

---

[31] "The common thread, the link, the unity of memory lies in the intentionality of acquisition, of transformation, and of recovery of our memories and of forgetfulness. This intentionality (which is different from the will: the will is a tool to actualize our intentions) is the primary mechanism that leads the choice of our sensations, our perceptions, and their interpretation" (Tadié 311) ["Le fil conducteur, le lien, l'unité de la mémoire réside dans l'intentionnalité d'acquisition, de transformation, de récupération de nos souvenirs et de l'oubli. Cette intentionnalité (qui est différente de la volonté: la volonté est un outil pour actualiser nos intentions) est le mécanisme primaire qui dirige le choix de nos sensations, de nos perceptions, de leur interprétation"] (Tadié 311).

[32] "Every function in the child's cultural development appears twice: first, on the social level, and later on the individual level; first, between people (interpsychological), and then inside the child (intrapsychological). This applies equally to voluntary attention, to logical memory, and to the formation of concepts" (Vygotskiĭ et al. 57).

are used in this chapter to underline the importance of the intentional memories characters experience in that it unifies the perception of the beings of fiction in the cognitive dimension of their dissonance. At the core of the storylines of the storyworlds presented, I therefore distinguish among different fictional minds whose intermental reading paths either punctuate, overplay, or identify with the actions of their intramental dissonant thinking based on (1) *knowledge*, in mainstream science fiction, (2) *duty*, in dystopian speculative diction, and (3) *deceptive ability*, in transfictions.

Intentional memory, which favors interpretation, is present at each decisive stage of the inner life of a character who is understood mainly through the modality of knowledge associated with the "fictional recentering" I mentioned earlier. For this type of memory, the intermental reading path punctuates the actions of the character's intramental dissonant thinking. This is the case of the "fictional recentering" specific to the character of Elisa in *The Silent City*, which begins with the learning of a "story" taught by Richard Desprats, when Elisa is a young child and still considers Desprats to be her grandfather:

> She knew the story by heart: it was about a little girl who lived in an enchanted castle where everyone was asleep. There were only machines in the castle, and even though they did everything the little girl wanted, they were still machines. One day the machines stopped. The little girl saw a big open door open and she went outside[33] (Vonarburg, *The Silent City* 8).

Besides the idea that Elisa evolves in her early days as a recluse in a City where sleep is close to death (for those who sleep surrounded by machines that will one day cease to function) what is important in this intertextual adaptation of *Sleeping Beauty* is the statement of a promise and a hidden message—an escape to the outside world—which Paul, as Elisa's main mentor and designer, cannot endorse.

For Paul, the geneticist (who sees this child above all as a laboratory subject, likely to regenerate the genetically modified human species in an outside world subject to all kinds of pollution), Elisa's departure should

---

[33] "Elle connaissait l'histoire par cœur: c'était la petite fille qui habitait un château enchanté où tout le monde dormait. Il n'y avait là que des machines, même si elles faisaient tout ce que désirait la petite fille. Un jour, les machines s'arrêtaient, et la petite fille voyait une grande porte s'ouvrir et elle allait *Dehors*" (Vonarburg, *Le silence de la cité* 9).

not worry her in any way. Indeed, in Paul's mind, Elisa must submit to the implementation of a project of eugenic repopulation designed to strengthen the power of an aging and technically advanced human race, which has remained sheltered in a closed society; indeed, this closed society reigned over the other humans in this post-apocalyptic world, whose life conditions have caused them to regress:

> Elisa smiles. That's like Grandpa's story. She tells Paul the story. Thinking he'll be pleased to find she already knows about it. But he looks cross, and she asks anxiously what she has said wrong. "It isn't that, exactly, "says Papa (Paul), "your grandfather, who wasn't your grandfather at all, any more than I'm your father, had some rather odd ideas about the city. [...] Paul drops on his haunches in front of her. He's so tall! "When I say 'you'll leave', I do not mean you, dearest. Nor your children. You'll have children, you know, lots of them. I'm speaking of your race. In a way, you'll be part of them, because they'll be your descendants and they'll have the same faculty. Do you understand?"[34] (Vonarburg, *The Silent City* 24).

When Pierre Desprats' "story" is discounted (for the time being), teenaged Elisa begins an apprenticeship of another kind with Paul, who starts by giving her access the central computer, "the City," so that she can help him to conduct genetic experiments. Unlike the paradigmatic and autonomously malignant Hal 9000 in *2001: A Space Odyssey* by Stanley Kubrick, this computer, which contains a lot of knowledge, is nevertheless an ambivalent agent in its interface with the minds and the bodies of the inhabitants it protects and who have somehow incorporated it.

While it is often reduced by its use to the consultation of a database of scientific knowledge, "the City" is an omnipresent collective artifact whose overflow of memory enacts, in an infernal no-exit, the lowering of self-consciousness due to the power of reification of images and screens. Elisa does not deny that this knowledge repository entity can be useful, but

---

[34] "Élisa sourit: c'est un peu ce que disait Grand-Père. Et elle lui raconte l'histoire, en pensant qu'il sera content de voir qu'elle est déjà au courant. Mais il a l'air fâché, et elle se demande avec inquiétude ce qu'elle a dit de mal. "Ce n'est pas tout à fait cela, dit Papa—Paul (...) Quand je dis 'vous sortirez', je ne parle pas de toi, ma chérie. Ni même de tes enfants. Car tu auras des enfants, beaucoup d'enfants. Je parle de ta race. D'une certaine façon, tu seras en eux, puisque ce seront tes descendants et qu'ils auront la même faculté que toi. Tu comprends ?" (Vonarburg, *Le silence de la cité* 35–36).

when she discovers both her origin as a "Subject. Of an experiment"[35] (Vonarburg, *The Silent City* 46) and the fact that she sometimes enters at night into a process of identity mutation as yet unknown to Paul, she realizes that she must hide. Elisa thus will leave the secluded world that is hers and that of her designer for fear of again becoming a man's guinea pig in a computer simulation.

Once outside of the City, Elisa's "story" moves forward, but does not unfold as Desprats had announced it. First of all, in order to deactivate other cities similar to the one they just left, she (having taken on the appearance of a man called Hanse) assists a robot that resuscitates the personality traits of the deceased Richard Desprats. Then at the end of this period and while still in her androgynous form, she has a short affair with a young girl named Judith, before she kills Paul, while he was trying to force Elisa-Hanse, Judith, and their future child to come (back) to his laboratory. A range of feelings, including loving admiration, sadness, and anger successively cross Elisa's mind. While these feelings contribute to enriching her intramental dissonant thinking, as self-knowledge and beyond a knowledge of her condition as an androgynous mutant, the essential milestone of her intermental reading path lies above all in the mediation of the book-object in the relationships that Elisa now has as an adult with the mainframe computer of her city of origin, a computer that she refuses to deactivate. When Elisa creates children with her genetic heritage, this mediation creates a distance between her memory and her knowledge about the City's screens, since this mediation is about questioning and transmission:

> She stares blindly at her book, frowning, as premises and theories surge through her brain. She'd have to go to the City herself again, use the learning machines. Those migraines …. But the knowledge of Desprats and Alghieri is still in the data banks, as is everything else[36] (Vonarburg, *The Silent City* 100).

---

[35] "Un sujet. D'expérience" (Vonarburg, *Le silence de la cité* 71).

[36] " Elle fixe son livre sans le voir, les sourcils fronces, tandis qu'hypothèses et théories s'échafaudent dans sa tête. Il faudrait... aller utiliser de nouveau elle-même la Cité; se servir des machines à apprendre—migraines en perspective... Mais le savoir de Desprats et d'Alghieri se trouve toujours dans les banques de données, comme tout le reste" (Vonarburg, *Le silence de la cité* 151).

Such a book is synonymous with Vonarburg's reflection on writing, which often associates the author's intention with that of her characters, but never reveals its title. It relays the "story" that once concerned Elisa when she was a child and becomes, in a way, paradigmatic of a comprehension of the world where reading strengthens the modified humanity of the fictional being and assures it of a certain form of clairvoyance in the comments that precede actions.

Hence it is through the reading of picture books representing "the Outside" that the androgynous "descendants" of Elisa are invited, even if this collective enterprise fails for a time, to separate from "[themselves] the truth of fantasy"[37] (Vonarburg, *The Silent City* 106), before this mediation by the book encourages the definitive liberation of Elisa, who regains control of her "history," when she withdraws from the influence of Richard Desprats' last computer avatar and puts the central computer of "the City" on standby. "There is no one to call to account but herself. It's her responsibility, the final act before closing the book ... and opening another"[38] (Vonarburg, *The Silent City* 206). Finally, the evocation of this figure of the book is of course not without coincidence given the continuous grouping of biblical motifs that assert themselves throughout Elisa's journey as I have already mentioned. However, the composition of Vonarburg's novel eludes this connection between biblical texts and characters as much as possible, and when it owns up to this connection, it is only so that the author can better dismantle it and depart from the framework of this association.

The objectification of the book, which gradually becomes the architect of the central character's memory in his or her quest for knowledge, characterizes both Vonarburg's Elisa and Bordage's Solman. Yet Solman's journey, which is transcribed in *Les Derniers Hommes*, differs in that he evokes the now-classic science-fiction theme of conflict with a computer program with criminal intentions and puts an end, at the closing of the novel, to the mediation of the world through the book as an object. Although Solman's "fictional recentering" is less allegorical than Elisa's, it too begins to be just as immaterial, since it is not the result of the

---

[37] "séparer d'[eux]-mêmes la vérité de la fantaisie" (Vonarburg, *Le silence de la cité* 161)

[38] "Elle n'a plus de comptes à demander qu'à elle-même. C'est elle qui fait ses comptes, la dernière opération sous le trait tiré, avant de fermer le livre—d'en ouvrir un autre" (Vonarburg, *Le silence de la cité* 321).

statement of a "story" but of the foresight of an imminent threat as expressed by the fear of the word "Apocalypse":

> He was certain that they [the criminal intentions] did not only encompass the diviners, not only the men and women of the Aquariot people, but all the peoples who were roaming freely over the vast territories of Europe. Like in his parents' tent eleven years earlier, he remained incapable of performing the slightest gesture and his scream remained stuck between his stomach and his throat. Then his last conversation with Raïma the Healer came back to his memory with a hurtful acuity. She had pronounced a strange word, derived from, according to her, the dominant ancient religion on the European continent, and that, in her mouth, had slammed like a terrible threat...: Apocalypse.[39]

From a word to its illustration in the form of a manuscript, the intermental reading path, which focuses on Saint John's *Apocalypse*, punctuates the decisive stages of Solman's inner life and actions of his intramental dissonant thinking framed here again by the modality of knowledge.

Solman's quest—initiated at the margin of the "water people's" society—begins with Raïma, the healer, who is inflicted like him with a physical handicap, but who is endowed with the necessary powers to protect the community of the Aquariots. It is with Raïma that Solman's sexuality awakens and becomes aware of the existence of the "Book of dead religions"[40] that explains the disorders of a world that is polluted and exhausted from the war in which his people and other nomadic tribes strive to survive.

At this first crossroads of intermental and intramental thinking, the complicity that is established for a time between Raïma and Solman matters in understanding the state of the beliefs of the "water people," against the backdrop of a confrontation between a "Nomadic Ethic" and

---

[39] "Il eut la certitude qu'elles [des intentions criminelles] ne cernaient pas seulement les sourciers, pas seulement les hommes et les femmes du peuple aquariote, mais l'ensemble des peuples qui parcouraient les vastes territoires de l'Europe. Comme dans la tente de ses parents onze ans plus tôt, il demeura incapable d'esquisser le moindre geste et son hurlement resta coincé entre son ventre et sa gorge. Puis sa dernière conversation avec Raïma la guérisseuse lui revint en mémoire avec une acuité blessante. Elle avait prononcé un mot étrange, tiré selon elle de l'ancienne religion dominante du continent européen et qui, dans sa bouche, avait claqué comme une terrible menace...: Apocalypse" (Bordage 15).

[40] "Livre des religions mortes" (Bordage 114).

the *New Testament*. In Raïma's plea about the importance of Solman's function as a "Giver," readers learn that while the *Apocalypse* may have happened in the past, from her point of view, the worst may not yet have happened:

> "Givers are the sentinels of the present time," says Raïma. "Listen to them from the depths of your soul, venerated mother, and you will see that there is no reason to be optimistic."
>
> "The Apocalypse took place almost a century ago, Raïma. The old religions died with the ancient world."
>
> "I am still waiting for the Last Judgement…"[41]

But once past the stage of these first murmurings of the language revealed by Raïma, Solman's intermental thinking and reading path only really takes shape when he meets protagonists such as Ismahil and Kadija, who both have a direct fictional relationship with the *Apocalypse* of the apostle Saint John. Ismahil and Kadija, welcomed by Solman among the "water people" when they were in danger, represent two key characters for understanding the meaning of the crimes and catastrophes that had just overwhelmed the Aquariots.

Described by Pierre Bordage as a paragon of wisdom inspiring compassion and brotherhood, the character of Ismahil, who plays the role of the "last man"—to the extent that he reveals to Solman the tenets of the "Apocalypse" and the "Last Judgment" that concern them—first teaches this young prophet that a literal reading of the text of the apostle Saint John is at the origin of the creation of a group of fanatical scientists: the "Eskato." Solman learns then that the members of this organization, who live in exile in space and under the sea, literally want to fulfill the prophecies of the "Revelation" by using technology to regenerate the human species, which means eliminating those who no longer resemble them.

In a complementary manner Kadija, who succeeds Raïma in the heart of the Aquariot visionary, then helps elucidate the narrative whose

---

[41] "Les donneurs sont les sentinelles du présent, dit Raïma. Écoutez-les du fond de l'âme, vénérée mère, et vous verrez qu'il n'y a aucune raison d'être optimiste.

 – L'Apocalypse a eu lieu il y a de cela presque un Siècle, Raïma. Les vieilles religions sont mortes avec l'ancien monde.
 – J'attends encore le Jugement dernier…" (Bordage 39–40).

beginning was told by Ismahil and the progressive understanding of which sustains Solman's intramental dissonant thinking to the point he eventually comes to know the intentions of the criminal organization. As an amnesic creature of the "Eskato" driven by the "Verb"—a computer program used in the execution of the "Last Judgement"—Kadija is in fact, in spite of herself, bait for Solman to whom the "Eskato" offer immortality in exchange for forgetting his community of origin. However, given the fact that prior to this offer, "Solman spent three days and three entire nights without eating or drinking in an empty trailer with, for his only company, Raïma's forbidden book, a flashlight, a mattress, and a woolen blanket"[42] his intermental reading path did not separate the text of the *Apocalypse* from the *New Testament* thanks to Ismahil, unlike that of the members of the "Eskato." His journey then finishes by anchoring the significance of his memory in the vision of a common humanity, a decision that saves the "water people," but for which Solman obviously pays with his sacrifice.

When the objectification of the book no longer follows the pace of a mutant becoming, the "sense of memory"—to recall the title of the essay of Jean-Yves and Marc Tadié about its intentional feature—that characterizes characters mainly understood through the modality of "duty or moral obligation" draws the contours of a community in direct contact with a history less marked by great tales with allegorical, symbolic, or religious tonalities. This objectification stresses more clearly other declensions of the figure of the book, such as the discovery of particular books, of a library, or of the exercise of writing. And, if there is a learning process, this one intersects all the emotional states of the beings of fiction in a successive way, less than in the two preceding science fiction novels. As such, reading can be assimilated to a form of companionship that strengthens the bonds of fellowship, friendship, or love between individuals and offers another perspective on their emotional life.

After looking at the previous example of a book I characterize as science fiction, I will now delve into an examination of *Globalia*, an example of dystopian speculative fiction. In the totalitarian society described in this novel, the exercise of freedom is just a masquerade. Minds are attached to both individual and insignificant collective celebrations, and excursions outside this society are controlled or banned to the point of having

---

[42] "Solman a passé trois jours et trois nuits entières sans manger ni boire dans une remorque vide, avec, pour toute compagnie, le livre interdit de Raïma, une lampe de poche, un matelas et une couverture de laine" (Bordage 524).

motivated its leaders to create enclosed natural spaces reserved for the outcasts, but forbidden to ordinary citizens, for fear of seeing them once again make "an identitarian use of History."[43] However, one book contradicts this inability to regain free movement. It is *Walden. Life in the Woods* by Henry-David Thoreau, which stands as a manifesto and produces multiple effects within this society. Perhaps the most important of these effects is the creation of an organization also called "Walden," a network of libraries, which encourages its members to fight against inertia and to reconnect with the very idea of History, whether it be through the consultation of novels or historical works. "In Globalia, everything seems to be both constantly moving and motionless at the same time. There are only two dimensions: the present, that is to say, reality, and the virtual where the imaginary, the future, and the little that is left of the past are all stuffed together."[44] It is therefore by pushing open the doors of this "book community" that the "recentering" of characters who have become aware of a lie or an injustice tends to become more political, following the example of Puig Pujol's journey.

Witness of the fact that the terrorist attacks perpetrated in Globalia are secretly organized by its leaders to keep the population in fear, Puig is a young unemployed journalist who finds explanations of the origins of the Globalian society by frequenting a library in the Walden network of libraries. He shares this discovery with Kate, a young woman whose companion, Baïkal, is unfairly regarded as the mastermind of these attacks. If reading transforms Puig's initial revolt into a commitment strengthened by the friendship he feels for Kate, the same goes for Kate who can, at the end of her journey to join her lover, better understand the latter's intentions and henceforth share them: "'In Globalia,' she says, dreamy, 'this book scarcely made sense to me. Happiness in nature. But here I am starting to understand. Wise used to say that it was the most powerful weapon available to human beings.'"[45]

---

[43] "usage identitaire de l'Histoire" (Rufin 333).

[44] "En Globalia, tout semble à la fois bouger sans cesse et rester immobile. Il n'y a que deux dimensions: le présent, c'est-à-dire la réalité, et le virtuel où l'on fourre tout ensemble l'imaginaire, le futur et le peu qu'il reste du passé" (Rufin 279).

[45] "En Globalia, dit-elle, songeuse, ce livre n'avait guère de sens pour moi. Le bonheur dans la nature. Mais ici, je commence à comprendre. Wise disait que c'était l'arme la plus puissante dont disposent les êtres humains" (Rufin 493).

But at the very end of the novel, the most intriguing (because it is off-beat) course holds more to a promise of reading than to its realization. As the main character and a public enemy in the media, having served unwillingly in the arrest or killing of opponents of the global society, Baïkal appears in effect as a rebel leader who the reading of *Walden* could transform into a revolutionary. This is in any case what the text seems to suggest in an open ending where Kate and Baïkal might find Puig "because they had chosen [him] and not because of the schemes"[46] of one of the leaders of Globalia.

In *Our Life in the Forest*, Marie, a psychologist, and her clone take a similar journey in her plan to escape from the city to the forest after she realizes that she lives under surveillance due to the suggestions and help of her former patient "the cliker"; however, on this journey, when literary references are made, the focus is more on specific authors than on the titles of the literary works that those authors had written. From the beginning, this project takes the form of a Notebook with an ongoing use of stream-of-consciousness writing, during which Marie—who chose Viviane as "fugitive name" (Darrieussecq, *Our Life in the Forest* 4), perhaps in a nod to Viviane, the character of the fairy in the Arthurian forest of Brocéliande—focuses on the importance of her writing as a testimony to analyze and recall the importance of the interpersonal relationships in her evolving awareness of the dystopian world in which she is engaged. Beyond the way Marie Darrieussecq multiplies literary references, often with humor, she points out that in "the forest, when an old clone dies, a whole library goes up in smoke. Ha!" (Darrieussecq 96) like the "Book People" in Ray Bradbury's *Fahrenheit 451*. In Darrieussecq's text, when authors are explicitly cited, they have a particular significance to the text, often counterbalancing a painful awareness related to Viviane's significant physical disability, with the goal of contrasting the two worlds (the Forest and the City) in which she still is connected to others.

Such is the case of the reference to the poet Sergei Yesenin whose verse, "I did not shoot the wretches in the dungeons," is placed as an epigraph to *Our Life in the Forest*. The first time Viviane quotes this verse, she does so to show empathy and restraint to the clones who mock her because of the way she walks like a penguin, as she struggles to survive in the difficult conditions of life in the forest, following an eye-removal surgery, and all of this despite the fact that she is a dedicated protector of her own "half":

---

[46] "parce qu'ils [l'] auraient choisi et non à cause des manigances" (Rufin 493).

It's difficult lifting up a half. A half is at the same time submissive and insolent, a bit surly. Impertinent and sly. I'm not crazy about halves, but we've had to come to terms with them. After all, we weren't about to eliminate them, "I did not shoot the wretches in the dungeons" is a line from the Russian revolutionary Sergei Yesenin, who is one of our Heroes. (There was a revolution in Russia at the beginning of the twentieth century.) Of course we're armed. Our pirated robots are weapons[47] (Darrieussecq, *Our Life in the Forest* 23–24).

This restraint is not shared in the city, to say the least, as Viviane notices ("You never know who will denounce you. You never know who will shoot the wretched in the dungeons" (Darrieussecq, *Our Life in the Forest* 115)[48]) when she leaves her apartment knowing that she also has implants in her arms and brain which report her movements. And when she understands, at the end of the novel, here again thanks to the cliker, that she—herself—is another clone whose eye has been harvested for a millionaire, from whom she has originated, who is around 160 years old, and who lives in a luxurious accommodation by the sea with "the one per cent of super-rich who own ninety-nine per cent of the world's wealth"[49] (Darrieussecq, *Our Life in the Forest* 141), her awareness changes, as do her worldview and posture. She quotes a passage[50] that precedes an important naval battle between the royalist camp and the republican camp from Victor Hugo's novel *Ninety-Three* about the period of the Terror during the French Revolution. And what this quotation suggests is no longer a question of empathy or lack of empathy, but a clear desire for a revolution and a revolt as a claim for her humanity

---

[47] " C'est très difficile à élever, une moitié. Une moitié c'est à la fois soumis et insolent, un peu chafoin. Impertinent et sournois. Je ne suis pas dingue des moitiés, mais il a bien fallu faire avec. On allait quand même pas les supprimer. 'Je n'ai pas fusillé le malheureux au fond des caves', c'est un vers d'un révolutionnaire russe, Essenine, qui fait partie de nos Héros (Il y a eu une révolution en Russie au début du XXe siècle" (Darrieussecq, *Notre vie dans les forêts roman* 36).

[48] "On ne sait jamais qui vous dénoncera. On ne sait pas qui fusillera le malheureux au fond des caves" (Darrieussecq, *Notre vie dans les forêts roman* 147).

[49] "… les 1% de super-riches qui possèdent 99% de la richesse du monde,…" (Darrieussecq, *Notre vie dans les forêts roman* 177).

[50] "A gloomy sense of expectation brooded over the sea. Suddenly amid this illimitable, tumultuous silence a voice was heard; exaggerated by the speakingtrumpet, as by the brazen mask of ancient tragedy" (Hugo 15).

in the face of the injustice that she, as a non-submissive clone, has suffered in her flesh:

> We have a book by Victor Hugo in the encampment (Victor Hugo was a nineteenth-century writer), in which I found this sentence: 'A strange sense of sombre expectation hung over the sea'. I say it over and over to myself. I don't know why, but this sentence makes me feel better. We can never listen to music here: the little battery power we have is reserved for more necessary functions.
> A strange sense of somber expectation hung over the sea. This sentence made it seem as if the sea was an immense reservoir of possibilities[51] (Darrieussecq, *Our Life in the Forest* 144).

The adversity characterizing the storyworld of *The First Century After Beatrice* by Amin Maalouf also associates a testimonial duty that tells the story from the point of view of the narrator's and characters' emotional lives with the objectification of the book. Just like Viviane at the end of Marie Darrieussecq's novel, who testifies to her commitment to writing to the point of being mummified, when she explains, "Sometimes, I imagine myself in the tin. I see myself in the tin, all squashed up, still alive, I have no idea how, still writing, all contorted, and no longer even managing to read what I'm writing" (Darrieussecq, *Our Life in the Forest* 149), the characters in Amin Maalouf's novel tend write in a testimonial fashion in which the "sense of memory" becomes more and more scriptural and corresponds in this way as much to resistance as to an extreme fragility, in the perspective of a disappearance.

For example, when asked to examine the reasons for a drastic decrease in the number of female births, the narrator's deciphering of a world that has become hostile is motivated by the reading experience that he owes to a member of his family:

> Ever since my childhood, whenever he gave me a book, he presumed that before our next meeting I would have read it carefully. 'Read it slowly', he recommended, ... [...] 'If, in twenty years, you've read, what I call seriously

---

[51] "On a un livre de Victor Hugo au campement (Victor Hugo était un écrivain du XIXe siècle), un livre où j'ai pêché cette phrase: 'Il y avait sur la mer on ne sait quelle sombre attente.' Je me la redis dans ma tête. Je ne sais pas pourquoi, cette phrase me fait du bien. Ici on ne peut jamais écouter de musique, le peu de batterie qu'on a est réservé à plus utile. 'Il y avait sur la mer on ne sait quelle sombre attente.' La mer avec cette phrase, on dirait un immense réservoir de possibles" (Darrieussecq, *Notre vie dans les forêts roman* 177).

read, forty real books, then, you'll be able to look the world in the face.' So I read 'what I call seriously read', that is re-read and chewed over his ten or so dispatches[52] (Maalouf, *The First Century After Beatrice* 45).

And so it is in his capacity as an informed reader that the narrator begins an investigation and follows the journalistic investigations of his companion Clarence, when she discovers that a "substance" designed by a Western pharmaceutical research team is the source of sugared almonds that ensure the primacy of male births over female births in the Third World, and then, irreversibly, everywhere else. Despite the fact that this writing project, which was reported in great detail in the diary kept by the same narrator, was able to alert the public opinion, it nevertheless remains unable to explain the underlying causes of the separation that occurs between scientific progress and civilizational development, from the moment when the diffusion of the so-called "substance" is amplified.

At the end of the novel, a disillusioned testimony borne by the determinism of the written word follows the continual interweaving of several writing projects: that of the diarist narrator, but also those of his companion, his friends, and his daughter Beatrice (let us recall on this point that the division of this novel into chapters is alphabetical and not numerical). From the point of view of the unfolding of the plot, the exercise of writing does not actually precede any action when it is identified only with the narrator's diary.

Such a determinism reduces an intermental reading path to intramental dissonant fictional writing. Indeed, the book whose final testimony explains in which circumstances Beatrice's father withdrew from the rest of the world, closes, in the dramatic orientation that the text takes, with the evocation of his estrangement and his next disappearance:

> And now I have nearly reached the last full stop, and I feel myself gradually relieved of a burden, which I never suspected of being so heavy. Will this text ever be published? Will someone be found to take an interest in it? And in how many years' time? That, I feel inclined to say, is no longer my problem. Whatever its fate, my role is over. When you cast a bottle into the

---

[52] "Depuis mon enfance, chaque fois qu'il m'offrait un livre, il présumait qu'avant la prochaine rencontre, je l'aurais lu de près, "lentement". (...) 'Si en vingt ans tu as lu, ce que j'appelle lu, quarante vrais livres, tu pourras regarder l'univers en face'. J'avais donc lu, "ce que j'appelle lu", c'est-à-dire relu et ruminé..." (Maalouf, *Le premier siècle après Béatrice* 77–78).

sea, you naturally hope someone will fish it out; but you don't swim after it[53] (Maalouf, *The First Century After Beatrice* 190).

Here again, as in Marie Darrieussecq's novel, the objectification of the book ultimately presupposes a fictional readership: from the narrator to the reading that other characters would undertake. The resulting discrepancy maintains an indecisive, resistant, and fragile emphasis, but still remains commensurate with our humanity.

For the forms of memory that result from a disturbance of intention, where a lack of empathy or suffering often takes precedence over other forms of affectivity, the inner life of a character is understood mainly through the modality of a deceptive ability associated with the "fictional recentering," the intermental reading path; this character identifies with the actions of his intramental dissonant thinking and produces a form of writing. Here, the "sense of memory" is irremediably scriptural and does not allow any shift in the order of the determinism of the written word.

This appears to be the narrative logic of *The Possibility of an Island*, which alternately tells the life story of Daniel and his clones (Daniel24 and 25) who are tasked with reading and commenting on the "life stories" of their original ancestor in order to give meaning to their immortality and to the "life stories" of their ancestors to "to prepare for the coming of a digital future"[54] (Houellebecq, *The Possibility of an Island* 156):

> A being is fashioned, somewhere in the Central City, that is similar to me; at least he has my features, and my internal organs. When my life ceases, the absence of a signal will be registered in a few nanoseconds; the manufacture of my successor will begin immediately. The next day, or the day after at the latest, the protective fence will be reopened; my successor will settle within

[53] "Me voici à présent tout proche du point final, et je me sens peu à peu délesté d'une charge dont je ne soupçonnais pas qu'elle fût si impérieuse. Ce texte sera-t-il publié un jour ? Se trouvera-t-il quelqu'un pour s'y intéresser ? Et dans combien d'années ? Ce n'est plus mon affaire ai-je envie de dire. Quel que soit son destin, mon propre rôle s'achève. Lorsque l'on lance une bouteille à la mer, on souhaite bien entendu que quelqu'un la repêche; mais on ne l'accompagne pas à la nage" (Maalouf, *Le premier siècle après Béatrice* 298).

[54] "préparer l'avènement d'un futur numérique" (Houellebecq, *La possibilité d'une île— Prix Interallié 2005* 220–21).

these walls. This book will be addressed to him[55] (Houellebecq, *The Possibility of an Island* 18).

The drama of this becoming mutant briefly summarized by Daniel24 is due to a lack of empathy revealed by this repeated identification with the book of a predecessor, since in this journey that encompasses the actions of fictional beings, neohumans are reduced to a memory limited by reading and writing, a notion that Lucie Clément qualifies as a "scriptural memory" in her essay entitled "Michel Houellebecq revisité" ("Michel Houellebecq revisited") (Clément 87).

At this crossroads of inseparable intermental and intramental thinking, perhaps the most significant point of the novel emerges from this programmed failure of reading and writing "life stories" which, moreover, anticipates and consolidates the emergence of poetry. Since the "rigorous duplication of the genetic code, meditation on the life story of the predecessor, [and] the writing of the commentary"[56] (Houellebecq, *The Possibility of an Island* 125) constitute the hermeneutic base of the project of society of the neohumans, the poetry that reevaluates the participation of a desiring "body" in this reading and writing indeed represents the greatest danger in this quest for immortality, in that it induces a permanent conflict of interpretations.

This duality, similar to the search for an "elsewhere," is essentially associated with Baudelaire's poetry. It is this poetry that inspires Daniel in his relationship with Marie, when he finds himself writing a few verses while watching a sunset and then finally glimpses "The possibility of an island"[57] (Houellebecq, *The Possibility of an Island* 300), before he commits suicide. The literal understanding of this metaphor of "the possibility of an island" then motivates Mary23's escape and then that of

---

[55] "Un être est façonné, quelque part dans la Cité centrale, qui est semblable à moi; il a du moins mes traits, et mes organes internes. Lorsque ma vie cessera, l'absence de signal sera captée en quelques nanosecondes; la fabrication de mon successeur sera aussitôt mise en route. Dès le lendemain, le surlendemain au plus tard, la barrière de protection sera rouverte; mon successeur s'installera entre ces murs. Il sera le destinataire de ce livre" (Houellebecq, *La possibilité d'une île—Prix Interallié 2005* 26–27).

[56] "duplication rigoureuse du code génétique, la méditation de vie sur le récit du prédécesseur (et) la rédaction du commentaire" (Houellebecq, *La possibilité d'une île—Prix Interallié 2005* 178).

[57] "La possibilité d'une île" (Houellebecq, *La possibilité d'une île—Prix Interallié 2005* 424).

Daniel25, and it is thus the effects of this poetry that pushes the latter to become aware of his limits as a doubly "coded" character: at the same time genetically programmed and enclosed in the "space of the book" of the first of the Daniels.

The "space of the book" also locks in the actions of Mevlido/ Mingrelian, the character of Volodine's "last man writer," but in a textualist perspective claimed in a militant way and mainly inherited from Russian formalism. The originality of Volodine's poetics and creation also lies in the fact that the author adds to this perspective other cultural borrowings, including a frequent reference to Tibetan Buddhism and its *Book of the Dead*, the *Bardo Thödol*, which he presents as the origin of post-exotic fiction:

> From its earliest proses, indeed, our literature has handled notions such as cyclical fate, non-death death and non-life life, transmigration, and reincarnation, and it has given support to action in the form of a reality made of multiple worlds, illusory and parallel. Post-exotic writers have described crossing dark space, the tetanization of time, walking through fire or in pain: the entire gamut of ordeals through which the chasms of time and space are vanquished. With great ease and since the beginning, characters in their books create pathways and portals from one soul to another, they wander from one dream to another, they slip from one universe to another. Post-exotic fiction rests on such crossings[58] (Volodine, *Post-Exoticism in Ten Lessons, Lesson Eleven* 65).

The fictional path of the eponymous character of Antoine Volodine's novel in this *Tibetan Book of the Dead* that "the representation of the world through libraries"[59] (Ruffel 113) reveals in a unique way is therefore illus-trative of the post-exoticism of the novel *Songes de Mevlido*.

Confronted with the traumatic memory of the slaughter of Verena Becker, the woman he loved and wishes to join, Mevlido is indeed that

---

[58] "Dès ses première proses, en effet, notre littérature a manié des notions telles que le destin cyclique, la mort non-mort et la vie non-vie, la transmigration, la réincarnation (…). Les écrivains post-exotiques ont décrit la traversée de l'espace noir, la tétanisation de la durée, les marches dans le feu ou dans la souffrance: toute la gamme des épreuves par quoi sont vaincus les gouffres du temps et de l'espace. Avec une grande aisance et depuis toujours, les personnages de leurs livres effectuent des allées et venues d'une âme à une autre, ils vagabon-dent d'un songe à l'autre, ils glissent d'un univers à un autre. Sur de tels franchissements repose la fiction post-exotique" (Volodine, *Le post-exotisme en dix leçons, leçon onze* 75).

[59] "la représentation du monde en bibliothèque" (Ruffel 113).

character whose actions Mingrelian, as the author, never ceases to "exhaust" in dreams and incessant reincarnations that only gain lucidity after Mevlido's death when his mind recalls his state of being of literary fiction:

> In an unexpected way when we think about the circumstances, his brain was suddenly visited by a literary reminiscence. His memory projected in himself a book chapter related to the current trial, a scene with which Mingrelian finished one of his fiction works. Because Mingrelian was also writing this kind of text, narrations that did not correspond to what the Organs were expecting from him or were commanding him to produce. Poetic narrations.[60]

Of all the dreamlike universes that Mevlido experiences, the one that is the least chaotic is in fact the world of the "Organs"—the world of "the materiality of books"[61] (Ruffel 113)—where Mingrelian the author lives. The other worlds Mevlido encounters are a dystopian world populated by mutant hens, old Bolsheviks, and child soldiers; a world in which Mevlido begins by dying; and a more shamanic world where he evolves in an altered way, until he finds himself in spirit in the form of an insect and finds Verena Becker again. The reminiscence of a scriptural and poetic memory is undoubtedly what brings his intermental thinking closer to his intramental thinking to reveal himself to be a focal character who knows himself to be an artifact, coded or written, but most humanly aware of his state and his impediments. For, provided that it is stamped with lucidity, this "fictional recentering" is accompanied in Volodine's characters by a predictable suffering that results from the deprivation of intentionality specific to the beings subjected to the determinism of the written word:

> Then Mingrelian hesitates. To conclude so many trials on a single episode does not please him [...] As if the black wind of the narration was, at this key moment, unable to find a satisfactory direction, the story weirdly withdrew, crouched, ready to pounce one more time, and suddenly it trembles on

---

[60] "De façon inattendue quand on pense aux circonstances, il avait soudain le cerveau visité par une réminiscence littéraire. Sa mémoire projetait en lui un chapitre de roman qui était en rapport avec l'épreuve actuelle, une scène sur quoi Mingrelian terminait un de ses ouvrages de fiction. Car Mingrelian rédigeait aussi ce type de textes, des narrations qui ne correspondaient à rien de ce que les Organes attendaient de lui ou lui commandaient. Des narrations poétiques" (Volodine, *Songes de Mevlido* 244).

[61] "la matérialité des livres" (Ruffel 113).

itself. Three versions then are going to coexist, independent and intertwined, three sequences from a same narrative dough with which Mingrelian skillfully shapes a clumsy ending for his story, as well as, for his hero, an unfinished eternity.[62]

For Mevlido who "is going to enter clandestinely into Verena Becker's dream"[63] (430) in the last of the three versions imagined by Mingrelian, we would therefore say that his lucid fictional mind proves to be the closest awareness not to the Book, but to the rumors of unfinished books that range from these three unfinished versions to the reduction of an entire world to mere libraries.

What can we take away from these intermental reading paths that either punctuate, overplay, or identify with the characters' intramental dissonant thinking, whose resulting actions are based on knowledge, duty, and deceptive ability? It is possible that the fictional minds as readers illustrate what I term *a longing to be written and its refusal*, thanks to the legacy of philosophical tales that started with Cyrano de Bergerac and Voltaire, works that start to reflect by literary means about determinism and self-determination. The next chapter examines how, through this longing and refusal, science fiction and its subgenres keep on telling the story of a *remediation* determined by the symbolism of the book (either open or closed) in its representations of a resistant humanity hoping to maintain an interpretation of its origins and its future. Indeed, rather than conceiving the numerous changes of identity in literature of anticipation as *intermediation*[64] activities, my hypothesis is that this same literature is rather the narrative of a *remediation*[65] determined by the metaphoric

---

[62] " Mingrelian alors hésite. Conclure tant d'épreuves sur un épisode unique ne lui plaît pas. (…) Comme si le vent noir de la narration était, à ce moment-clé, incapable de trouver une direction satisfaisante, l'histoire se replie bizarrement, se ramasse, prête à bondir encore une fois, et soudain elle tremble sur elle-même. Trois versions vont alors coexister, indépendantes et inextriquées, trois séquences issues d'une même pâte narrative avec quoi Mingrelian façonne habilement une fin maladroite pour son récit, ainsi que, pour son héros, une éternité inaboutie" (Volodine, *Songes de Mevlido* 427).
[63] "va rentrer clandestinement dans un rêve de Verena Becker" (Volodine, *Songes de Mevlido* 430)
[64] "…this entanglement of the bodies of texts and digital subjects is one manifestation of… 'intermediation,' that is, complex transactions between bodies and texts as well as between different forms of media" (Hayles 7).
[65] "*remediation*. Defined by Paul Levenson as the 'anthropotropic' process by which new media technologies improve upon or remedy prior technologies" (Bolter and Grusin 273).

expressions of the symbolism of the book—whether it be the book of the universe, the book of the world, the book of nature, or the book of life—that gives all its meaning to this longing and technological desire.

BIBLIOGRAPHY

Bolter, Jay David, and Richard Grusin. *Remediation: Understanding New Media.* MIT Press, 2003.

Bordage, Pierre. *Les derniers hommes.* J'ai Lu edition, 2005.

Clément, Murielle-Lucie. *Michel Houellebecq revisité: l'écriture houellebecquienne.* L'Harmattan, 2007.

Darrieussecq, Marie. *Notre vie dans les forêts roman.* P.O.L., 2017.

———. *Our Life in the Forest.* Translated by Penny Hueston, The Text Publishing Company, 2018.

Doležel, Lubomír. *Heterocosmica: Fiction and Possible Worlds.* Johns Hopkins University Press, 1998.

———. "Narrative Modalities." *Journal of Literary Semantics,* vol. 5, no. 1, 1976.

Hayles, N. Katherine. *My Mother Was a Computer Digital Subjects and Literary Texts.* University of Chicago Press, 2005.

Herman, David, et al. *Routledge Encyclopedia of Narrative Theory.* Routledge, 2008.

Houellebecq, Michel. *La possibilité d'une île.* Fayard, 2005.

———. *The Possibility of an Island.* Translated by Gavin Bowd, Knopf, 2006.

Hugo, Victor. *Ninety-Three.* TheClassics.us, 2013.

Jouve, Vincent. *L'effet-personnage dans le roman.* Presses Universitaires de France, 1998.

Lavocat, Françoise. *La théorie littéraire des mondes possibles.* CNRS Éditions, 2011.

Maalouf, Amin. *Le premier siècle après Béatrice: roman.* Grasset, 1999.

———. *The First Century After Beatrice.* Translated by Dorothy S. Blair, Abacus, 1994.

Palmer, Alan. *Fictional Minds.* University of Nebraska Press, 2004.

Ruffel, Lionel. *Volodine post-exotique.* Ed. Cécile Defaut, 2007.

Rufin, Jean-Christophe. *Globalia.* Gallimard, 2005.

Ryan, Marie-Laure. *Possible Worlds, Artificial Intelligence, and Narrative Theory.* Indiana Univ Press, 1992.

Saint-Gelais, Richard. "Ambitions et limites de la sémantique de la fiction." *Acta Fabula,* vol. 2, n° 2, Automne 2001, https://www.fabula.org:443/revue/document11007.php.

———. *L'empire du pseudo: modernités de la science-fiction.* Nota bene, 1999.

Schuknecht, Mattison. "The Best/Worst of All Possible Worlds? Utopia, Dystopia, and Possible-Worlds Theory." *Possible Worlds Theory and Contemporary Narratology,* edited by Alice Bell and Ryan, Marie-Laure, University of Nebraska Press, 2019, pp. 225–48.

Stockwell, Peter. *The Poetics of Science Fiction*. Routledge, 2000.

Tadié, Jean-Yves. *Le sens de la mémoire*. Gallimard, 1999.

Volodine, Antoine. *Le post-exotisme en dix leçons, leçon onze*. Gallimard, 2010.

———. *Post-Exoticism in Ten Lessons, Lesson Eleven*. Translated by J. T. Mahany, Open Letter, 2015.

———. *Songes de Mevlido*. Seuil, 2007.

Vonarburg, Elisabeth. *Le silence de la cité*. Editions Alire, 1998.

———. *The Silent City*. Translated by Jane Brierley, Tesseracts Books, 2002.

Vuarnet, Jean-Noël. "L'utopie inverse. Notes sur la prolifération des utopies 1408 du pire." *Saint-Denis: Presses et Publications de l'Université de Paris VIII Vincennes à Saint-Denis*, vol. Théorie-Littérature Enseignement n°3, 1984.

Vygotskiĭ, L. S., et al. *Mind in Society: The Development of Higher Psychological Processes*. Harvard University Press, 1981.

CHAPTER 4

The Idea of the Book and Its Symbolism in Times of Change

Having extended the notion of the traditional literary figure of the "book within the book," it is clear now that what is at stake in the storyworlds I have been focused on so far is an idea of the book which is both a medium and, as I will explain in detail in this chapter, a powerful metaphor whose symbolism informs the fictional minds and bodies and their subsequent worldviews in the near and far futures of futuristic novels. But how can the book be both a medium and a metaphor altering and defining who we are? As Allison Muri points out in her book *The Enlightenment Cyborg: A History of Communications and Control in the Human Machine, 1660–1830*, there is a history of the human mind and identity either altered[1] by the book and its pages in its materiality or on a metaphoric register as an assimilation of the metaphors of the book to the human body and mind. This latter approach is inherited from the humanist conceptual framework for which although "the body is a book to be read, the mind is imagined as a page to be inscribed"; this approach is enrooted in

---

[1] "Since the arrival of television and the personal computer, the presentation of our ideas via configuration of electron beams rather than fixed upon a more palpable page has inspired repeated commentary upon not only lamentation for the loss of the texture of the book, but also how *we* will change. Whether a exultation for a supposed new traversing of boundaries and freedom from hierarchical structures, a predominant conclusion has been that we are altered by our media" (Muri 229).

© The Author(s), under exclusive license to Springer Nature Switzerland AG 2022
E. Buzay, *Contemporary French and Francophone Futuristic Novels*, Studies in Global Science Fiction, https://doi.org/10.1007/978-3-031-16628-0_4

a religious understanding of which Alberto Manguel gives a clear example in his *A History of Reading* quoting a sixteenth-century Spanish mystic, Fray Luis de Granada, who compares human beings to illuminated and living letters of the book of the universe:

> Human beings, made in the image of God, are also books to be read. Here, the act of reading serves as a metaphor to help us understand our hesitant relationship with our body, the encounter and the touch and the deciphering of signs in another person (Manguel 169).

I will take Manguel's point and explore how it might function in the genre of futuristic novels. Therefore, I ask: How does "the act of reading serve[ ] as a metaphor to help us understand our hesitant relationship with our body, the encounter and the touch and the deciphering of signs in another person" (169) in futuristic novels? And to what understanding of the world do the reading paths we identified in the previous chapter refer? What is the focus of this imaginary of the book that invariably counterbalances the instability of the dystopian worlds of science fiction literature? As they are perceived and then interpreted by the fictional minds of my book selection, the intelligibility of these fictional storyworlds is built on the acceptance or rejection of the conceptual[2] metaphors of the book of nature and the book of the world in the sense that these metaphors symbolize a "totality" or favor (by their weakening) the emergence of an open "rumor" about an unlimited world.

In the antechamber of totalitarian media devices as in that of images of computer and genetic coding, where to be coded is first of all to be "written," the importance of the enclosure of and the departure from the symbolism of the book lies in the fact that it determines the metamorphoses that the human race wishes or fears. Consequently, throughout this chapter, I explore the hypothesis that the metaphors of the book and the metalepsis correlated to the use of computer science and genetics share the coherence or incoherence of the fictional storyworlds, based on the extent of the characters' resistance.

---

[2] "Conceptual metaphor allows inferences in sensory-motor domains (e.g., domains of space and objects) to be used to draw inferences about other domains (e.g., domains of subjective judgment, with concepts like intimacy, emotions, justice, and so on). Because we reason in terms of metaphor, the metaphors we use determine a great deal about how we live our lives" (*Metaphors We Live by* 244).

The main interest of this articulation lies, according to my hypothesis, in the fact that this acceptance accounts for a humanity inclined toward the defense of what it considers to be its very limits, while the rejection describes the situation of mutants or clones confronted for better or for worse with the limits of their humanity. Finally, still from the paradigmatic point of view of these metaphors of the book, my last analyses of humankind's mutations will take into account the relations that the imagination of science fiction literature maintains concerning the animality of insects and spiders as a mode of expressionist representation of coding and a sociality competing with human history and its evolution.

METAPHORS OF THE CLOSED SYMBOLISM OF THE BOOK

As I have already retraced the evolution of the metaphors of the book in the section, "The broader scope of the Books of Nature and the World," in my first chapter, I will now expand on how philosophical tales and the science fiction inherited from this questioning have appropriated this concept by secularizing it. What exactly do I mean by books of nature and the world? As expressions of the sacred nature of writing at its origins, these metaphors of the book, whose symbolism goes back beyond the holy texts "of Christianity, of Islam, of Judaism to the ancient Orient—the Near East and Egypt" (Curtius et al. 304), refer to collective representations that were mainly elaborated in philosophy, theology, and literature from antiquity to the Renaissance and beyond, to speak of the creative intention and coherence that participate in the organization of nature and the world, from a monotheistic point of view.

As Jesse M. Gellrich outlines in *The Idea of the Book in the Middles Ages*, the growing importance of these metaphoric expressions in the Middle Ages reinforced a notion that "[t]he idea of the Book readily corresponds to the medieval conception of the Bible" (Gellrich and Cornell University Press 31–32). These notions reinforce the metaphors inspired by the acts of reading and writing that became commonplace until finally coinciding in the seventeenth century with the idea of traveling or traversing the world in search of explanations and adventures, according to the well-known formulation of the philosopher René Descartes excerpted from his *Discourse on the Method*:

This is why, as soon as age permitted me to emerge from the control of my tutors, I entirely quitted the study of letters. And resolving to seek no other science than that which could be find in myself, or at least in *the great book of the world* (I underlined) I employed the rest of my youth in travel, in seeing courts and armies, in intercourse with men of diverse temperaments and conditions, in collecting varied experiences, in proving myself in the various predicaments in which I was placed by fortune, and under all circumstances bringing my mind to bear on the things which came before it, so that I might derive some profit from my experience (Descartes et al. 8).

From this still hushed skepticism to the satirical evocation of the marvelous mechanical book which summarizes the materialist laws of another world in Cyrano de Bergerac, a certain hexagonal rationalism has never ceased to criticize the conception of such providential writing, a critique that in the French philosophical tradition has recently culminated in Jacques Derrida's enterprise of deconstruction, for whom the idea of the book (of the nature, of the world, etc.) is perceived as "the encyclopedic protection of theology and of logocentrism against the disruption of writing; against its aphoristic energy, and, […] against difference in general" (Spivak and Derrida 18).[3] The philosophical tale makes this perspective of doubt even more explicit in Voltaire's *Micromégas* in the eighteenth century, before subsequently being relayed by futuristic novels, without the latter perhaps ever having truly abandoned this paradigm of the *liber mundi* as a frame of reference for the plotting of its detective narratives. One can verify this trend by the persistence of this symbolic weaving in the composition of the storyworlds of the novels studied in this chapter. Exploring these storyworlds in order to feel the ambivalence of the longing and refusal to be written is often tantamount to fueling the hermeneutic reception of a dissonance that pleads against the determinism of beings, nature, and the world, through the interposition of characters taking several forms of choice and contestation.

Before seeing themselves technologically assimilated to a mode of writing or coding, many characters in speculative fiction are in fact the first to distinguish themselves by their ability to read the book of nature in order to escape from the enterprise of reification of the dystopian worlds they inhabit. This reading of nature, which emphasizes the symbolism of the book in its most circumscribed version, generally translates into the use of motifs such as the metaphors of the tree of knowledge and of the circle or

---

[3] "… la protection encyclopédique de la théologie et du logocentrisme contre la disruption de l'écriture, contre son énergie aphoristique et, (…) contre la différence en général" (Derrida 31).

sphere of knowledge (which are recurring motifs in Chap. 3 "Le livre cyclique" of Domon's book *Le Livre imaginaire* (*The Imaginary Book*)) to describe a garden—in positive or negative reference to that of the biblical Eden—through the expansion of which the characters access a unitary vision of the worlds they intend to reevaluate. In addition, these metaphors invite readers to draw on their personal memories, since "[their] conceptual structure is not merely a matter of the intellect—it involves all the natural dimensions of our experience, including aspects of our sense experiences: color, shape, texture, sound, etc." (Lakoff and Johnson 235). Their hermeneutic reception is singular in that the reader is free to dismantle or regroup the motifs of a biblical scenography according to questions more secular than theological about the future, the reemergence, or the fall of humanity.

The novel by Jean-Christophe Rufin thus willingly compares the Globalian society to a garden under surveillance where History, which "is a tenacious plant when it is not uprooted,"[4] has practically no more reason to be: "In this immense garden that Globalia had become, a close guard was set up around this potentially dangerous species that was man. Fortunately, society agreed to control it"[5] (131). Of all the characters who try to leave this sanitized "garden," Baïkal and Puig, who meet each other through Kate, complement each other in the "reading" of the book of nature that they each undertake in their own way, to lay, almost in spite of themselves, the foundations of a revolutionary action whose instigator suggests at the end of the novel that it could succeed if these two men were to work more closely together on a long-term basis.

Chosen by Ron Altman, one of the directors of Globalia, to play the role of a terrorist who must federate against himself the opinion and ingenuity of Globalia's leaders in exchange for greater freedom outside this totalitarian society, Baïkal appears first as a fugitive whose desire for adventure could have made him turn into the "scapegoat" of this political machination if he had not evolved in contact with a wilderness and learned much about himself this way. From this perspective, Baïkal's history is that of an individual reconquest supported by the promises of a romantic elsewhere: "Around the river, downhill, the caress of gusts of wind made silver

---

[4] "...est une plante tenace quand on ne l'[en] extirpe pas"(Rufin 299).

[5] "Dans cet immense jardin qu'était devenu Globalia, une garde étroite était montée autour de cette espèce potentiellement dangereuse qu'était l'homme. Heureusement, la société s'entendait à le contrôler" (Rufin 131).

waves roll over the fleece of large willows. But all of this was about the distant, that is to say, the outside."[6] This way of being, which makes him a poet rather than a man of action, is not, however, only limited to landscapes, since it extends to the outcasts living in the "no-zones," which for him have the appearance of "dry, gnarled vine stalks that are nonetheless still capable of exploding into flowers and fruit"[7] (173); it is in fact part of a continuum, that of a poetic vision woven in the solitude of an idealistic relationship between man and the world mediated by nature, which recalls, in Rufin's writing, the great spiritual tradition of nineteenth-century American transcendentalist writers and essayists, whose best-known authors are Ralph Waldo Emerson and Henry David Thoreau. If Thoreau's essay, *Walden or Life in the Woods*, is a key text for understanding Globalia before it is even mentioned by Puig and members of the "Walden society" of protesting readers, it is because in many ways it sheds light on the dissatisfaction and the desire for adventure embodied in the character of Baïkal: this relationship to books and the knowledge that results from them cannot be compared to reading the book of nature, which alone engages the body and measures erudition with its lucidity and perceptiveness. This attitude, mentioned by Emerson in a lecture entitled "The American Scholar," in reaction to the predominance of European culture in nineteenth-century America, and taken up and then detailed by Thoreau, is known to have various qualities, including the ability to conceive of "futurity":

> What is a course of history or philosophy, or poetry, no matter how well selected, or the best society, or the most admirable routine of life, compared with the discipline of looking always at what to be seen? Will you be a reader, a student merely, or a seer? Read your fate, see what is before you, and walk onto futurity (Thoreau 119).

The approach to this aptitude for perceptiveness also shared by Puig Pujol's character is more cerebral, and thus supplements Baïkal's approach in the hypothesis of an alliance between the two men. As a trained journalist, Puig reads *Walden* and rediscovers handwriting thanks to the Walden

---

[6] "Autour de la rivière, en contrebas, la caresse des bourrasques faisait courir sur la toison de grands saules des ondes argentées. Mais tout cela concernait le lointain, c'est-à-dire le dehors" (Rufin 21).

[7] "...sarments secs, noueux et pourtant capables encore d'exploser en fleurs et en fruits" (Rufin 173).

Association before its president introduces him to reading history books and maps. It is under the guidance of this association, whose members are all political opponents of Ron Altman's regime, that Puig discovers with Kate that "Globalia, contrary to a generally accepted idea—and which was in fact an element of propaganda—, did not cover the whole world but corresponded to a territory—or rather territories—, more or less grouped islets, strictly delimited and ultimately quite small"[8] (338–339). Less poetic than the reading of the book of nature undertaken by Baïkal, and perhaps also less extensive insofar as Baïkal is about to reach the Amazonian Forest with Kate to hide there, Puig's reading is nonetheless more perceptive about the fault lines of a totalitarian system whose geocriticism could incite others to future civil disobedience.

The imaginary that emerges from the reading of the "great book of nature" in Marie Darrieussecq's novel *Our Life in the Forest* is that it almost combines the attitudes of Baïkal and Puig through their respective poetic and geocritical readings in the pursuit of civil disobedience that is in itself the story of the Notebook of the character of Viviane/Marie, but with a more pessimistic tone. And this reading of nature intersects with the symbolism of the book, as I previously noted, with the use of the metaphor of the tree of knowledge, which is associated with the forms of the circle and the sphere in order to recall a phantasmagoric Edenic garden.

In Darrieussecq's novel, this garden first remains in Viviane's mind and corresponds to her childhood memories, as for her "safe place [...] [she] visualized a forest that [she] went to as a child. [Lying] just beyond [her] grandparent's garden. In a vanished world" (Darrieussecq, *Our Life in the Forest* 36).[9] Then comes the cliker, Viviane's former patient and later lover, who sets her free and whose "safe place" during the therapy he underwent with her was also a forest. In the plot, this character is the one who makes Marie—who is not yet Viviane—realize that she lives under surveillance and that her multiple surgeries, which include a removal of an eye and a kidney, as well as the implants she received under the skin of her arm and in her head, are very problematic. Feeling depressed or burned out after

---

[8] "Globalia, contrairement à une idée reçue—et qui était en fait un élément de propagande—, ne couvrait pas le monde entier mais correspondait à un territoire—ou plutôt des territoires—, des îlots plus ou moins groupés, strictement délimités et finalement assez réduits" (Rufin 338–339).

[9] « Mon lieu sûr. Je voyais une forêt. (...) je voyais une forêt que j'ai connue enfant. Elle s'étendait en bas du jardin de mes grands-parents. Dans un monde disparu » (Darrieussecq, *Notre vie dans les forêts roman* 51).

teaching human behaviors to robots, the cliker's limitations and resistance as a duty- and compassion-oriented character helps Marie to write and see their dystopian world as it is by overcoming her own physical handicaps. Thus, they switched roles—the caretaker becoming the cared-for, and vice versa—when the forest turned out to be a beautiful physical refuge and not just a mental safe place. In this way, the cliker stands by a tree as the loving embodiment of Marie-becoming-Viviane's perceptiveness:

> The forest was astonishing. Tiny little bright green leaves, a green so natural that it looked artificial, the green you think of when you think of green: tiny little leaves growing at the ends of absolutely every single branch. I wanted to touch them, to be touched by this foliage that was soft and velvety and SO green. And I couldn't hear anything apart from the sound of the wind in the trees, and occasionally, yes, a bird. Astonishing. I was trembling, breathing, no tension, nothing. Just the call of the wind, the trees and the birds, and the sun. And of the dog, whom I was following, and who had the tact to act as if he was following me.
> Standing under a tree was the clicker (Darrieussecq 116–117).[10]

While Viviane's journey is a form of clear-sightedness supported by her writing, this writing exercise does not aim to summarize their love story by itself, as she makes clear: "My patient and me. That could have been the title of this notebook, assuming it needs a title, but I don't want to talk about that at all. I want to talk about our life in the forest" (Darrieussecq 22–23). In fact, she feels the obligation to testify about the city's danger in her writing because of the cliker's resistance. Her writing compensates for her physical handicaps, providing her new insights, and does so in two stages: one stage when she explicitly quotes authors like Sergei Yesenin and Victor Hugo, who express her compassion and desire for revolt and justice (as I indicated in Chap. 3), and a second stage where her capacity

---

[10] « La forêt était étourdissante. De toutes petites feuilles d'un vert très clair, d'un vert tellement naturel qu'il me semblait artificiel, le vert quand on pense au vert: de toutes petites feuilles qui poussaient au bout d'absolument toutes les branches. On avait envie de les toucher., d'être touchée par ce feuillage doux et velu et si vert. Et le fait de ne rien entendre dans l'oreille que le bruit du vent dans l'oreille que le bruit du vent dans les arbres, et occasionnellement, oui, un oiseau. Pas de sollicitations, rien. Juste l'invitation du vent, des arbres et des oiseaux, et du soleil. Et du chien, que je suivais, et qui avait l'élégance de faire comme si c'était lui qui me suivait.

Debout, sous un arbre, il y avait le cliqueur » (Darrieussecq, *Notre vie dans les forêts roman* 149).

for reading the books of nature and the world empowers her with a form of foresight that recalls Thoreau's "futurity" and enables her to see the other side of the world:

> Today, I need to write. *I don't know if it does me any good to write, but I can see. I see what they're doing to us. I feel it. With the rest of my body.* "I'm lying under the trees as I write, my back against a mound of earth. I'm making an effort to breathe slowly. It's a sunny day even if we always stay in the shade. Every now and again I tip my head back and try to concentrate on the foliage. *With my head upside down, and my single eye, I try to see things from the other side, as they say.* (I underlined) You can't feel the wind at ground level, and the trees above seem to be moving by themselves. They're swaying their arms, their branches; they're waving their green hands; they're doing the helicopter. I try to empty my mind. To breathe. The air is marvellous here. It smells green. It smells like sap. It's so good. Between the leaves, I glimpse confetti pieces of sky. Sequins of sky. It's raining blue sky. The blue sky settles over me" (Darrieussecq 111) (my italics).[11]

Concerning this perceptiveness entailed here by her writing practice, it is important to note that the literal translation of "…j'essaie de voir comme qui dirait l'envers du monde" (Darrieussecq, *Notre vie dans les forêts roman* 143) is closer to "I try to see, as one would say, the other side *of the world*" (my italics), instead of the official translation of "I try to see things from the other side, as they say," in which the phrase "of the world" is clearly not mentioned, while the term "things" is unnecessarily added. As observed by Hélène Domon in her essay *Le Livre imaginaire* (*The Imaginary Book*), the reading of the books of nature and the world has its own limits, which are tied to the images of the *circle* and the *sphere*, since culturally our "historical rootedness in the book allow us to consider it as

---

[11] « Aujourd'hui j'ai besoin de l'écrire. Je ne sais pas si ça me fait du bien, de l'écrire, mais je vois. Je vous ce qu'on nous a fait. Je sens. Avec ce qui me reste de corps. J'écris allongée sous les arbres, adossée à un monticule de terre. Je m'applique à respirer lentement. C'est un jour de soleil, même si nous restons toujours à l'ombre. De temps en temps je relève la tête et j'essaie de me concentrer sur le feuillage. La tête à l'envers, avec mon œil unique, j'essaie de voir comme qui dirait l'envers du monde. Le vent n'est pas sensible au ras du sol, et les arbres là-haut semblent bouger tout seuls. Ils balancent leurs bras, leurs branches, ils agitent leurs mains vertes, ils font l'avion. J'essaie de ne penser à rien. De respirer. L'air est merveilleux ici. Il sent le vert. Il sent la sève. C'est bon. Entre les feuilles on devine des confettis de ciel. Des paillettes de ciel. Il pleut du ciel bleu. Le ciel bleu se dépose sur moi » (Darrieussecq, *Notre vie dans les forêts roman* 142–143).

the metaphor of any myth of closure."[12] It is this aspect that is put to the test and takes a dramatic turn when, with her expanded faculty of concentration, Viviane tries "to see the *whole* sea" (Darrieussecq, *Our Life in the Forest* 136)[13] in a video that the cliker shows her to make her understand that she is—like her half, the term used for clones in this novel—just another clone. It is as if during this dramatic event her microcosmic and macrocosmic vision, which once provided her with a poetic, compassionate form of foresight, collided and collapsed to deny her singular humanity, as she summarized it: "An eye like the sea, the sea where she cavorted like a happy-go-lucky sea lion. What did she see? I saw the sea she saw. It was my eye, my missing eye."[14] (Darrieussecq 139). And this loss takes on even more dramatic proportions when Viviane understands that she is no longer, or rather not at all, at the center of the humanist vision she deployed and from which she told her story as one of damned who are living in the shadow of the most fortunate:

> I wanted to look at the old woman. The pureblood. The woman from whom I was born. The one from whom Marie and I, and perhaps others exactly like us, were born. I found the whole thing difficult to take on board. For weeks, I found it difficult. It seemed so hard to believe. It requires a radical change of thinking, really, to no longer see yourself at the centre of things—at the centre of your own vision of the world. To understand that you are nothing more than a peripheral offshoot. Required by people very far away, light years away from you. Who have decided, *bingo*, that you would be born, that you would be harvested, then taken to pieces. I felt like Copernicus […] who worked out that the Sun doesn't orbit the Earth, but that the Earth orbits the Sun (Darrieussecq 145).

What's left of Viviane's notebook then is worse than disappointment, but her final statement matters when she claims that "They say you have to turn the page […] Before turning that page, I'd like us to read to the bottom of it" (Darrieussecq 148). This suggests that in her death, she is becoming the very fabric of her notebook that is worthy of being read,

---

[12] « … enracinement historique dans le livre permet que nous considérions celui-ci comme la métaphore de tout mythe de clôture » (Domon 53).

[13] « … voir *toute* la mer » (Darrieussecq, *Notre vie dans les forêts roman* 172).

[14] « Un œil comme la mer, la mer où elle s'ébattait façon otarie insouciante. Qu'est-ce qu'elle voyait? Je voyais la mer qu'elle voyait. C'était mon œil, l'œil qui me manquait » (Darrieussecq, *Notre vie dans les forêts roman* 142–143).

either to sympathize with the dignity she has recovered with this writing exercise that somehow reclaims her humanity or to serve as a starter for a rebellion by transmitting a final message as a footnote to her wish to see her notebook read entirely (by whoever will find it) after her death. The message itself is not supposed to be able to understood by the robots or the algorithms in her time because of the use of triple negations, as indicated earlier: "And don't go thinking that I am not certain I am not a non-person" (Darrieussecq 148),[15] a resistant and coded message, which means "I am certain that I am a person," that is only addressed to humans of the future.

The interweaving of the tree of knowledge metaphors are described in a tragic way by the narrator father of Beatrice in *The First Century After Beatrice*, as he observes the insects that represent for him the animated alphabet of the book of nature. On one side, therefore, there is a tree that represents a sum of knowledge that is not clearly delimited; within the text, "a pernicious substance" is termed a literal "fruit" of this metaphorical tree, a fruit that causes the genetic engineering experiments that exclusively favor the birth of boys:

Hatred has today taken the form of a pernicious substance, the fruit of legitimate research, the fruit of this same genetic research which allow us to combat malformations and tumours, the fruit of the same genetic engineering which allow us to improve our food resources. But a pernicious fruit which has brought out the worst instincts in everyone[16] (Maalouf, *The First Century After Beatrice* 126).

And on the other side, the human race as summarized by another scientific character named Emmanuel Liev, known for his work on fruit trees—this detail is of course not insignificant—who "devoted his life to the genetic improvement of plants"[17] (Maalouf, *The First Century After*

[15] « Et ne croyez pas que je ne sois pas sûre d'être une non-personne » (Darrieussecq, *Notre vie dans les forêts roman* 186).

[16] La haine a pris la forme d'une substance pernicieuse, fruit de recherches légitimes, fruit de ces mêmes recherches génétiques qui nous permettent de combattre les malformations ou les tumeurs, fruit de ces mêmes manipulations génétiques qui nous permettent d'améliorer et de multiplier nos ressources alimentaires. Mais fruit pervers, qui a permis à chacun de révéler ses pires instincts (Maalouf, *Le premier siècle après Béatrice* 202).

[17] "consacré sa vie à l'amélioration génétique des plantes" (Maalouf, *Le premier siècle après Béatrice* 86).

Beatrice 51), and for whom humankind is considered to be "all the men and women of the six continents, [who] are only a thin layer, a minute layer of flesh and conscience on the face of the earth" (Maalouf, *The First Century After Beatrice* 125),[18] according to the narrator's account of a lecture given at the United Nations headquarters in New York to make a plea for the preservation of a common humanity. All the dramatization of the narrative in the fictional mind of the entomologist narrator in the novel points toward an opposition between the darkening of a human nature whose instinct for survival "gets lost in a dark forest of ideas"[19] (Maalouf, *The First Century After Beatrice* 75), when this nature does not give birth to a "jungle of hostilities"[20] (Maalouf, *The First Century After Beatrice* 92), and the impossible clarity or radiance of a garden linked to the symbolism of the book's enclosure, which makes Emmanuel Liev say that he represented an ideal to be reached when he found himself "thinking that the Earthly Paradise mentioned in the Scriptures is not a myth of the olden times, but a prophecy, a vision of the future"[21] (Maalouf, *The First Century After Beatrice* 127). This opposition between the obscuring of a human nature and the impossible clarity of a paradisiacal garden can be explained, from the narrator's point of view, by a "line of disunion" between the two hemispheres of the terrestrial globe which could no longer share the same horizon to think or simply to communicate:

Without wishing to linger over the euphoria of the last years of the past century, I would like to emphasize the fact that, as the two wings of the developed world joined, and the gap between their values, institutions, language, way of life closed, so the deep gap which divided the world, the 'horizontal fault-line' responsible for so many tremors, had been thrown into violent relief. On the one side of the divide, all the wealth, all the freedom, all the hope. On the other, a maze of dead-ends: stagnation, violence, rage, and storms, spreading an epidemic of chaos, and salvation through a massive

---

[18] "nous tous les hommes et les femmes, qu'une mince couche, une couche de chair et de conscience sur la face du monde" (Maalouf, *Le premier siècle après Béatrice* 201).

[19] "...instinct de conservation se perd chez les hommes dans une sombre forêt d'idées" (Maalouf, *Le premier siècle après Béatrice* 124).

[20] "jungle des haines" (Maalouf, *Le premier siècle après Béatrice* 150).

[21] "... penser que le Paradis terrestre mentionné dans les Écritures n'est pas un mythe des temps passés mais une prophétie, une vision d'avenir" (Maalouf, *Le premier siècle après Béatrice* 203).

exodus to the paradise of the North[22] (Maalouf, *The First Century After Beatrice* 84).

As a fault line between a radiant northern hemisphere sure of the fluidity of its exchanges and development and a southern hemisphere in recession immersed in fear and anger, the "horizontal fault-line" metaphorically marks the end of the writing of a common history. In the end, it is thus on the basis of this observation of powerlessness that the narrator envisages his disappearance after having identified, this time at the book level of the world, a communicative symbolic component that no longer manages to articulate itself on a natural order, which paradoxically hints at a humanity perhaps reduced to appearing only within the framework of testimonial writing.

Less deterministic and more explicit in its use of metaphors linked to biblical intertexts to signify the closure of the symbolism of the book, mainstream science fiction goes, so to speak, straight to the point in the plotting and permanent redistribution of the metaphors of the knowledge of the tree and the circle. The plot of Pierre Bordage's novel *The Last Men* is most enlightening on this point when, at the end of the story, it describes how the space of a clearing is invested by the architectural avatar of a computer program inspired by a literal reading of the *Book of Revelation*. Here the objective of this program is to establish the advocates of a post-humanity and to liquidate the "last men" facing them, in the heart of a forest that is moreover presented as a dreaded territory throughout the novel.

The story of "Solman the crippled" is the story of the fight against this substitution project. As a prophet, or more exactly "Giver," Solman must protect the "water people" to which he belongs from the actions of an organization of exiled scientists in space and under the oceans, the Eskato, which pursues, as I have already mentioned, the objective of exterminating the last human tribes still remaining on earth in order to take their

---

[22] Sans vouloir m'attarder sur l'euphorie des dernières années du siècle passé, je voudrais souligner le fait que les retrouvailles entre les deux ailes du monde développé, cette convergence vers des valeurs, des institutions, un langage, un mode d'existence similaires, avaient brutalement mis en relief le fossé vertigineux qui partageait le monde, cette "faille horizontale" responsable de tant de secousses. D'un côté, toute la richesse, toutes les libertés, tous les espoirs. De l'autre, un labyrinthe d'impasses: stagnation, violence, rages et orages, contagion du chaos, et le salut par la fuite massive vers le paradis septentrional (Maalouf, *Le premier siècle après Béatrice* 203).

place. To recount this unequal struggle, Pierre Bordage multiplies biblical intertexts and lends his characters metaphors that he extracts from the symbolism of the sacred books where, as Hélène Domon reminds us, "books and fabrics remind communities of their belonging to a single text (…), distinguish them from the rest of men and circumscribe their enclosure."[23] Therefore, the meaning of the Aquarius' fight against the members of the Eskato shifts very quickly to a metaphorical terrain. Whereas the Eskato groups together angels or creatures without defect "marked with a Seal"[24] (355) by the "Verb," a computer program adapted from a literal reading of the Apocalypse, the representation of the water people reverses the pattern of this election in the eyes of a Solman, who very early on undertook a less conclusive reading of the *New Testament*:

> His vision was unfolding on them, dragging, like a net with extraordinarily fine mesh, their memory, their feelings, their suffering (…). He filled himself with their history like bitter water, and his cup overflowed, because he was like them, only a human being, only a tiny fragment of the creation …[25]

The battle between Solman and the Eskato is in many ways confined to this reading exercise that attempts to pierce the original meaning of the text as the "textus," in the sense of a weft or fabric, in the form of the "writing" of the books of nature and the world that relate mythologically to the formation of mankind. And when, against all expectations, the Eskato proposes to the "Giver" to be transformed into a perfect and immortal man, "to be the ultimate redeemed one of humanity, to strip himself of the shreds of his past, to drink from the source of living water, to stretch out under the branches of the tree of life"[26] (653), Solman decides to escape the networking of the "Verb" and to oppose it with the metaphorical vision of a human weft that closes its memory before acting within it like a virus that comes into being by incarnating "the Book" in a

---

[23] "livres et tissus rappellent aux communautés leur appartenance à un texte unique (…), les distingue du reste des hommes et circonscrit leur clôture" (Domon 58).

[24] "marqués d'un Sceau" (Bordage 355).

[25] "Sa vision se déployait sur eux, draguait, comme un filet aux mailles extraordinairement fines, leur mémoire, leurs sentiments, leurs souffrances (…). Il s'emplissait de leur histoire comme d'une eau amère, et sa coupe débordait, parce qu'il n'était comme eux, qu'un humain, qu'un éclat infime de la création… (366–367)" (Bordage 366–367).

[26] "d'être l'ultime racheté de l'humanité, de se dépouiller des lambeaux de son passé, de boire de la source d'eau vive, de s'étendre sous les branches de l'arbre de vie" (Bordage 653).

Christ-like way even going so far as to sacrifice himself for humanity's sake: "Raïma the transgenic was the thread by which the human weft was reconstituted, consolidated itself. Then Solman closed himself to the gentle supplication of the Verb and unfurled his vision."[27] While Bordage uses the Christ-like character of Solman as a pretext to oppose the song of a destructive intelligence to a more authentic "weft," because the latter is more faithful to the idea of human nature, it is less to emphasize the traditional religious meaning of the tree of knowledge than to perhaps suggest to readers that the idea of humanity is once again based on an act of semiotic foundation, this time giving to writing, before speech or the enlarged perspective of a communication, a substantially human trait that would apply to the books of nature and the world.

Once Solman is killed and absorbed by the Verb, the *Bible* he possessed is cremated with him in order to prevent the last remaining men from falling back into the past and engaging once again in an "apocalyptic" adventure, in the literal sense of the word.

Knowing that the end of this novel has not necessarily been interpreted in a religious way, any more so than the other of my selected works for that matter, what is, therefore, the interest of playing this scenario of the use of the metaphors of knowledge of the tree, the circle, and the sphere in loops to signify the closure of the symbolism of the book? In its approach to the media, as it is monopolized by the question of the use of books or screens, whether television or computers, it would seem that futuristic novels go back, whenever they can, by circuitous but nevertheless reaffirmed ways to better reevaluate themselves, using the great mythologies of the Mesopotamian, Jewish, and Greek civilizations which made the first writings the true *doubles of humanity*.

As the linguist and archaeologist Clarisse Herrenschmidt explains in Chapter V, "Writing as the double of humanity," of her essay *Les trois écritures: langue, nombre, code (The Three Scriptures: Language, Number, Code)*, each myth that explains the emergence of the human race in these three ancient cultures shows "some analogy between the modalities of the emergence of the human race and the writing system that notes the

---

[27] "Raïma la transgénosée était le fil par lequel la trame humaine se reconstituait, se consolidait. Alors Solman se ferma à la supplique doucereuse du Verbe et déploya sa vision" (Bordage 659).

language in which it was written."[28] If in these three cultures, "the metaphor of modelling common to Mesopotamia, Greece, and Israel" (202)[29] accompanies the practice of these early writings, only the text of *Genesis* (2.5–9) explicitly mentions the presence of significant trees (life and knowledge) in a garden:

> On the day Lord God made earth and heavens, no shrub of the field being yet on the earth and no plant of the field yet sprouted, for the Lord God had not caused rain to fall on the earth and there was no human to till the soil, and wetness would well from the earth to water all the surface of the soil, then the Lord God fashioned the human, humus from the soil, and blew into his nostrils the breath of life, and the human became a living creature. And the Lord God planted a garden in Eden, to the east, and He placed there the Human He had fashioned. And the Lord God caused to sprout from the soil every tree to look at and good for food, and the tree of life was in the midst of the garden, and the tree of knowledge, good and evil (Alter 13–14).

At the beginning of this myth that has deeply marked the imagination of Western civilization, the "prototypal Adam, made from clay from the moistened soil, is embodied by his name, which is not yet a proper name since it is determined by the article, with this soil: in the Hebrew language Adam (*'dam*), 'specific man', and 'soil' (*'adamah*) are related; the myth depicts the linguistic relationship."[30] It is this prototypical Adam who pushes back the determinism of his inscription in the ground thanks to a breath of life that biblical exegesis identifies with breathing and the ability to speak and then write in order to arrive at individuation and the necessarily written reformulation of his own history. Such is the myth revived or transformed in a secular way by science fiction literature and its sub-genres, which perceive writing as an "engineering that treats languages and substantifies them into a physical body that carries the signs, inspires the emergence of the human according to its operations and makes of him a

---

[28] "quelque analogie entre les modalités de l'émergence de l'humain et le système d'écriture qui note la langue dans laquelle il fut rédigé" (Herrenschmidt 193).

[29] "la métaphore du modelage commune à la Mésopotamie, à la Grèce et à Israël" (Herrenschmidt 202).

[30] "L'Adam prototypal, fabriqué à partir d'une glaise du sol humidifié, fait corps par son nom, qui n'est pas encore un nom propre puisqu'il est déterminé par l'article, avec ce sol: dans la langue hébraïque Adam (*'dam*), 'Homme spécifique', et 'sol' (*'adamah*) sont apparentés; le mythe met en scène la parenté linguistique" (Herrenschmidt 201).

double artifact, at the same time human creature (…) and [a] text-creature, [a] humanoid engineering"[31] (Herrenschmidt 218) whose Promethean screens seek a priori the computer or genetic double and which gives substance to a *fictional remediation* that I will study further on in this chapter.

METAPHORS AND METALEPSES OF THE OPEN SYMBOLISM OF THE BOOK

If the "becoming mutant" of Élisabeth Vonarburg's characters also is tied to the symbolism of the book, it is however quite different since it is, so to speak, based on its openness.

In *The Silent City*, the humanity portrayed at the beginning of the novel, which is a post-apocalyptic pastoral narrative, is divided into two main groups. On the one hand, there are many "primitive" men who have regressed on almost all levels, and on the other, there is a group of scientists who live hidden in an underground city in order to prolong their existence through a few robots and to exploit the fear they inspire in the so-called "primitives" in order to carry out experiments of genetic regeneration. First perceived as a laboratory project, Elisa is considered as the "fruit" of one of these experiments of genetic regeneration which has been so successful that its designer, Paul, says that her birth places her and the "Project" she embodies at the periphery of the tree of evolution:

> The baby squirms under his caress. Paul lifts one of the miniature hands, looks closely as it closes on his index, and gives a little tug. Such a strong grip for such tiny fingers. *You're not in a tree now, you're at the end of evolution. Do you know that, you technogenitic miracle? No, of course you don't*[32] (Vonarburg, *The Silent City* 11).

At the "other end of the evolution" of this tree, which is also a tree of knowledge, Elisa emerges as the character of "disaffection," and her

---

[31] "…ingénierie qui traite les langues et les substantifie en un corps physique qui porte les signes, inspire l'émergence de l'humain selon ses opérations et fait de lui un double artefact, à la fois créature humaine (…) et [un] texte-créature, [une] ingénierie humanoïde" (Herrenschmidt 218).

[32] "Le bébé gigote sous la caresse. Paul prend une main minuscule, la regarde se refermer sur son index, tire un peu. Une prise si tenace, pour de si petits doigts… *Tu n'es pas dans un arbre, tu es à l'autre bout de l'évolution, le sais-tu, miracle de la technogénétique? Mais non, bien sûr*" (Vonarburg, *Le silence de la cité* 14).

apprenticeship lies in the fact that throughout the novel she effectively disaffects herself from the influence of the "stories" as well as the computer and genetic programming of two men, Richard and Paul, whom she calls grandfather and father respectively, at the beginning of her life. The interest of the narrative of this disaffection is that it is inscribed in a feminist perspective which corresponds, still using Domon's terminology, to "an authentic restitution of the rumor, extremely 'written' but opposed to the notion of the book [in its symbolism], seeking to reclaim the surplus of the spoken word according to a modern theme of opening rather than closing."[33] While continuing to make use of the metaphors (tree of knowledge and circle), the originality of this opening lies in the use of fictional ontological metalepses[34] to transcribe the changes that matter most to the focal character of Elisa.

Several remarks are necessary on this kind of metalepsis. First, they disrupt the readers' participation in the storyworld that they construct for themselves throughout the pages of the novel, and these metalepses interfere with, or more precisely divert, in the perspective of interest here, the emotional or sentimental transfer—which is a game of metaphors—towards a reflection on the limits of the storyworld that these readers have in mind and that they compare to the actuality of a world that they perceive as the expression of their reality. The objective of these metalepses is therefore to insinuate a doubt about the boundary that distinguishes these two worlds and to suggest to readers that they could be fictitious or fictional entities comparable to the characters whose paths they observe, as summarized by Marie-Laure Ryan:

> Metaleptic texts make us *play* with the idea that we are fictional, the product of a mind that inhabits, a world closer to the ground level than we do, but they cannot turn themselves into the command language that scripts our lives, into the matrix of irreality that envelopes our existence, and in the end, they cannot shake our conviction that we inhabit the only world that exists "for real," because this world is the one that we inhabit corporeally. We can

---

[33] "…une authentique restitution de la rumeur, extrêmement 'écrite' mais opposée à la notion de livre [dans son symbolisme], cherchant à reconquérir le surplus de la parole selon une thématique moderne de l'ouverture plutôt que de la clôture" (Domon 24).

[34] "Ontological metalepsis' occurs when character, author or narrator are relocated across the boundary of the fictional world; 'rhetorical metalepsis', when they only glance or address each other across this boundary" (Kukkonen and Klimek 2).

visit other worlds in imagination, but our bodies tie us to the base of the stack (Ryan, *Avatars of Story* 230).

In relation to the question of computer and/or genetic coding, these same metalepses are thus considered ontological and it is for this reason that they predominate in *The Silence of the City* each time Elisa dreams of being absorbed by a "pink blob"[35] (Vonarburg, *The Silent City* 17), which represents the City as a numerical matrix governing the lives of its inhabitants, or that she finds herself overwhelmed by the expression of her feelings. The emotional outbursts, in this second case, which use the metaphor of the knot to translate in a few words the condition of a metaleptic disaffection are undoubtedly the most interesting on this precise topic. In Vonarburg's writings, it seems that the knot refers to this "desire for a sphere, totality, capacity, [and] receptacle"[36] (Domon 89) thwarted by a sudden awareness that in some way wishes to surpass it. This is why Elisa feels "a knot of anger"[37] that in the official English translation of the book has been reformulated to read, "[a]nger swells in Elisa's chest" (Vonarburg, *The Silent City* 86) before she murders Paul in order to free herself definitively from his influence. And it is this feeling, preceded by a strong feeling of anguish, which is a sign in her eyes that she belongs to the human condition, however mutant and androgynous she may be:

She lies down, but the tight knot of anxiety holds her sleepless. She knows she can control her body, eradicate the emotion, but it would be a lie. No, she must accept the anxiety, study the reason for it, admit she's human. She's done it hundreds of times in the last four years[38] (Vonarburg, *The Silent City* 73).

The ambiguity of the feelings translated by these "threaded metaphors" that assume a metaleptic transgression is explained by two other texts by Élisabeth Vonarburg. The first is an article I already discussed in Chap. 2, which describes the condition of "ontological artifacts" where, she writes,

---

[35] "masse rose" (Vonarburg, *Le silence de la cité* 25).

[36] "… désir de sphère, de totalité, de contenance, [et] de réceptacle" (Domon 89).

[37] "… un nœud de colère" (Vonarburg, *Le silence de la cité* 113).

[38] "Elle se couche, mais le nœud d'angoisse ne se défait pas. Elle sait qu'elle pourrait contrôler son corps, effacer cette émotion, mais ce serait un mensonge. Non, il faut accepter cette angoisse, en examiner la cause, accepter d'être humaine" (Vonarburg, *Le silence de la cité* 110).

for "all, female and male artifacts, the desired evolution goes from dependence-subjection to liberation: to become, so to speak, auto-artifacts by integrating and transcending these different fabrication plans" (Vonarburg, "Les femmes en tant qu'artefactes dans la science-fiction moderne" 155). The second text is a short story entitled "The Knot" which gives her previous theoretical considerations a more fictional consistency:

> They don't tell you a lot, in the Center, but they talk to you of the universes. The universes that the Bridge opens to us are... like a tree born of multiple roots. Its trunk divides itself in multiple branches; each knot of the causality makes another possible one shoot up, one which is another tree, with multiple branches, each tree studded with knots and with branches, too. It is not really a tree, however, it does not bear either leaves or fruits, and it doesn't grow straight in front of itself: at the end of its innumerable offshoots, it may be its roots that grow, and it perpetuates itself thus, our tree-to-universe, born of itself and closed on itself [...] And this universe exists because it is the one that I came back to. I am the knot.[39]

Because it entails a permanent metaleptic transgression, this metaphor of the knot, sometimes a relay between the branches of a tree and sometimes a point of contact between the ramifications of a network, continues to clarify for Elisa the expression of anguish and anger in many other scenes where computer science and the idea of coding literally refer to the tree of knowledge in *Genesis*. In the City, "at the garden gate, [...] the communication column disguised as a tree"[40] (Vonarburg, *The Silent City* 53) teaches Elisa in the voice of a computerized "grandfather" avatar that Paul has gone crazy and that for this reason she must go into exile. Then, once she is back from that painful exile that inspired her to commit a mur-

---

[39] "Ils ne vous disent pas grand-chose, au Centre, mais ils vous parlent des univers. Les univers que nous ouvre le Pont sont... comme un arbre né de multiples racines. Son tronc se divise en multiples branches; chaque nœud de la causalité fait jaillir un autre possible, qui est un autre arbre, aux branches multiples, constellées elles aussi de nœuds et de branches. Ce n'est pas vraiment un arbre, cependant, il ne porte ni feuilles ni fruits, et il ne pousse pas droit devant lui: au bout de ses innombrables ramifications, ce sont peut-être ses racines qui poussent, et il se perpétue ainsi, notre arbre-à-univers, né de lui-même et refermé sur lui-même, (...) Et cet univers-ci existe parce que c'est celui où je suis revenue. Je suis le nœud" (Vonarburg, *Le jeu des coquilles de nautilus* 194–195).

[40] "... à l'entrée du jardin, la colonne de communication, déguisée en arbre" (Vonarburg, *Le silence de la cité* 83).

der, it is again "in the little garden beside the communication-tree"[41] (Vonarburg, *The Silent City* 91) that the same avatar leaves her alone to make the decision to close or to continue using the City.

Finally, in the end of the novel, on the battlefield which opposes an army of women with an army of men, it is "[w]ithin the magic circle around the apple tree"[42] (Vonarburg, *The Silent City* 193) which joins together the bodies of two previously married warlords, that Elisa, in her male form, gains some essential insight. Wounded by a bullet, she dreams, which allows her to pierce the mystery of the computer matrix on which she still depends in order to move away from it: "She perceives the whole City, like a gigantic, multicellular organism stretching its pseudopods in all directions, numberless ducts wherein the breath and blood of the City circulates, the infinitely ramified networks of electronic circuits, the eyes and ears of the City"[43] (Vonarburg, *The Silent City* 194).

Elisa's becoming mutant, which occurs in this passage in which the metaphors of the tree and the circle shift to that of the metaphor of the knot, is a literary treatment that could be illustrated by a precise concept borrowed from information and communication sciences. This concept, which I reformulated and to which I gave a fictional meaning, is that of *remediation*,[44] in the sense that the book in the symbolism of its closure could be remediated by the code in an opening to programming or to a reticular coding applied to the network device. Before explaining how the fictional illustrations of this concept also summarize almost all the semiotic considerations underlying the idea of a resistant humanity, it is necessary to note with Peter Stockwell that the poetics of science fiction has this singularity that it often conceives of metaphors in their literal sense:

> The construction of such alternative (views of) realities is the business of science fiction. From a moving time-machine, the sun *is* 'a streak of fire, a

---

[41] "… dans le jardin, près de l'arbre-console" (Vonarburg, *Le silence de la cité* 141).

[42] "… dans un cercle magique autour du pommier" (Vonarburg, *Le silence de la cité* 298).

[43] "elle perçoit [alors] toute la Cité, comme un gigantesque organisme multicellulaire qui étend ses pseudopodes dans toutes les directions—les innombrables conduits par ou circulent le souffle et le sang de la Cité, le réseau infiniment ramifié des circuits électroniques, les yeux et les oreilles de la Cité" (Vonarburg, *Le silence de la cité* 300).

[44] "In *The Soft Edge* (1997), Paul Levinson uses the term *remediation* to describe how one medium reforms another (104–114). Levinson's intriguing theory is teleological: media develop "anthropotropically"—that is, to resemble the human. For Levinson, remediation is an agent of this teleological evolution, as we invent media that improve on the limits of prior media" (Bolter and Grusin 59).

brilliant arch' (Wells 1953: 24); in a science fictional universe, emotions *can* be dialled (Dick 1972: 8–9); stars, planets, ships and computers can be animate and intelligent, and abstract concepts can be dramatised in narrative. Fundamentally, science fiction literalises metaphors (Stockwell 196).

What, then, should we think about the metaphors that apply to the characters in my selected texts and whether they can be remediated or not? My hypothesis is that any change implying the perspective of reification, or the idea of coding, is for our imagination a remediation of the metaphor of the *liber mundi* which mobilizes in all its paradigmatic extension the books of life, nature, the world, and the universe, and translates, from the point of view of these same characters, into the ambivalence of a longing and a refusal to be written. As defined by Paul Levinson in his essay *The Soft Edge: A Natural History and Future of the Information Revolution*, this hypothesis is largely based on an anthropological conception of the media and their use, including the imagination of science fiction, which plays with the idea of a remediation of body and mind and for which we would be a *narrative species*. In *The Roots of Civilization*, as "Alexander Marshack (1972) puts it, humans are a story-telling species. We can be defined in contrast to other species by the fact that we weave ourselves in narratives; and we can be distinguished, among ourselves, by the kinds of narratives we weave" (Levinson 86).

The fictional remediation of the body and mind is the one that most concerns science fiction. Contrary to Solman's character, who considers for a time the possibility of being remediated by the "Verb," a computer program adapted from a literal reading of the *Apocalypse*, but who refuses to do so in order to destroy it at the price of his own life, Elisa's character somehow accepts being a remediated "fruit" of the tree of knowledge, if she can maintain a certain distance and also conceive of its autonomy, an approach which stems from Vonarburg's feminist perspective. This choice is one that Marie/Viviane cannot make once she realizes that she is a clone growing from the *souche* of a tree that nearly rejects her singularity and certainly instrumentalizes her; indeed, she explains in detail, "We don't think enough about what a tree is. Indeed, the root of the word clone is the Greek word for κλών, which means 'twig'"[45] (Darrieussecq, *Our Life in the Forest* 79). The French word *souche* is polysemous, meaning not just

---

[45] « On ne pense pas assez à ce que c'est un arbre. D'ailleurs le mot clone a pour racine le grec κλών qui veut dire « jeune pousse » (Darrieussecq, *Notre vie dans les forêts roman* 103).

the base of a tree (a stock (as it is translated in the English version of the novel) or stump), but also an ancestor from whom descendants are born and the origin of something. Thus, when Marie-Viviane explains that the cliker has told her that clones are grown from old rich people who are called "*souches*," the richness of this extended metaphor is emphasized, in that the clones are the twigs stemming from these *souches*:

> Judging from the average age of those old, rich creatures, whom we call (so the clicker told me) the pureblood stock, there is not just one but several Generations, so instead of refereeing to halves, we have to say thirds, or quarters, probably even tenths. They use one clone, then two, then three, then four, et cetera. They dissect them one after the other [...] Only the planet's super-rich can afford clones (Darrieussecq, *Our Life in the Forest* 140).[46]

Here, the remediation of the self-image is tied to the body, as well as self-perception, thus situating this book at the edge of the speculative fiction genre. The reason for this is that the remediation of the self-image, which precedes those of the body and the mind, is at the heart of the debates of speculative fiction, in that it anticipates an enterprise of reification of the human race which would precede a dystopian remediation of the body. In the two works of speculative fiction, *Globalia* and *The First Century After Beatrice*, we can see a closing of the book's symbolism. This is how Baikal and Puig in *Globalia*, as well as the narrator of Maalouf's novel, turn away from the "screens" on the grounds that screens trap them in a propaganda discourse, not to mention, of course, the electronic eye and the general surveillance from which Viviane turns away in *Our Life in the Forest*. In short, the remediation of the self-image by new media is fought all the more by these characters as the mediation by the book is a guarantee of humanity and resistance.

Finally, transfictions combine the remediation of the body and the self-image in the most intriguing way possible. In *The Possibility of an Island* and *Songes de Mevlido*, the remediation of the bodies of their respective focal characters is presented as if it could no longer be the subject of any

---

[46] "Au vu de l'âge général de ces vieillards riches, qu'on nomme (m'a dit le cliqueur) *les souches*, il n'y a pas une, mais plusieurs générations, donc il ne faut pas parler de moitiés mais de tiers ou de quarts, voire probablement de dixièmes. Ils usent un clone puis deux puis trois puis quatre, etc. Ils les dépiautent en série. (...) Seuls les super-riches de la planètes peuvent se payer des clones" (Darrieussecq, *Notre vie dans les forêts roman* 176).

real debate, unlike Solman's or Elisa's journeys. The series of Daniels and Mevlido have indeed already been remediated against their wills, and it is all the energy those characters put into finding meaning in the fragmentation of their self-image that causes the reader to reflect on the loss of their humanity. Bearing in mind they are more (*textual*) *corpuses* than *mutant bodies*, nothing that physically constitutes them can be reversed; although driven by the promise and rumor of technological remediation, they are and remain "written" at the limits of the *liber mundi* paradigm.

What are these limits in *The Possibility of an Island* and how are they expanded by the joint use of ontological metalepses and metaphors as expressions of the openness of the symbolism of the book? The pleasant surprise with Michel Houellebecq's novel is that the biblical referent changes. It is no longer explicitly informed by the metaphor of the tree and its associations with knowledge, although it is broadened in the dreams that characterize the characters of Daniel and his clones:

> ...our dreams could be insights into other *branches of the universe*, [...] i.e., other bifurcations of observable phenomena that appeared at the same time as certain events in the day [...] According to other interpretations, some of our dreams are of a different order from those experienced by mankind; of artificial origin, they are the spontaneous productions of mental half-forms engendered by the modifiable interweaving of the electronic elements of the network. A gigantic organism could have demanded to be born, to form a common electronic consciousness,... (Houellebecq 155–156)[47] (my italics).

Explicitly, the titles of the chapters from Daniel 1:1 to Daniel 1:28 can be understood as intertextual references to the book of the prophet Daniel, known for his ability to interpret dreams but also for his apocalyptic visions of the resurrection of the dead mentioning "open books"[48] (Daniel 7:10),

---

[47] "... nos rêves seraient des aperçus sur d'autres *branches d'univers existantes* (C'est moi qui souligne) (...), c'est-à-dire d'autres bifurcations d'observables apparues à l'occasion de certains événements de la journée (...). D'après d'autres interprétations, certains de nos songes sont d'un autre ordre que ceux qu'on a pu connaître les hommes; d'origine artificielle, ils sont les productions spontanées de demi-formes mentales engendrées par l'entrelacement modifiable des éléments électroniques du réseau. Un organisme gigantesque demanderait à naître, à former une conscience électronique commune,..." (Houellebecq, *La possibilité d'une île—Prix Interallié 2005* 220).

[48] "A river of fire was flowing and went out before Him. Thousands upon thousands ministered to Him, and myriad upon myriad stood before Him. The court was seated and the books were opened" (Alter 778).

the books of life and death, of which only "the book of life" will be taken up again with a view to a final judgment by the Christian canon (Revelation 20:11–15). But more implicitly Daniel24's belief in the "Return of the Humid [that] will be the sign of the coming of the Future Ones"[49] (Houellebecq, *The Possibility of an Island* 79), a belief that is adopted and commented on by his double Daniel25 who throws himself, at the end of the novel, into the sea to survive. This belief also invites readers to reread *Genesis* in order to remember that the "prototypal Adam," as the archaeologist Clarisse Herrenschmidt calls him, is that creature, made or rather molded from a word and a piece of clay, fashioned from water vapor rising from the earth (*Genesis* 2:5–8), which then precipitated the creation of the Garden of Eden.[50] From this mythical point of view, the story of Daniel24 and Daniel25 is thus the story of a mysterious, collective, literal drying up, which makes Daniel24 say that the "Great Drying up was a necessary parable, teaches the Supreme Sister; a theological condition for the Return of the Humid"[51] (Houellebecq, *The Possibility of an Island* 79), a statement that is to be read and elucidated in the story of the individual disappointment of Daniel25 as a "creature-text" (Herrenschmidt 218) that remains dry:

> As I consider the night sky my thoughts turn to the Elohim, to that strange belief that was finally, in a roundabout away, to unleash the Great Transformation. Daniel1 lives again in me, his body knows in mine a new incarnation, his thoughts are mine; his memories are mine; his existence actually prolongs itself in me, far more than man ever dreamed of prolonging himself through his descendants. My own life, however, I often think, is

[49] Le "Retour de l'Humide [qui] sera le signe de l'avènement des Futurs" (Houellebecq 113).

[50] "On the day the LORD God made earth and heavens, no shrub of the field being yet on the earth and no plant of the field yet sprouted, for the LORD God had not caused rain to fall on the earth and there was no human to till the soil, and wetness would well the earth to water all the surface of the soil, then the LORD God fashioned the human, humus from the soil, and blew into his nostrils the breath of life, and the human became a living creature. And the LORD God planted a garden in Eden, to the east, and He placed there the human He had fashioned" (Alter 13–14).

[51] "Le Grand Assèchement était une parabole nécessaire, enseigne la Sœur suprême; une condition théologique au Retour de l'Humide. La durée du Grand Assèchement sera longue, enseigne également la Sœur suprême" (Houellebecq 113).

far from the one he would have liked to live (Houellebecq, *The Possibility of an Island* 288).[52]

For Daniel25, who speaks these disillusioned words, the drying up of the neohumans is part of a remediation that has obviously gone wrong and that results from a confrontation between two writing practices practiced by the clones of Daniel1 and his companions. On the one hand, "life stories" are supposed to correct and improve neohumans, in relation to the desires of the one whose memory they perpetuate, from an initial remediation to an intermediation, then from one intermediation to another until the advent of a digital future where they would exist only as computer avatars. While on the other hand, the practice of poetry revives the memory of these same desires that, in the amplification of the rumor of a reticular writing, are consecrated by the disintegration of the self-image and then the wandering of these neohumans. The metaleptic aspect of this drying up is particularly well illustrated by the exchange of snapshots of life between the clones of Daniel1 and those of Marie1 who make use, in the absence of any physical contact, of a network that transforms the little sexual desire they maintain into sources of anxiety, as is shown at the beginning of the novel through Marie22's message:

12, 12, 533, 8467.
The second message from Marie22 was worded thus:
I am alone like a silly cunt
With my
Cunt
245535, 43, 3. When I say "I," I am lying. Let us posit the "I" of perception—neutral and limpid. Put it next to the "I" of intermediation—when you look at it this way, my body belongs to me; or, more exactly, I belong to my body. What do we observe? An absence of contact.

---

[52] "Il m'arrive en considérant le ciel nocturne de songer aux Elohim, a cette étrange croyance qui devait finalement, par des voies détournées, déclencher la Grande Transformation. Daniel1 revit en moi, son corps y connait une nouvelle incarnation, ses pensées sont les miennes, ses souvenirs les miens; son existence se prolonge réellement en moi, bien plus qu'aucun homme n'a jamais rêvé se prolonger à travers sa descendance. Ma propre vie pourtant, j'y pense souvent, est bien loin d'être celle qu'il aurait aimé vivre" (Houellebecq 405–406).

Fear what I say (Houellebecq, *The Possibility of an Island* 7–8).[53]

These encrypted sequences introduced by a network addressing of the IP (Internet Protocol) type are significant because they maintain a metaleptic relationship with the poem and its commentary, to the extent that they "entangle the level of the textual data and that of the instructions which make them visible to the reader";[54] this amounts, according to Marie-Laure Ryan, to a reflection on human language that sketches out a poetry of code based on the hierarchical nature of computer architecture in its information processing. The originality of such poetry as "a new idiom that will erase the difference between the human and the machine"[55] is undoubtedly to amplify the weight and scope of the metaphors that literally weigh down the consciousness of neohumans, as in the example of this poem by Mary23 sent to Daniel25, which shortly precedes the announcement of Mary23's defection from the neohuman community: "*The burdened membranes / Of our waking dreams / Have the muffled charm / Of sunless days*"[56] (Houellebecq, *The Possibility of an Island* 265).

The metaphorization that can be read in this neohuman poem is emblematic of a process that evolved between Daniel1, Mary1, and their "descendants," in that it appears to be essentially deceptive. As Roger Célestin noted, "in Proust the metaphor communicates *with an afterlife*. In contrast, Houellebecq's style is inscribed in *the flat*, in our present where the style must be trimmed, rid of its metaphors in order to be able to reflect this present with a certain degree of success—at least according

---

[53] "12, 12, 533, 8467.
Le second message de Marie22 était ainsi libellé:
Je suis seule comme une conne
Avec mon
Con.
245535, 43, 3. Quand je dis "je", je mens. Posons le "je" de la perception—neutre et limpide. Mettons-le en rapport avec le "je" de l'intermédiation en tant que tel, mon corps m'appartient; ou, plus exactement, j'appartiens à mon corps. Qu'observons-nous? Une absence de contact. Craignez ma parole" (Houellebecq 13–14).

[54] "enchevêtre[ent] le niveau des données textuelles et celui des instructions qui les rendent visibles au lecteur" (Ryan, "Logique culturelle de la métalepse, ou la métalepse dans tous ses états" 216).

[55] "… nouvel idiome qui effacera la différence entre l'humain et la machine" (Ryan, "Logique culturelle de la métalepse, ou la métalepse dans tous ses états" 218).

[56] "*Les membranes alourdies / De nos demi-réveils / Ont le charme assourdi / Des journées sans soleil*" (Houellebecq 374).

to Houellebecq."[57] This is not the trend illustrated by *The Possibility of an Island*, contrary to *Whatever* or *The Elementary Particles*. Why is that? Deprived of their bodies, or more exactly of the singularity of a use of the world through their bodies, it would seem that neohumans were no longer able to understand how metaphorization was part of a cyclical form of writing[58] opposed to the metaleptic and immanent aim of their condition. As a result, like the members of the Eskato in Pierre Bordage's novel *The Last Men*, they are victims of a literal reading of the world, except that the deceptive metaphorization that informs this reading is the cause of their wandering, not of their destruction. Misled by this metaphorization strongly inspired by Esther's love for Daniel, Marie23 followed by Daniel25 are two neohuman characters who cut themselves off from their community of origin in order to leave in search of the mythical island of Lanzarote.

It is this possibility of an island (*"There exists in the midst of time / The possibility of an island"*[59] (Houellebecq, *The Possibility of an Island* 300)) as "the most common figure of the totality, [… the] most perfect illustration of the desire of the sphere"[60] (Domon 75) which, though enlarged to the extreme, will plunge Daniel25 back into the greatest disappointment

---

[57] "chez Proust la métaphore communique avec un *au-delà de la mort*. Par opposition, le style de Houellebecq s'inscrit dans *le plat,* dans notre présent où le style doit être élagué, débarrassé de ses métaphores pour pouvoir avec un certain degré de succès—du moins selon Houellebecq—refléter ce présent" (Clément et al. 345).

[58] Cyclical writing, writes Hélène Domon, is "a taming. It creates essential ties between the book and the universe that spreads out from it. While the sacred book radically establishes the possibility of community, cyclical writing puts into movement and makes turn between them, in their very closing, the three cosmoses that are the book, the human body (of which the eye is the specular organ), and the universe, superposing them to the point that there are no longer three, but one single cosmos that reflects itself infinitely in the two others, in big and in small, 'microcosm' or 'macrocosm'" (Domon 61) [L'écriture cyclique, écrit Hélène Domon, est "un apprivoisement. Elle crée des liens essentiels entre le livre et l'univers qui s'étale à partir de lui. Alors que le livre sacré instaurait radicalement la possibilité de la communauté, l'écriture cyclique met en mouvement et fait tourner entre eux, dans leur clôture même, les trois cosmes que sont le livre, le corps humain (dont l'œil est organe spéculaire) et l'univers, les superposant au point qu'il n'y ait plus trois, mais un seul cosmos qui se reflète à l'infini dans les deux autres, en petit ou en grand, 'microcosme' ou 'macrocosme'" (Domon 61).

[59] *"il existe au milieu du temps / La possibilité d'une île"*] (Houellebecq 424).

[60] "… figure la plus commune de la totalité, (…) illustration la plus parfaite du désir de la sphère" (Domon 75).

as he knows that he "had not found deliverance"[61] (Houellebecq, *The Possibility of an Island* 336) and was reduced to the teachings that the Supreme Sister was giving to Daniel24:

> I now know that I will not finish my commentary. I will leave with no real regret an existence that brought me no real joy. Considering death, we have reached a state of mind that was, according to the monks of Ceylon, the one sought by the Buddhists of the Lesser Vehicle; our life at the moment of its end "is like blowing out a candle." We can also say, to use the words of the Supreme Sister, that our generations follow one another "like flicking the pages of a book" (Houellebecq, *The Possibility of an Island* 116).[62]

In comparison to Houellebecq, Antoine Volodine is more radical in his undertaking of a restitution of the written rumor since in his work this rumor is revolutionary. Volodine is an author who also seeks to "write the outside of the book: to write the rumor of the beginning, the wandering word, the incessant murmur, the muffled roar from the bottom of the being, the chaos, the madness, the abyss..."[63] (Domon 109). In *Songes de Mevlido*, his eponymous character "goes crazy"[64] (102) in his inability to distinguish between dream and reality, and everything is blurred in the succession of fictional ontological metalepses—here the story of his dreams—that describe Mevlido's troubled life. If we reread the remarks made by Daniel25 on the defining character of dreams in the potential formation of a computer network likely to become more autonomous and to resemble a "City," as Elisa understood it at the end of her apprenticeship, we can see that Antoine Volodine does not develop new ideas by

---

[61] "... *j'étais indélivré*" (Houellebecq 473). Let us note that there is a potential wordplay here in French that is extremely hard to translate since the sound of the word *livre* (book) is contained in *indélivré* which literally means "undelivered", as if the physicality of the book was the prison itself.

[62] "Je sais à présent que je n'achèverai pas mon commentaire. Je quitterai sans vrai regret une existence qui ne m'apportait aucune joie effective. Considérant le trépas, nous avons atteint à l'état d'esprit qui était, selon les textes des moines de Ceylan, celui que recherchaient les bouddhistes du Petit Véhicule; notre vie au moment de sa disparition "a le caractère d'une bougie qu'on souffle". Nous pouvons dire aussi, pour reprendre les paroles de la Sœur suprême, que nos générations se succèdent "comme les pages d'un livre qu'on feuillette" (Houellebecq 164).

[63] "...écrire le dehors du livre: écrire la rumeur du commencement, la parole errante, le murmure incessant, le grondement sourd du fond de l'être, le chaos, la folie, l'abîme..." (Domon 109).

[64] "sombre fou..." (Volodine 102).

reducing Mevlido's metaleptic condition to its dreamlike state. Perhaps it would be more accurate to observe that he pushes this condition back into its final retrenchments when the network is no longer figurative other than by the imprint it leaves in the consciousness of his character in the form of a *labyrinth*.

The reiterated scrolling of Mevlido's dreams gives substance to this labyrinth and makes one think, especially after Mevlido's death, of a scaffolding of the "metaleptic process of the feedback loop (or retroactive loop) [to which] artificial intelligence owes the possibility of creating so-called 'emergent' systems, that is, systems producing objects capable of adapting dynamically to their environment or of transforming themselves in an unpredictable manner,"[65] which constitutes a simulated reality for which the text suggests that Mevlido accesses it in reincarnation "by obeying a program etched in the most tortuous layers of his being."[66]

Although Volodine distanced himself from science-fiction as a genre after his fourth novel to work on his formalist and elaborated narratives, the influence of the science fiction model on Volodinian novels remains significant. As Mélanie Lamarre points out, when Volodine was questioned about his science fiction readings, he "mention[ed] a considerable list of names—among them [...] the Americans H.P. Lovecraft, Kurt Vonnegut, Ray Bradbury, Isaac Asimov, Roger Zelazny, Robert Sheckley, Clifford Simak, Lucius Sheppard, Frank Herbert, or J.G. Ballard. These references testify to a dialogue maintained with a vast science-fiction subtext more than with any one author in particular, and images from science fiction permeate his work."[67] With *Mevlido's Dreams* that I termed a "transfiction" in the introduction, the innovative approach of Antoine Volodine, in the spirit of what remains of the scaffolding of these

[65] "...processus métaleptique de la feed-back loop (ou boucle rétroactive) [auquel] l'intelligence artificielle doit la possibilité de créer des systèmes dits 'émergents', c'est-à-dire des systèmes produisant des objets capables de s'adapter dynamiquement à leur environnement ou de se transformer de manière imprévisible" (Ryan, "Logique culturelle de la métalepse, ou la métalepse dans tous ses états" 214).

[66] "en obéissant à un programme gravé dans les plus tortueuses couches de son être" (Volodine 267).

[67] "Antoine Volodine mentionne une liste considérable de noms–parmi lesquels (...) les Américains H.P. Lovecraft, Kurt Vonnegut, Ray Bradbury, Isaac Asimov, Roger Zelazny, Robert Sheckley, Clifford Simak, Lucius Sheppard, Frank Herbert ou J.G. Ballard. Ces références témoignent d'un dialogue entretenu avec un vaste sous-texte science-fictionnel plus qu'avec un auteur en particulier, et les images venues de la science-fiction imprègnent son œuvre,..." (Lamarre 35).

"retroactive loops," appears to inscribe the exhaustion of his character at the heart of an imaginary qualified as post-exotic made of shamanic magic, interrogations, and a triangulation between author, narrator, and character: "Mevlido was programmed to incarnate in a baby man, but the incarnation took place at a calamitous period in human history, even more calamitous than the others, since it marks the beginning of a prolonged death throes for the species."[68]

To do this, Volodine was informed by the treatise *The Tibetan Book of the Dead* (the *Bardo Thödol*), not because he granted any spiritual prevalence to this branch of Buddhism, but because the shamanism from which he draws his inspiration determines the main orientations of his poetic imagination. If there is a science fiction book and author that particularly emphasize *The Tibetan Book of the Dead* to the point of making it appear as a paradigm of the *liber mundi*, it is indeed that of Philipp Dick in his *Ubik* (and consequently, a reference to a significant science fiction subtext concerning simulated reality). Furthermore, as I have already explained, *Ubik*, among other of Dick's novels, was an inspiration for the sub-genre of transfiction novels. Besides the frequent mention of *The Tibetan Book of Death* in both *Songes de Mevlido* and *Ubik*, the points they have in common are numerous. First of all, there is against a backdrop of outdated technology, this "half-life" experience, as Dick terms it, is "an unnatural place, [...]. Halfway between the world and death" (Dick 92) that refers to a state of "Ubiquity" (Dick 132); it is in just such a state that Mevlido's murder occurs. Another similarity between Dick's and Volodine's works is that both include a common empowered enemy embodied by the moon. In addition, Dick's and Volodine's characters evolve in altered realities in which they communicate between two worlds using poetic sentences that pop up randomly as warnings or calls to action, even if at the end of both novels only an experience of time with multiple layers that embraces the traumatic dimensions of the human condition matters, which makes one of *Ubik*'s protagonists say: "The past is latent, is submerged, but still there, capable of rising to the surface once the later imprinting unfortunately— and against ordinary experience—vanished. The man contains—not the boy—but earlier men, [...]. History began a long time ago" (Dick 138–139). It is within this scope that, according to *The Tibetan Book of the*

---

[68] "Mevlido a été programmé pour s'incarner dans un bébé homme, mais l'incarnation s'est effectuée à une période calamiteuse de l'histoire humaine, encore plus calamiteuse que les autres, puisqu'elle marque le début d'une agonie prolongée de l'espèce" (Volodine 267).

Dead, "death is not an end, but the beginning of another existence according to altered modalities, which can itself know a term, then be prolonged on another plane, until the definitive death of the individual."[69] If there is a metaphorical focus of the human in this condition, it is around light and flames that we see in *Songes de Mevlido.* This light cannot be reflected in the example of the moon, which strangely attracts threats of attacks on it, suspected as it is of metamorphosing "the night into a dream."[70] It must set fire to—and bring together in the same metalepsis—a character and its author, like Mevlido and Mingrelian in the most metafictional aspect of this novel:

> The boiler rumbled on the lower floor.
> It rumbled thus until Mevlido dozed off, and, even then, the vibration continued, the music of the flames did not fall silent, this melody of destruction and travel that in any case is in us, from the beginning, and which at the moment of sleeping everyone confuses sometimes with his own existence, sometimes with his own death.
> "The music of the flames did not fall silent," Mingrelian wrote later in his report, "this melody of destruction and travel, this guttural, harmonious, regular, likely to make the unknown and the unknowable understood and loved, this somber clamor which in any case is in us, has always been in us."[71]

And it is to this fiery clamor, outside the closing of the book and its symbolism, that, at the end of the novel, Volodine / Mingrelian / Mevlido will entrust the meaning of the action: "LITTLE SISTERS DRESSED IN FLAMES, UNDRESS, STRIKE!"[72]

---

[69] "...la mort n'est pas une fin, mais le début d'une autre existence selon des modalités altérées, qui peut elle-même connaître un terme, puis se prolonger sur un autre plan, jusqu'au décès définitif de l'individu" (Ruffel 206).

[70] "la nuit en rêve" (Volodine 151).

[71] "La chaudière grondait à l'étage inférieur.
Elle gronda ainsi jusqu'à ce que Mevlido s'assoupisse, et, même alors, la vibration se prolongea, la musique des flammes ne se tut pas, cette mélodie de destruction et de voyage qui de toute façon est en nous, depuis toujours, et qu'au moment du sommeil chacun confond tantôt avec sa propre existence, tantôt avec sa propre mort.
La musique des flammes ne se tut pas, écrivit plus tard Mingrelian dans son rapport, cette mélodie de destruction et de voyage, ce chant guttural, harmonieux, régulier, propre à faire comprendre et aimer l'inconnu et l'inconnaissance, cette clameur sombre qui de toute façon repose en nous depuis toujours..." (Volodine 223).

[72] "PETITES SŒURS HABILLÉES DE FLAMMES, DÉVÊTEZ-VOUS, FRAPPEZ!" (Volodine 462).

METAMORPHOSES AND HUMAN MUTATIONS: THE RELATIONSHIP TO INSECT ANIMALISM

The figure of insects and spiders represents a break in the remediation process I have just described because it calls into question the idea of the exercise of a unitary consciousness [73] shaping the human race. This last section of this chapter questions how this figure of insects and spiders sheds light on the meaning of human mutations with regard to the symbolism of the book of nature and the book of the world, and then what their metamorphosis or hybridization reveals to the characters facing them in this selection of novels. The animality of insects and spiders is often presented as a form of sociality so independent from that of humans that it becomes a competitor. More numerous, preceding the emergence of any form of human civilization, and undoubtedly still of this world if we were to disappear, insects and spiders intrigue us in that their collective intelligence develops in symbiosis with nature, whereas the human species struggles to organize itself there. Even if literature and cinema relay insects' and spiders' characteristics, the interest of these animals as they are represented mainly rests, from my point of view, elsewhere in another function in that they *prefigure*, in the literal sense of the term, a reflection on genetic and computer coding.

In these works, as in English-speaking science fiction works of the cyberpunk and post-cyberpunk movements, it is clear that the representations of the stakes related to genetics, data processing, and data processing networking are often accompanied by the presence of insects and spiders which define the enigmatic feature of the worlds that the characters experience, sometimes frightened, sometimes fascinated, by the essential otherness that these animals end up having in their own apprehension of the world.

While "[c]onfused images of wasps and spiders rose in Case's mind..." (Gibson 182), when this young hacker evolves within a computer "[m]atrix" in William Gibson's *Neuromancer*, the representation of insects

---

[73] "Swarms, metamorphoses, and weird sensations are easily produced by digital technologies of imaging, but this theme is not reducible to technological possibilities. Hence, there is also a philosophical side to these simple animals, (...) The insect becomes a philosophical figure for a cultural analysis of the nonhuman basics of media technological modernity, labeled not by the conscious unity of Man but by the swarming, distributed intelligence of insects, collective agents, and uncanny potentials of the 'autonomity of affect'" (Parikka XXXV).

and spiders culminates in Dan Simmons' more recent novel series *The Hyperion Cantos*. As a character, whose personality and memory are the exact computerized replica of the poet John Keats, discovers his origins, he manages to give an explanation of the conflict that opposes a mutant humanity with insectoid forms, that of the "Ousters," evolving in swarms in interstellar space, to a more traditional human race that has renounced mutations and has regrouped in an expansionist and conquering confederation called "Hegemony." What does the character discover? In summary, he finds that the artificial intelligence programs that make up a "TechnoCore" want to eliminate all forms of humanity, mutant or not, and that thwarting the purpose of this entity implies dislodging it from the computer and teletransportation network that the inhabitants of the Hegemony use permanently, while knowing that such a network resembles "an elaborate latticework of singularity-spun environments in which the TechnoCore AIs move like wondrous spiders, their own 'machines,' the billions of human minds tapped into their datasphere at any second" (Simmons 415).

Insects and spiders reveal a conception of the world in the continuity of which many possible worlds in science fiction literature are inscribed, but what is this conception? Regardless of the technological and scientific variations that science fiction authors can imagine, this conception could refer to a collective representation elaborated in philosophy, theology, and literature from Antiquity to the Renaissance, which states that nature, the world, and life are the result of writing and narratives whose main form has become, in the long run, that of the *book*.

In his chapter "The Book as Symbol" from his seminal work, *European Literature and the Middle Ages*, Ernst Robert Curtius thus recalls that the wisdom of insects astounded Renaissance thinkers who were careful to learn "to read in the book of nature or the world" (Curtius et al. 319) and that a commentator like Sir Thomas Brown in his *Religio Medici* (1643) went so far as to perceive an intelligence superior to our own in these most minute animals:

> Indeed, what Reason may not go to the school of Bees, Ants, and Spiders? What wise hand teacheth to do what Reason cannot teach us? [...] in these narrow Engines there is more curious Mathematicks; and the civility of these little Citizens more neatly sets forth the Wisdom of their Maker... (Curtius et al. 323).

During the seventeenth century, the Dutch biologist Jan Swammerdam assimilated the history of the evolution of insects with the very idea of the composition of the book of nature itself in a treaty of insect anatomy translated in English as *The Book of Nature, or, The History of Insects.*[74] In addition, under the influence of Galileo, Swammerdam conceived of the universe as a great book "written in a mathematical language, and the characters are triangles, circles, and other geometrical figures" (Curtius et al. 324). Furthermore, scientific observations of these insects were then also enriched by optical techniques such as the microscope, and from the Enlightenment period onwards, these optical techniques anchored the scientific imagination in the field of scopic knowledge that constantly pushed back the limits of the observation of these animals with "curious mathematics." My hypothesis is that in the most contemporary actualizations of the "conjectural novelistic treatment of the 'images of science'"[75] (Langlet 168) to which science fiction literature lends itself, insects and spiders embody in an expressionist manner the ideograms, the alphabet, or the coding of a determinism peculiar to the symbolism of the book of nature and the world; the specificity of this figure is interesting in that it is not only found in traditional French and Francophone mainstream science fiction, but also inspires the general literature influenced by the subgenres of speculative fiction and transfiction.

On this subject, science fiction makes the figure of insects and spiders a recurring motif. The insects in Pierre Bordage's novel *The Last Men* foreshadow a reflection on genetic coding as well as on the intentions that promote their dissemination. In this story, where the insects are first described as a biological weapon used during a third world war, the picture presented by Solman, a young man endowed with the faculty of clairvoyance to protect the "water people" to which he belongs, is reminiscent of the *Bible*'s phraseology when it comes to "plagues" and "calamities":

Solman had heard of grasshoppers[GM], like all Aquariot children, but until then, they had never had any reality in his eyes, they had always seemed to him to belong to that phantasmagorical bestiary from which the Aquariots populated their stories and their songs. [...] The old ones affirmed that the armies of the two camps, after having taken the precaution to protect

[74] Swammerdam, Jan, 1637–1680. *The Book of Nature, or, The History of Insects*. London: C.G. Seyffert, 1758. https://digital.lib.usu.edu/digital/collection/History_sci/id/71.
[75] "traitement romanesque conjectural des 'images de la science'" (Langlet 168).

themselves from the lethal stings with the appropriate vaccinations, had used the insects as exterminating legions during the Third World War.[76]

Yet the entire plot of this work revolves precisely around the question of the extent to which insects foreshadow the "final judgment" of a conclusive apocalyptic episode, which a criminal organization of now-posthuman scientists has long planned so as to eradicate what remains of humanity in its original form. Perhaps the originality of Bordage is to have enlarged at the end of the novel the faculty of metamorphosis of these insects on the horizon of a world in suspense, a new Eden or a guaranteed hell, depending on whether the characters belong to this posthumanity that I have just mentioned, or to the community of the last men who have to face them to survive:

> The plain provided false information about the distances, seeming sometimes to shorten them to better lengthen them the following instant. They crossed veritable hails of insects of all sizes and of all forms that were relentlessly preparing the coming of a new worldly order.[77]

This world presented as the parousia of a completion between mutants and a matrix computer citadel that came to sit in the heart of a deep forest before embarking on the extermination of human groups excluded from it, is one that Solman puts in check. By his sacrifice in acting with the help of other members of his community of origin like a virus within this grouping, if he resists a regeneration of the insectoid type within this matrix, it is because this implied the elimination of his memory and his identity. The terror inspired by the figure of the insect in science fiction is thus due to a symbiotic determinism, as if what was better organized, better programmed, or finally better written—of which the figure of the insect is in every way paradigmatic—was tainted by a perfectly inhuman

---

[76] "Solman avait entendu parler des sauterelles^GM, comme tout enfant aquariote, mais jusqu'alors elles n'avaient recouvré aucune réalité à ses yeux, elles lui avaient semblé appartenir à ce bestiaire fantasmagorique dont les Aquariotes peuplaient leurs récits et leurs chants. (…) Les anciens affirmaient que les armées des deux camps, après avoir pris la précaution de se prémunir des piqûres mortelles avec des vaccins appropriés, avaient utilisé les insectes comme légions exterminatrices lors de la Troisième Guerre mondiale" (Bordage 200–201).

[77] "La plaine délivrait de fausses informations sur les distances, semblait parfois les raccourcir pour mieux les rallonger l'instant suivant. Ils traversaient de véritables grêles d'insectes de toutes tailles et de toutes formes qui préparaient sans relâche l'avènement du nouvel ordre terrestre" (Bordage 622–623).

determinism that had to be amended, circumvented, or destroyed in order to preserve the attribute of human singularity.

In a less scientific register of the dystopian speculative fiction that the authors of general literature are fond of trying to extrapolate, it is striking to note that insects continue to foretell a world in the making that approaches the question of the determinism of the written word in a different way.

Such is the case with Amin Maalouf's novel *The First Century After Beatrice*, whose narrator brags that he is an entomologist and understands better than anyone else the dystopian order in which the society of his time is basing itself, following the consumption of a "substance" that only favors the birth of male children by most of the members of this society. This "reading [of] the "symptoms"[78] (Maalouf, *The First Century After Beatrice* 54) in the great book of nature is one he owes essentially to his sense of observation of metamorphoses:

> From the larva to the insect, from the ugly, crawling caterpillar to the magnificent butterfly with its true colours displayed, we have the impression of passing from one reality to another; and yet, everything which will form the beauty of the butterfly is there in the caterpillar. My job allows me to read the image of the butterfly or the scarab or the trap-door spider in the larva. I look at the present, and I perceive the future, isn't that wonderful?[79] (Maalouf, *The First Century After Beatrice* 35).

The ordering of this perspicacity coupled with this character's solid practice of reading is very important (and holds the attention of the attentive reader), so much so that it inspires the narrator to a surprising writing project that constitutes the very backbone of Maalouf's novel. By replacing numbers with the limited number of letters of the alphabet, the division of this account—which takes the form of a diary—into chapters, reminds us that this testimony is perhaps ordered according to a code

---

[78] "lecture des symptômes" (Maalouf, *Le premier siècle après Béatrice* 51).

[79] "De la larve à l'insecte, de la chenille disgracieuse et rampante au superbe papillon aux couleurs déployées, nous avons l'impression de passer d'une réalité à l'autre; pourtant, il y a déjà dans la chenille tout ce qui fera la beauté du papillon. Mon métier me permet de lire dans la larve l'image du papillon, ou du scarabée, ou de la mygale. Je regarde le présent, et je discerne l'image du futur, n'est-ce pas merveilleux?" (Maalouf, *Le premier siècle après Béatrice* 36).

which one can imagine broadens the relationship to the animality of insects on the horizon of a finite world.

Finally, closer to science fiction but in a poetic detour from the conjectural treatment of the "images of science," transfictions also appropriate the figure of insects and spiders no longer to relate an externalized conflict where characters may or may not still occur in the order of a world, but instead to reveal an internalized conflict where they are already inscribed in the order of nature and a world derived from it. This is illustrated by the "becoming mutant" of characters found in Michel Houellebecq's *The Possibility of an Island*, Aurélien Bellanger's *Information Theory* (*La Théorie de l'information*, a response to Houellebecq's novel), and Antoine Volodine's *Songes de Mevlido*. The first of these novels describes the failure of a collective enterprise of cloning supposed to remove the remainder of belonging to the human race from a posthumanity by means of mediation and reading of "life stories," which lead from an individual to the clones that were developed from that individual. This novel is perfectly summarized by one of the participants who identifies himself in this project by a poem incorporating the figure of the insect:

> *Insects bang between the walls,*
> *Limited to their tedious flight*
> *Which carries no message other*
> *Than the repetition of the worst*[80]
> (Houellebecq, *The Possibility of an Island* 124).

In the second novel, *Information Theory*, insects occupy a more prominent place, but this time Bellanger assigns a completely different function to poetry about them. In *Houellebecq, écrivain romantique*, the essay Bellanger wrote before his own novel in response to Houellebecq's, he first stresses the importance of the relations that exist between science and poetry to fully understand Houellebecq's writing. Michel Houellebecq, who wrote one of his first essays on Howard Philips Lovecraft before becoming a successful novelist, was able to carefully cultivate this posture, which starts from the observation that "human actions are as free and

---

[80] "*Les insectes se cognent entre les murs, / Limités à leur vol fastidieux / Qui ne porte aucun message / Que la répétition du pire*" (Houellebecq 178).

meaningless as the free movements of elementary particles,"[81] to then willingly appeal to poetry and science in order to see a certain despair overcome by the exercise of novel writing. From his point of view, there are indeed complementary relationships between poetry and science in a dematerialized world gaining ground by pushing back the limits of our conscious life. And that is why Houellebecq writes "science fiction, [...] prais[es] Auguste Comte, the inventor of positivism, the most scientific of all 19th-century philosophies: his romanticism, essentially Baudelairian, always [leaves] itself anchor points in the field of positive truths."[82] I consider that Houellebecq's understanding of science fiction as a form of "scientifically aided"[83] romanticism provided Aurélien Bellanger with an explicit reading grid or interpretative framework for his first novel *The Information Theory*, which he summarized as follows:

> In essence predictive, science only deals with the future of things; a world that would be scientifically known in its entirety would instantly become limitless. The paradigm of matter is then succeeded by the paradigm of information [...] The ancient world had a history, natural or human, which literature could largely describe. The world to come will no longer have a history, because it will be all possible (hi)stories accomplished together: only mathematical tools dedicated to the study of complex phenomena will be able to describe it—poetry being one of these tools.[84]

Extended to the quest for digital immortality fostered by the use of computers, this grid or framework of appreciation, which resonated with Bellanger when he wrote *The Information Theory*, particularly in reference

---

[81] "Les actions humaines sont aussi libres et dénuées de sens que les libres mouvements des particules élémentaires" (Houellebecq, *H.P. Lovecraft contre le monde, contre la vie* 18).

[82] "la science-fiction tout en faisant l'éloge d'Auguste Comte, l'inventeur du positivisme, la plus scientiste de toutes les philosophies du XIXᵉ siècle: son romantisme, d'essence baudelairienne, se [ménage] toujours des points d'ancrage dans le domaine des vérités positives" (Bellanger, *Houellebecq, écrivain romantique* 43).

[83] "scientifiquement aidé" (Bellanger 38).

[84] "Essentiellement prédictive, la science n'a affaire qu'au futur des choses; un monde qui serait scientifiquement connu en totalité deviendrait instantanément illimité. Au paradigme de la matière succède alors le paradigme de l'information (...) Le monde ancien avait une histoire, naturelle ou humaine, que la littérature pouvait largement décrire. Le monde qui vient n'aura plus d'histoire, car il sera toutes les histoires possibles réalisées ensemble: seuls des outils mathématiques voués à l'étude des phénomènes complexes pourront le décrire—la poésie étant l'un de ces outils" (Bellanger 289).

to other science fiction novels such as William Gibson's *Neuromancer* and more recently Greg Egan's *Permutation City*, allowed him to rethink and decompose the American mathematician Claude Shannon's information theory into three parts in his novel: Steampunk, Cyberpunk, and Biopunk. These three parts, which correspond to three periods in the history of information and communication sciences revisited by Bellanger, are theoretical inserts that explain how his main character Pascal Estranger, an Internet provider and computer billionaire, came closer step-by-step to an understanding of Claude Shannon's theory of information. Thanks to this understanding and his own financial power, Estranger was able to transform "human computer dust"[85] in order to give to the human race an insectoid immortality that reduces it to a message whose value cannot be known through repetition and which no longer presents any form of singularity:

> Pascal had indeed succeeded in projecting human society onto an animal society [...] Humanity would thus survive, in the winged recombinations of its last messages, and could be reborn at any time. Information theory would be a time machine.[86]

Antoine Volodine also differently combines this determinism with the exhaustion of his character, who is in a way consubstantial with the dystopian world that carries it under the gaze of the spiders. Indeed, at the beginning of the novel, spiders populate Mevlido's room before coming out of it and invading the planet he lives on at the end of this story, while he is metamorphosed and reunited as a cockroach with the memories of a woman he loved in another room:

> She goes to the second room. It is a blind room, with a small cot, a table, a hot plate, a chair, a sink, a toilet, a central light bulb. One could be detained or sheltered there for centuries. Verena Becker lights the lamp. A cockroach

---

[85] "poussières informatiques humaines" (Bellanger 513).

[86] "Pascal était en effet parvenu a projeter la société humaine sur une société animale (...) L'Humanité survivrait ainsi, dans les recombinaisons ailées de ses derniers messages, et pourrait renaître à tout moment. La théorie de l'information serait une machine à voyage dans le temps" (Bellanger, *La théorie de l'information* 523–524).

runs at the foot of the wall, takes refuge under the bed. She doesn't recognize me. She sits on the bed.[87]

What does the sense of memory teach us in this last example about the figure of the insect? Probably that it prefigures the extreme "otherness" that which becomes one, technologically speaking, [88] with the immanence of the world in which it is inscribed. But the question that this metamorphosis may also raise is how to know, ultimately, the effects of removing the limits between a body and the world.

In light of a resistant humanity, the stakes related to the remediation of the body between the closing and the opening of the symbolism of the book could roughly be summarized as follows. While the *postures* of Baikal, Viviane, and Beatrice's father presuppose a causal link between their reading of the book of nature and their fragile rejection of a reified world, the *mutant bodies* of Elisa and Solman are still able to evade or subvert such determinism, which leaves the *bodies* personified by the Daniels and Mevlido only the possibility of a testimony against the march of a world whose rewriting participates in their erasure, as long as this rewriting knew how to or could, at the time of a final overthrow, incorporate these two characters.

BIBLIOGRAPHY

Alter, Robert. *The Hebrew Bible: A Translation with Commentary*. Norton, 2019.
Bellanger, Aurélien. *Houellebecq, écrivain romantique*. L. Scheer, 2010.
———. *La théorie de l'information: roman*. Gallimard, 2012.
Bolter, Jay David, and Richard Grusin. *Remediation: Understanding New Media*. MIT Press, 2003.
Bordage, Pierre. *Les derniers hommes*. J'ai Lu edition, 2005.
Clément, Murielle Lucie, et al. "Du style, du plat, de Proust et de Houellebecq." *Michel Houellebecq sous la loupe*. Rodopi, 2007.

[87] "Elle va vers la seconde pièce. C'est une chambre aveugle, avec un petit lit de camp, une table, un réchaud, une chaise, un lavabo, une cuvette de cabinets, une ampoule centrale. On pourrait y rester détenue ou à l'abri pendant des siècles. Verena Becker allume la lampe. Un cafard court au pied du mur, se réfugie sous le lit. Elle ne me reconnaît pas. Elle s'assied sur le lit" (Volodine 460–461).

[88] "...with insects the artifice, the 'tool,' is not distinguished from the body acting, coupling, and affecting within the world. As a medium in itself, the insect differed from the intellectual orientation of the human being. Humans (as a mode of thought and action) are able to reflexively select their tools, which gives them a guaranteed advantage" (Parikka 28–28).

Curtius, Ernst Robert, et al. *European literature and the Latin Middle Ages.* Princeton University Press, 2013.

Darrieussecq, Marie. *Notre vie dans les forêts roman.* P.O.L., 2017.

———. *Our Life in the Forest.* Translated by Penny Hueston, The Text Publishing Company, 2018.

Derrida, Jacques. *De la grammatologie.* Les Éditions de Minuit, 1967.

Descartes, René, et al. *Discourse on the Method and Meditations on First Philosophy.* Yale University Press, 1996.

Dick, Philip. *Ubik.* First Mariner books ed. Houghton Mifflin Harcourt, 2012.

Domon, Hélène. *Le Livre Imaginaire.* Summa Publications, 2000.

Gellrich, Jesse M., and Cornell University Press. *The Idea of the Book in the Middle Ages: Language Theory, Mythology, and Fiction.* Cornell University Press, 1988.

Gibson, William. *Neuromancer.* Ace, 2020.

Herrenschmidt, Clarisse. *Les trois écritures: langage, nombre, code.* Gallimard, 2007.

Houellebecq, Michel. *H.P. Lovecraft contre le monde, contre la vie.* J'ai lu, 2007.

———. *La possibilité d'une île.* Fayard, 2005.

———. *The Possibility of an Island.* Translated by Gavin Bowd, Knopf, 2006.

Kukkonen, Karin, and Sonja Klimek. *Metalepsis in Popular Culture.* De Gruyter, 2011.

Lakoff George and Mark Johnson. *Metaphors We Live By.* University of Chicago Press, 1980.

Lamarre, Mélanie. *Ruines de l'utopie: Antoine Volodine, Olivier Rolin.* Presses universitaires du Septentrion, 2014.

Langlet, Irène. *La science-fiction: lecture et poétique d'un genre littéraire.* A. Colin, 2006.

Levinson, Paul. *The Soft Edge: A Natural History and Future of the Information Revolution. Routledge, 1998.*

Maalouf, Amin. *Le premier siècle après Béatrice: roman.* Grasset, 1999.

———. *The First Century After Beatrice.* Abacus, 1994.

Manguel, Alberto. *A History of Reading.* Penguin Books, 2014.

Muri, Allison. *The Enlightenment Cyborg: A History of Communications and Control in the Human Machine, 1660–1830.* University of Toronto Press, 2007.

Parikka, Jussi. *Insect Media: An Archaeology of Animals and Technology.* University of Minnesota Press, 2010.

Ruffel, Lionel. *Volodine post-exotique.* Ed. Cécile Defaut, 2007.

Rufin, Jean-Christophe. *Globalia.* Gallimard, 2005.

Ryan, Marie-Laure. *Avatars of Story.* Univ. of Minnesota Press, 2009.

———. "Logique culturelle de la métalepse, ou la métalepse dans tous ses états." *Métalepses: entorses au pacte de la représentation,* edited by John Pier and Jean-Marie Schaeffer, Éditions de l'École des hautes études en sciences sociales, 2005.

Simmons, Dan. *The Fall of Hyperion.* Bantam Books, 1995.

Spivak, Gayatri Chakravorty, and Jacques Derrida. *Of Grammatology*. The Johns Hopkins University Press, 1998.

Stockwell, Peter. *The Poetics of Science Fiction*. Routledge, 2000.

Thoreau, Henry David. *Walden, or, Life in the Woods and On the Duty of Civil Disobedience*. Pocket Books, 2004.

Volodine, Antoine. *Songes de Mevlido*. Seuil, 2007.

Vonarburg, Elisabeth. *Le jeu des coquilles de nautilus*. Editions Alire, 2003.

———. *Le silence de la cité*. Editions Alire, 1998.

———. "Les femmes en tant qu'artefactes dans la science-fiction moderne." *Science-fiction et imaginaires contemporains*, edited by Francis Berthelot and Philippe Clermont, Bragelonne, 2007, pp. 153–67.

———. *The Silent City*. Translated by Jane Brierley, Tesseracts Books, 2002.

CHAPTER 5

Regaining Humanity by Learning from Escapes and Detours

The space crossed by characters of futuristic novels often reveals what can make them singular during or at the end of their journey. Therefore, the novels in my corpus link the crossing of this space to the end of an investigation that sees the affirmation of an "Evidential Paradigm," to quote the title of a chapter "Clues. Roots of an Evidential Paradigm"[1] in *Clues, Myths, and the Historical Method* by Carlo Ginzburg; this chapter, based on an article whose French title was "Racines d'un paradigme de l'indice,"[2] generated much commentary in French academic circles. To define this paradigm, I agree with Denis Mellier's interpretation, in which he applied this paradigm to analyze the specificities of detective novels as thrillers, arguing that fictional abduction can be explained by a hunting or cynegetic origin of literature:

> Ginzburg proposes tracing this paradigm back to an immemorial cynegetic knowledge thanks to which the hunter reads the tracks of his prey on the ground, transforming the signs constituted by marks, hairs, excrement or drool into clues signifying its passage, its nature, its direction. It is in this reading of the hunter, which is the transparent source of all the metaphors of the book-world, that the very experience of the story originates. It is born in the observation that "someone has been there". In an implicit teleology

---

[1] (Ginzburg, *Clues, myths, and the historical method* 96–113).
[2] (Ginzburg, "Racines d'un Paradigme de l'indice").

© The Author(s), under exclusive license to Springer Nature Switzerland AG 2022
E. Buzay, *Contemporary French and Francophone Futuristic Novels*, Studies in Global Science Fiction, https://doi.org/10.1007/978-3-031-16628-0_5

of the literary form, all that is left to do is to slip from the observation to the question and to dramatize this passage into a questioning of the identity that the trace signifies, so that the seduction of the fictional is born.[3]

In Chap. 2, I borrowed Irene Langlet's definition of science fiction as the "enigma genre, where the elucidation concerns not the culprit of a crime but the coherency of a world or an imaginary world"[4] (Langlet 51) in large part because of my interpretation of the origins of this genre. From my perspective, the philosophical tale engages similar questions of coherency, as they are related to the enigmatic aspects of a world. This perspective of doubt becomes even more explicit in Voltaire's *Micromégas* and other philosophical tales in the eighteenth century, before being relayed by subsequent futuristic novels, in which the paradigm of the *liber mundi* continues to serve as a frame of reference for the plotting of these narratives that require detection on the part of the reader. For this reason, in science fiction, like in detective novels, "this narrative of origin puts to work, in retrospective abduction, an idea of literature that represents it as attached to the enigma of the letter, to the translation of the sign and to the hermeneutic production of the solution, whether in the narrative mode or in the commentary mode"[5] and represents the core of this hermeneutic endeavor.

From the enigma to the clue and then from the clue to the trace (a term whose specific meaning I will describe later), throughout the fiction works in my corpus, the act of reading allows the fictional minds of the characters and consequently the readers to construct hypotheses, through the

---

[3] « Ginzburg propose de faire remonter ce paradigme à un savoir cynégétique immémorial grâce auquel le chasseur lit les traces de sa proie à même le sol, transformant les signes que constituent les marques, les poils, les excréments ou la bave, en autant d'indices signifiant son passage, sa nature, sa direction. C'est dans cette lecture du chasseur, qui est source transparente de toutes les métaphores du monde-livre, que l'expérience même du récit s'origine. Elle naît dans le constat que « ... quelqu'un est passé par là ». Dans une implicite téléologie de la forme littéraire, il n'y aura plus qu'à glisser du constat à la question, et dramatiser ce passage en une interrogation sur l'identité que signifie la trace, pour que naisse la séduction du romanesque » (Bessière et al. 111).

[4] « ... genre[s] à énigme, où l'élucidation concerne non pas le coupable d'un crime mais la cohérence d'un monde ou d'un imaginaire » (Langlet 2006, 51).

[5] « ..., ce récit de l'origine met en l'œuvre, dans l'abduction rétrospective, une idée de la littérature qui la représente comme attachée à l'énigme de la lettre, à la traduction du signe et à la production herméneutique de la solution, que ce soit sur le mode du récit ou sur le mode du commentaire » (Bessière et al. 113).

interpretation of metaphors, using a hermeneutic approach. In this chapter, therefore, my objective will be to show how the idea of the detour that favors the reading of the book-world and that often takes the form of long walks produces a human singularity that can be seen from two perspectives: that of manhunts inscribed in a territory, most often outside the city, and that of projects for information or knowledge societies, which instead represent the vocation of the city in its utopian communicational attributions.

THE METAPHYSICAL MANHUNT

In the same way that insects occupy the possible worlds of anticipation with an otherness contrary a priori to the principal characteristics of the human species, the hunts for man abound in these same fictional storyworlds as "[e]very hunt is accompanied by a theory of [its] prey that explains why, by virtue of what difference, of what distinction, some men can be hunted and others not"[6] (Chamayou, *Manhunts* 2).

The recurrence of this theme linked to the treatment of otherness goes far beyond the genre of French and Francophone science fiction literature alone, given that the model of the manhunt is abundantly present in the "classics" of Anglophone science-fiction literature. Without going in depth into the multiple television and film productions (*X-files*, *Alien*, *Matrix*, *Avatar*, etc.) that regularly exploit this model, I also note that this model is included in key literary works such as Philip K. Dick's *Do Androids Dream of Electric Sheep?* and *Hyperion* by Dan Simmons, whose famous "Shrike" (a monstrous robot made of knife blades) places the hunt for man within the framework of a metaphysical reflection on the value and meaning of human sacrifice.

As for this theme of an encounter with the "other" in its status of predator or prey, the originality of French and Francophone anticipation literature is undoubtedly due to the variations of roles between the hunters and the hunted included in the full range of subgenres that require detection, going from science fiction to transfiction through speculative fiction, all of which function to portray an "other" alienness.

---

[6] « Toute chasse s'accompagne d'une théorie de [leur] proie, qui dit pourquoi, en vertu de quelle différence, de quelle distinction, certains peuvent être chassés et d'autres pas » (Chamayou, *Les chasses à l'homme* 8).

In mainstream science fiction, the manhunt stimulates the unfolding of the plot of the science fiction story by establishing a chronological order that often goes so far as to envisage the inversion or abolition of the predatory relationship between the "hunters" and the "hunted." Following multiple quests, *Les Derniers Hommes* by Pierre Bordage wonderfully illustrates the first of these tendencies because the spirit of the hunt animates both the Aquariots in their search for water-filled underground aquifers and their numerous adversaries: solbots (robot soldiers), dogs, Slangs (the opposing tribe), and genetically modified insects, whose mission is to eliminate the Aquariots. While the diviners of this tribe must rely on their taste to detect the presence of cyanide in the groundwater during strange ceremonies called "rhabde[s]" (Bordage 11), the tribe's seer, Solman, develops other hunting skills in order to preserve his people from imminent danger.

By going back to the source of a criminal animus that assails his clan, Solman's skills take the form of a clairvoyance that identifies all those who gang up against the "last men" as simple *intermediaries* distributed at the cardinal points of a vast manhunt, a form of organization that the philosopher Grégoire Chamayou depicts as the most accomplished form of predation relationships specific to the hunt: "Whereas in the master-slave dialectic the relationship of consciousness had a fundamentally dual structure, in the hunting situation the master almost never confronts his prey directly. He uses intermediaries, mercenary hunters or hunting dogs. This a schema with three terms rather than two"[7] (Chamayou, *Manhunts* 67). This is how Solman's character begins to become aware that he is being stalked and that he will have to explain himself in order to understand and then "transcend [his] status as prey and begin a movement of liberation"[8] (Chamayou, *Manhunts* 58):

> Sitting in the grass, he observed for long hours the movements of the foliage agitated by the breeze. He perceived a form of coherence, of intelligence in this apparently chaotic, inextricable tangle. An intelligence that had nothing

---

[7] « Alors que, dans la dialectique du maître et de l'esclave, le rapport de conscience avait une structure fondamentalement duelle, dans la situation de chasse, le maître ne se confronte quasiment jamais directement à sa proie. Il utilise des intermédiaires, chasseurs mercenaires ou chiens de chasse. C'est un schéma à trois termes plutôt qu'à deux » (Chamayou, *Les chasses à l'homme* 98).

[8] « ... dépasser son statut de proie et amorcer un mouvement de libération » (Chamayou, *Les chasses à l'homme* 86).

to do with natural order: it evoked the maneuvering skill of the dogs a few days earlier, as if the horde and the forest were inhabited by a single consciousness. He felt the same sensation of presence, of vigilant, evil attention, he sensed the same background, the same destructive intention.[9]

The explanation of this tracking will consequently include most of the characters that surround him. Ismahil reveals to Solman that the Eskato refers to a group of scientists who have decided to orchestrate the end of the world by themselves in the advent of a post-humanity of which they are the sole representatives. As for Kadija, she plays the role of "bait," under the cover of an analogy between man-hunting, or woman-hunting, and amorous desire, which participates in a final reversal, in the blurring of the relation between the "hunters" and the "hunted." Because he perceives in his lover Kadija, "this fundamental inspiration to break the rampart of amnesia erected by the Eskato, to reinsert himself in the original framework,"[10] Solman is going to follow this same impulse and to allow himself to be incorporated by the computer program of this organization in order to better destroy it from the inside and to prevent, through his sacrifice, the enterprise of the extermination of the last men.

In the same way, Élisabeth Vonarburg's novel *The Silent City* aims at the minimum of incompleteness as a storyworld. In this work, a vast manhunt is also organized with intermediaries, and the rhetoric of the hunt aligns with that of desire evolving in the description of a war of the sexes where the state of androgyny confirms the erasure of the relations of predation between the "hunters" and the "hunted." The beginning of the novel clearly sets the tone for this, when the founder of a city that houses scientists who survived a nuclear winter, Marquande de Styx, blames her son Paul, with whom she wants to continue what appears to be an incestuous relationship, for not having "anything better to do at night

---

[9] « Assis dans l'herbe, il observa pendant de longues heures les mouvements des frondaisons agitées par la brise. Il percevait une forme de cohérence, d'intelligence dans cet enchevêtrement en apparence chaotique, inextricable. Une intelligence qui n'avait rien à voir avec l'ordre naturel: elle évoquait l'habileté manœuvrière des chiens quelques jours plus tôt, comme si la horde et la forêt étaient habitées par une conscience unique. Il éprouvait la même sensation de présence, d'attention vigilante, maléfique, il captait le même arrière-plan, la même intention destructrice » (Bordage 75).

[10] « cette inspiration fondamentale à briser le rempart d'amnésie érigé par l'Eskato, à se réinsérer dans la trame d'origine » (Bordage 665).

than hunt wild muties"[11] (Vonarburg, *The Silent City* 8). If the reasons for this hunt are legitimized from Paul's point of view by the pursuit of a scientific project called the "Project," his motivations respond in part to the lack of horizon caused by incestuous violence:

> Paul smiles at Serena and reflects inwardly that it marks another birthday: the Project. Did it give it this name right away? To be honest, he must admit he didn't. It was more a pastime at first. Or a whim. Or a sort of joke. As he had watched the blood flow slowly from his slashed wrists on the day he turned twenty-six, he'd suddenly thought of this embryonic capacity for autoregeneration discovered by accident in the mutants of the Exterior, and he had decided to create a new race out of them. What was that, if not a sign of humor? As he'd watched the blood flow from his wrists. Perhaps it wasn't humor, after all. He hadn't been very humorous in those days [...] Now he begins to understand Marquande's reaction when she came into his room and saw him bleeding. In her place he'd have laughed too[12] (Vonarburg, *The Silent City* 13).

In practice, this manhunt, which is in service to the "Project," requires robots as *intermediaries* called "ommachs." When commanded by Paul, these ommachs go outside the City and act as predators to select a batch of guinea pigs on which Paul carries out dissections and experiments. If the ommachs are an extension of the body of the men of the City, their use appears problematic or at least worrying as soon as the men forget themselves or when, upon their deaths, what remains of them takes refuge in the ommachs, in order to continue to intervene in the current political affairs of the populations outside the City:

[11] « ... rien de mieux à faire la nuit que d'aller à la chasse aux mutants sauvages » (Vonarburg, *Le silence de la cité* 8).

[12] « Tout en souriant à Serena, Paul se dit que c'est aussi un autre anniversaire: celui du Projet. L'a-t-il appelé ainsi tout de suite? En toute honnêteté, il doit reconnaitre que non. C'était plutôt un passe-temps, au début. Ou un caprice. Ou une sorte de plaisanterie. Le jour de ses vingt-six ans, regarder le sang couler lentement de ses poignets tailladés, penser soudain a cette capacité auto-régénératrice embryonnaire découverte par hasard chez des mutants de l'Extérieur, et décider de créer à partir d'eux une nouvelle race, qu'était-ce, sinon une manifestation d'humour? En regardant le sang couler de ses poignets. Ce n'était peut-être pas de l'humour après tout. Il n'en avait guère à cette époque. (...) Maintenant, il comprend mieux la réaction de Marquande quand elle l'a vu en entrant dans sa chambre. Lui aussi il aurait ri, à sa place » (Vonarburg, *Le silence de la cité* 17).

Paul sets the system on automatic and throws himself back with a sight as the screens dim. In an hour the specimens will be in the City. For a moment Paul lies motionless under the network of wires covering his head and body. Then, one by one, he detaches the electrodes. The robot's eyes, nose, ears; the robot's voice, hands, legs. As usual he feels somewhat empty, a little weak, cut off from a body that is stronger than his could ever be, and equipped with senses he could never have. At times like these he can almost understand why some people in the City no longer live except through robots[13] (Vonarburg, *The Silent City* 6).

With the birth of Elisa, constituting the culmination of the "Project," the ommachs change their functions. On the one hand, they prepare Elisa's "descendants," who are, like her, androgynous, to repopulate an outside world lacking in men; on the other hand, they perpetuate a hunt for men or women, according to the camps that use them, in the context of a war of the sexes that rages on the Outside between the men of Vietelli and the women of Libera, without readers being able to know, at first glance, which human memory these ommachs perpetuate. Finally, the end of the "Project," decided by Elisa's "descendants" after incessant discussions about its colonialist reasonings, coincides with the end of the conflict between the men and women of the Outside, as well as participating in the erasure of the predatory relationships between the "hunters" and the "hunted." This new horizon relegates the male and female ommachs to the rank of faithful servants of the memory of the City that saw Elisa's birth, and it is thus that, pacified, they now exist in harmony with a humanity that is nearly androgynous.

Outside the prism of the mutant future and the technologies that science fiction presupposes, manhunts remain at the heart of other anticipation stories, but they no longer confer the same completeness or depth to the texture of their plots. The postures adopted by the focal characters of speculative fiction are in this respect revealing. For Baïkal, Marie/Viviane, and the entomologist narrator, Beatrice's father, desire is

---

[13] « Paul enclenche l'automatique et se renverse en arrière avec un soupir tandis que les écrans s'éteignent; d'ici une heure, les spécimens arriveront à la Cité. Il demeure un moment immobile dans le fin réseau de fils qui recouvre sa tête et son corps, puis détache une à une les électrodes: les yeux du robot, le nez, les oreilles, la voix du robot; les mains du robot, ses jambes... Comme d'habitude il se sent un peu vide, un peu mou, amputé de ce corps plus puissant que ne le sera jamais le sien, et pourvu de sens qu'il ne possèdera jamais. Dans ces moments-là il peut presque comprendre ceux qui dans la Cité ne vivent plus que par l'intermédiaire des robots... » (Vonarburg, *Le silence de la cité* 6).

no longer a part of the manhunt, because these characters who take blows or avoid them learn above all to permanently internalize their status as a hunted person in the unstable worlds in which they evolve and in which the distinction between the "hunters" and the "hunted" is very fragile.

Of the three focal characters who internalize this function of a hunted human being, Baïkal alone embodies this "art of effective flight, insofar as it presupposes an intellectual mastery of cynegetic logic, [that] paves the way for a reversal of the hunting relationship"[14] (Chamayou, *Manhunts* 71). He owes this conjuration of fate mainly to Fraiseur, whom he meets in the "no-zones" at the beginning of his forced exile from Globalia, while he is on his way to a village controlled by the mafia to sell the tribe's Amazonian Forest ozone production. After noticing that outside of Globalia Baïkal sees almost everything but knows nothing, even though he is loaded with technology, Fraiseur is the character who teaches him to decipher the terrain, starting by asking him to change his dress code in order to learn to blend in:

> "Mind your manners, damn it! You can't go on acting so elegant."
> Baïkal looked down at his clothes, which were beginning to harden from sweat and mud.
>
> Elegant! Me?
> Don't quibble. Elegance may not be the word. In any case, it's not right. You have the clothes of a lord or a mobster and you wear them dirty and sloppy like a tribe[15] (168).

Motivated at first by the need to act as a "tribe" to better grasp the laws of an unprotected world that attracts and repels him at the same time, Baïkal then accepts all the more the nomadic teachings of his companion as he realizes that he is at the center of a manhunt that turns out to be a

---

[14] « … art de la fuite efficace, en ce qu'il suppose la maîtrise intellectuelle de la logique cynégétique, [qui] prépare un retournement de la relation de chasse » (Chamayou, *Les chasses à l'homme* 104).

[15] « Soigne un peu tes manières, sang diable! Tu peux pas continuer à jouer les élégants comme ça.

Baïkal baissa les yeux sur ses frusques que la sueur et la boue commençaient à durcir.

– Élégant! Moi?

– Chicane pas. Élégance c'est peut-être pas le mot. En tout cas, ça va pas. T'as des habits de seigneur ou de mafieux et tu les portes sales et négligés comme un tribu » (Rufin 168).

machination far surpassing his strengths and abilities. The media campaign that makes him play the role, in spite of himself, of a "New Enemy [having] appropriately fulfilled his function"[16] in tracking down all the adversaries of the global society, forces him to flee for the second time. But at the end of Jean-Christophe Rufin's novel, when Baïkal makes the decision to venture with Kate into the heart of the Amazonian forest, he does so under the influence of his reading of Thoreau's *Walden* with a view to reuniting with his friend Puig, from whom the text suggests that he should learn from his condition of "bait" in order to gain maturity and continue their struggle. It should be noted that if the inversion or the abolition of the predation relationships between the "hunters" and the "hunted" is not as explicit in speculative fiction as in mainstream science fiction, it is more a question of denouncing the instrumentalization of the characters than of tracing their becoming, with the example of Elisa's dream that frees her from the organic character of the City or of Solman's intrusion into the "Verb" of the Eskato.

The instrumentalization that brings the executors closer to the sponsors or the victims closer to the intermediaries is of a different nature in speculative fiction since it translates into a dystopian hold of the media and communication technologies that reinforce their control; this creates a blurring of the level of responsibility of each and every one of them, as much as the plot can delay the disclosure of it. In *Our Life in the Forest*, predation is an essential component of the dystopian society this novel describes, but this notion advances in a hidden manner, which explains that just like surveillance, which I will discuss later, predation is internalized and the "hunters" as well as the "hunted" or prey have to be found by the reader. This storyworld indeed illustrates the Latin proverb *Homo homini lupus est* that can be translated succinctly as "Man is wolf to man" and which can be applied in the context of this novel to the category of "human beings" who prey upon each other. The hunters who are first mentioned do not appear in the daily life of the protagonists, but in Marie's clone's nightmares that seem to clearly depict the nature of the threat of having her organs harvested, which is a reason for the anguish communicated to Marie herself who is watching over her clone when she sleeps: "Sometimes I'd wonder about the limbo she was held in; perhaps it was not some sort of white material but rather a black abyss, in which she was chased by hunters. A stifling universe, where she saw organs throbbing, decomposing

---

[16] « Nouvel Ennemi [ayant] rempli convenablement sa fonction » (Rufin 168).

or ready to swallow her. I woke up with a start. I was having Marie's nightmares"[17] (Darrieussecq, *Our Life in the Forest* 65).

These nightmares are key to understanding how predation organizes the society; the predators (the wolves, in a metaphoric sense) are the wealthiest ones and barely represent 1% of the society at the top, the robots (and by extension the algorithms) are the intermediaries of the rich, and, at the bottom of the chain, there are the human and animal clones, both of whom are not aware of their cloned condition. What makes this form of manhunt metaphysical is the search for those traces of memory that allow the reader to understand the secrets kept by this society; this search is based on the narrative of the journal written by Marie/Viviane who must go against the norm by escaping to a forest to find who she is. This stream of consciousness journal not only reveals how she found herself in this predatory organization, but also explores the grey zone of the fragile distinction between the "hunters" and the "hunted" and the uncanny worldview that emerges from it, as the ambiguity of the "safe place" therapy illustrates:

> My safe place was already a forest. So it's not surprising that the clicker and I got on well. I think it defined us as human animals. [...] But the forest is traditionally a rather disturbing place. I think so. Remember fairy tales like 'Hansel and Gretel. And the myth of the wolf. The wolf is among us, now, today. In the city, in the zone, and in almost all the safe places. I'm talking metaphorically. If you get my drift[18] (Darrieussecq 35–36).

This disturbing insight about "safe place" therapy seems to be at the heart of a denunciation of the politics of the care provided in many respects both by the doctors, who seem like robots and who care for sleeping clones like Marie's, which are kept in hospitals, and by Marie herself in her work as a psychologist who must teach her patients to overcome their

---

[17] « Je me disais parfois que les limbes qui la tenaient n'étaient pas du coton blanc mais un abîme noir Qu'elle était poursuivie par des chasseurs. Un univers irrespirable, où elle voyait des organes palpitants, en décomposition ou prêts à l'avaler. Je me réveillais en sursaut. Je faisais les cauchemars de Marie » (Darrieussecq, *Notre vie dans les forêts roman* 86–87).

[18] « Mon lieu sûr c'était déjà une forêt. Pas étonnant qu'on s'entendait bien, avec le cliqueur. Je pense que ça nous définissait comme animaux humains. (...) Mais la forêt est traditionnellement un lieu plutôt inquiétant. Je crois. Si on pense aux contes genre Petit Poucet. Et au mythe du loup. Le loup est parmi nous aujourd'hui. Il occupe la ville, la zone, et presque tous les lieux sûrs. Je parle métaphoriquement. Si vous me suivez » (Darrieussecq, *Notre vie dans les forêts roman* 50–51).

traumas in order to adapt to the demands of society and continue to be productive. Following this blurring of the boundaries between the "hunters" and the "hunted" that needs to be unveiled, even kindness becomes suspicious, as Marie noticed that psychologists delivered a cloned dog—one who she will later call "Wolf"—the day her mother died in a suspicious way, before adding "It's a form of orphan benefit. Supportive relationships are the key to neuronal integration. Obviously, orphans have a harder time of it. The shrinks used a certain number of compassionate strategies. There are a lot of orphans, so they have to breed up a lot of dogs"[19] (Darrieussecq 51). Still the unique bond with animals through compassion is likely to be the start of an awareness supported by the cliker in Marie/Viviane's mind that leads her to the truth of her human condition, one step before discovering that she is nothing more than raw materials potentially ready for substitution: "The cloning of non-human animals is nothing more than slaughter—that's what I've been told in the forest"[20] (Darrieussecq 55). It is next to her cloned dog/wolf and then with a natural dog found in nature by her side that Marie/Viviane perceives the space of the forest as a necessary lucid rewilding where this hunting that is becoming metaphysical will enable her to nourish the specificities of her writing in the aftermath of a desire for revolt and perhaps a revolution.

In *The Possibility of an Island* the situation is different since Michel Houellebecq stages the impossibility of a reversal in the hunting relationships, which first takes the form of a systematic killing of humans who have returned to a savage state by clones with an ideologically motivated post-humanity, like Daniel24:

> When I kill a savage who, more audacious than the others, lingers too long at the protective fence—it is usually a female, with prematurely sagging breasts, brandishing her baby like a supplication—I have the sensation of accomplishing a necessary and legitimate act. […] The human species will

---

[19] « C'est une sorte d'avantage acquis des orphelins. L'intégration neuronale n'est possible que grâce à des relations soutenantes. Forcément pour les orphelins c'est plus dur. Les psys prenaient certaines mesures compassionnelles. Les orphelins sont nombreux et il faut usiner beaucoup de chiens » (Darrieussecq, *Notre vie dans les forêts roman* 86–87).

[20] « Le clonage des animaux non humains, c'est de l'abattage ni plus ni moins, c'est ce qu'on m'a dit dans la forêt » (Darrieussecq, *Notre vie dans les forêts roman* 74).

disappear, it must disappear so that the words of the Supreme Sister can be accomplished[21] (Houellebecq, *The Possibility of an Island* 48).

It should be noted that the manhunt—or more accurately a "womanhunt"—which begins at the start of the novel and to which Daniel24 devotes himself, is more of a slaughter than an organized hunt, and goes hand in hand with the beginnings of this character's reflection on the desire conveyed by the poetry of his ancestor Daniel1. The effects of this poetry that motivates Marie22 to strip naked in front of the camera during her "intermediations" with Daniel24 and to write on these occasions short aphorisms on the crises which she experiences, have this essential aspect: in the long run, they will push Daniel25 and Marie23, the successors of the two above-mentioned characters, to leave their respective dwellings and to launch an irrational, unusual race-chase. This transfiction thus implicitly revives the analogy between the hunt and the love conquest, but it defuses its dynamism in order to keep only the ambiguity cultivated at the end of the novel by Daniel25, who is on the trail of Marie23, even if he recognizes a priori that he feels no attraction for her:

> I had felt no physical attraction to Marie23 [...] I was convinced that neither Marie23, despite her departure, nor Marie22, despite the strange episode preceding her end, related by my predecessor, had known desire either. On the other hand what they had known, and in a singularly painful way, was nostalgia for desire, the wish to experience it again, to be irradiated like their distant ancestors with that force that seemed so powerful[22] (Houellebecq, *The Possibility of an Island* 294).

Indeed, despite his denials, Daniel25 at least desires the prospect of that which is foreign to him in the pursuit of a woman. And when he

[21] « Lorsque j'abats un sauvage, plus audacieux que les autres, qui s'attarde trop longtemps aux abords de la barrière de protection—il s'agit souvent d'une femelle, aux seins déjà flasques, brandissant son petit comme une supplique—, j'ai la sensation d'accomplir un acte nécessaire, et légitime. (…) L'espèce humaine disparaitra, elle doit disparaire, afin que soient accomplies les paroles de la Sœur suprême » (Houellebecq, *La possibilité d'une île 2005* 68).
[22] « Je n'avais ressenti aucune attraction physique pour Marie23 (…). J'étais persuadé que ni Marie23, malgré son départ, ni Marie22, malgré l'étrange épisode précédant sa fin, relaté par mon prédécesseur, n'avaient elles non plus connu le désir. Ce qu'elles avaient par contre connu, et cela de manière singulièrement douloureuse, c'était la nostalgie du désir, l'envie de l'éprouver à nouveau, d'être irradiées comme leurs lointaines ancêtres par cette force qui paraissait si puissante » (Houellebecq, *La possibilité d'une île 2005* 415–416).

leaves his house armed with a rifle in the company of his dog, he travels in the outside world toward Marie23, who no longer wants to live in the loops of her "ancestor's" memory, just as Daniel25 wants to escape his own "ancestor's" memory. As he progresses toward the ocean, the practice of traditional hunting is imposed on him so that he can feed his dog the game that crosses their path, recognizing, however, that with the pleasure he experiences in pursuing and killing animals, that "perhaps [he] had, in the worst sense of the term, become human"[23] (Houellebecq, *The Possibility of an Island* 322). But this pleasure is short-lived when he encounters men who have returned to a "savage" state and who kill his dog with an arrow. Overwhelmed by this loss and unable to find Marie23, he goes on a manhunt without real joy. Equipping his rifle to shoot quickly and automatically at all those he encounters, Daniel25 thus heads for the outskirts of the "Great Gray Space"[24] (Houellebecq, *The Possibility of an Island* 328), a space covered in ashes, between a ruined city and the sea, whose crossing will illuminate the hunting referent of his quest—to which I will return later—with a completely different meaning.

The practice of hunting human beings also occurs in Antoine Volodine's novel *Songes de Mevlido*. The first of these practices, devoid of any analogy between hunting violence and the triggering of desire, concerns the memory that the character of Mevlido keeps of the pursuit and execution of his wife Verena Becker by child soldiers:

He had begun to think about Verena Becker, his wife who had been assassinated twenty years earlier by child soldiers during the racist fighting in Zone Five, in Djaka Park West. Assassinated twenty years earlier by child soldiers. Verena Becker. The image of Verena Becker was about to become clearer, in his memory the doors were opening and threatening to open wide. The child soldiers were there, almost on the threshold, with their human ear necklaces and their multicolored vinyl wigs. Mevlido, too, was standing on the threshold. Only one more step to take, and he would be

---

[23] « … peut-être, dans le plus mauvais sens du terme, humanisé » (Houellebecq, *La possibilité d'une île* 2005 454).
[24] « Grand Espace Gris » (Houellebecq, *La possibilité d'une île* 2005 462).

able to venture into the pain of grief. Into the pain and the ashes. He was going to enter there again and sink there into the unbearable images.[25]

As in Houellebecq's novel, the maximum of incompleteness evoked by the practice of hunting women or men under Volodine's pen is no longer about the intermediation that would have supposed a reconciliation between the character of Marie23 and that of Daniel25, but about the memories associated with the *intermediaries* of hunts, in the pay of a hunting power or violating that power, that constantly replay scenes of murder in Mevlido's mind. The child soldiers who capture Mevlido's attention and dreams are monstrous. Not only does Mevlido seek to overcome the trauma of his wife's death, but he must also confront one of these child soldiers in the person of Alban Glück in order to kill to his past obsessions and find the Verena Becker he loved through a cycle of different reincarnations. These child soldiers are therefore unavoidable, but they are not the only intermediaries, since in this transfiction the manhunt temporarily turns against the child soldiers' main employers, thanks to the strength of a young revolutionary named Sonia Wolguelane:

> Like many of us, Sonia Wolguelane wandered in underbelly of the failed revolution. [...] From time to time, when the opportunity arose, she would kill a child soldier, but usually she reserved her ammunition for former genocidaires and warlords who had turned to self-sufficient wealth management or the mafia, or a combination of both when they belonged to the circles close to central power. She killed a lot.[26]

---

[25] « Il avait commencé à penser à Verena Becker, sa femme assassinée vingt ans plus tôt par des enfants-soldats, pendant les combats racistes de Zone Cinq, à Djaka Park West. Assassinée vingt ans plus tôt par des enfants-soldats. Verena Becker. L'image de Verena Becker était sur le point de se préciser, dans sa mémoire les portes s'entrouvraient et menaçaient de s'ouvrir grandes. Les enfants-soldats étaient là, presque sur le seuil, avec leurs colliers d'oreilles humaines et leurs perruques en vinyl multicolore. Lui aussi Mevlido se tenait sur le seuil. Plus qu'un pas à faire, et il allait pouvoir s'aventurer dans la douleur du deuil. Dans la douleur et les cendres. Il allait de nouveau entrer là-dedans et s'y abîmer, dans les images insupportables » (Volodine 36–37).

[26] « Comme nombre d'entre nous, Sonia Wolguelane errait dans les bas-fonds de la révolution manquée. (...) De temps en temps, quand l'occasion se présentait, elle tuait un enfant-soldat, mais en général, elle réservait ses munitions aux anciens génocideurs et chefs de guerre qui s'étaient reconvertis dans la gestion autarcique des richesses ou dans la mafia, ou dans un combiné des deux quand ils appartenaient aux cercles proches du pouvoir central. Elle tuait beaucoup » (Volodine 56–57).

In addition to the fact that Sonia Wolguelane's vengeful wake revives the analogy between the hunt and the desire for love,[27] the admiration of which she is the object and which is expressed in the first person plural, with the use of *we* in its political meaning in Volodine's work, anticipates the explanations given about Mingrelian's writing, writing in the form of fictions in which Mevlido evolves at the end of the novel as a character; this *we* is also the designation of a community of post-exotic writers.

What does this substitution of writing practices for the portrait of a hunter tell us? Or what is the relationship between the art of hunting and the consuming pleasure of letting the letters of the alphabet flow on a sheet of paper? By restating some of the conclusions I reached about the semantics of possible worlds in Chap. 3 and about the idea of a remediation of the symbolism of the book in Chap. 4, I would like to explain how the symbolic function of space explores a paradigmatic duality in anticipation literature that Ginzburg identified in his chapter, "Clues. Roots of an Evidential Paradigm," that deals largely with the hypothesis of a shared semiotics between the practice of reading or writing and that of hunting. To understand this cynegetic reference of which Sonia Wolguelane's portrait, in Mevlido's eyes, and that of the preceding characters of Marie/Viviane and Daniel25 are the signs, it is necessary to imagine them framed by the threat of a death and the search for an immortality (or the threat of a dystopian reification) that they resist and from which they conceive their singularity by escaping and detouring.

---

[27] "Sonia Wolguelane is an important figure of our night, and at that time we were all in love with her to the point of death. (…) As an image, now, the photograph of a young marginal, a girl of small size, with narrow hips, with a not very exuberant chest, an extremely attractive girl, with short very dark hair, very curly, a face of a small southern goddess with white teeth, and eyes able to look daggers or to drive crazy with love, and an admirable skin, perfect but equivocal, of such uncommon texture that we had a different perception of it according to the circumstances, according to the exaltations or the frustrations which seized us in her presence, according to our fantasies, according to our memories…" [« Sonia Wolguelane est une figure importante de notre nuit, et à l'époque nous étions tous et toutes amoureux d'elle à en mourir. (…) Pour image, à présent, la photographie d'une jeune marginale, une fille de petite taille, aux hanches étroites, à la poitrine peu exubérante, une fille extrêmement séduisante, avec des cheveux courts très sombres, très bouclés, un visage de petite déesse méridionale aux dents blanches, et des yeux capables de fusiller ou de rendre fou d'amour, et une peau admirable, parfaite mais équivoque, de si peu commune texture que nous en avions une perception différente selon les circonstances, selon les exaltations ou les frustrations qui nous saisissaient en sa présence, selon nos fantasmes, selon nos souvenirs… »] (Volodine 55–56).

Of these two anthropological orientations, which from my point of view correspond to the "evidential paradigm" and the "Galilean paradigm" identified by Ginzburg, the first one prevails at the beginning of my approach since, "thanks precisely to the literature of the imagination the conjectural paradigm [...] enjoyed a new and unexpected success" (Ginzburg, *Clues, myths, and the historical method* 105) from the nineteenth century until today. What I mean by "evidential paradigm" coincides with a mode of investigation that considers any trace as an index in the individualizing perspective of a knowledge whose indirect character of deciphering goes from the particular to the general.

While the investigation of the traces of this "evidential paradigm" knew its hours of glory in the nineteenth century with Sigmund Freud (symptoms), Conan Doyle (clues in Sherlock Holmes), and the art critic Giovanni Morelli (pictorial signs)—the common point between these three men being that each of them was a doctor at a given moment of his life—its origins go back to the first times of hominization, which allows the historian to formulate a double hypothesis as regards its foundation. By Ginzburg's admission, the first part of this hypothesis is mythical, which sees in the original hunter the one who "would have been the first to 'tell a story' because he alone was able to read, in the silent, nearly imperceptible tracks left by his prey" (Ginzburg, *Clues, myths, and the historical method* 93), but this first part is directly seconded by another, more historical part, which is presented as what comes from cynegetic or hunting knowledge:

> ..., if we abandon the realm of myth and hypotheses for that of documented history, we are struck by the undeniable analogies between the venatic model just discussed and the paradigm implicit in the Mesopotamian divination texts, which began to be composed in the third millennium B.C. [...] It has been noted, in particular, how profoundly the invention of writing shaped Mesopotamian divination. In fact, among other royal prerogatives, the power to communicate with their subjects by means of messages was attributed to the gods—messages written in the heavens, the human bodies, everywhere—which the divines had the task of deciphering (a notion destined to issue in the ageless image of the "book of nature") (Ginzburg, *Clues, myths, and the historical method* 94).

The hypothesis I pursue in this chapter is that not only does this symbolism of the book explain the emphasis on hunting actions in the literature involving detection that we have just surveyed, but that such symbolism is furthermore subject to remediation, in the sense that I have already used this word in Chap. 4, in terms of the historical formation of what Ginzburg calls the "Galilean paradigm." While more abstract, deductive, and scientific, this second perspective reveals the part of the imaginary that concerns the exact sciences, whether it is the formation of otherness in the figure of the insect, as examined previously, or the extension of this quantifying and impersonal perspective to the more political question of the technological emergence of a *universal thought* echoing the philology of Galileo:

> Significantly, Galileo turned to philology in the very moment that he was founding modern natural science through an equally drastic reduction. The traditional medieval juxtaposition of world and book was based on evidence that both were immediately decipherable, while Galileo, instead, stressed that "philosophy … written in this great book which is always open before our eyes (I call it the universe) … cannot be understood if we do not first learn the language and the characters in which it is written" namely, "triangles, circles, and other geometrical figures" (Ginzburg, *Clues, myths, and the historical method* 97–98).

TRACES AND MEMORIES IN INFORMATION AND KNOWLEDGE SOCIETIES OF THE FUTURE

The emergence of a universal thought that would result from a collective scientific intelligence having finally gone beyond the stage of framing individual specificities is at the base of the social utopias that could create information and knowledge societies. In these utopias of individuals' transparency to others, which began in French anticipation literature in the eighteenth century with Louis Sébastien Mercier's *The Year 2440. Dream If It Was Ever*, the "first utopia about the universal community from an existing media, the press"[28] (Mattelart, *History of the Planetary Utopia* 65), the communication and the exchanges of information prefigure the establishment of a form of knowledge of the world founded on the development of the sciences. Many dystopias of speculative fiction contradict this idyllic vision when they remind us that information societies control the traceability of the citizens who inhabit them and the coverage

---

[28] « … première utopie à traiter de la communauté universelle à partir d'un média existant, la presse… » (Mattelart 65).

of the events that constitute their daily lives, without these activities benefiting in any way whatsoever an improved and pacified conception of knowledge. How can this discrepancy be explained? That which the semiotic composition of manhunts continually contests in information and knowledge societies, whose evolution can be explained first by an "evidential paradigm" and then by a "Galilean paradigm," is a sense of memory. This sense that is related to the dystopias of speculative fiction refers to a technological memory whose invasive character serves individuals who can no longer "read" the book of the world, this book that previously specified their humanization and their progression in time and space.

In *Globalia*, the permanent control of society and its public space by "surveillance receivers that transmit image and sound"[29] (59) is an obvious fact that Ron Altman does not even try to hide from Baïkal when Altman offers Baïkal the opportunity to become the enemy the former needs order for Baïkal to regain his freedom. But escaping from Globalia is not an easy task, even when one is pushed into it, since the media coverage of a society that presents itself as planetary and therefore global has replaced the knowledge of the underlying geopolitical truth of the maps of history and geography, as well as their handling.

From this amplification of the means of communication and information perceived as technologies of an impersonal memory, the temptation is great for dystopian speculative fiction to tighten the trap that only the intuition of a path strewn with pitfalls can truly thwart. This is how the information society in Marie Darrieussecq's novel can be seen and approached from inside its main characters. The global surveillance in *Our Life in the Forest* is different since it is already internalized by the characters, and the originality of the novel lies in that the reader is invited to discover the different layers of this internalization in both Marie/Viviane's stream of consciousness narration and her journal. Needless to say, the forest reveals the internalization of the global surveillance when as a "safe place therapy" it turns out to be a refuge away from the omnipresence of the information and communication technologies of the city to make Marie/Viviane realize, as shown in Chap. 4, that she comes to the conclusion that as a clone, she is literally one of the "twigs" ready to be sacrificed for the well-being of the "stump" from which she originated. It is in this capacity that the glance given by Marie, who says that she is "nostalgic for the

---

[29] "récepteurs de surveillance qui transmettent image et son" (Rufin 59).

future"[30] (Darrieussecq 29), matters the most, and this glance highlights the importance given to the motif of the eye in this novel.

In a society where the second-class clone citizens live, while "the watchful robotic eye and the robotic memory, [and given] the endless time that machines have, their endless capacity for crosschecking"[31] (Darrieussecq 22) operate autonomously and keep track of everything, the clones, such as Marie, do not have such abilities since their use of sight seems to be linked to oblivion. It is interesting to note that as a psychologist, Marie, who is not yet Viviane, is involved almost despite herself in this trend, and that she uses behavioral therapies such as "(*Eye Movement Desensitisation and Reprocessing EMDR*)" (Darrieussecq 11) to help her patients overcome and somehow forget their traumas in order to be able to "function" again and to play the social roles assigned to them. But these types of therapy clearly reach their limits, first when her patient whose family died in a plane accident, who she "had [...] make eye movements in order to reprogram her brain"[32] (Darrieussecq 29), commits suicide, and then when the cliker, who will turn Marie's world upside down refuses to undergo this therapy, calling it an "Extreme Morbid Delirious Response"[33] (Darrieussecq 31).

But the morbidity that is a joke to the cliker soon becomes a reality for Marie, when one of her eyes is removed:

When it came to facial recognition, I was confusing vertical and horizontal lines. Morbid prosopagnosia. I contracted a serious degenerative disease in one of my eyes. They're considering a new transplant in the not-too-distant future.

I have green eyes, quite an unusual green that verges on turquoise, with a golden halo around the pupil. I really like my eyes.

---

[30] « J'ai de la nostalgie pour le futur » (Darrieussecq, *Notre vie dans les forêts roman* 42).

[31] « C'était sans compter sur l'œil et la mémoire robotiques, sur le temps infini qu'ont les machines, sur leurs infinies capacités de recoupement » (Darrieussecq, *Notre vie dans les forêts roman* 34).

[32] « ... je lui faisais faire les mouvements oculaires pour reprogrammer son cerveau » (Darrieussecq, *Notre vie dans les forêts roman* 43).

[33] « Mort De Rire,... » (Darrieussecq, *Notre vie dans les forêts roman* 45).

I don't mind telling you that the news was very unwelcome. And to think Marie would be disfigured, one-eyed, thanks to me[34] (Darrieussecq 72–73).

And after this surgery that represents a turning point, Marie's "missing eye" will paradoxically be the agent of transformation that triggers her quest to see the world differently, once she is no longer an instrumentalized human being who previously processed facial recognition according to the marking of "vertical and horizontal lines" like a computer. Instead, with only one eye left, her own individuality stands out more strongly when she tries to "see things from the other side"[35] (Darrieussecq 111) of the world and—in the most iconic instance, which subverts the importance of the eye as a literary motif—she wants "to see the *whole* sea"[36] (Darrieussecq 136). It is at this moment when she finally realizes that her eye was falsely claimed to be dysfunctional for the greater benefit of her "stump" (the human from which she was cloned); that being said, this "stump" seems actually to be less human than her own clone, the narrator Marie/Viviane, when the "stump" cruelly gains this new eye, or rather, takes Marie's eye for her own use. In the tension between Marie's remaining eye that serves an example of a resistant humanity and her other "stolen" eye that results from and aligns itself with the eye-camera of the global surveillance, the beneficiary of the surgery appears less human than her clones, as well as more "domesticated" by the technologies she endorses.

The autonomy of the eye-camera, which suggests in these circumstances that the dark side of this device's use is due to a lack of humanity on both sides of the screen, also translates a pessimistic point of view regarding the disempowerment of information societies that Amin Maalouf similarly relays in *The First Century After Beatrice*. While the narrator of this novel admires the work of his girlfriend, an investigative journalist, he criticizes the lack of reasoning in the media, which, he believes, should have helped their audiences understand the effects of the abortion-causing substance

---

[34] « Je mélangeais les lignes verticales et les lignes horizontales, en matière de reconnaissance faciale. Prosopagnosie morbide. Un de mes yeux était affligé d'une maladie dégénérative grave. A moyen terme, il faudrait envisager une nouvelle greffe. J'ai les yeux verts. D'un vert assez rare qui tire sur le turquoise, avec une couronne dorée autour de la pupille. J'aime bien mes yeux. J'aime autant vous dire que la nouvelle ne m'a pas fait plaisir. Et imaginer Marie défigurée, borgne par ma faute » (Darrieussecq, *Notre vie dans les forêts roman* 95–96).

[35] « …j'essaie de voir comme qui dirait l'envers du monde » (Darrieussecq, *Notre vie dans les forêts roman* 143).

[36] « … voir *toute* la mer » (Darrieussecq, *Notre vie dans les forêts roman* 172).

that plunges their world into chaos; the media could have prevented the consumption of this substance and at the same time stopped the practice of riotous manhunts, if only it had provided more analytical information. The "media is responsible for a casual attitude as surely as light is responsible for shadow [says the narrator before adding]… we have to put ourselves into the minds of the people at the time, when you had to be instantly affected by everything and never to worry about anything"[37] (Maalouf, *The First Century After Beatrice* 26).

This distrust has led him to subvert the notion of "network," in the media sense of the term, without referring at this stage to the use of computers, to reassess the sociality of the scholarly communities of the time when they were still the linchpins of public policies modeled on the nineteenth-century positivism in Western Europe. In this way, mention is made of a "'Network of Sages', which would cover a great many countries and whose role would be to alert public opinion and the different authorities to the dangers arising from the irmanipulation of the human species"[38] (Maalouf, *The First Century After Beatrice* 95). If the narrator clearly perceives the incongruity of such a formulation, he does not consider it less relevant and provocatively and prosaically summons the "wisdom" in the matter:

But did he not think the title "Network of Sages" somewhat pompous, a trifle ridiculous? 'Not at all' he flashed back. 'Wisdom is the forgotten virtue of our times. A scientist who is not a wise man is either dangerous or, at the best useless. And the word "Network" has an aura of mystery, ambiguity, something a bit provocative which will excite people's curiosity. No, André

---

[37] Les « … moyens d'information répandent l'inconscience aussi sûrement que la lumière répand l'ombre, [dit ce narrateur avant d'ajouter] (…) c'était une époque où il fallait s'émouvoir instantanément de tout et ne se préoccuper durablement de rien » (Maalouf, *Le premier siècle après Béatrice* 48–49).

[38] « 'Réseaux des sages', qui s'étendrait sur un grand nombre de pays et aurait pour rôle d'alerter l'opinion et les diverses autorités sur les dangers qu'entraîne la manipulation irresponsable de l'espèce humaine » (Maalouf, *Le premier siècle après Béatrice* 84).

was right, the "Network of Sages" is a good name. I'm for it[39] (Maalouf, *The First Century After Beatrice* 96).

How can we explain this mistrust of the prefiguration of a networked society in the age of audiovisual information and the written press? As an entomologist, the narrator obviously recognizes a collective intelligence in insects that he does not transfer to the "infosphere" that is imposed on human societies in the twenty-first century. Rather than seeing in it a simple outdated attitude, what Beatrice's father seems to denounce in the lethargy inspired by this "society of the spectacle," as Guy Debord termed it, corresponds perhaps to the imperfect arrangement of memory and of the most recent media. One can imagine—and the intellectual posture of the character lends itself to it—that for this entomologist the success of a media or a technological project concretized by a tool "is really only in the 'gesture which makes it effective' and [...] the operative synergy between the one and the other supposes the existence of a memory in which is inscribed the program of the behavior [...]; this patient evolution of the tools-gestures-memory [being] constitutive of the human adventure of planetization."[40]

Perhaps it is for this reason that the knowledge societies of science fiction and transgressive fiction explore the possibility of more operative, though often troubled or problematic, connections between human memory and technology from the perspective of what I should now call post-humanity. This concept designates an ideology which bets on a symbiosis between the human and the machine and/or which conceives the improvement of a humankind through information technology and genetic modification.

---

[39] « Mais ne pensait-il pas que l'appellation "Réseau des sages" avait quelque chose de pompeux, d'un tantinet risible?—Pas du tout s'enflamma-t-il. La sagesse est la vertu oubliée de notre temps. Un savant qui n'est pas un sage est soit dangereux, soit, dans le meilleur des cas, inutile. Et puis le mot "réseau" a un relent de mystère, d'ambiguïté, de coquinerie qui piquera la curiosité des gens. Non, André ne s'est pas trompé, le Réseau des sages est une bonne enseigne. Je marche! » (Maalouf, *Le premier siècle après Béatrice* 85).

[40] « ... n'est réellement que dans le 'geste qui le rend efficace' et [que] la synergie opératoire entre l'un et l'autre suppose l'existence d'une mémoire dans laquelle s'inscrit le programme du comportement (...); cette patiente évolution des outils-gestes-mémoire [étant] constitutive de l'aventure humaine de la planétisation » (Mattelart, *Histoire de la société de l'information* 51).

What does this post-human ideology pursue? Post-humanism pursues the quest for immortality with, as intermediate phases, the improvement of human capacities, such as intelligence, which would eventually free itself from the body, as well as fusion between the human race and the computer among other machines. Even if this ideology began in the 1970s under the name of transhumanism, the text that really revealed it to the general public is the one that the American writer Vernor Vinge wrote, "The Coming Technological Singularity: How to survive in the Post-Human Era" (1993), which was devoted to the overtaking of the human being by the acceleration of technological progress before feeding the debate that began in 2000, in the USA, between one of its opponents, in the person of the computer scientist Bill Joy, and one of its most fervent defenders, namely Ray Kurzweil. Many essays have, of course, taken a stand on this desire for a radical transformation of the human condition. Most of them are alarmed by the premises of this ideology, like Jürgen Habermas in *The Future of Human Nature* (2003), while others temper it by reminding us, like the astrophysicist Chris Impey in *How It Ends: From You to the Universe* (2010) that it is, rather, the expression of a utopia based on the model of the epic of *Gilgamesh*, which corresponds well to an "immemorial imaginary," as explained in the first chapter:

> Gilgamesh was enough of a god to taste the benefits of power and longevity, but he couldn't make the transition to immortality. Ray Kurzweil plans to do better. [...] In Kurzweil's vision, computation and medical technology will converge in a capability to repair and replace our bodies from within. He argues that a central trope of science fiction—man versus machine—is wrong. Instead, we'll meld with technology and *become* the machine. We'll have many millions of blood cell-sized robots, or nanobots, swarming through our bodies, patrolling for pathogens, and repairing our bones, muscles, arteries, and brain cells. Kurzweil says, "Death is a tragedy." These indefatigable repair crews will destroy disease, rebuild organs, and remove natural limits to our intelligence. Genetic improvements will be downloaded from the Internet. It's a classic Utopian vision (Impey 102–04).

But mostly what is fascinating is that posthumanism as an ideology is also backed by several other mythological narratives. In that sense Prometheus plays a key part almost as a referee to the point that Michael Hauskeller in *Mythologies of Transhumanism* stated that "Prometheism, which presents itself as the '21st century Religion of Transhumanism', [...] is supposed to be founded not on myth and superstition, but on reason and science, and is dedicated to, unsurprisingly, Prometheus" (Hauskeller 165). While I certainly consider the mythological figure of Prometheus as an essential figure in my approach, my focus will go beyond his heroic action to include Pandora and before all Epimetheus, Prometheus's brother and Pandora's husband, to fully explore the threshold of transhuman and, as a final stage, posthuman ideologies. As related by Jean-Claude Heudin in *Les Créatures artificielles. Des automates aux mondes virtuels*, at first sight the myth narrates the story of Prometheus who wants to create a living being to compete with the gods. With water and clay, Prometheus then crafts a creature that can use the resources that nature can offer it, and to complete his work, on the advice of Athena, he goes to steal a source of fire that gives life from the gods. In order to punish Prometheus after that, Zeus asks Hephaitos to create another clay creature: Pandora with a box or a jar containing all the troubles of the earth and who Prometheus will not accept, but who his brother, less on his guard, will accept as a wife. Heudin notes that five characteristic features could summarize this narrative: (1) the clay associated with water is what serves as a basis for Prometheus's initial attempt, (2) sculpture is an art mastered by Prometheus, (3) Athena embodies here the prototype of divine intervention, (4) Prometheus is judged guilty by Zeus, and (5) Zeus punishes men (through Pandora) and also punishes Prometheus by inflicting an eternal punishment. The combination of these features causes Heudin to conclude that "[w]e find this narrative structure in the Jewish legend of the Golem, in Mary Shelley's famous novel *Frankenstein*, and even in Hollywood films such as the *Terminator* saga, to name but a few examples."[41] With a focus on the interpretation of the relations between Prometheus, Epimetheus, and Pandora, my reading is more allegorical to fully develop the significance of this myth, following in this sense Bernard Stiegler in his *Technics and Time, 1. The Fault of Epimetheus*, when he brings into play the two polarities that constitute the *logos* and the *technique* as they act within the post-humanist ideology and drive the great metaphysical questions that science fiction develops:

> The being of humankind is to be outside itself. In order to make up the fault of Epimetheus, Prometheus gives humans the present of putting them

---

[41] « Nous retrouvons cette structure narrative dans la légende juive du Golem, dans le célèbre roman de Mary Shelley *Frankenstein*, et jusque dans les films hollywoodiens comme la saga *Terminator, pour ne citer que quelques exemples* » (Heudin 28).

outside of themselves. Humankind, we may say, puts into effect what it imagines because it is endowed with reason, with *logos*—that is also with language. Or should we rather say that it because it realizes what it imagines—as we said a moment ago, because it lies outside itself—that humanity is endowed with reason, that is, with language? Is it tekhnè that arises from logos, or the reverse? Or rather, is it not that logos and tekhnè are modalities of the same being-outside-oneself? (Stiegler 193).

As an early form of posthumanism, the cyberpunk aesthetic, in an attempt to coincide with technologies deployed in the fields of computer science, genetics, or robotics, thus focuses on the evolution of societies that debate, in the mode of epic or drama, knowledge that is sometimes mobilized by the opposition between the individual and technological singularities, and sometimes is summarized by these singularities' assimilation. If talking about distinctive features from an individual point of view does not *a priori* present difficulties, this is not the case for the notion of "technological singularity" (or Singularity) that corresponds to a very precise idea to describe the acceleration of a technological progress whose ultimate stage supposes a surpassing of humankind as we currently know it. It is in this sense that the "Singularity" can be associated either with the disappearance of our humanity and its civilizations, or with a radical technological reconfiguration of humankind as a definitively transformed living species. In relation to my selected texts, two fictional perspectives emerge from these two possibilities that link posthumanity to the "technological singularity." While in an epic way science fiction over-powers the advent of a posthumanity and of the technological singularity that is correlated to it in *Les Derniers Hommes*, and this genre arranges the advent of a posthumanity and of the technological singularity in *The Silent City*, the transfiction genre assimilates these two trends to each other in *The Possibility of an Island* and in *Songes de Mevlido* to better signify the drama that is played out in the mutations of a human race whose loss of control of History and evolution brings out identity crises more than the benefits of a supposedly unequaled technoscience.

Whether it is a cyberpunk aesthetic of the event or that of a fusional reduction, the same referent to the mythologies of a "writing as a double of mankind" pushes science fiction and transfiction to look for traces of humanity in the ambivalence of the desire and the refusal to be written of their main characters. How does this ambivalence become transparent? I argue that for science fiction and transfiction, the pursuit or quest involved in manhunting becomes a query of knowledge societies about their sense of memory in the hypothesis of a remediation of the symbolism of the book and its enlargement to the problematic of computer and genetic coding. Formulated in an explicit way, this kind of request is addressed in the case of science fiction, specifically in *Les Derniers Hommes*, to the technological legitimacy of post-human societies, to the example of the invasion of the earth that, according to Solman, the members of the Eskato started by the first stage of their becoming mutant:

- – Do you really think that Kadija and her tribe are in tune with Mother Nature?
- – They use a language that we don't know, or that we have forgotten. But if they sent Katwrin and Kadija, it is because they are missing something. Something they don't have or that they have lost. We are marked by the mistakes of our ancestors, of our history, while they have lost their way in a blocked, frozen future.
- – The future is never fixed or else one would have to despair of everything.
- – If they did not despair, Moram, they would not have condemned man to extinction.[42]

Indeed, in Pierre Bordage's storyworld, which aims at the minimum of incompleteness, almost everything is said about the origins of the Eskato and its intentions. And this also includes its shortcomings, at the risk of making this memorial request too explicit and sometimes appearing too didactic for the narrator: "The Verb of which Raïma spoke had failed to extirpate the previous memory of those he had chosen as Righteous. If, according to the words of Ismahil, men, those evolved animals, kept in

---

[42] « – Tu penses réellement que Kadija et ceux de sa tribu sont en accord avec mère Nature?.

Ils utilisent un langage que nous ne connaissons pas, ou que nous avons oublié. Mais, s'ils ont envoyé Katwrin et Kadija, c'est que quelque chose leur manque. Quelque chose qu'ils n'ont pas ou qu'ils ont perdu. Nous, nous sommes marqués par les erreurs, de nos ancêtres, de notre histoire, eux ils se sont fourvoyés dans un avenir bloqué, figé.

L'avenir n'est jamais figé ou alors ce serait à désespérer de tout.

S'ils ne désespéraient pas, Moram, ils n'auraient pas condamné les hommes à l'extinction » (Bordage 624).

themselves traces of their primitive nature, the Saints remained stitched in the human fabric."[43]

In the same way, Elisa's becoming mutant is outlined in the perspective of the disappearance of the "memory banks"[44] of the City (Vonarburg, *The Silent City* 26); knowing that Elisa's apprenticeship only really progresses insofar as she learns to reformulate the request of this knowledge society in its collective sense of memory, before distancing herself from it and then discarding her "descendants" as much as possible. To do this, the request that deals with the meaning of the City's memory is all the more explicit as it serves as a framework for the exchanges between the "last men" embodied by Paul or Richard Desprats and the "men from the Outside" between whom Elisa plays the role of referee by asking herself many questions. What help does she wish to bring to the Outsiders? What is the content of this help, taking into account the influences exerted on her personality by the two already-mentioned men? And above all, how do her "children" perceive this "Project"? All these questions, which give rise to so many event sequences which must be understood from the point of view of the discovery, and then the mastery of her androgyny, are still an essential interrogation that could be summarized as follows: who is she exactly to decide the disappearance of the City? A most crucial question, if there is one, since after having murdered Paul and justified her act by self-defense, Elisa is quite conscious that a definitive ending of the City would, this time, mean the total disappearance of her creator, of his intentions, and, in spite of her gesture, of the affection she still has for him:

> Elisa can't think of any words as Paul's coffin advances slowly toward the door of the cremation oven. She doesn't know whether one is supposed to say anything. She feels numb, her mind filled with disjoined images, fragments of memory, Paul's face, a smile, an expression of tenderness or anger, his forehead, a glimpsed profile. But she can't bring it all together, can't see him whole; already she's losing him. And yet those images of him

---

[43] « Le Verbe dont parlait Raïma avait échoué à extirper la mémoire antérieure de ceux qu'il avait choisis pour Justes. Si, selon les paroles d'Ismahil, les hommes, ces animaux évolués, gardaient en eux des traces de leur nature primitive, les Saints restaient piqués dans la trame humaine » (Bordage 612).

[44] « ... banques mémorielles » (Vonarburg, *Le silence de la cité* 38).

lie sleeping, intact, in the City's memory. They too will disappear when the City stops[45] (Vonarburg, *The Silent City* 92).

As evidence of the explicit transfer of the constitutive elements of the "evidential paradigm" (trace, imprint, sign, etc.) to the "Galilean paradigm" in the opening of the symbolism of the books of nature and of the world, let us observe that the haunting of the destruction of the memories, whose remediation is very precisely qualified as "traces" in the French language (and not as "images," as proposed by Jane Brierley's translation), is also attested to by a second disappearance, that of Richard Desprats' computerized avatar: "PROGRAM DISCONTINUED. At the end of half an hour, after she's tried every possible code she can think of, she's forced to give up. There's not a trace of the program of programs that made up the pseudo-personality of Desprats in the City's memory banks"[46] (Vonarburg, *The Silent City* 93–94). Apart from the suffering and then the surprise that Elisa experiences when faced with the disappearance of these two "last men," the computerized traces of Paul and Richard Desprats evoke above all the actions that these characters left behind and suggest that the City could always update their skills if necessary, as if the dead who characterized this society of knowledge in their survival never ceased to compete for Elisa's conscience and never stopped intervening in the affairs of the living.

None of this pretension that the heroine of Vonarburg's novel ends up turning to her advantage remains, however, in the transfiction narratives that cast a real discredit on intentional action. In the absence of subjects conscious of a world that would evolve according to their cognitive aim, the drama played out in *The Possibility of an Island* and *Songes de Mevlido* involves a reduction of the characters to the world they inhabit, knowing

---

[45] « Elle ne sait pas quoi dire pendant que le cercueil de Paul avance lentement vers la porte qui masque le brasier. Elle ne sait s'il convient de dire quelque chose. Elle se sent tout engourdie, des images disjointes passent dans son esprit, des lambeaux de souvenirs, des morceaux du visage de Paul, un sourire, une expression de tendresse, ou de colère, le front, ou un profil perdu, elle n'arrive pas à l'évoquer en entier, il se perd, déjà. Toutes ces images de lui, pourtant, qui dorment, intactes, dans la mémoire de la Cité. Ces traces-là aussi vont s'effacer, quand la Cité s'arrêtera » (Vonarburg, *Le silence de la cité* 142).

[46] « PROGRAMME DISCONTINUÉ. Au bout d'une demi-heure, après avoir essayé toutes les approches qu'elle a pu imaginer, elle doit se rendre à l'évidence: il n'y a plus trace du ou des programmes qui constituaient la pseudo-personnalité de Desprats dans les banques mémorielles de la Cité » (Vonarburg, *Le silence de la cité* 145).

that such a fictional universe is itself diminished or reduced, according to traditional cyberpunk aesthetics, to a social organization that recomposes itself in a race to mutations or technological innovations. In contrast to science fiction works, the city is no longer an expanding political entity in the novels of Houellebecq and Volodine. For instance, Daniel24 and Daniel25 live in a house that cuts them off from the rest of the world, while Mevlido oscillates between the city center of an unnamed country, which keeps the appearance of a normal place of sociality, and a ruined building in the course of his ramblings.

Formulated in an implicit way, the goal of the knowledge societies of transgressive fiction concerns the "naturalization" of the intentional aim of its characters, this sense of memory that pushes readers to apprehend them not in their becoming mutant—as was previously the case for Solman and Elisa—but as real *corpora* that fluctuate in the computerized or genetic looping of the memories they have of themselves and of their society. A maximum of incompleteness therefore surrounds this drama between, on the one hand, ideologically motivated memorial requests to which Houellebecq's and Volodine's characters must submit (writing comments from their "ancestor's" life story, as far as Daniel24 and Daniel25 are concerned, and political and psychological interrogations, as far as Mevlido is concerned), and, on the other hand, their actions that amount to nothing more than expectations: those of a sign, for Daniel25, near the sea, and of an inclusion of Mevlido in one of his wife's dreams. This disproportion is important because it makes the transfiction aphoristic—in the sense that Carlo Ginzburg understands it—in the description of the crises that these characters go through:

> The decline of systematic thought has been followed by the success of aphoristic reasoning [...] The very term *aphoristic* is in itself revealing. (It is a clue, a symptom, a lead: there is no getting away from the paradigm.) *Aphorisms* was, in fact, the title of a famous work by Hippocrates. [...] Aphoristic literature is, by definition, an attempt to formulate evaluations of man and society on the basis of symptoms and clues: a man and a society that are sick, *in crisis* (Ginzburg, *Clues, Myths, and the Historical Method* 112).

A very particular poem on the meaning of this reduction of a memory that turns in loops emerges from these crises which are more fusional than eventful in that they testify to a tracing of the characters onto their world. In Houellebecq's work, aphoristic poetry thus corresponds particularly to

Marie22's states of mind, which are often relayed by Daniel24's attempt to understand them:

> *Beneath the sun of the dead bird,*
> *Spread infinitely the plain;*
> *There is no death more serene:*
> *Show me some of your body.*
> 4262164, 51026, 21113247, 6323235. At the address indicated there was nothing, not even an error message; a completely blank screen[47] (Houellebecq, *The Possibility of an Island* 98).

The character of a "shifted exchange" also subject to multiple interpretations, Mevlido is for his part a being of fiction whose narrator amuses himself by listing the emotions, either in Volodine's aphoristic poetry, in which a series of variations on the same word occurs, or in a listing that appears even more clearly since it is introduced by the typographical use of a bullet point in order to express the wish or the hope of an action that is a political revendication:

- BEFORE BEING REBORN, ONLY THE FIRE, BECOME THE ONE WHO BURNS!
- ENTER INTO THE STRANGE IMAGE, BECOME THE ONE WHO BURNS!
- WHEN YOU HAVE BURNED, UNDRESS, BE REBORN, STRIKE![48]

Whether it manifests the invasive character of technology or questions the legitimacy and crisis of posthuman societies, the sense of memory as related to speculative fiction, science fiction, and transfiction thus accounts for a resistance in characters who redefine the limits of their humanity. And if it asserts itself throughout their trajectories when they take their distance both with the pursuit of the manhunts and with the building of

---

[47] « *Sous le soleil de l'oiseau mort/Étale infiniment, la plaine;*
Il n'y a pas de mort sereine:/Montre-moi un peu de ton corps.
4262164, 51026, 21113247, 6323235. À l'adresse indiquée il n'y avait rien, pas même de message d'échec;
un écran entièrement blanc » (Houellebecq, *La possibilité d'une île 2005* 139).
[48] « AVANT DE RENAÎTRE, SEUL LE FEU, DEVIENS CELLE QUI BRÛLE!
ENTRE DANS L'IMAGE ÉTRANGE, DEVIENS CELLE QUI BRÛLE!
QUAND TU AS BRÛLÉ, DÉVÊTS-TOI, RENAIS, FRAPPE! » (Volodine 459).

information or knowledge societies, it is very often to measure the "evidential paradigm" in comparison to the meaning of the walk, the literary wandering representing the apogee of a liberating detour in the literature of anticipation by its reconquest of space.

THE TRIAL OF WALKING

In the detour that consists of escaping from one's pursuers as well as from an enterprise of reification, the walk becomes an ordeal for the focal characters of my selection of works who make their entry in a space where walking requires the "crucial element of engagement of the body and the mind with the world, of knowing the world through the body and the body through the world." (Solnit 29). Indeed it is by walking, which generates in them "senses of place" (Solnit 4), that these characters show resistance, reappropriate the world, and also take the measure of the possibilities offered by their body, in that this activity "represents one of the first fights of man with nature, as if the simple fact of walking was not part of the order of things"[49] (Carpentier and L'Allier 16). Finally, moving upright and remaining in this posture for the duration is really what characterizes humans, what makes the walk an almost-always-significant test in anticipation literature. The act of reading the great book of nature— "reading with one's feet" (Solnit 70)—begins at first in prospective fiction by an uprooting of the original clay that recalls the emergence of humankind. This mythological aspect of literary wandering is particularly well illustrated in *Globalia*, when Baïkal discovers the territory of the "no-zones" for the first time, after having failed with his companion Kate to escape from an indoor hiking building:

The red of the earth suggested the rising of a sun from the ground, not the dawn of a day but the dawn of time. Baïkal felt like the first human offered to the world; the first to whom the world was offered. It was necessary for a cry to reach him in order for him to decide to interrupt this solitary and blissful wedding. It was a distant croaking sound that was muffled by the humid air. It came from a large bird, which crossed a corner of the sky with a wobbly flight. This signal set in motion the whole mechanics of life. Baïkal began by lifting his feet one after the other to remove them from the suction of the mud. Then he started walking. [...] Between his escape from the

[49] « ... représente un des premiers combats de l'homme avec la nature, comme si le simple fait de marcher n'était pas inscrit dans l'ordre des choses » (Carpentier and L'Allier 16).

trekking room and this liberation on an unknown desert plateau, there was a similarity that made these two moments like one.[50]

If one of the attributes of walking in science fiction literature is to very quickly embody a form of protest practice, it is because it can be likened to a deciphering activity that invites the reader to a different use of the world from that which is *a priori* wanted and organized by the whole of society. Because its main function is to drive a wedge into the dystopian order of the storyworld, walking requires characters who have a shifted view of what the object of a quest or of questioning is, like Baïkal's fellow traveler, Fraiseur, who practices what is called the *art of memory* during their journey together.

Traditionally, the art of memory is a mnemonic procedure practiced since antiquity, which consists of associating images or places with textual or numerical sequences that one seeks to memorize. Initially conceived as an aid to rhetoric and then to writing, this process, which was taught until the Renaissance, was inspired by a legend that Cicero mentions in his *De Oratore* to describe the hypothetical circumstances in which the Greek poet Simonides of Ceos remembered the names of guests invited to a banquet, on whom a roof had collapsed in his absence because of an affront committed against the twin gods Castor and Pollux. Having remembered the place occupied by these guests around a table before the catastrophe, Simonides would have been able to designate each of the unrecognizable bodies by their name and summarize this process in a mnemonic method called "places." Concerning the analogy between walking and reading, Rebecca Solnit suggests in her essay *Wanderlust: A History of Walking* that the art of memory has, in these conditions, very early impregnated the culture of walking for which to "walk the same route again can mean to think the same thoughts again, as though thoughts and ideas were indeed fixed objects in a landscape one need only

---

[50] "Le rouge de la terre suggérait le lever d'un soleil sorti du sol, non pas aube d'une journée mais aube des temps. Baikal se sentait comme le premier humain offert au monde; le premier auquel le monde était offert. Il fallut qu'un cri lui parvienne pour qu'il se résolût à interrompre cette noce solitaire et béate. C'était un coassement lointain qu'atténuait l'air humide. Il provenait d'un grand oiseau, qui traversa un coin de ciel d'un vol bancal. Ce signal enclencha toute la mécanique de la vie. Baikal commença par soulever l'un après ses pieds pour les soustraire à la succion de la boue. Puis il se mit en marche. (…) Entre son escapade hors de la salle de trekking et cette libération sur un plateau inconnu et désertique, existait une parenté qui faisait de ces deux moments comme un seul" (Rufin 130).

know how to travel through. In this way, walking is reading" (Solnit 77). This situation summarizes the posture of Fraiseur, who is confronted with the natural and urban landscapes that he rediscovers in Baïkal's company and who does not escape the observations of the latter who sees there the possibility of reappropriating a singular word, even if it is anecdotal or legendary:

> While they walked side by side, Baïkal let him talk. Fraiseur knew a great number of legends, anecdotes that came to him according to what the landscape gave him to see. It was all the more surprising in that this landscape itself did not speak: the advertisements that invaded the space in Globalia were completely missing.[51]

Such a path, which is doubled in Baïkal by an aptitude for clairvoyance and which tends moreover toward a reading of *Walden* by Thoreau, at the end of Rufin's novel, gives consistency to what I termed (in Chap. 4) a conception of the world borrowed from the closing of the symbolism of the book. Still dealing with speculative fiction, I observe that this closure becomes much more encyclopedic under the pen of Maalouf since the focal character of his novels survey the Jardin des Plantes as a book of nature and "landscape of the memory" (Solnit 77).

In *Our Life in the Forest*, walking also goes hand in hand with the stream of consciousness and the questioning of a memorial landscape that sets the parameters of Marie's involvement in freeing her "half" (that is, her clone) when she recalls how she used to visit her clone, taking a "walk along the train tracks. That long walk to go and see Marie—let's not call it a stroll— did me good. When it comes to the shrinks' talk of pathological attachment, I wonder if I wasn't addicted to walking. To the movement of my legs and also to the unfolding of the landscape"[52] (Darrieussecq, *Our Life in the Forest* 77). Considering this statement helps readers better understand

---

[51] "Pendant qu'ils marchaient côte à côte, Baïkal le laissait parler. Fraiseur connaissait un grand nombre de légendes, d'anecdotes qui lui venaient au gré de ce que le paysage lui donnait à voir. C'était d'autant plus surprenant que ce paysage lui-même ne parlait pas: les publicités qui envahissaient l'espace en Globalia faisaient là totalement défaut" (Rufin 219).

[52] « … marche le long des rails. Cette longue marche pour aller voir Marie, on ne peut pas parler de promenade, me faisait du bien. Quand les psys évoquaient un attachement pathologique, je me demande si je n'étais pas devenu un accro à la marche elle-même. Au mouvement de mes jambes et aussi au déroulé du paysage » (Darrieussecq, *Notre vie dans les forêts roman* 100–101).

why freeing her "half" occurs through the actions of "verticalizing" and "walking" which, if we add the ability to speak, defines the character of what is properly human: "A few of us got together to verticalize our halves. We held their legs and shoulders by propping them up against a tree [...]. Next came walking. Like a baby. It didn't take long; it was as if their mode of life had somehow instilled in them a certain amount of human data—first walking upright then speech"[53] (Darrieussecq, *Our Life in the Forest* 3–4).

These vertical positionings and crossings of spaces are important because they testify to decisive changes in the psyches of the characters who can be viewed as having an evolving reading of the books of nature and the world in the course of their peregrinations. In *The First Century After Beatrice*, this is also the case of the narrator for whom the "Jardin des Plantes" constitutes an encyclopedic referent.

From the point of view of this entomologist comparing the limits of the human race to those he has observed in insects, walking is an activity of recollection that helps him to take stock, to the point of representing, at the end of the story, a gesture of resistance for this scholar of a discreet nature who is most often in agreement with a deterministic vision of History:

> I often think of those lost futures. Sometimes, as sunk in my daydreams I take my daily walk along the mountain paths, I go back sixty years, long before the beginning of the Century of Beatrice, and I try to imagine what different paths this irksome species to which I belong could have followed. Then, in the space of one walk, I build a different world[54] (Maalouf, *The First Century After Beatrice* 191).

In continuity with the deciphering of this closing of the symbolism of the book, science fiction cannot, however, be satisfied with the only posture that would affect its focal character, since from that character's

---

[53] « On verticalisait nos moitiés en s'y prenant à plusieurs. On leur tenait les jambes et les épaules en les calant contre un arbre. La marche, ensuite. Comme un bébé. Ça allait vite, à croire que leur genre de vie les avait quand même informés d'un certain *data* humain, la marche debout et plus tard la parole » (Darrieussecq, *Notre vie dans les forêts roman* 12–13).

[54] « Je pense souvent à ces avenirs révolus. Parfois même au cours de mes promenades quotidiennes dans les sentiers de ma montagne, emporté par mes rêveries, je reviens soixante ans en arrière, bien avant le début du siècle de Béatrice, et j'essaie d'imaginer les chemins qu'aurait pu suivre l'irritante espèce à laquelle j'appartiens. (...) Je reconstruis alors, l'espace d'une promenade, un monde différent » (Maalouf, *Le Premier siècle* 300).

point of view it is especially a question of giving an account of a becoming mutant that supposes an explicit confrontation with what could incarnate the symbolism of the *liber mundi*, from the book of the life to that of the world by including the book of the nature. The example of "Solman the lame"—who appears at the beginning of Pierre Bordage's novel *Les Derniers Hommes*, at the time of an expedition organized with the aim of detecting underground water tables—illustrates this deciphering and a confrontation with the order of a world literally inspired by the symbolic space of the book. Although perceived as "a visionary mind in a feeble body,"[55] Solman is that character who finally overcomes the infirmities of his body, first by leading his people, then by taking the lead in a long and fraught journey to thwart the replacement of the "last men," to whom he belongs, by the proponents of a posthumanity who seek to eliminate him and his people. The last phase of this quest, which sees him leading a forced walking expedition to the gathering place of his posthuman enemies, is by far the most intriguing because the endurance and physical efforts involved in this walk allow him to feel, before he faces his adversaries, in full control of his body, and this despite his disgrace and handicap:

> He didn't stare at the forest, he didn't look behind him, he just had to be aware of his movements, of the regular swinging of his legs, of his arms, of the rhythm of his breathing and of his heart. He was now enjoying the lightness he had always dreamed of, the unequalled happiness of running in the bosom of Mother Nature, this perfect harmony between intentions and actions.[56]

Even if temporary, such a change, which magnifies the will, only takes on real significance insofar as it counterbalances a host of clues that herald a new world in which the metamorphosis of the Île-de-France forest precedes the appearance of "a gigantic esplanade in the center of which stands a cube-shaped building that [shines] with the splendor of fire."[57]

---

[55] « …un esprit visionnaire dans un corps débile » (Bordage 75).

[56] « Il ne fixait pas la forêt, il ne regardait pas derrière lui, il lui suffisait d'être conscient de ses mouvements, du balancement régulier de ses jambes, de ses bras, du rythme de sa respiration et de son cœur. Il jouissait maintenant de cette légèreté dont il avait toujours rêvé, de ce bonheur inégalable de courir dans le sein de mère Nature, de cet accord parfait entre les intentions et les actes » (Bordage 636).

[57] « … une gigantesque esplanade au centre de laquelle se [dresse] une construction de forme cubique qui [resplendit] avec le faste du feu » (Bordage 650).

The consistency of the closure of the symbolism of the book, which allows a return to the space of the biblical book, thus objectifies the meaning of its struggle in a well-defined place where decisive transformations take place:

> And then, suddenly, they entered another world [...]. The trees were now clothed in sparkling leaves, as if gorged with the brightness of the sun. Green, blue, red, yellow, purple, they shone with more brilliance than the precious stones and the gold of the Leote people. They adorned the day with gleaming, shimmering reflections, sketching sumptuous arches of light constantly modified by the whims of the breeze. It was from them, moreover, that these musical sighs came, these more or less low chords which, all together, composed a choir with a bewitching harmony.
> "Thee rampart of the new Jerusalem," murmured Kadija.[58]

For as soon as he crosses this rampart, Solman, who follows in Kadija's steps as she is "sucked into the heart of the forest,"[59] finally discovers his artifact-adversary, which takes the form more of a "flamboyant construction [...] which [shelters] the source of living water, the tree of life"[60] than that of a non-embodied reticular computer device, in what I have called in Chap. 4 the recovered radiance of the tree and the garden. From the human fabric to the "book of life" that became a tree, it is thus that the return to the key mythologies occurs. These mythologies are based, according to Clarisse Herrenschmidt, on a parallel between the emergence of humankind and the systems of writing that recount it, before envisaging the possibility of the resistance of these systems to mutations in the language of code.

If one observes the literary wandering that agrees with the opening of the symbolism of the book, it is necessary to note that it no longer leads

---

[58] « Et puis, subitement, ils pénétrèrent dans un autre monde (...). Les arbres se vêtaient à présent de feuilles étincelantes, comme gorgées de la clarté du soleil. Vertes, bleues, rouges, jaunes, violettes, elles brillaient avec davantage d'éclat que les pierres précieuses et l'or du peuple léote. Elles paraient le jour de reflets rutilants, chatoyants, esquissaient de somptueuses arches de lumière sans cesse modifiées par les caprices de la brise. C'était d'elles, en outre, que provenaient ces soupirs musicaux, ces accords plus ou moins graves qui, tous ensemble, composaient un chœur a l'harmonie envoutante. "Le rempart de la Jérusalem nouvelle", murmura Kadija » (Bordage 645).

[59] « ... aspirée par le cœur de la forêt » (Bordage 650).

[60] « ... construction flamboyante (...) qui [abrite] la source d'eau vive, l'arbre de vie » (Bordage 656).

to *the tree*, whatever its encyclopedic figuration, but to *the labyrinth*, which already suggests the imprint of coding or networking. Contrary to the long march of Bordage's novel, which supports an explicit confrontation with a computer entity, the one revealed by the epilogue of Michel Houellebecq's novel, *The Possibility of an Island*, gives an account of a much more implicit confrontation in that it ends with the exhaustion of the neo-human character of Daniel25 in the pathways of his interior labyrinths.

In this transfiction that alternately tells the story of Daniel1 and his clones in charge of commenting on their ancestor's "life stories" in an attempt to make sense of their own existence, Daniel25 decides to leave the protective environment of his villa, following in the footsteps of Marie23, and to set off on an adventure for a journey that would seem to have no return. Following this escape, the discovery of new spaces resembles at first multiple scenes of hunting for this character, who then submits himself to the test of a long walk to discover himself differently in his condition of being artifact. By trying thus to retrace the "evidential paradigm" of the metaphysical desire of the old humanity from which he seeks to be freed, he then discovers what remains of the sea and the oceanic feeling which is associated with it. When he leaves the surroundings of the old city of Madrid for the desert after numerous hunts, Daniel25 first of all abandons his rifle and approaches the crossing of the Big Grey Space as if it were a blank page that his body, which was now invested with a cynegetic knowledge, was going to be able to read. Besides, conceiving himself as one of the "incomplete beings, beings in transition, whose destiny was to prepare for the coming of a digital future"[61] (Houellebecq, *The Possibility of an Island* 156), no doubt he hopes to participate in a new form of writing in this space that invites a stripping down:

> I was not, strictly speaking, certain I wanted to live, but the idea of death had no substance. I saw my body as a vehicle, but it was a vehicle for nothing.

---

[61] « Nous étions nous-mêmes des êtres incomplets, des êtres de transition, dont la destinée était de préparer l'avènement d'un futur numérique » (Houellebecq, *La possibilité d'une île 2005* 220–221).

I had not been able to reach the Spirit; I continued, however, to wait for a sign[62] (Houellebecq, *The Possibility of an Island* 330).

However, the ordeal that pushes him to his limits during this walk does not produce the expected effect, because at the end of his investigations, he finds himself in the incapacity to divest himself of Daniel1's "life stories" that make Daniel25, according to his own terms, an "undelivered" being, all the more without reference points in that he chooses to end his journey by immersing himself in pools of salt water. Immobile, only his dreams then measure the incompleteness of his existence and remind him, in their labyrinthine dimension, of the time when he understood them as if they could be "insights into other branches of the universe, [...], other bifurcations of observable phenomena that appeared at the same time as certain events in the day" (Houellebecq, *The Possibility of an Island* 155).[63] To play on Albert Camus' challenge in *The Myth of Sisyphus*, that of imagining Sisyphus happy, here we see that from the point of view of this neo-human who lives in the despondency of a naturalized awareness, we must now imagine Sisyphus unhappy:

Happiness was not a possible horizon. The world had betrayed. My body belonged to me for only a brief lapse of time; I would never reach the goal I had been set. The future was empty; it was the mountain. My dreams were populated with emotional presences. I was, I was no longer. Life was real[64] (Houellebecq, *The Possibility of an Island* 337).

By contrast, the literary wanderings in Élisabeth Vonarburg's and Antoine Volodine's novels, which are also in line with the opening of the book's symbolism, emphasize much more the function of dreams and daydreams, while also remaining more faithful to what Rebecca Solnit calls

---

[62] « Je n'étais pas, à proprement parler, certain de vouloir vivre, mais l'idée de la mort n'avait aucune consistance. Je percevais mon corps comme un véhicule, mais c'était un véhicule de rien. Je n'avais pas été capable d'accéder à l'Esprit; je continuais, pourtant, à attendre un signe » (Houellebecq, *La possibilité d'une île 2005* 465).

[63] « ... des aperçus sur d'autres branches d'univers existantes (...), c'est-à-dire d'autres bifurcations d'observables apparues à l'occasion de certains événements de la journée » (Houellebecq, *La possibilité d'une île 2005* 220).

[64] « Le bonheur n'était pas un horizon possible. Le monde avait trahi. Mon corps m'appartenait pour un bref laps de temps; je n'atteindrais jamais l'objectif assigné. Le futur était vide; il était la montagne. Mes rêves étaient peuplés de présences émotives. J'étais, je n'étais plus. La vie était réelle » (Houellebecq, *La possibilité d'une île 2005* 474).

"the moral of mazes: sometimes you have to turn your back on your goal to get there" (Solnit 69). The reason is that this kind of wandering participates fully in a learning process that places Elisa and Mevlido in a position not to master but to accomplish a symbolic journey, although they have not often had the opportunity to decide on the bodily mutations causing their displacement.

The first maze of dreams that loses both Elisa's character and her reader in *The Silent City* concerns above all access to this computer matrix that contains the bodies of those who now live only through the interface of robots. It is in reaction to her childhood dream that pushes her to open a succession of doors in spite of her fears and to walk toward a "pink mass"— which is the very heart of the City's project in the undifferentiation of its inhabitants—that Elisa first seeks to acquire an identity, a face of which she knows she is deprived:

Elisa managed to turn and run. But once back in the corridor she had to open the other doors. And in each room were pink blobs that smiled and talked to her, and the voices belonged to Mario, to Serena, to—. The blobs had no eyes, no mouths, no faces, but they were alive, alive. The last one had Papa's voice, and Elisa couldn't stop herself from going toward it, from going to it, her hands, her legs, her head, her whole body melting and mingling with the pink blob. Elisa woke up screaming[65] (Vonarburg, *The Silent City* 17).

In adulthood, other dreams deprive her of a singular face when Paul, her creator, who has become her lover, confuses her with another woman he knew in the past and who answers to the name of Séréna, at the moment when Elisa mutates and unconsciously changes her identity at night in order to take on the aspect of this other woman he has loved. But if the labyrinth easily traverses the domain of dreams inside of the City, it is not the same outside it, where this labyrinth covers a more geographic reality: "The ommach, guided by infrared vision, threads his way through the labyrinth of haystacks, woodpiles, machinery and other material. Elisa

---

[65] « Élisa arrivait à faire demi-tour et à se sauver. Mais dans le couloir, il fallait qu'elle aille ouvrir les autres portes. Et dans chaque pièce des masses roses lui... souriaient, et elles lui parlaient, et c'était la voix de Mario, de Serena... sans yeux, sans bouche, sans visage, mais vivantes, vivantes. Et à la fin c'était la voix de Papa, et Élisa s'avançait malgré elle vers la masse pulsante et elle y entrait, et ses mains, ses jambes, sa tête, tout son corps se fondait, se confondait avec la masse rose. Élisa se réveilla en hurlant » (Vonarburg, *Le silence de la cité* 24–25).

follows" (Vonarburg, *The Silent City* 66),[66] just like when she travels in her androgynous form through the city of Vietelli in the company of a robot before trying to return to her city of origin and confront Paul who has fallen into madness. And in fact, after many events, including Paul's death and a dreamlike struggle that makes her definitively eliminate this "pink mass" from her personality, the labyrinth materializes all the more because it signifies Elisa's disengagement from this computer entity, in the physical form of a protective retreat between her "children" and the City that she has managed to silence:

> Much later, when she has finished giving all her instructions to the City, Elisa gets up and Abram does the same. Together they walk through the corridors and along the galleries, the lights going out behind them. [...] Elisa and Abram walk on, their steps in unison as they thread their way through the underground labyrinth that leads to the caves and up to the daylight[67] (Vonarburg, *The Silent City* 208).

The science fiction literature conceived in the opening of the symbolism of the book does not therefore suppose the disappearance of the fable at the limits of the psychic life of its characters. The fact that the labyrinth serves as an imprint of the crossroads of consciousnesses confronted with the identity questions of computer coding explains that it refers to what I previously called in Chap. 4 a remediated form of the symbolism of the book, which cannot for this reason totally discard the metaphorical conception of a life assimilated to a story, contained in the play of metaphors such as the books of life, of nature, and of the world. This explains why the labyrinth can be understood in fiction according to *a variable geometry*, perhaps returning it to one of its first cultural functions, at the time when it was "thus a three-dimensional anthology in which walking, reading, and looking united into a journey into the fables' morals and meanings" (Solnit 75).

---

[66] « Élisa suit l'ommach et sa vision infrarouge dans ce labyrinthe, et ils arrivent enfin au bâtiment habité » (Vonarburg, *Le silence de la cité* 98).

[67] « Longtemps après, quand elle a fini de donner toutes ses instructions à la Cité, Élisa se lève, et Abram en fait autant. Ensemble, ils traversent des couloirs et des galeries, et les lumières s'éteignent derrière eux. Ils arrivent au bout du chemin, et pour la dernière fois les sas s'ouvrent et se referment sur eux. (...) Élisa et Abram s'éloignent du même pas dans le labyrinthe souterrain qui mène aux cavernes, puis au jour » (Vonarburg, *Le silence de la cité* 324).

As a transfiction that insists less on the necessity of a focal character with a unitary consciousness, Antoine Volodine's *Songes de Mevlido* also evokes the variable geometry of the labyrinth, which refers as much to the maze of the streets of Poulailler Quatre that the policeman Mevlido walks as to his inner labyrinths. But if the maze of the streets serves as a setting for the assassination of his character by a former child soldier, and then echoes the incessant reincarnations that occur in equally labyrinthine places, only his inner labyrinths and their resorptions in a bedroom in the presence of Verena Becker allow us to understand this "moral of the labyrinth" that Rebecca Solnit has detected in the choice of turning back in order to achieve his ends. Before readers learn about Verena, at the beginning of the novel, Mevlido cohabits with a certain Maleeya Bayarlag in a room populated by spiders:

> Suddenly they had started to walk each for himself, at a great distance from each other. They were no longer communicating. Mevlido in turn was retreating into his own labyrinths. He neglected what connected him to Maleeya Bayarlag, his current life with her, this fatalistic sharing of the fall. He had begun to think of Verena Becker, his wife who had been assassinated twenty years earlier by child soldiers during the racist fighting in Zone Five, in Djaka Park West.[68]

While the two roommates only have in common the experience of mourning the loss of a loved one, Mevlido's dreams, namely his own labyrinths, are going to materialize in a series of stories including other characters, until returning at the end of the novel to a scene of a room to be shared, not with Maleeya Bayarlag, but with Verena Becker, through the prism of her own memories. This is how literary wandering reduces madness to memory in this novel with a refined cyberpunk aesthetic. But then why turn back and what could this "moral of the labyrinth" intimated by technological mutations be? Thinking about coding through these mutations or through a networking in the labyrinth's imprint, it is undoubtedly to make the choice of feeling for a humankind whose sense of memory orchestrates not its abstract virtualization, but its resistance.

---

[68] « Soudain ils s'étaient mis à cheminer chacun pour soi, à grande distance l'un de l'autre. Ils ne communiquaient plus. À son tour Mevlido reculait vers ses propres labyrinthes. Il négligeait ce qui le reliait à Maleeya Bayarlag, sa vie actuelle avec elle, ce partage fataliste de la chute. Il avait commencé à penser à Verena Becker, sa femme assassinée vingt ans plus tôt par des enfants-soldats, pendant les combats racistes de Zone Cinq, à Djaka Park West » (Volodine 36–37).

BIBLIOGRAPHY

Atwood, Margaret. *In Other Worlds: Sf and the Human Imagination*. Anchor Books, 2012.

Bessière, Jean, et al., editors. "'Paradigme de l'indice' et Certitudes de La Fiction: Discours de l'Histoire et Origines de La Littérature." *Savoirs et Littérature: Literature, the Humanities and the Social Sciences*, Presses de la Sorbonne nouvelle, 2002.

Bordage, Pierre. *Les derniers hommes*. J'AI LU edition, Editions 84, 2005.

Carpentier, André, and Alexis L'Allier. *Les Écrivains Déambulateurs: Poètes et dédembulateurs de l'espace urbain*. Figura, Centre de recherche sur le texte et l' imaginaire, 2004, p. 199.

Chamayou, Grégoire. *Les chasses à l'homme: histoire et philosophie du pouvoir cynégétique*. Fabrique, 2010.

———. *Manhunts: A Philosophical History*. Princeton University Press, 2012.

Darrieussecq, Marie. *Notre vie dans les forêts roman*. P.O.L., 2017.

———. *Our Life in the Forest*. Translated by Penny Hueston, The Text Publishing Company, 2018.

Ginzburg, Carlo. *Clues, Myths, and the Historical Method*. Johns Hopkins Univ Press, 2013.

———. "Racines d'un Paradigme de l'indice." *Le Débat*, vol. 6, no. Signes, traces, pistes, 1980, pp. 3–44.

Hauskeller, Michael. *Mythologies of Transhumanism*. Springer International Publishing, 2016.

Heudin, Jean-Claude. *Les créatures artificielles: des automates aux mondes virtuels*. O. Jacob, 2008.

Houellebecq, Michel. *La possibilité d'une île*. Fayard, 2005.

———. *The Possibility of an Island*. Translated by Gavin Bowd, Knopf, 2006.

Impey. *How It Ends: From You to the Universe*. John Wiley and Sons, 2010.

Langlet, Irène. *La science-fiction: lecture et poétique d'un genre littéraire*. A. Colin, 2006.

Maalouf, Amin. *Le premier siècle après Béatrice: roman*. Grasset, 1999.

———. *The First Century After Beatrice*. Translated by Dorothy S. Blair, Abacus, 1994.

Mattelart, Armand. *Histoire de la société de l'information*. La Découverte, 2003.

———. *Histoire de l'utopie Planétaire: De La Cité Prophétique à La Société Globale*. La Découverte, 2009.

Rufin, Jean-Christophe. *Globalia*. Gallimard, 2005.

Solnit, Rebecca. *Wanderlust: A History of Walking.* Verso Books, 2007.
Stiegler, Bernard. *Technics and Time.* Stanford University Press, 1998.
Volodine, Antoine. *Songes de Mevlido.* Seuil, 2007.
Vonarburg, Elisabeth. *Le jeu des coquilles de nautilus.* Editions Alire, 2003.
———. *The Silent City.* Translated by Jane Brierley, Tesseracts Books, 2002.

CHAPTER 6

Encounters with Bodies and Narratives: A Matrix of Contemporary Philosophical Quests

It is in their focus on the body that some recent contemporary French and Francophone futuristic novels reformulate the topics examined thus far, but with a much more explicit reference to specific philosophers. Throughout this chapter, I will discuss three of these works—*Sulphuric Acid* (2008) by Amélie Nothomb, *The Horde of Counterwind* (*La Horde du Contrevent* (2004)) by Alain Damasio, and *Latium* (2016) by Romain Lucazeau—to illustrate how I can extend the hypotheses of this current study to a wider range of French and Francophone science fiction novels. In *Variations on the Body*, Michel Serres wrote "like the body and the world, life appears as an immense memory whose reserves are exploited by today's technological revolution [...] In the objects of the world as well as in living creatures, a manner of knowing resembling our corporal postures [...] is revealed, a manner our arts will try to resemble. Positions, first alphabets: Diderot called these bearings and attitudes hieroglyphs" (Serres and Burks 81). These manners of knowing that resemble our corporal postures as "attitude hieroglyphs" serve as a matrix for contemporary philosophical quests in the dystopian speculative fiction and two science fiction novels mentioned above that focus differently on the value and power of speaking and writing.

While in *Sulphuric Acid* the threat of violence and the suffering question the use of speech and the value of literature as fragile gatekeepers of humankind's conception of an intrusive deployment of surveillance

E. Buzay, *Contemporary French and Francophone Futuristic Novels*, Studies in Global Science Fiction, https://doi.org/10.1007/978-3-031-16628-0_6

cameras, in *The Horde of Counterwind* and *Latium* writing and being able to narrate stories based on a corporeal standpoint delimit the capacities of an embodied consciousness, whether it be human or mutant. Thus, Hannah Arendt's approach can be employed to help readers understand the telegenic suffering caused by a reality television show, in addition to integrating philosophical notions from the works of Spinoza, Nietzsche, Plato, and Leibniz in an exploration of the potentialities of consciousness guided by narratives.

THE VALUE OF SPEECH AND LITERATURE UNDER THE THREAT OF VIOLENCE IN AMÉLIE NOTHOMB

To begin, I will examine the case of the dystopian speculative fiction work *Sulphuric Acid* by the Belgian writer Amélie Nothomb, who revives the practice of writing as a renewal of the intertwining of self-narrative and anticipation. Marianne Chaillan sees in this fiction—in addition to the general Nietzschean undertone that her essay clearly indicated by its title *Ainsi philosophait Amélie Nothomb*[1] (*Thus Philosophized Amélie Nothomb*), a nod to Nietzsche's *Thus Spoke Zarathustra*—an illustration of the thesis of Hannah Arendt's *Eichmann in Jerusalem: A Report on the Banality of Evil* (1964) and Stanley Milgram's *Obedience to Authority: An Experimental View* (1974), which concern the banality of evil that spares no viewer, extended to the violence and cruelty of reality TV in Nothomb's work. In this novel, through dialogues that question the nature of evil—with irony regarding the role of the media—the confrontation is direct with a dystopian society that recreates the concentration camp universe of the Nazi camps, through a reality TV show called "Concentration." In the show, the voyeurism of the viewers and the aggressiveness of some "kapos" are focused on a group of people chosen at random in the street. In a struggle between the media and those dehumanized characters whose suffering has become well-suited to the medium of television—"The time came when the suffering of others was not enough for them; they needed the spectacle of it, too" (Amelie Nothomb, *Sulphuric Acid* 3)—such a battle is embodied by a female character named Pannonique, who is known by the identifier CKZ 114 and whose beauty is matched only by her courage when she refuses for a time to reveal her first name.

---

[1] Chaillan, Marianne, and Raphaël Enthoven. *Ainsi Philosophait Amélie Nothomb.*, 2019. 45–60.

In Chaillan's book, which stages an imaginary trial that puts Arendt on the stand to determine whether Nothomb should be called a philosopher or not in a phantasmagoric place that looks like some kind of paradise where Spinoza and Sartre already wander, Chaillan states that *Sulphuric Acid* particularly succeeds in illustrating today how the ordinary human stops thinking, "stops this silent dialog with himself,"[2] because of the banality of evil that can apply to Nothomb's novel. Doing so, Chaillan imagines Arendt taking Nothomb's defense explaining that as much as herself and Stanley Milgram, this Belgian writer and philosopher's speculative fiction has undergone heavy criticism although "she had simply understood in depth, she too, the banality of evil"[3] at work in recent reality television programs that combine together in prime-time humiliation, contempt, and instrumentalization. While this concept of banality of evil—embodied by Eichmann's claim that everything he did was just to follow orders during the Holocaust—and its implication through the Milgram experiments[4] have been criticized in scholarly works, such as the article written by Paul Hollander, "Revisiting the Banality of Evil: Contemporary Political Violence and the Milgram Experiments,"[5] to question the limitations of the obedience experiments, I think that the understanding of this idea by Nothomb remains nonetheless relevant.

In *La Barbarie des hommes ordinaires* (*The Barbarity of Ordinary Men*), Daniel Zagury, who is a psychiatrist and a current expert for the French judiciary system in charge of analyzing the psychic processes triggering

---

[2] « …[il] cesse ce dialogue silencieux avec lui-même… » (Chaillan 51).

[3] « …, elle avait simplement compris en profondeur, elle aussi, la banalité du mal » (Chaillan 53).

[4] The conditions under which Milgram's experiments were conducted are reported in his book *Obedience to Authority: An Experimental View (1974)*. To study how obedience and authority apply to ordinary people, Milgram asked 40 male participants playing the role of "teachers" involved in his experiments to deliver high voltage shocks—from 15 volts to 450 volts—to a "learner" in another room that they did not know that he was an actor. Despite the learner's scream and protests at 150 volts and the fact that he became silent after 330 volts, obeying the experimenter, 65% of these male participants went as far as 450 volts even the learner was not responsive.

[5] Hollander, Paul. "Revisiting the Banality of Evil: Contemporary Political Violence and the Milgram Experiments." *Society*, vol. 53, no. 1, Feb. 2016, pp. 56–66.

crimes on a large scale, pays a large tribute[6] to Arendt's works. Throughout his last chapter entitled "La banalité psychique du mal" ("The psychic banality of evil"), Zagury *narrows down* an absence of thought with an absolute lack of empathy which paves the way for a denial of humanity in others steadily reduced to the status of things or objects. Yet, this reification process described in detail by the psychiatrist also collides with another definition of evil that Arendt coined as "radical" in *The Origins of Totalitarianism* (1951):

> There is only one thing that seems to be discernible: we may say that radical evil has emerged in connection with a system in which all men have become equally superfluous. [...] Totalitarian solutions may well survive the fall of totalitarian regimes in the form of strong temptations which will come up whenever it seems impossible to alleviate political, social, or economic misery in a manner worthy of man (Arendt, *The Origins of Totalitarianism* 459).

It is precisely this radical evil preceding its psychic banality when reality television shows prey on democracy using surveillance cameras in a concentration camp that Nothomb describes in *Sulphuric Acid* where "No skill was required to be arrested" (Amelie Nothomb, *Sulphuric Acid* 3). The fact that Nothomb combines this philosophical approach with considerations about television as a form of media allows her not only to explore the power of this kind of entertainment that compensates for inadequacies of a society in crisis both in terms of complexity and injustice, but also to address the importance of the body which, when not subjected to the spectacle of violence, regains its individuality using speech and the support of literature and artistic values.

Concerning the television and media component of these issues, another essay written by Arendt: *The Human Condition* (1958) addresses totalitarianism as a product of modernity from a complementary angle. In her Chap. 3 in which she focuses on the long-standing differences dating

---

[6] "…Hannah Arendt is obviously present in the title I have chosen, as in each of my developments, because she had the intuition of what the criminological clinic does not cease to confirm: it is initially in the emptiness of thought, in the incapacity to elaborate our conflicts or more prosaically to contain them psychically, that evil is inscribed." [« … Hannah Arendt est évidemment présente dans le titre que j'ai choisi, comme dans chacun de mes développements, car elle a eu l'intuition de ce que la clinique criminologique ne cesse de confirmer: c'est d'abord dans le vide de la pensée, dans l'incapacité à élaborer nos conflits ou plus prosaïquement à les contenir psychiquement, que s'inscrit le mal »] (Zagury 11–12).

back from ancient Greek times in which life in the public realm promoted action in contrast to life in the private realm, Arendt relates the conditions of the emergence of a "growing social realm, [against which] the private and intimate, on the one hand, and the political (in the narrower sense of the word), on the other, have proved incapable of defending themselves" (Arendt, *The Human Condition* 47). When the private realm takes the dimensions of the public realm, and this public realm is erased to the exclusive benefit of the social sphere, opinions can no longer take refuge in the spectacle of suffering made intimate, in Nothomb's novel, and therefore are responsible for the consequences of this situation. This is the whole point of Avril Tynan's study "Please Watch Responsibly: The Ethical Responsibility of the Viewer in Amélie Nothomb's *Acide Sulfurique*"[7] in which she discusses this novel as a criticism of contemporary bystander behavior where the reality television show *Concentration* "presents a self-sufficient spectacle of human suffering, packaging socially acceptable forms of evil to provoke moral outrage in order to engage the viewer" (Tynan 138). It is the ins and outs of this dilemma that I will now examine.

The confrontation between Pannonique and those who inflict torments on her and her companions in distress is a quasi-theatrical posture that reminds us of the confrontational character of Antigone who says "no" and stands by her principles in her conflict with Creon, who represents a totalitarian power in Jean Anouilh's play, when she claims: "I can still say no to anything I don't like, and I alone am the judge" (Anouilh et al. 38). Indeed, it is through dialogue that the character of Pannonique, who is the main heroine of the program on which she is known by the prisoner number CKZ 114, best illustrates her radical opposition to the autonomy of a spectacle[8] that is supposed to condemn her and her fellow sufferers to certain death, under the eye of a camera. Although the plot tends toward the denouement of the relationship that a kapo named Zdena seeks to establish with CKZ 114, as well as the identification of the chain of responsibility for the commissioning of a program such as "Concentration," this perception of an autonomous and cruel show is essential in this dystopian society, since it is the basis for the exercise of power over the prisoners:

---

[7] Tynan, A. "Please Watch Responsibly: The Ethical Responsibility of the Viewer in Amélie Nothomb's *Acide Sulfurique.*" *French Forum.* 44.1 (2019): 133–147.

[8] "...the spectacle is not identifiable with mere gazing, even combined with hearing. It is that which escapes reconsideration and correction by their work. It is the opposite of dialogue" (Debord 6).

The prisoners didn't know which of them were being filmed, or which the viewers saw. That was part of their torture. Those who cracked were terribly afraid of being telegenic: along with the pain of their torment there was the shame of becoming an attraction. And The Camera did not scorn the moments of hysteria (Nothomb *Sulphuric Acid* 11).[9]

Facing what Michel Foucault identified in *Discipline and Punish: The Birth of the Prison* (1975) as a "panoptic mechanism"[10] inspired by the architect Bentham's Panopticon, through which prison guards can see without being seen, CKZ 114 is that character who sets out to re-establish intersubjective distance, through dialogue, in order to combat the prison subjugation framed by the kapos and informally commissioned by the viewers. Dialoguing in these conditions is illustrated in many ways and highlights before all a continuous tension between Zdena and CKZ 114, as the latter tries to convince the kapo to free her and her companions without resorting to emotional blackmail, which can particularly be seen in CKZ 114's rants, such as in this apostrophe to the viewers on the implications of their voyeurism:

Viewers, switch off your televisions! You are the guiltiest of all! If you didn't provide this monstruous programme with such a huge audience, it would have gone out of existence long ago! You are the true kapos! And when you watch us die, you eyes are our murderers! You are our prison, you are our torture (Nothomb *Sulphuric Acid* 71).[11]

Here the stalking that surveillance cameras allow in *Sulphuric Acid* is not reserved for a few anonymous technicians under the orders of a

---

[9] "Les prisonniers ne savaient pas lesquels d'entre eux étaient filmés ni ce que les specta-teurs voyaient. Cela participait de leur supplice. Ceux qui craquaient avaient affreusement peur d'être télégéniques: à la douleur de la crise de nerf s'ajoutait la honte d'être une attrac-tion. En effet, la caméra ne dédaignait pas les moments d'hystérie" (Nothomb *Acide Sulfurique* 19).

[10] "The panoptic mechanism arranges spatial unities that make it possible to see constantly and to recognize immediately. In short, it reverses the principle of the dungeon; or rather of its three functions—to enclose, to deprive of light and to hide—it preserves only the first and eliminates the other two. Full lighting and the eye of a supervisor capture better than dark-ness, which ultimately protected. Visibility is a trap" (Foucault 200).

[11] "Spectateurs, éteignez vos télévisons! Les pires coupables, c'est vous! Si vous n'accordiez pas une si large audience à cette émission monstrueuse, elle n'existerait plus depuis longtemps! Les vrais kapos, c'est vous! Et quand vous nous regardez mourir, les meurtriers, ce sont vos yeux! Vous êtes notre prison, vous êtes notre supplice!" (Nothomb *Acide Sulfurique* 109).

totalitarian society, but for a larger public that are more hunters than sadists, and for whom the camera kills from a distance, first by delegation and then directly. While at the beginning of the program the camp's kapos act as intermediaries and take charge of designating who is to be eliminated from among the randomly selected candidates—the violence of this manhunt being marked at first by a total indeterminacy of those it targets—the search for a better audience rating and the televisual interactivity that accompanies it explain that at the end of the novel it is the viewers themselves who carry out the selection of the prisoners sent to their deaths.

In opposition to the totalitarian system that Arendt's philosophy elucidates, the character of Pannonique is the one who embodies, in these circumstances, the value of speech and literature under the threat of violence mediated by surveillance cameras. Among the linguistic elements that are staged in the development of Pannonique as a character, who moves from becoming a "marble statue" (Nothomb *Sulphuric Acid* 3)[12] in front of the cameras to finally "[inhabiting] syllables that form a whole [that] is one of life's great concerns"[13] (Nothomb *Sulphuric Acid* 63), are the importance given to first names, naming itself, the use of polite language (that is using the formal *vous* (you) form when speaking) to create distance between characters, and discussions of the value and potential of literature in dehumanizing situations.

After being rounded up with others to participate in the reality show *Concentration* and deported to the show's concentration camp, CKZ 114/Pannonique is faced with the terrible Kapo Zdena and develops a relation with Pietri Livi (EPJ 327). In this context, the faculties of naming and dialogue permanently refer to relations of power or respect, whether it is a matter of dominating or, more rarely, of protecting or pleasing. This is the reason why the "name is a rampart"[14] (Nothomb *Sulphuric Acid* 40) against dehumanization—as is the use of the *vous* form—since "[n]ot for nothing do human beings bear names rather than numbers: the first name is the key to personality"[15] (Nothomb *Sulphuric Acid* 19). Readers intrigued by the unusual use of the heroine's first name and could discover that the term "pannonique" is used to qualify a geological era, to name a

---

[12] "Elle resta donc de marbre..." (Nothomb *Acide Sulfurique* 10).

[13] "Habiter des syllabes qui forment un tout est l'une des immenses affaires de la vie" (Nothomb *Acide Sulfurique* 96).

[14] "... un nom est un rempart" (Nothomb *Acide Sulfurique* 61).

[15] "Ce n'est pas pour rien que les humains portent des noms à la place des matricules: le prénom est la clé de la personne" (Nothomb *Acide Sulfurique* 31–32).

part of the upper Miocene in Central Europe, and to designate in geography the Pannonian plain of the center and southeast of this same continent, leading to questions about the natural determiners that characterize
this character. But they would probably be even more surprised to discover that "Pannonic" refers above all to the first name of Baroness
Pannonica de Koenigswarter, a young Jewish aristocrat famous in the
American jazz and Bebop scene, whose entomologist father had chosen to
name her after a species of extremely rare moth that he himself had identified in Europe.

What follows the revelation of Pannonique's first name triggers both an
ongoing struggle with Zdena, until she decides to help Pannonique and
other prisoners to escape the camp, and a loving relationship with Pietri
Livi—who "found her [Pannonique] as magnificent as her first name"[16]
(Nothomb *Sulphuric Acid* 39)—that fully unfolds a focus on literature
and its value. As Pannonique gets closer and closer to Pietri Livi, who
appears very quickly to be a fictional double of the Italian chemist and
writer Primo Levi, well known for his book *If This Is a Man* (1947) and
whose perspective is close to Arendt's understanding of the banality of evil
in concentration camps during WWII that I commented upon above,[17]
Livi helps Pannonique realize she should pursue the objective of insisting
on the importance of precisely naming everything and dialoguing with
respect to protect her co-detainees' "epic weapon of [their] interior
narrative"[18] (Nothomb *Sulphuric Acid* 43).

Thanks to Pietri Livi, Pannonique discovers an essential way of acting
to save both her own humanity and that of the other prisoners. Livi does
this by telling Pannonique the story of the French writer Romain Gary
who recounted how in a Nazi concentration camp, one of the inmates like
him "invented the character of the lady"[19] (Nothomb *Sulphuric Acid* 43)
to maintain vital signs of civility, a practice quickly accepted by everyone
around him. Livi explains that he identifies Pannonique's behavior with

---

[16] "Il la trouvait aussi magnifique que son prénom" (Nothomb *Acide Sulfurique* 59).

[17] "We must remember that these faithful followers, among them the diligent executors of
inhuman orders, were not born torturers, were not born (with a few exceptions) monsters:
they were ordinary men. Monsters exist, but they are too few in number to be truly dangerous. More dangerous are the common men, the functionaries ready to believe and to act
without asking questions, like Eichmann; like Hoss, the commandant of Auschwitz; like
Stangl, commandant of Treblinka" (Levi and Woolf 228).

[18] "… les armes épiques de son récit intérieur" (Nothomb *Acide Sulfurique* 66).

[19] "… il inventa le personnage de la dame" (Nothomb *Acide Sulfurique* 64).

that of the lady, which helps sustain Pannonique's efforts to maintain her way of being, a way that therefore echoes the fictional lady's behavior in Gary's literary account. The significance of literature and writing goes even further when Pannonique wonders what God's role in the world was after creation, as well as how she could emulate it, since for her "the absence of God was beyond discussion":[20]

> [W]hat was the task of God? Probably that of a writer when his book is published: publicly to love his text, to receive compliments, jeers and indifference on its behalf. To confront certain readers who denounce the work's shortcomings when, even if they are right, it would be impossible to change it. To love it to the bitter end. That love was the sole concrete help that one would be able to bring to it (Nothomb 45).[21]

Thus, Nothomb suggests that God is, in fact, the writer of the world, but that this role has limits once the work is "written," indeed, that all that concretely remains for God-as-writer to do is to assume the consequences of His work. But Pannonique's attempt to continue God's work by being God fails, when Pannonique is confronted with the evil done by an old lady identified as ZHF 911, and consequently Pannonique gives up this attempt. Instead, she develops an awareness that to "hate humanity was to hate a universal encyclopaedia"[22] (Nothomb *Sulphuric Acid* 44), an awareness that allows her to consolidate the epic weapon of her own interior narrative and overcome her fear to confront the viewers in a situation that ultimately benefits her. Once she has escaped from the camp, Pannonique is joined by Pietri Livi and ultimately undergoes a final metamorphosis when she decides to learn the cello instead of continuing her studies in paleontology because, she says, "it's the instrument that most closely resembles the human voice"[23] (Nothomb *Sulphuric Acid* 127). Let us note that this optimistic tone that closes Nothomb's cycle of dystopian

---

[20] "... l'absence de Dieu était établie" (Nothomb *Acide Sulfurique* 68).

[21] "... quelle était la tâche de Dieu? Sans doute celle d'un écrivain quand son livre est édité: aimer publiquement son texte, recevoir pour lui les compliments, les quolibets, l'indifférence. Affronter certains lecteurs qui dénoncent les défauts de l'œuvre alors que, même s'ils avaient raison, on serait impuissant à la changer. L'aimer jusqu'au bout. Cet amour était la seule aide concrète que l'on pourrait lui apporter" (Nothomb *Acide Sulfurique* 69).

[22] "Haïr l'humanité revenait à haïr une encyclopédie universelle" (Nothomb *Acide Sulfurique* 68).

[23] "... c'est l'instrument qui ressemble le plus à la voix humaine" (Nothomb *Acide Sulfurique* 193).

speculative fictions including *Les Combustibles* (1994) and *Péplum* (1996) in which the fictional value of literature in their respective plots was placed under the sign of destruction by an auto-da-fé.[24]

WRITING AND WALKING THE WILDERNESS AS A SCRIBE IN ALAIN DAMASIO

At the crossroads of science fiction and fantasy Alain Damasio's novel *La Horde du Contrevent* (*The Horde of Counterwind*[25]), published in 2004, describes an alternate world that opposes the major technological orientations of the post-humanist ideology that has inspired a number of futuristic novels of our time. In this text, which could also be described as a philosophical tale in which the bodies submitted to a harsh ordeal assert themselves as matrices of meaning through walking, the novelist recounts the deeds, gestures, and words of a group of characters constituted as a "Horde," who set out on foot against multiple powerful winds in search of an "Upper Reaches" that is supposed to correspond to the mythical stories of the origin of their world. In a 2014 interview in *Télérama* with journalist Kora Saccharin, Damasio explained the motivations that pushed him to write a novel like *The Horde of Counterwind* and denounced a closure to the world in the transhumanist movement and the posthumanist ideology that constitutes its culmination: "Transhumanism is a frustrated closure to the world because the human being has not yet delivered all its flavor, its greatness, and its sensitive intelligence, which springs from the junction of flesh and spirit. Our intellect is infinite, of course, but as Spinoza said, there is something even more fascinating: *'we don't know what a body can do'*. So

---

[24] *Les Combustibles*, literally the "fuels or combustibles", later translated in English under the title of *Human Rites* (2005), tells the story of a professor, his student, and the student's girlfriend who are trapped in a city at war who make the decision to burn books to get warm and discuss the value of books that are thrown into the flames, while *Péplum* features the character of Amélie Nothomb projected in the future following a surgical operation and confronted with a scientist named 'Celsius' in an allusion Ray Bradbury's *Fahrenheit 451* (1953) with whom the fictional Nothomb discusses the significance of Celsius' genocidal actions and the value of her novels.

[25] A sample of the official translation in English by Alexander Dickow is available at: https://www.frenchrights.com/the-horde-of-counterwind. All translations of the novel included here are his own.

let's learn."[26] To illustrate how this philosophical statement applies to *The Horde of the Counterwind*, I will first indicate the breadth of its philosophical underpinnings, from Spinoza to Nietzsche, as their philosophies are understood and illustrated by Damasio, before examining the character of the scribe named Sov and addressing the trial of an epic march in this novel written as a polyphonic narrative that portrays a resistant in the face of the adversity of the natural world that they traverse. To clarify Damasio's philosophical perspective, the statements he referred to concerning Spinoza's philosophy are what the latter wrote in *The Ethics* (Part 3, II):

> ...no one has yet determined what the Body can do, i.e., experience has not yet taught anyone what the Body can do from the laws of nature alone, insofar as nature is only considered to be corporeal, and what the body can do only if it is determined by the Mind (Spinoza and Curley 115).

Beyond the fact of pointing out a relation of equality between the body and the spirit which marks a clear difference with the dualism between body and mind seen in the approaches of philosophers from Plato to Descartes, Spinoza's argument indicates that the body does not maintain a relation of subordination with the mind, but instead expresses an unpredictable power which is subject to change. This disposition of the body determines its *affectivity*, "that which allows us to build a knowledge that can compose our encounters in the world into 'euphoric' experiences; [...], experiences that are carried well and where the body can express itself" (Pethick 18) and echoes a desire of overcoming which leads Stuart Pethick to argue that with "this extremely nuanced approach, Spinoza thus makes an unlikely precursor for Nietzsche's genealogical philosophy" (Pethick 18). After quoting Spinoza, Damasio also clearly situates *The Horde of the Counterwind* under Nietzsche's influence, which he specifies in these terms during an interview where he again attacks the transhumanist movement that he perceives as the new religion of a world that is becoming more and more devitalized: "each one exists through the collective, in the form of the horde. It is a humanist book, it is Man with his

---

[26] Interview with Alain Damasio by Kora Sacchrin, *La liberté d'utiliser ou de repousser la technologie est inexistante aujourd'hui*: « Le transhumanisme est une fermeture frustrée au monde parce que l'humain n'a pas encore livré toute sa saveur, sa grandeur et son intelligence sensible, qui jaillit à la jonction de la chair et de l'esprit. Notre intellect est infini, certes, mais comme le disait Spinoza, il y a plus fascinant encore: '*on ne sait pas ce que peut un corps*'. Alors apprenons. » https://www.telerama.fr/idees/la-liberte-d-utiliser-ou-de-repousser-la-technologie-est-inexistante-aujourd-hui-alain-damasio-ecrivain-de-science-fiction,109555.php.

sensitive forces, his energy, his will, who goes all the way. The Man who exploits his forces: it is a very Nietzschean book."[27] Considered from this point of view of the forces, the "horde" is therefore composed of members who overcome their physical abilities through walking, and one of its members—the scribe—who rethinks the limits of their condition by observing the wind in its many forms and recording it in writing. Following their quest, readers are witnesses of what the Horde's bodies can do both on an individual and on collective level to form a "Lance" with Golgoth the trailbreaker at the top and the spurs at the bottom (see the calligram below) in a fight against the wind.

Ω Golgoth, trailbreaker	Ω
π Pietro Della Rocca, prince	Δ >
) Sov Strochnis, scribe	) ¬ π
¿' Caracole, troubadour	∧ ',)- ˇ•
Δ Erg Machaon, defender	∞ x (·) ◇ ∞
¬ Talweg Arcippé, geomaster	¿' ∫ ◊ ~ ∂
> Firost de Toroge, brace	≈]] √
∧ The Austringer, bird-hunter	(Dickow 19)
', Steppe Phorehays, florian	
)- Arval Redhamaj, scout	
ˇ• The Falconer, bird-hunter	
∞ Horst and Karst Dubka, flanks	
x Oroshi Melicerte, aeromaster	
(·) Alme Capys, mender	
◇ Aoi Nan, gatherer and dowser	
∫ Larco Scarsa, sky-poacher	
◊ Learch, smithy	
~ Callirhoé Deicoon, kindler	
∂ Boscavo Silamphre, woodsmith	
≈ Coriolis, spur	
√ Sveziest, spur	
]] Barbak, spur (Dickow 1)[a]	

[a]« La Horde Ω Golgoth, traceur π / Pietro Della Rocca, prince /) Sov Strochnis, scribe / ¿' Caracole, troubadour / Δ Erg Machaon, combattant-protecteur / ¬ Talweg Arcippé, géomaître / > Firost de Toroge, pilier / ∧ L'autoursier, oiselier-chasseur / ', Steppe Phorehys, fleuron /)-Arval Redhamaj, éclaireur / ˇ• Le fauconnier, oiselier-chasseur / ∞ Horst et Karst Dubka, ailiers / x Oroshi Melicerte, aéromaître / (·) Alme Capys, soigneuse ◇ Aoi Nan, cueilleuse et sourcière / ∫ Larco Scarsa, braconnier du ciel / ◊ Léarch, artisan du métal / ~ Callirhoé Déicoon, feuleuse / ∂ Boscavo Silamphre, artisan du bois / ≈ Coriolis, croc / √ Sveziest, croc /]] Barbak, croc" (Damasio, *La horde du contrevent* 704)

[27] « ...chacun existe à travers le collectif, sous la forme de la horde. C'est un livre humaniste, c'est l'Homme avec ses forces sensibles, son énergie, sa volonté, qui va jusqu'au bout. L'Homme qui exploite ses forces: c'est un livre très nietzschéen. » Alain Damasio: « Le hacker est l'homme cultivé du présent et du futur": https://usbeketrica.com/fr/article/alain-damasio-le-hacker-est-l-homme-cultive-du-present-et-du-futur

Applying a Nietzschean grid to Damasio's novel as he invites us to do means that it is worthwhile to consider some passages from *Thus Spoke Zarathustra*, especially section IV of Part 1 entitled "On the Despisers of the Body" (Nietzsche 22). Against the unifying power of consciousness inherited from the dualism between body and mind in Plato and Descartes, the body is at the same time a vector of pluralism as well as of a will to power: "The body is a great reason, a multiplicity with one sense, a war and a peace, one herd and one shepherd" (Nietzsche 23), an aphorism that could at best describe the Horde's will to overcome obstacles. This readiness to meet obstacles goes hand in hand with a will to power that grows in a fight that is an increasingly violent confrontation with the different forms of wind during the Horde's quest. As such, the body is a dynamic but stable marker: "More honestly and more purely speaks the healthy body, the perfect and the perpendicular body, and it speaks the meaning of the earth" (Nietzsche 22). This statement explains that the body is in itself a source of knowledge insofar as the body's knowledge does not form concepts, but instead evaluates situations of conflict for which it represents a form of infallibility that has to be constantly tested, to the extent that it aims at the whole universe and is part of a cosmology form that Damasio creates at the very start of his novel with a rewriting that has biblical connotations of the origin story: "In the beginning there was speed, pure elusive motion, the 'wind-lightning.' Then the cosmos slowed, brought forth form and substance, until survivable densities arose, until there was life, until there was you."[28] In this windy world that distinguishes three categories of inhabitants: the sheltered (les "abrités"), the Freoles (les "Fréoles"), and the hordlings (les "hordiers"), the wind has six external forms (zephyrine, slamino, stesch, choon, blizzard, and the threshgale) and two inner forms that can be seen as the breathing of its inhabitants, the Quick (le "vif") and the ninth form. This wind therefore has symbolic value and constitutes a discriminating factor within these populations. While the sheltered try to protect themselves as much as possible, this is not the case of the Freoles, designers of mechanized flying artifacts, or the hordlings, whose bodies are subjected to intensive training so as to pursue a single goal: to go back to the origin of the wind in order to attain the Upper Reaches.

---

[28] « À l'origine fut la vitesse, le pur mouvement furtif, le 'vent-foudre'. Puis le cosmos décéléra, prit consistance et forme, jusqu'aux lenteurs habitables, jusqu'au vivant, jusqu'à vous" (Damasio 703).

Of all the differences that emerge from the abilities of these last two groups (Freoles and hordlings), the power to be able to "counter" the wind, whatever the form that it manifests, constitutes without any doubt the essential quality of the hordlings who must be able to fight the winds to accomplish their mission and quest. Such fighting abilities presuppose an organization that Damasio details at the beginning of his novel by assigning to the 24 hordlings of the 34th Horde both a function necessary for the consolidation of the group and a symbol specific to each of them. As a group, when these characters are in battle position against the omnipresence of the wind, the composition of the Horde is designed as a "Lance"—as in the illustration above—, while the symbols representing each character are used throughout the text in place of our alphabet to signal who is speaking in this polyphonic narrative. In a similarly symbolic manner, the narrative is remarkable in its inverted numbering of the pages, with the novel starting at page 704 and ending on page 0, one reading of which could be that this decreasing numbering signals a return to the origin of the wind.

Alongside the most emblematic character of the Horde named Golgoth, who occupies the role of a trailbreaker in that he decides the group's route and remains permanently at the head of this formation, is another pivotal character: the scribe named Sov, who is represented by a close parenthesis) and who records all the memories of the Horde in a document called a "counterwork logbook" ("carnet de contre") when he is not transcribing all the forms of the wind that this group meets during its peregrinations. This character of the scribe is one of the most elaborated and refers to another character of a scribe in another of Damasio's works, a short story entitled "El Levir and the Book" ("El Levir et le Livre" (2001))—El Levir being the anagram of the French word "le livre," which means "the book"—where a man confronts his own limits to complete the calligraphy of a book that has never been written—The Book—that requires him to be the substance or the "human ink" while traveling the world:

The true Book is written with the shadow cast by a light so intense that no hand can sustain its bite. The true Book is written with fire, but no fire lasts, so that it must be fed with flesh [...]

"The scribes write with the turned blood of others. But are you THE Scribe, El Levir, the color of the ink of the Book? For the Book has an ink and the Book has a surface, which is not paper..."[29]

This character of the scribe may well reflect another Nietzschean stance: "I love those who do not know how to live unless by going under, for they are the ones who cross over" (Nietzsche 7), which summarizes all the requirements of Damasio's project about writing. The character of the scribe El Levir foreshadows the character of Sov, in that the latter invests himself without restraint in the writing of The Book which, as in *The Horde of the Counterwind*, is "the absolute matrix of all the links woven or that can be woven."[30] As Stéphane Martin and Colin Pahlisch have analyzed in *The Crossroad of Gusts. The Horde of the Counterwind by Alain Damasio* (*La Croisée des souffles. La Horde du Contrevent d'Alain Damasio* 2013), this writing process is of course identified with that of the author Alain Damasio himself and unfolds completely by echoing "a fertile metatextual exploration through the intermediary of three mises en abyme relating to the exercise of writing: a cosmogony as the birth of the act of writing, an ontology making a character the process of an orality, and finally the notations of the wind assimilated to a syntax, flow, poetic breath."[31] That being said we can better understand that in *The Horde of the Counterwind*, which was indeed inspired both by a short story by Ray Bradbury "The Long Rain" and by some poems by Stéphane Mallarmé, including "Un coup de dés" and "Hérodiade," the world exists to lead to a book, echoing the famous aphorism of that poet—*le Monde est fait pour aboutir à un livre* (*The World Is Made to Result in a Book*)—and the character of the scribe embodied by Sov has the function of reading and transcribing the fluctuation of the winds in their interactions with other members of his group. In this book of the world, Sov becomes, by his role,

---

[29] « Le vrai Livre est écrit avec l'ombre projetée par une lumière si intense qu'aucune main n'en soutient la morsure. Le vrai Livre est écrit au feu, mais nul feu ne dure, si bien qu'il faut l'alimenter à la chair [...]—Les scribes écrivent avec le sang tourné des autres. Mais es-tu LE Scribe, El Levir, la couleur de l'encre du Livre? Car le Livre a une encre et le Livre a une surface, qui n'est pas du papier... » (Damasio, *Aucun souvenir assez solide* 230).

[30] « ... la matrice absolue de tous les liens tissés ou tissables » (Damasio, *Aucun souvenir assez solide* 239).

[31] « ... une féconde exploration métatextuelle par le truchement de trois mises en abyme ayant trait à l'exercice de l'écriture: une cosmogonie comme naissance de l'acte de l'écriture, une ontologie faisant d'un personnage le processus d'une oralité et finalement les notations du vent assimilées à une syntaxe, flux, souffle poétique » (Martin and Palisch 52).

a more and more significant character in that he is called to witness and testify about the writing process as a weaving and living experience in the *Horde of the Counterwind*: "No ideal in my heart, be it the most universal on our Earth – I mean: finding the Origin of the Wind – would ever be worth the textile, animal bond, the prehuman miracle of being woven from the fiber of another"[32] (Damasio 163). The fight of the hordlings against the wind under its nine forms culminates in many ways in this exercise of reading done by Sov who tries to pierce the original meaning of the textus, in the sense of frame or fabric, in the reading and then the "writing" of a book of the world that mythologically relates to the formation of the human race and its extension in a humanity that wants to be resistant. Thus, this faculty makes the scribe the most lucid character since, as his lover Oroshi, the Horde's aeromaster, reminds him, he will ultimately be the only one to survive this journey in order to testify to the inhabitants who pushed them—he and the other members of his group—to accomplish this mission when they were still only children, that the Upper Reaches and the Lower Reaches meet and that only a thread of humanity would be able to survive this journey: "Since Alticcio, I've been following it very closely: you gain power every month, Sov, you unfurl! One day, you'll be just as intense as an Erg, after your fashion, through your spirit, your strength in bonding. You should have seen yourself in the veramorph: you possess a fairly unique weaving force, you're woven into others. And you heard Caracole: you're the one who will survive!"[33]

Walking parallels the writing process and this teaching in *The Horde of the Counterwind* occurs essentially in the process that determines a way of being in the world that is becoming that the character of Sov depicts as well:

Even before I was born, I think we were walking. We were already standing, the entire horde spread out in an arc, already firm on our femurs, and we advanced with our scraped-up bodies and our ribs bare, our shoulder-joints rusted with sand, scrabbling at the rock with our tarsi. We have walked for a long time this way, all together, to seek the first of all our prairies. We have never had parents: the wind made us. We appeared gradually in the midst of

---

[32] « Aucun idéal à mon cœur, fut-il le mieux partagé de notre Terre—j'entends: trouver l'Origine du Vent—ne vaudrait jamais le lien textile animal, ce miracle préhumain d'être tramé en fil de l'autre » (Damasio 163).

[33] « Depuis Alticcio, je suis ça de très près: tu gagnes en puissance chaque mois, Sov, tu de déploies! (...) tu possèdes un pouvoir assez unique de tissage, tu es tramé aux autres. Et puis, tu as entendu Caracole: tu es celui qui survivra! » (Damasio 163).

the fallow land of the high plateaus, with great scoops of fluttered earth caught in our bones, through the accumulation of bits of flowers, it is also said, upon this surface that was to become our skin.[34]

In this test of humans confronted with the winds, walking is defined as the act in which the "world-body" and the "body-world" agree on a use of a disconcerting world that refuses technological reification with its consequences of exponential scientific progress that is nourished by a desire of death while also trying to escape it. In the gradation of the hardships faced by members of the Horde all along their march from the city of Aberlaas in the Lower Reaches to the mountain range of Norska in the Upper Reaches, no doubt it is for this reason that the last forms of wind (after all those listed above) are interior and not able to be transcribed, as if to close the chapter of this paradoxical existential attitude. This ninth form of the wind is also the one that confirms Sov's vocation as a scribe: "*The ninth form is sure to kill the camel. It wounds the lion to the point of death. But the child that you may be able to become will be able to survive it.*"[35] And to understand this prediction, one needs to refer the first section, "The Three Metamorphoses," of the first part of *Thus Spoke Zarathustra* in which the camel represents morality, the lion willpower, and the child both innocence and oblivion, which like a wheel in motion conforms a will of overcoming and introduces an eternal return as an ultimate form of resistance.

In light of this resistant humanity, issues related to the extension of the body's powers and the recomposition of self-images in *The Horde of the Counterwind* could be roughly summarized as well. While a rereading of the world in which the postures affected by the sheltered and the Freoles no longer occur could benefit them, the body and spirit of the hordlings constantly reinvent the means of evading a desire of a lethal progress, but they pay a high price for it by a cruel delusion. As it progresses, the horde loses indeed many hordlings. Only eight survivors finally make it to the Upper Reaches where, contrary to their mythologies and legends, they discover neither the origin of the wind which was at the origin of their

---

[34] "Avant de naître, je crois que nous marchions. (...) Nous avons marché ainsi, tous ensemble, à chercher la première de toutes nos prairies. Nous n'avons jamais eu de parents: c'est le vent qui nous a faits. Nous sommes apparus doucement au milieu de la friche armée des hauts plateaux, à grandes truellées de terre voltigée pris dans nos ossements, par l'accumulation des copeaux de fleurs, dit-on aussi, sur cette surface qui allait devenir notre peau" (Damasio 251).

[35] "La neuvième forme tue à coup sûr le chameau. Elle blesse le lion. Mais l'enfant que tu sauras peut-être devenir pourrait lui survivre" (Damasio 8).

quest nor gods. At the end of this journey or it turns out that this 34th Horde is not the only one to have arrived at this point, since the hordlings find traces of the 31st Horde which had arrived before them. Four hordlings lose their lives in an accident, three commit suicide by jumping into the void, and Sov, the only survivor, resists this temptation to end up discovering against all odds half-medusa half-plant parachutes that make him suppose for a while that there is an unknown civilization living on the resources of the wind and the clouds, but when he rushes toward one of these parachutes, one of its extremities becomes a metallic cable to which he clings for hours whirling in violent winds until he falls and loses consciousness. When Sov wakes up his surprise is considerable because he finds himself back where his world had started. He learns this when the people he meets tell him that he is at the foot of the cliff of Aberlaas in the Lower Reaches: "West suburb of Aberlaas, Lower Reaches, Boundary Cliff! That enough for ya? Were you just born, or what?"[36] The scorn with which they treat his questions thus contrasts with his surprise and disbelief at finding himself in that physical location.

Thus, the scribe is an emblematic character of the eternal return, for in *Thus Spoke Zarathustra* in Part 3. *The Convalescent* we can read a reference to the eternal return (or eternal recurrence) that is reminiscent of Sov's path: "I come again eternally to this identical and selfsame life, in its greatest and its smallest, to teach again the eternal return of all things" (Nietzsche 178). The scribe is thus reborn under the sign of lucidity: the Upper and Lower Reaches are one and the same, and all the deaths and the values that inspired them may seem vain in the face of this terrible truth, unless Sov tells another story and starts writing to do so.

Shifting Determinism with the Reminiscent Body of an Artificial Intelligence in Romain Lucazeau

In the vein of Dan Simmons' *Hyperion*, Romain Lucazeau's *Latium* is a uchronistic space opera novel that features artificial intelligences in the form of interstellar ships wandering in interstellar space following the disappearance of the human species during an episode described as the "Hecatombe," before one of these artificial intelligences receives a mysterious message and decides to incarnate in a human body.

---

[36] "Banlieue oust d'Aberlaas, Extrême-Aval, Falaise des Confins! Ça te va pour le topo? Tu viens de naître ou quoi?" (Damasio 0).

As a new kind of creature named Plautine, she sets out on a quest to find what may be the "last man" in the company of her former lover and new ally, an intelligent automaton named Othon, who is considered a god by a people of mutant dogs fit for battle and war, in this Leibniz-infused retelling of Pierre Corneille's play *Othon* (1664), which stages the ways in which Platonism characterizes Roman nobility of this uchronic world. Endowed with a body that allows her to dream and to reconnect, almost in spite of herself, with palace intrigues that guide her in this quest to the point of finding the entity responsible for planning the disappearance of the human race and eliminating it, Plautine then becomes a character whose body appears to be the main matrix of the exercise of a power that is searching for and forging itself between dilemmas and inner convictions.

The objective of this section is first to examine the borrowings of this uchronic work from the philosophy of Leibniz and Corneille's tragedy *Othon*, before examining how the bodies of insects, dog-men, and androids resulting from artificial intelligence play a primordial role in the exercise of a power in search of incarnation that never ceases to roam and to seek to conquer outer space. To do this, I will explore what is unique to the humanoid incarnation of the character of Plautine, who is, strangely enough, committed to Platonism, then I will conclude with a discussion of how Plautine's incarnation gives her the power of narration, as opposed to simply regurgitating information.

While many science fiction authors choose to "digitalize" the minds of their characters or even to download them onto digital media like William Gibson in *Neuromancer* or Greg Egan in *Permutant City*, Romain Lucazeau envisages in a way the opposite path by imagining artificial intelligences in the form of gigantic naves in a post-apocalyptic uchronia where the Roman Empire would never have ended—hence the title of the novel "Latium." Lucazeau then goes on to give one of those gigantic naves the possibility of dreaming of an anthropomorphic incarnation in order to pursue its quest as a zealous servant of a paradigmatic "last man."

There are several points of encounter between the deployment of the most inescapable mechanics of power described in the tragedy of Corneille's *Othon* and the conceptions of necessity or constraint of a world that sheds new light on the image of Leibniz as the thinker of a network where nomads circulate. The function of these nomads is specified by the artificial intelligence Oikè through Plautine, an entity that she has created in these terms:

> The world [she says] is made of spiritual atoms, of monads. Like an immense number of clocks, each set to follow its path, and so well matched to the others that they appear to form a whole and interact. This system is arranged so that each point can be seen as a perception and expression of the whole.[37]

And Romain Lucazeau clarifies this point: "I recommend to SF fans reading Leibniz's *The Monadology*, from which I draw much inspiration (…). He describes a world made up not of atoms, but of spiritual corpuscles, which are all coordinated with each other and which constitute a gigantic cosmic machine, fabulously complex—that went well with a novel whose characters are automatons."[38]

The characteristic of a "nomad" for the author of *The Monadology* (1714) is to align the expression of a force with the growth and potentialities of an organic body that culminates in a power. This notion is illustrated—from my point of view—by a tirade in Corneille's play *Othon* (Act I, scene 4), which, although not included in the novel, helps clarify Lucazeau's intentions. In Corneille's tirade, the character Plautine addresses Othon in the following terms, under the pretext of a love sacrificed to the expectations of the political: "And ne'er forget, when thou shalt be Rome's master, / 'T was I who forced you and helped thee to be that" (Corneille and Lockert 269). Also, the play has a particular relationship with the idea of providence—a theme dear to Leibniz, author of *Theodicy* (1710)—as analyzed by Robert Emory in his article, "The Providential Universe of 'Othon,'" which has brought to light a tension between the characters of Plautine and Othon which remains relevant to the understanding of Lucazeau's novel: the "situation demands a return

---

[37] "Le monde [dit-elle] est fait d'atomes spirituels, de monades. Comme un nombre immense d'horloges, chacune réglée pour accomplir son chemin, et si bien appariée avec les autres qu'elles paraissent former un tout et interagir. Ce système est agencé de sorte que chaque point peut être considéré comme une perception et une expression du tout" (Lucazeau *Latium 1* 328).

[38] "… je recommande aux fans de S.-F. de lire *La Monadologie* de Leibniz, dont je m'inspire beaucoup (…). Il décrit un monde constitué non pas d'atomes, mais de corpuscules spirituels, qui sont tous coordonnés entre eux et constituent une gigantesque machine cosmique, fabuleusement complexe—cela allait bien avec un roman dont les personnages sont des automates." in Interview 2016: Romain Lucazeau pour *Latium*. https://www.actusf.com/detail-d-un-article/Interview-2016-Romain-Lucazau-pour.

to the providential hero, as Plautine observes: 'l'univers a besoin qu'un vrai héros y monte' [the universe needs a real hero to rise up] (v. 534) but Othon is powerless to act on his volition, the hesitant hero who is a pawn for men and gods"(Emory 250). Indeed, in *Latium*, the quest of providential order, whose goal is the search for the "last man," is still significant for Plautine, even if she ultimately changes its goal, while Othon remains a character immersed in political intrigues only compatible with his ambition.

Yet it is this idea of strength expressing in its vital impulse the alliance of a complete being to an organic body that is precisely the object of a debate and antagonism that serve as a framework for the plot developed in *Latium*. Automatons animated by artificial intelligences oppose barbarians, who have chosen a post-humanity, although the automatons are not able to eliminate these barbarians due to the little bit of humanity that resides in them, protecting them from any aggression because of a set of laws called "Carcan," which are reminiscent of Isaac Asimov's three laws of robotics:

> Ecosystem against ecosystem, vital impulse against vital impulse: the struggle was not driven by the will to power, but by biology. And in this game, the barbarians would eventually win. They did not have the means to fight in one go, nor even the will. From their point of view, they were just dealing with old machines with inadequate programming, the annoying remnant of a vanished civilization.[39]

In their relationship to power, which is essentially a vital impulse, the bodies of the insects, of mutant men called dogmen, and of Plautine, as an intelligence embodied in a humanoid form, question throughout the plot the order imposed by this "Carcan," hence the need to examine the power relations that are organized by all these bodies whose actions are limited by these restrictive laws, whether they follow the orders or end up bypassing them. At the bottom of the hierarchy of mechanical and corporal incarnations are the insect and spider automatons, which are inferior nomads that traverse interstellar vessels to maintain them, as well as

---

[39] "Écosystème contre écosystème, élan vital contre élan vital: la lutte n'avait pas pour moteur la volonté de puissance, mais la biologie. Et, à ce jeu-là, les barbares finiraient par gagner. Ils n'avaient pas les moyens d'en découdre d'un seul coup, ni même la volonté. De leur point de vue, ils n'avaient affaire qu'à de vieilles machines à la programmation inadé-quate, au reliquat agaçant d'une civilisation disparue" (Lucazeau *Latium 1* 166).

serving as means of communication, because of their continual displacements, that the artificial intelligences decline.

As explained in Chap. 4, if the literature of science fiction relays these characteristics, it is because the interest of these animals as they are represented resides mainly, from my point of view, in another function in that they "pre-figure," in the proper sense of the term, a reflection on genetic and computer coding. Thus, if the representations of the stakes linked to data processing and the networking of that data processing are often accompanied, in numerous works of science fiction, by the presence of insects, which define the enigmatic character of the worlds that the characters, who are sometimes frightened and sometimes fascinated by the otherness of these animals' understanding of the world, nothing of the sort appears in *Latium* since these insect or spider automatons are the basic elements of computational intelligences. As Plautine prepares to leave the ship where she was created during a war between insectoid automatons, a form of compassion prevails in this character who almost recognizes herself in their condition:

> She was no better than them. No less a product of the Nave than they were, she had no valid reason to throw them away to ensure her survival. In the smallest repair beetle was some aspect, at least minimal or partial, of that vast whole which had been called Plautine, and which had transcended its various parts—as the subtle sound of a violin is neither glue, nor strings, nor humble wood, nor horn, but all of these and much more. And something that could, handled according to the rules of art, come close to an immanent form of divinity. This was what she was about to sacrifice.[40]

The dogmen are the next characters that are designed to circumvent the Carcan's rules. These creatures to whom the artificial intelligence Othon has given birth exist to fight the barbarians. Frequently compared to Greek warriors, the dogmen, for whom Eurybiades is the spokesperson to the other artificial intelligences, do not operate for long under the

---

[40] "Elle ne leur était pas supérieure. Pas moins issue de la Nef qu'eux-mêmes, elle n'avait aucune raison valable de les jeter en pâture pour assurer sa survie. Dans le moindre scarabée de réparation se trouvait quelque aspect, à tout le moins minimal ou partiel, de ce vaste tout qui s'était appelé Plautine, et qui en avait transcendé les différentes parties—comme le son subtil d'un violon n'est ni la colle, ni les cordes, ni l'humble bois, ni la corne, mais tout cela et bien plus. Et quelque chose qui pouvait, manié selon les règles de l'art, frôler une forme immanente de divinité. C'était cela qu'elle s'apprêtait à sacrifier" (Lucazeau *Latium 1* 362).

illusion of their actual condition: "The humanity of these strange creatures did not withstand scrutiny for long. They were a strange kind of dogs, put on two legs to resemble men, and endowed with a kind of chubby hands."[41] These dogmen find in Plautine a strong ally who sought both their emancipation and their help in the quest that pushed her to seek the last man or men, who alone could reform the laws of the Carcan and again give meaning to the life of the artificial intelligences. But what the dogmen share the most with Plautine is that they are all in evolution, in terms of their mutations. Indeed, as a reminder, Plautine first held the shape of a spaceship that was several kilometers long, before one of the nomads who constituted her made the decision to create a replica of the automaton she used in the past, but with the notable difference that this new Plautine was provided with a humanoid body of flesh and blood. First of all, following the idea to find the "last man" who would allow her to give a legitimacy to a posthuman civilization again, this new Plautine with her embodiment surprises those who accompany her in her quest as her incarnation gives her the ability to remember and to dream following some kind of mystical Platonism, which inspires in her not only a certain sense of moral courage, but also the desire to stand up against injustice. It is this inner strength affected by dilemmas that make her such a special heroine, one who will break and emancipate herself from the determinism of her first condition.

It is therefore through this incarnation that Plautine gradually becomes aware of her function and her role by dint of dreams and reminiscences, which are the only influences likely to divert her from a quasi-biological determination in the pursuit of exclusive power, so that she acquires a personal point of view on the History of humanity and seeks, against all odds, to render justice and punish those responsible for the Hecatombe who made her disappear:

> Not dreams, she realized, but a serial reminiscence, a plunge into the abyss of her own machine autobiography, a gradual revelation of a hidden meaning in her automaton past. And this experience, she did not want it, she was afraid of it. And yet, another part of her was consumed with the need to know. Not because of intellectual curiosity, but because of the unbearable

---

[41] "L'humanité de ces étranges créatures ne résistait pas longtemps à l'examen. Il s'agissait d'une étrange sorte de chiens, mis sur deux jambes pour ressembler à des hommes, et dotés d'espèces de mains potelées" (Lucazeau *Latium 1* 435).

idea that justice had been flouted, that a crime had gone unpunished, and therefore because of a visceral need to act, to repair.[42]

Here the idea of "reminiscence" is a key reminder of the importance of Platonism in the narrative of *Latium* as an explicit influence, as many characters follow Plato's ideas, while simultaneously not knowing themselves to be characters created through the influence of Leibniz's philosophy. Plato's notion of reminiscence assumes that the soul has learned things or more precisely was exposed to ideas in another life, as can be seen in his texts *Meno* (a Socratic dialogue about virtue) and *Phaedo* (a Socratic dialogue regarding the soul through an exploration of the death of Socrates), that explore the idea that knowledge proceeds from a recollection by which the soul rediscovers knowledge that it had already possessed in a previous life. In *Latium*, what seems to be crucial to Plautine in the experience of reminiscence is a need for justice, since through reminiscence in *Phaedo* "the reality is, [...], that temperance, and justice, and courage are a kind of purification from everything like this, and that wisdom itself is a kind of rite to purify us" (Plato 56), which leads to an insatiable desire for truth. Without doubt the originality of the plot conceived by Lucazeau lies in the effect of surprise associated with the incarnation of Plautine, who does not follow the temperance, which would be the assumed tendency that she would follow, based on the experience of reminiscence. Indeed, at the end of the novel when Plautine discovers that the last man, who she and her companions had so sought after in order to serve him, as the rules of the Carcan oblige her to do, is in fact Berenikè, the cruel Empress at the origin of the Hecatombe, who wants to recreate humanity in her own image by means of genetic cloning. It is through an act of rage understood as a passionate outburst that Plautine puts an end to the existence of this *Imperatrix mundi* before considering, after having been surprised by her own audacity, all the advantages that her body now offers her:

---

[42] "Non pas des rêves, réalisa-t-elle, mais une réminiscence en série, plongée dans l'abîme de sa propre autobiographie de machine, révélation progressive d'une signification cachée dans son passé d'automate. Et cette expérience, elle n'en voulait pas, elle en avait peur. Et pourtant, une autre partie d'elle-même était rongée par le besoin de savoir. Pas par curiosité intellectuelle, mais à cause de l'idée insupportable que la justice avait été bafouée, qu'un crime restait impuni, et donc par un besoin viscéral d'agir, de réparer" (Lucazeau *Latium* 2 53–54).

She imagined an entire human race coming out of her womb, out of her flesh. Or perhaps she could give stem cells to the dog people and Atticus? Such humans would undoubtedly be different from their predecessors. And, therefore, endowed with other moral values, with an alternative vision of the world. She, Plautine? All these dreams seemed to her delusional, and at the same time possible, which was even more absurd. For there were still other possibilities, other ways, just as crazy.[43]

This contrast is interesting and somehow reinforced when it is also revealed to readers at the end that Berenikè belonged to a Platonician cult that believed that human salvation only resides in a computational transcendence, that is to say, a total human digitalization where human souls are stocked and trapped in hard drives. Indeed, millions of years earlier, while Berenikè was preserved in a tower called a "Tempus nullum" or "T-nullum" considered to be "a pure place of the mark of becoming, a concept. A platonic essence"[44] that guarantees a form of immortality since time does not pass, she had sent a signal to Plautine, when the latter was still a spaceship.

Finally, in another intriguing idea associated with the perception of Plautine's body as a matrix of power, attentive readers will notice that the automatons in Lucazeau's work are part of what Philippe Breton calls in his book *A l'image de l'homme. From the Golem to the virtual creatures* a "global narrative" in which Plautine discovers her mediatic genealogy:

Between the invention of silent reading and the development of printing, more than a thousand years. Between printing and the emergence of the first network four to five centuries. And still the transported information, which was coded in the form of optical signals, was extremely weak. Then came electricity. Two centuries later, the first draft of the noosphere was created. One hundred and fifty years, and a stammering Intelligence—that which we call Achinus, the Gardener—took shape. It took fifty years to crystallize into a self-awareness—right here, according to the legendvand then a mere

---

[43] "Elle s'imagina une race humaine tout entière sortie de son ventre, de sa chair. Ou peut-être pourrait-elle confier des cellules-souches aux hommes-chiens et à Atticus? De tels humains seraient incontestablement différents de leurs prédécesseurs. Et, de ce fait, dotés d'autres valeurs morales, d'une vision alternative du monde. Elle, Plautine? Tous ces songes lui semblaient délirants, et en même temps possibles, ce qui était encore plus absurde. Car il y avait encore d'autres possibles, d'autres voies, tout aussi folles" (Lucazeau *Latium 2* 613–614).

[44] "… un lieu pur de la marque du devenir, un concept. Une essence platonicienne" (Lucazeau *Latium 2* 546).

twenty years before explaining to humans how they could integrate their thoughts, directly and not via more or less rudimentary interfaces.[45]

In the case of Plautine, this media component deserves close examination given her humanoid incarnation. On the one hand, she is a coded entity designed to respond as a program to a call; this she recalls when she says: "It was implanted in me at birth. I had to, since before the Hecatombe, wait for this signal [this signal indicating the presence of a last man] and to go to the rescue of the last Man,"[46] but on the other hand the attribution of a body makes her a singular automaton because she is endowed with the power of narration: "[o]nly she could report it, could narrate the story, rather than amassing raw facts, thanks to the strange succession of dreamlike experiences that sketched out a new relationship with the past—narrative rather than direct access to information."[47] Perhaps it is this particularity that brings her closer to humanity when Plautine, thanks to her body, remembers "in the manner of humans, who relive the past and grasp its meaning, and not like intelligent machines, which can only replay the recording of facts, without reconstructing a narrative framework."[48] One would expect nothing less in the way of subversion from an author such as Lucazeau, inspired as he was in this novel by the philosopher of the "book of fates"[49] in *Theodicy*.

[45] "... Entre l'invention de la lecture silencieuse et le développement de l'imprimerie, plus d'un millier d'années. Entre l'imprimerie et l'émergence du premier réseau quatre à cinq siècles. Et encore l'information transportée, qui était codée sous forme de signaux optiques, était-elle extrêmement faible. Puis vint l'électricité. Deux siècles plus tard, la première ébauche de noosphère était créée. Cent cinquante ans, et une Intelligence balbutiante—celui que nous appelons Achinus, le Jardinier—prenait forme. Il mit cinquante ans à se cristalliser en une conscience de soi—ici même, selon la légende—puis une vingtaine d'années à peine avant d'expliquer aux humains comment ils pouvaient intégrer leur pensée, de manière directe et non pas via des interfaces plus ou moins rudimentaires » (Lucazeau *Latium 2* 213).

[46] "... C'était implanté en moi à ma naissance. Je devais, dès avant l'Hécatombe, attendre ce signal et me porter au secours du dernier Homme" (Lucazeau *Latium 2* 553).

[47] « Mais elle seule pouvait en faire état, en narrer l'histoire plutôt que d'amonceler des faits bruts, grâce à l'étrange succession d'expériences oniriques qui esquissaient un rapport inédit au passé—narration plutôt qu'accès direct à des informations » (Lucazeau *Latium 2* 252).

[48] « ... à la manière des humains, qui revivent le passé et en saisissent le sens, et non comme les machines intelligentes, qui ne peuvent que rejouer l'enregistrement des faits, sans reconstituer de trame narrative » (Lucazeau *Latium 2* 556–557).

[49] "There was a great volume of writings in this hall: Theodorus could not refrain from asking what that meant. It is the history of this world which we are now visiting, the Goddess told him; it is the book of its fates" (Leibniz and Farrer 376).

BIBLIOGRAPHY

Anouilh, Jean, et al. *Antigone*. Methuen, 2009.

Arendt Hannah et al. *The Human Condition*. University of Chicago Press, 2018.

———. *The Origins of Totalitarianism. New Ed. with Added Prefaces*. Harcourt Brace Jovanovich, 1973.

Chaillan, Marianne, and Raphael Enthoven. *Ainsi philosophait Améie Nothomb*. Albin Michel, 2019.

Corneille, Pierre, and Lacy Lockert. *Moot Plays of Corneille;* Vanderbilt University Press, 1959.

Damasio, Alain. *Aucun souvenir assez solide*. Gallimard, 2015.

———. *La horde du contrevent*. Gallimard, 2012.

Debord, Guy. *Society of the Spectacle*. AK Press, 2018.

Emory, Robert. "The providential universe of 'Othon.'" *Romancenotes Romance Notes*, vol. 20, no. 2, 1979, pp. 248–55.

Foucault, Michel. *Discipline and Punish: The Birth of the Prision*. Vintage Books, 1977.

Leibniz, Gottfried Wilhelm, and Austin Farrer. *Theodicy: Essays on the Goodness of God, the Freedom of Man, and the Origin of Evil*. Wipf and Stock, 2007.

Levi, Primo, and Stuart Woolf. *The Reawakening: The Companion Volume to Survival in Auschwitz*. Touchstone Book, 1995.

Lucazeau, Romain. *Latium 1*. Denoël, 2018. .

Martin, Stéphane, and Colin Palisch. *La croisée des souffles. La horde du contrevent d'Alain Damasio*. Archipel Editions, 2013.

Nietzsche Friedrich Wilhelm et al. *Thus Spoke Zarathustra: A Book for All and None*. Cambridge University Press, 2006.

Nothomb, Amélie. *Sulphuric Acid*. Faber and Faber, 2008.

———. *Acide sulfurique: roman*. Albin Michel, 2005.

Pethick, Stuart. "Spinoza: Discovering What the Body Can Do." *Affectivity and Philosophy after Spinoza and Nietzsche: Making Knowledge the Most Powerful Affect*, edited by Stuart Pethick, Palgrave Macmillan UK, 2015, pp. 18–67.

Plato and D. N Sedley. *Meno; and Phaedo*. Cambridge University Press, 2011.

Serres, Michel, and Randolph Burks. *Variations on the Body*. Univocal, 2011.

Spinoza, Benedictus de, and E. M. Curley. *The Collected Works of Spinoza*. Princeton University Press, 1985.

Tynan, Avril. "Please Watch Responsibly: The Ethical Responsibility of the Viewer in Amélie Nothomb's Acide Sulfurique." *French Forum French Forum*, vol. 44, no. 1, 2019, pp. 133–47.

Zagury, Daniel. *La barbarie des hommes ordinaires: ces criminels qui pourraient êre nous*. Editions de l'Observatoire, 2018.

CHAPTER 7

Conclusion

There is no myth more innocent than that of a knowledge innocent of myth
Michel Serres

How can I summarize the breakthrough of the imaginary that leads
from the tree to the labyrinth, and where literary wandering recognizes in
each of the journeys of the characters of these selected texts a singular tracing that supposes a detour, an uprooting, or a more or less accepted break
with the conception of a nature to be read or of a book of the world? As
Herrenschmidt reminds us in her book *Les trois écritures: langue, nombre,
code* (*The Three Scriptures: Language, Number, Code*), the "stage of the
mythical emergence of the human, analogous to the manufacture of a
tablet, format of cuneiform writing, takes [initially] all its meaning"[1] in
Mesopotamia. As an abundant natural resource provided by the Tigris and
Euphrates Valleys of ancient Mesopotamia, the clay that was used to make
most of the utensils of everyday life was nonetheless a noble material suit-
able for the design of writing tablets, as well as a symbol of a vision of the
world through which "writing became, handled and reflected by the

---

[1] L'"étape de l'émergence mythique de l'humain, analogue à la fabrication d'une tablette,
support de l'écriture cunéiforme, prend [d'abord] tout son sens" (Herrenschmidt 198).

© The Author(s), under exclusive license to Springer Nature   223
Switzerland AG 2022
E. Buzay, *Contemporary French and Francophone Futuristic Novels*,
Studies in Global Science Fiction,
https://doi.org/10.1007/978-3-031-16628-0_7

intellectuals of Mesopotamia, a matrix in which to think Man, a mold in which was cast the history of his conception":[2]

> Contemplating their landscape of clay and water, the thinkers of ancient Mesopotamia, those of the ancient Sumerian city of Eridu in the southern marshes, and later those of Babylon, attributed to it the quality of a primordial element. Enki, the god of Eridu, master of the ocean of fresh water which supports the earth and pours its fertilizing waters into the dry bed of the rivers to produce silt, created man from a lump of earth.[3]

From this account of the emergence of humanity as well as other texts from the ancient East, from which Herrenschmidt has tried to "show that writing, in its material and linguistic aspects, participated in the construction of the myths of the birth of humans in three ancient cultures, the Mesopotamian culture of Akkadian expression, the Hebrew culture according to the Bible, and the Greek culture in the work of Hesiod,"[4] it seems that a teleological structure of the written word (writing) was set up and consolidated from Antiquity to the Renaissance in the formulation of the metaphors of the books of life, nature, the world, and the universe. As I have demonstrated throughout this book, my hypothesis is that the subversion of this structure of the written word, which in the long run became that of a meta-book in keeping with life, nature, the world, and the universe, first undertaken by Cyrano de Bergerac's work *The States and Empires of the Moon*, then continued in other philosophical tales during the eighteenth century, explains the hermeneutic character of science fiction literature, which brings into play metafictionality and makes a litera-

---

[2] L'"écriture devint, maniée et réfléchie par les intellectuels de Mésopotamie, une matrice où penser l'Homme, un moule où couler l'histoire de sa conception" (Herrenschmidt 199).

[3] "En contemplant leur paysage d'argile et d'eau, les penseurs de l'antique Mésopotamie, ceux de la vieille ville sumérienne d'Eridu dans les marais du Sud, puis ceux de Babylone, lui attribuèrent la qualité d'élément primordial. Enki, le dieu d'Eridu, maître de l'océan d'eaux douces qui soutient la terre et déverse ses eaux fertilisantes dans le lit desséché des cours d'eau pour produire le limon, créa l'homme à partir d'une motte de terre. André Salvini, Béatrice. "L'Aventure des écritures. Matières et formes: écriture cunéiforme. L'argile, support-mémoire de l'écriture cunéiforme." *La Bibliothèque nationale de France.* n.d. Web.2 Apr. 2012. <http://classes.bnf.fr/dossisup/supports/11art.htm>.

[4] "montrer que l'écriture, en ses aspects matériel et linguistique, participa de la construction des mythes de la naissance des humains dans trois cultures antiques, la culture mésopotamienne d'expression akkadienne, la culture hébraïque selon la Bible et la culture grecque dans l'œuvre d'Hésiode" (Herrenschmidt 192).

ture of detection of it. From this point of view, which suggests that there is another world to see in the fragmentation of the limits of the symbolism of the book, I have explained in what ways cyberpunk aesthetics, preceded by dystopias evoking the fears of a reified humankind, have more to do with the closing of this symbolism or, via its opening, with the remediation of the written word by code, than with a departure into a techno-scientific imaginary of which one would a priori ignore the whys and wherefores.

If it appears difficult to exhaustively unpack the meaning of this symbolism of the book in its relation to the mythology of the modeling of the human being, taking into account the fact that the text of *Genesis*, for example, cannot be summarized as the expression of a determinism, but is, quite the contrary, illustrated by an uprooting of a matrix conception of writing, a more targeted reflection about the meaning of this technical activity imposes itself all the same on our reasoning in order to understand what I mean by the *desire and refusal to be written*. Far from appearing as an exclusively positive motivation, since it designates at the same time, in the characters of this selection of works, a traditional resistance to technological invasions and the temptation of immortality, this desire and this refusal to be written as a form of "technical activity takes [...] its source in the human desire to transmit oneself to oneself by passing through the world, to return to oneself by alienating oneself from the world; to transmit oneself via the real, by making fragments of nascent languages express themselves, bits of memory that articulate themselves, become autonomous, serve as support and restraint."[5] In a resistant humanity, the sense of memory, which is split between this desire and this refusal to be written, cannot correspond to the ideology of an exponential scientific progress. This ideology of a technological determinism often is only seen as having the meaning of an illustration of a regime of possibilities in science fiction. Contrary to this doxa of technological determinism, my framework of reading has consequently endeavored to identify a certain number of "markers": the use of book metaphors (of nature, of the world, etc.), of which the figures of insects and spiders is one of the most intriguing expressions, and the functions of man-hunting and literary wandering,

---

[5] "activité technique prend (...) sa source dans le désir humain de *se transmettre à soi-même en passant par le monde*, de revenir à soi en s'aliénant au monde; de se transmettre via le réel, en les faisant s'exprimer, des fragments de langues naissantes, des bouts de mémoire qui s'articulent, s'autonomisent, servent d'appui et de retenue" (Sibony 16).

which are an integral part of the imaginary of French and Francophone
science fiction literature, regardless of its type, and in which the function
of the body is re-evaluated because it goes beyond the mind/body dualism to often gain a singular and collective embodied consciousness.
Indeed, if the departure from the body or the will to free oneself from it
does not constitute in itself a positive experience in French and Francophone
literature, it is not the case in many English-speaking science-fiction novels, for example, William Gisbson's novel, *Neuromancer*, which launched
cyberpunk, where the main character Case is first described as being a
character who is condemned to live in his body as if it were a prison:

> For Case, who'd lived for the bodiless exultation of cyberspace, it was the
> Fall. In the bars he'd frequented as a cowboy hotshot, the elite stance
> involved a certain relaxed contempt for the flesh. The body was meat. Case
> fell into the prison of his own flesh (Gibson 6).

This positive conception of the body from a French and Francophone
point of view is perhaps due to the notion of a social contract in which the
physical appreciation of the world plays a role; indeed, as David Le Breton
summarizes very well in his article, "Homo Silicium or the hate of the
body," this "vision of the world which liquidates the body, erects a cult to
the spirit, suspends the man as a secondary, even superfluous, hypothesis
is confronted with a strong social resistance. A humanity out of body is
also a humanity without sensoriality, amputated from the flavor of the
world."[6]

To illustrate these conclusions I have just developed, I will now return
to my selected texts and some of the key examples it includes. In *The Last
Men*, it is because Solman is confronted with the rediscovered flavor of a
world rejuvenated by posthumans, but which could just as easily benefit
the nomads of the old humanity he is in charge of, that he decides to sacrifice himself and rejects the idea of a purity without memory or differences. In the same way, in *The Silent City*, Elisa favors the direct experience
of the world and of sexuality for her androgynous descendants, over the
mastery of technologies which could have, if they had fully mastered them,
made them override many other natural laws, at the risk or at the

---

[6] Cette "vision du monde qui liquide le corps, érige un culte à l'esprit, suspend l'homme
comme une hypothèse secondaire, voire même superflue, est confronté à une forte résistance
sociale. Une humanité hors corps est aussi une humanité sans sensorialité, amputée de la
saveur du monde" (Le Breton 137).

advantage, according to the point of view one adopts, of developing into robots, or even of creating one or several bodies from the same entity. On this point, it is interesting to observe that this reticence to lose one's body has been variously appreciated in the American feminist milieu, following the publication of Donna Haraway's *Cyborg Manifesto*,[7] as Jenny Wolmark testifies:

> Vonarburg fails to give the Project a context other than that of Paul's original genetic ambitions, and despite Elisa's personal vision, it remains in those negative politics. It is at odds with the quite different politics implied by the metaphor of gender metamorphosis, in which possibilities for the redefinition of gender identity and social relations are explored. In the end, Vonarburg's text remains disappointingly unclear about exactly where the narrative emphasis should lie (Wolmark 137).

In the Mothers' Land,[8] which constitutes the continuation of the novel *The Silent City*, there is indeed metamorphosis, but in a social contract that includes a physical appreciation of the world where the bodies will be, this time, administered according to a model of society of social insects: that of the hive.

In French and Francophone science fiction literature, the body is tendentially linked to the world. More appreciated than considered in terms of its total engagement with the world, the physical bodies in dystopian speculative fiction are particularly valued for their poetic perception of the world. This can be seen, for example, in *Globalia*, when at the end of his journal in the non-zones, Baïkal becomes a poet, and in *Our Life in the Forest*, Marie acquires a form of poetic clairvoyance because of the limitations that her many handicaps progressively impose on her. The abandonment of the body is not much better accepted in examples of the transfiction subgenre, insofar as the reiteration of the same individual through cloning provides material for a very strange dramaturgy. In the case of Houellebecq's work, *The Possibility of an Island*, the cloned bodies express the impossibility of being able to truly ignore the flavor of the world, and even if it is the source of many disappointments, it is invariably poetry that leads to the world, and the effects of poetry are that Daniel25 leaves his home. In addition, in *Mevlido's Dreams*, the departure from Mevlido's original body

---

[7] Haraway, Donna J. *Cyborg Manifesto*, 2018.
[8] Vonarburg, Elisabeth, and Jane Brierley. *In the Mothers' Land*. New York: Bantam Books, 1992.

during his insectoid metamorphosis is only conceivable, in the words of Volodine, insofar as the couple "Mevlido-Verena Becker" reunited in a room finally pays attention to the rumor of the world, which takes the form of a protest march inviting the continuation of the struggle against the commodity society, in which case the body of Mevlido perhaps designates in itself the beginning of a collectivist utopia. In *Sulphuric Acid* by Amélie Nothomb, *The Horde of Counterwind* by Alain Damasio, and *Latium* by Romain Lucazeau, bodies are even more clearly identified as manners of knowing that dialogue in turn with philosophers including Arendt, Spinoza and Nietzsche, and Leibniz and Plato because they serve as a matrix for contemporary philosophical quests that either question the use of speech and the value of literature as fragile gatekeepers of humankind or delimit the capacities of truth and consciousness in writing and being able to narrate stories from a corporeal perspective. In short, contrary to the modulable, supernumerary, or absent bodies of posthuman futures, the bodies in the novels of these selected works remain "what draws and makes live a world, 'our general means to have a world'" (Marzano 47), perhaps with the goal of pointing out that our interactions with the world are relational and embodied, notions that could be explored further through additional research.

To conclude I would like to turn, beyond these selected books, to authors who have recently approached the mythologies of writing through the lens of an embodied consciousness and who have profiles similar to Jacques Perriault or Marie-Laure Ryan, that is, who have crossed professional boundaries from computer science to communication sciences or narratology, but who might also have a background in the hard sciences. For this reason, I have assessed French and Francophone authors to try to find if there are any who might resemble the American science fiction writer and computer scientist Ted Chiang, whose collection of short stories,[9] including "Tower of Babylon" (1990) and "Story of my life" (1998) (that inspired the movie *Arrival* (2016), directed by Denis Villeneuve), shed a new light on the mythologies of writing. Could people well versed in the sciences take myths and legends seriously to enrich their scientific paths? If so, would the myths and legends be those of the ancient narratives of Western history, or would other cultures' narratives be included, too? While there may be other French and Francophone authors with scientific backgrounds who are also engaged in hard science fiction,

---

[9] Chiang, Ted. *Stories of Your Life and Others.* 2016.

the one I found who fit the criteria of my research is David Elbaz, astrophysicist and director of the Cosmology and Evolution of Galaxies Laboratory at the French Atomic Energy Commission or CEA. Elbaz has published two scientific novels: *Le Vase de Pépi* (*The Vase of Pépi*) in 2007 and *...et Alice Tao se souvint du futur* (*... and Alice Tao Remembered the Future*) in 2010, and more recently a popular science work about astronomy *La plus belle ruse de la lumière* (*The Most Beautiful Trick of Light*) in 2021.

While *...and Alice Tao Remembered the Future* corresponds in some ways to a futuristic novel, *The Vase of Pépi* as retrospective scientific fiction explores the same topic of taking into consideration the memory of bodies that keep a trace of the notion that "the world is a story," to use a motto attributed to Descartes that David Elbaz comments on in *The Most Beautiful Trick of Light*:

> *Mundus est fabula,* "the world is a story", says the discoverer of the Big Bang, Georges Lemaître, in an article from 1949, taking up the motto attributed to René Descartes (...) The history of the universe unfolds before our eyes when we become aware of the succession of physical processes implemented by matter to respond to the propensity of light to proliferate, and thus also to the increase in entropy of the universe. Since the Big Bang, from the formation of the first particles of matter and antimatter, to the birth of the Earth, through the genesis of atoms, molecules, stars and interstellar dust, the history of the universe unfolds according to a direction that has never been refuted.[10]

In *The Vase of Pépi*, Elbaz creates a new legend where, thanks to a dream, an anthropologist, named Michel Saramo, with his friend Ernesto, who helps him in his archaeological excavations, discovers near Louksor in Egypt a cave that houses not a sarcophagus, but a vase that tells the life story of a certain Pepi, a famous painter and illuminator of the time of

---

[10] « *Mundus est fabula,* 'le monde est une histoire', rapporte le découvreur du Big Bang, Georges Lemaître, dans un article de 1949 en reprenant la devise attribuée à René Descartes. (...) L'histoire de l'univers se déploie devant nos yeux quand on prend conscience de la succession des processus physiques mis en œuvre par la matière pour répondre à la propension de la lumière à proliférer, donc aussi à l'augmentation d'entropie de l'univers. Depuis le Big Bang, dès la formation des premières particules de matière et d'antimatière, jusqu'à la naissance de la Terre, en passant par la genèse des atomes, des molécules, des étoiles et de la poussière interstellaire, l'histoire de l'univers se déroule selon un sens jamais démenti » (Elbaz, *La plus belle* 121).

pharaoh Ramses II. Using shamanic techniques, Saramo reconnects with Pépi's memories and the atomic structure of iron, where the infinitely large meets the infinitely small, to find out among other discoveries that one must keep, like Ernesto, an "open look that dives inside the 'skin of the world'"[11] that "[e]ach of us is a book with a secret language, [and we each] contain[] the whole history of humanity, since the birth of the first human being. A book written in atomic letters."[12]

Based on exchanges among French, American, and Chinese cultures, ...and Alice Tao Remembered the Future, in a story that alternates between the twenty-first and twenty-second centuries, expands the theme of the memory as the "future of the past," to quote the French poet Paul Valéry, as does Elbaz. In this book, a young man from the twenty-second century, Michel Marosa, has the memory of a young Chinese astrophysicist named Alice Tao from the twenty-first century. Because it contains the memory of events that it has not experienced, Marosa's brain is therefore the subject of multiple studies by a neurologist, Professor Malthus, who has been hired to do this work by a mafia organization—the UNUN—based in China, before both Marosa and Malthus escaped thanks to a Chinese journalist and the detailed knowledge that Marosa acquired about the history of Chinese calligraphy and the importance that the body can play in these circumstances which helped him to better understand his condition. From the twenty-first century on her side, the young Chinese astrophysicist whose memory Marosa has inherited is also helped by a young French acupuncturist Daniel, another specialist in the history of Chinese writing and the importance it has represented and still has for Chinese power, and it is the combination of Marosa's and Daniel's knowledge of the "spells of writing" that pushes them at the end of the novel to use an ancient automaton/clock which delivers written messages, once wound up, that could perhaps teach men that through this automaton "there [is] a bridge through which one [can] reach one's ancestors and talk to them as if they were still alive."[13]

---

[11] « ... un regard ouvert qui plonge à l'intérieur de la 'peau du monde' » (Elbaz and Cassé 66).

[12] « Chacun de nous est un livre au langage secret, qui contient toute l'histoire de l'humanité, depuis la naissance du premier être humain. Un livre écrit en lettres atomiques » (Elbaz and Cassé 261).

[13] « ... apprendre aux hommes qu'il existait un pont par lequel on pouvait rejoindre ses ancêtres et leur parler comme s'ils étaient toujours vivants » (Elbaz, ... et Alice Tao 338).

Mundus est fabula and depending on our atomic composition, our mutations, or our condition in the past, present, or future, there are other mythological imponderables which undoubtedly deserve to be explored in which the *world is a story* that futuristic novels and science fiction invite us to appropriate so that we can tell our own.

Bibliography

Elbaz, David. *... et Alice Tao se souvint du futur.* Odile Jacob, 2010.

———. *La plus belle ruse de la lumière: et si l'Univers avait un sens...* Odile Jacob, 2021.

Elbaz, David, and Michel Cassé. *Le vase de Pépi ou Les mémoires d'un noyau d'atome: roman.* O. Jacob, 2007.

Gibson, William. *Neuromancer.* Ace, 2020.

Herrenschmidt, Clarisse. *Les trois écritures: language, nombre, code.* Gallimard, 2007.

Le Breton, David. "Homo silicium ou la haine du corps." *Thérapie psychomotrice et recherches: revue trimestrielle,* 2004.

Marzano, Michela. *Philosophie du corps.* PUF, 2016.

Sibony, Daniel. *Entre dire et faire: penser la technique.* B. Grasset, 1989.

Wolmark, Jenny. *Aliens and Others: Science Fiction, Feminism and Postmodernism.* University of Iowa Press, 1994.

AUTHOR INDEX[1]

[1] Note: Page numbers followed by 'n' refer to notes.

© The Author(s), under exclusive license to Springer Nature   233
Switzerland AG 2022
E. Buzay, *Contemporary French and Francophone Futuristic Novels*,
Studies in Global Science Fiction,
https://doi.org/10.1007/978-3-031-16628-0

Subject Index[1]

A

Abduction, 19, 20, 23, 25, 66, 151, 152
Accessibility (of fictional worlds), 63
Alethic domain, 84
Alethic modality, 83
Alethic system(s), 75
Alethic world(s), 75, 76, 76n7,
   79, 80, 86
Algorithms, 36, 117, 160
American transcendentalist writer, 112
Androgynous mutant, 78, 90
Anticipation, 17, 21, 27, 30, 35, 41,
   45, 47, 48, 52, 72, 74, 87, 104,
   153, 157, 165, 167, 181, 196
Anti-utopia, 27, 28, 30
Aphoristic literature, 179
Aphoristic reasoning, 179
Apocalypse, 22, 47, 47n30, 48, 49, 53,
   55, 66, 79, 91, 92, 92n39, 93,
   94, 120, 128

Artifact, 25, 35, 36, 50, 56, 70, 87,
   89, 103, 123, 126, 187, 207
Artificial intelligence, 136,
   140, 212–220
Art of memory, 182
Auto-da-fé, 45, 46, 204
Automaton, 5–7, 25, 213–217, 219,
   220, 230

B

Barbarian(s), 28n14, 215, 216
Bardo Thödol, 11, 102, 137
Becoming artifact, 22, 27, 34,
   46, 56
Bees, 140
Behavioral therapies, 169
Bible, 10, 11, 23, 40, 54, 77, 79, 109,
   121, 141, 224, 224n4
Biopunk, 146

[1] Note: Page numbers followed by 'n' refer to notes.

Printed by Printforce, United Kingdom